PLAGUE
GARDEN

HALLOWED KNIGHTS

WARHAMMER
AGE OF SIGMAR™

PLAGUE GARDEN

JOSH REYNOLDS

BLACK LIBRARY

For Dan, Ben, Kenny, Tyler and the rest of the Faithful.

A BLACK LIBRARY PUBLICATION

Hallowed Knights: Plague Garden first published in 2017.
This edition published in Great Britain in 2017 by
Black Library,
Games Workshop Ltd.,
Willow Road,
Nottingham,
NG7 2WS, UK.

10 9 8 7 6 5 4 3 2 1

Produced by Games Workshop in Nottingham.
Cover illustrations by Matthias de Muylder.

See Black Library on the internet at

blacklibrary.com

Find out more about Games Workshop
and the worlds of Warhammer at

games-workshop.com

Printed and bound by CPI Group (UK) Ltd, Croydon, CR0 4YY

From the maelstrom of a sundered world, the
Eight Realms were born. The formless and the divine
exploded into life.

Strange, new worlds appeared in the firmament, each one
gilded with spirits, gods and men. Noblest of the gods was
Sigmar. For years beyond reckoning he illuminated the realms,
wreathed in light and majesty as he carved out his reign. His
strength was the power of thunder. His wisdom was infinite.
Mortal and immortal alike kneeled before his lofty throne.
Great empires rose and, for a while, treachery was banished.
Sigmar claimed the land and sky as his own and ruled over a
glorious age of myth.

But cruelty is tenacious. As had been foreseen, the great
alliance of gods and men tore itself apart. Myth and legend
crumbled into Chaos. Darkness flooded the realms. Torture,
slavery and fear replaced the glory that came before. Sigmar
turned his back on the mortal kingdoms, disgusted by their
fate. He fixed his gaze instead on the remains of the world he
had lost long ago, brooding over its charred core, searching
endlessly for a sign of hope. And then, in the dark heat of
his rage, he caught a glimpse of something magnificent. He
pictured a weapon born of the heavens. A beacon powerful
enough to pierce the endless night. An army hewn from
everything he had lost.

Sigmar set his artisans to work and for long ages they toiled,
striving to harness the power of the stars. As Sigmar's great
work neared completion, he turned back to the realms and saw
that the dominion of Chaos was almost complete. The hour
for vengeance had come. Finally, with lightning blazing across
his brow, he stepped forth to unleash his creations.

The Age of Sigmar had begun.

CHAPTER ONE

THE SEA OF STARS

The sigmarite runeblade gleamed in the soft glow of infinity, as it etched complex patterns upon the air. Wherever the blade passed, light followed. The light, that of ancient stars and newborn suns, glimmered briefly but brightly before fading away. There was a lesson in that, the blade's wielder mused, as he swept the sword around in a curving slash. But then, lessons were all around, for the attentive student.

And Gardus of the Steel Soul was nothing if not attentive. The Lord-Celestant of the Hallowed Knights was clad only in a simple blue tunic, marked with the sign of the twin-tailed comet. His limbs were bare of all save sweat and scars, and his white hair was cropped short. His armour, gleaming silver and crafted of the same holy metal as his runeblade, lay nearby, alongside his tempestos hammer, stacked neatly against one of the long marble benches that lined the walls, biding its time. Soon, he would once again don the panoply of war, and the man would be subsumed beneath the warrior.

But for now, he was simply a man, hard at his labours, joyful and content.

Through the soles of his feet, Gardus could feel the omnipresent rumble of the storms that raged eternally over the aetherdomes of the Sigmarabulum. Overhead, the High Star Sigendil gleamed, an eternal beacon in the black seas of infinity that stretched outwards around the celestial ramparts of Sigmaron. This place had ever called to him, stirring something inside. It was where he felt the most at ease, on the edge of all that was.

The weight of the blade in his hand was a comfort. The pull of his muscles, the growing ache from his exertions. The sweat in his eyes. All of it served to ground him. To anchor him to this place, this moment. There was peace here, for a time. A purity of purpose, simple and uncomplicated. He turned, letting the hilt of the runeblade slide through calloused palms. The mystic steel was an extension of his arm, of his soul.

As he moved, his flesh began to shimmer with an eerie radiance, like sunlight across new-fallen snow. It shone from every pore, filling the air. The light welled up, only to then fade away as he instinctively mustered his will and forced it back down inside himself. He slid forwards, moving gracefully despite his size. With god-given strength came elegance as well. Such were the gifts of Sigmar. But they did not come without a price.

There was always a price. Both physical and otherwise. At times, Gardus felt as if he were a broken vessel, badly repaired, and all that he had been was leaking away. Perhaps that was the origin of the light he had just banished – perhaps it was his soul, seeking escape. The thought unsettled him.

Sometimes, his mind thrummed with fragments – snatches of conversations he could not recall having, faces without names and names without faces. Embers of old emotion flared to new life, before guttering away once more. The ghosts of those he'd known – those he'd failed. Those he'd killed.

He felt phantom heat wash over him. Heard the pad of feet over marble floors, and the guttural howls of the Skin Eaters. His skin prickled as the howls grew louder. The candlesticks were heavy in his hands. The doors of the hospice burst inwards and…

He breathed out. His grip on his runeblade tightened, and he drew strength from the steel, surety from its purpose. Not a candlestick, this. He turned, slicing the air, letting the weight of the blade do the work, as he'd been taught. Banishing the Skin Eaters back to oblivion. But they had not come alone.

A hand, vast and reeking of rot, reached for him. He jerked back, sword slicing up. He heard the rumble of daemonic laughter as the image wavered and dispersed. Another broken memory, though he could put a name to this one – Bolathrax.

'Much is demanded of those to whom much is given,' he said, forcing the memory down. Bolathrax was gone. Cast back into the void by Alarielle. He repeated the words. The mantra had a calming effect on his troubled mind. His voice echoed across the platform, its echoes merging with the roar of the storm, even as the reflection of his blade merged with the glow of the stars above. He slowed his movements, falling into a more elegant rhythm. His runeblade moved lazily, with less precision, as he let his muscles relax and his attention wander away from old hurts.

Here, on the precipice of the Sigmarabulum, he was as close as any save the gods could come to the celestial canvas. It was a sea of colour and light, impossibly vast and terrible in its cosmic ferocity. Stars pinwheeled through the fraying strands of pulsing nebulas, and immense coronas flashed in the deep.

And, nestled within its tides, the still-beating heart of a broken world. He looked up.

Mallus. The world-that-was. The last breath of all that had come before. A fragment of forgotten grandeur, casting strange shadows over the vast forges, armouries and soul-mills of Sigmaron. The broken world was at once a reminder and a promise for all those who dwelled in Sigmaron.

Gardus turned away, unable to bear the weight of the sight for very long. In any event, he needed no reminding of what was at stake; he would keep his promise, whatever the cost.

He was a Stormcast Eternal, and he could do no less. The embodiment of the tempest, forged anew to wage war in Sigmar's name. To fight and die, and fight again, until either ultimate victory was achieved, or the foundations of all that was at last crumbled. The thought brought him little pleasure. Victory was not certain, and sometimes the price seemed more than he could bear. He pushed the thought aside, and concentrated only on the runeblade in his hand, and the light of the stars as they played across its edge. Like the weapon he had been forged for a purpose, and he would fulfil it.

He fell into a defensive stance, rolling his wrists, letting the runeblade rise. As he brought it down a moment later, he moved, stepping to his left. Like the storm, it was best to always be in motion. Lessons learned in Ghyran, the Realm of Life, had taught him that standing still often led to being overwhelmed. A warrior must be fluid, like water, else he would inevitably be worn down, as happened to even the tallest mountains.

He paused, sword raised, sensing a new presence just behind him.

'You employ that blade of yours the way an artist employs his brush, Steel Soul.'

Gardus turned, lowering his sword as he did so. 'And your voice carries even over the roar of the storm eternal, Beast-Bane. We all have our talents.'

Zephacleas Beast-Bane laughed boisterously. The Lord-Celestant of the Astral Templars did everything boisterously, much to the chagrin of some. 'Too true,' Zephacleas said as he came forwards, grinning. 'When I heard you were back, I decided to come and pay my respects. It has been too long since last we spoke.' They clasped forearms.

He was bigger than Gardus, big even for a Stormcast Eternal, and brutal-looking despite his cheerful demeanour. In his mortal life, the man who would become Zephacleas had been a barbarian chieftain of the Ghurlands, a brawling, bellowing giant of a man. Apotheosis had refined him somewhat, but the veneer of civilization was a thin one. And, indeed, thinner now than it had been the last time they'd met.

He had his helmet tucked under one arm, leaving his head bare. His hair was long and bound in thick braids, as was his beard. His battered features would never be handsome, but his eyes gleamed with merriment, and his smile was genuine, despite the gaps in his teeth.

Like his face, his bruise-coloured war-plate was scarred by hard use. Its gilded edges were faded and dull, and the plates were now marked by savage adornments. Fangs and claws taken from the slain bodies of monstrous beasts rattled against the holy sigils of Azyr. The skull of an orruk had been mounted on one of his shoulder-plates, the thick bone etched with primitive runes.

Gardus gestured to it. 'That's new.'

'This? This is Drokka.' Zephacleas knocked on the skull with his knuckles. '*Was* Drokka, I should say. A gift from the Fist of Gork himself.'

'I heard you'd been sent to parley with the orruks. I'm glad to see you made friends.' Gardus laid the flat of his sword over his shoulder. 'I was worried they might take offence to you and send you back in pieces.'

'You just have to know how to talk to them.' Zephacleas motioned to Gardus' hair. 'Gone shock-headed, have we? Last time I saw you, it was black.'

Gardus reached up and ran a hand through his hair. 'The Athelwyrd,' he said simply.

Zephacleas' smile faded. He knew what Gardus was referring to. They'd fought side by side in the hidden vale, in defence of Alarielle, the Queen of the Radiant Woods, embodiment of Ghyran, the Realm of Life. And during that battle, Gardus had... died.

'That'd do it, I suppose.' Zephacleas peered at Gardus, as if searching his face for something. 'Do you... remember any of it? After, I mean.'

Gardus frowned. Bits and pieces of the last scattered moments rose to the surface of his mind – he smelled the foetid stench of the Great Unclean One as it scooped him up, rotting fingers tightening painfully about his battered form. He felt his bones crack and burst as the daemon sought to wring the life from him. And he felt again the pain as a bolt of searing lightning carried him from the killing grounds, and back to the celestine vaults of Sigmaron. There, formless and broken, he had been forged anew by the hand of the God-King himself, and made fit for duty once more.

Hammer stroke after hammer stroke had shaped the shards of his soul. Each blow, a tempest, drawing forth memory and instinct from what remained. Who he had been was the fire used to fuel his rebirth. Was he even the same being who had undergone those tribulations that still haunted his dreams, or was he but the barest memory of that warrior, recast and given the same name? A memory of a memory, clothed in borrowed flesh.

'Gardus?' Zephacleas said softly, startling him from his reverie. He sounded concerned. There was a keen mind beneath that brutish exterior. Zephacleas played the fool, but he was more observant than many gave him credit for.

Gardus shook his head. 'Some. Pain. Thunder. And Sigmar's voice, like a bell tolling on high, drawing me up from the depths.' He hesitated. 'It hurt worse than death. I was glad when it was done, and I would not go through it again for anything.' He fell silent. He had died, in the Athelwyrd. And on the Anvil of Apotheosis, he had been Reforged. That was all there was to it. And no benefit to be had in dwelling on it.

Zephacleas looked as if he wished to ask more questions but, thankfully, he kept them to himself. He clapped Gardus on the shoulder. 'I am glad you are back, my friend. And I am sorry I was not able to fight beside you on your last foray.'

Gardus nodded. The battle for the Great Green Torc had been fierce, and many warriors, both Hallowed Knights and otherwise, had fallen on the sky-borne toroid. They had been victorious but, as ever, there had been a cost. 'It was your sort of battle, more so than mine. There were giant spiders.'

'I miss all of the good fights,' Zephacleas said mournfully. He broke into a grin. 'Still, there's always tomorrow.'

'Unfortunately.'

Gardus went to where he'd left his war-plate and began to pull it on. Other Lord-Celestants were more than content to allow chamber serfs to help them with their armour, but Gardus had no patience for such indulgences. He would do it himself, or not at all. He dressed slowly, the warmth of the sigmarite easing the ache from his muscles. 'But perhaps not forever.'

Zephacleas grunted and scratched his chin. 'You're rejoining your chamber in Ghyran soon, I hear. A last push across the Plains of Vo, or so go the rumours.'

'You shouldn't listen to rumours,' Gardus said. He was looking forward to rejoining his chamber. And he wasn't alone in that. Other warriors, some newly Reforged, would be returning to Ghyran with him. It had been too long since the Steel Souls had fought as one, and, reunited, they might just be able to swing the war in the Jade Kingdoms in Alarielle's favour. Or so he hoped.

'Grymn must be beside himself with joy,' Zephacleas said.

Lorrus Grymn, Lord-Castellant of the Steel Souls, had assumed overall command of the warrior chamber after Gardus' fall in the Athelwyrd. The Lord-Castellant had led the Steel Souls to continue their mission in the Jade Kingdoms, and defend Alarielle from the diseased servants of the Plague God, Nurgle. Their efforts had culminated in a final stand against the forces of the Rotbringers at Blackstone Summit, and the subsequent rebirth of Alarielle.

'He has acquitted himself well,' Gardus said, smiling slightly as he thought of the taciturn warrior. Grymn was the Steel Souls' shield, where Gardus was its sword. Where he chose to plant his standard, no enemy would prosper, as the servants of the Ruinous Powers had learned to their cost, most recently during the siege of the Living City. 'The sylvaneth sing his praises.'

'The least they could do, given all that you have both done for them and that goddess of theirs,' Zephacleas said. He picked up Gardus' hammer and gave it an experimental swing. 'But then, gods aren't ones for gratitude.'

Gardus stood and sheathed his runesword. He picked up his helmet and took his hammer from Zephacleas. Whatever

Zephacleas thought, Gardus knew that Alarielle owed them little. For, in their ignorance, it was the Stormcast Eternals who had inadvertently cost the goddess her last sanctuary in Ghyran. Whatever debts lay between them were paid, or as good as. 'It is not for us to question the gods, my friend. Merely to do their will, whatever it might be. Much is demanded...'

Zephacleas laughed. 'Of course we should question the gods. How else will they know we're listening?' He poked Gardus in the chest. 'Eh? Answer me that.'

Gardus chuckled. 'As much as I've missed arguing with you, I fear I have somewhere a good deal less cheerful to be.' He looked past Zephacleas. 'Isn't that right, sister?'

'Punctuality has always been one of your more pleasing virtues, Steel Soul,' the newcomer said, as she drew close. The Lord-Celestant was as large as Gardus, and her silver war-plate was marked with a profusion of blessed prayer scrolls. Her helmet hung from her belt, and her round, dark face was set in a look of stern disapproval as she studied Zephacleas. 'But your choice of such disreputable friends has ever been your greatest failing. Take care, lest they lead you into impropriety.'

'My Lady Cassandora, a pleasure as ever,' Zephacleas said, making an attempt at a courtly bow. He peered up at her as he did so. 'How's that for respect?'

'Adequate,' she said, smiling slightly. 'Barely.'

Lord-Celestant Cassandora Stormforged had been among the first of their Stormhost to wage war in the Mortal Realms. It was by her hand that the Queen of Swords had been cast down, and the ancient rim-citadel of Ytalan claimed in Sigmar's name, during the Crater-War. The Stormforged struck like lightning, and left nothing standing in their wake. 'Still as foolish as ever, Beast-Bane. I recall it was almost the death of you, in Klaxus.'

'And yet, here I stand,' Zephacleas said, gesturing expansively.

'Yes, thanks to me,' Cassandora said. 'You're welcome, by the way.' She looked at Gardus, as Zephacleas spluttered. 'It's time, brother. The Shadowed Soul requests our presence. The lords of the fourth Stormhost gather in the Sepulchre of the Faithful.'

Gardus nodded. 'Yes.' He tapped Zephacleas' shoulder-plate with his hammer. 'It was good to see you again, brother.'

'So it was,' Zephacleas said. He caught Gardus up in a rib-rattling bear hug, squeezing him hard enough to make his sigmarite creak. 'Go with Sigmar, my brother. And if you need help, I shall be there, come death or ruin.'

Cassandora coughed politely. 'Time runs swift, brother.'

'Indeed it does,' Gardus said. He extended his hammer. 'Lead on, sister. The Sepulchre of the Faithful awaits us.'

The celestine vaults of Sigmaron rang with the sounds of eternal industry as Tornus the Redeemed strode swiftly after his Lord-Celestant. The Knight-Venator tried his best to hide his uncertainty as he said, 'I am not understanding, my lord. It is being a – a funeral?'

'Of sorts,' Silus the Untarnished said, not unkindly. He led Tornus along the high outer platform, past the great emptiness of the universal sea. In the distance, the aetherdomes crackled with captured lightning, funnelling the fury of the storm into the forges of the citadel. Tornus flinched inwardly as he heard what might have been the faint screams of those undergoing their Reforging, beneath the growl of distant thunder.

'But we are not dying. We are being Reforged.'

'Yes.'

Tornus looked up as the shadow of shimmering wings passed over him, and caught sight of his star-eagle, Ospheonis, gliding overhead. The bird accompanied him everywhere. It had become his constant companion since his Reforging. When no further explanation seemed forthcoming from Silus, he asked, 'Who is to be dead?'

Silus stopped. His shoulders sagged slightly as he turned. 'A brother of our Stormhost. Tarsus Bull Heart.'

'I am not knowing him,' Tornus said. Even now, he knew precious few of his new-found brothers. None had been unwelcoming of him, but few sought him out. He found no fault with them for this reluctance. He was who he was, and who he had been.

'No. He met his fate before you were Reforged.'

Tornus noted a hesitation in Silus' answer. He nodded slowly. 'Before I am being Tornus again, you mean,' he said softly. Silus frowned.

'You were always Tornus. Everything else was a lie.'

'It was not feeling like a lie at the time,' Tornus said. He smiled, to show it was a joke. Though there was precious little humour to be found in his situation. The few memories he still possessed of his time as defender of the Lifewells, and then later of his imprisonment in the Pit of Filth, welled up unbidden, and he took a deep breath. For seventy-six days, he had resisted the miasmic attention of Nurgle's chosen, until his stubborn refusal to succumb became the very thing which spelled his doom.

On the seventy-seventh day, Tornus had died. And Torglug the Despised had emerged from the ruin of him, like a maggot from a wound. The things he had done as Torglug still haunted him... He remembered clearly the drowning of the Athelwyrd and the toppling of the Moon-Oak, the screams of his own people and the rasping cries of the tree-kin... All crimes committed by his hand. He had been the Woodsman, the sharp edge of Nurgle's axe pressed against the bark of the World Tree.

Until the Blackstone Summit, and the coming of the Celestant-Prime. Tornus could still feel the heat of the divine warrior's first and final blow, as it burnt away the rotten husk of Torglug and freed the dwindled spark of Tornus within. That spark had flourished on the Anvil of Apotheosis, hammered and shaped into a weapon of vengeance and redemption. And yet, he still heard the screams of the innocent who'd perished by his hand. Sometimes he wondered if he had been left those memories for a purpose. A reminder, perhaps, of how far he'd fallen. Or a warning of what awaited him should he fail again.

Silus made as if to clasp Tornus' shoulder, but stopped short. 'Whatever you once were, Tornus, you are a Stormcast Eternal now.' He let his hand fall. 'You are a Hallowed Knight. A scion of the fourth Stormhost, one of the faithful. Who will stand, when all others fall?'

'Only the faithful,' Tornus said. He was all of those things, to be sure. But Silus had never once called him brother. None of them had, as yet. Perhaps it would come with time. He hoped so. In the interim, he was determined to do all that he could to earn it.

'Only the faithful,' Silus echoed. 'Now come, it is time you knew what that truly entails. It is time for you to learn the true price of faith.'

Tornus nodded, but said nothing. He was already familiar with the price Silus spoke of, but saw little reason to insist on it. 'Where are we going?' he asked.

'The Sepulchre of the Faithful,' Silus said. 'All Stormhosts have such mausoleums, though they call them by different names. A place of quiet contemplation, where the truly dead are honoured, and the memories of our mortal lives are recounted and recorded so that even if we… forget, those moments are not lost.'

Tornus shivered slightly. 'I am thinking my memories are best forgotten, yes?'

'No,' Silus said, firmly. 'Do you think you are alone in your darkling past? There are many among us who found their faith only in their final moments, or who discovered the light only after a lifetime of darkness.' He glanced at the Knight-Venator. 'None fell so far as you, Tornus, but some… came close. That is why Sigmar placed you with us.'

Tornus fell silent. He had his own suspicions as to why he had been inducted into the ranks of those he had, until recently, been trying his level best to kill. Another lesson. Another reminder. This new world was full of them.

Somewhere, the Great Mourning Bell was ringing, sounding a eulogy for the fallen. Stormcasts from other Stormhosts moved to and fro about their own business, and Tornus studied them. He could not help but compare them to those corrupt warriors he had fought alongside in the Jade Kingdoms. Here, there was little of the incessant bickering that afflicted the servants of the Ruinous Powers. Rather than a horde of individuals, each warrior fighting for his own glory, the Stormcasts were truly united, both in war and peace. Indeed, so too were most of those who inhabited Sigmar's realm.

Sigmaron was not only inhabited by Stormcast Eternals these days. Representatives from Azyrheim, engineers of the Ironweld Arsenal, even envoys from the reclusive clans of the Dispossessed, moved about their business everywhere Tornus looked. In the dark days when the assaults of Chaos had set the Mortal Realms reeling, many had sought refuge in Azyr. As the war had progressed, the descendants of those refugees now prepared themselves to reclaim that which had been lost.

JOSH REYNOLDS

Silus nodded in a friendly fashion to certain of these mortal envoys – among them a tall, dark-skinned warrior-priest, clutching a heavy tome to his chest, a soldier of the Freeguilds, his helmet resplendent with plumage, and a grim-faced duardin warrior, clad in finely crafted armour and carrying a rune-inscribed hammer – though he spoke to none of them. Tornus studied the duardin wonderingly. He had fought such beings before, in darker times. Torglug the Woodsman had hewn apart the ironwood shields of the root-kings, and cast down their stoneoak citadels. The Lord-Celestant noticed Tornus' fascination with the mortals and said, 'We are the storm, and these the seeds that flourish in the wake of our rains.'

'There are being so many of them,' Tornus said. 'My folk, the guardians of the Lifewells, were being few in number. As the land grew sick, so too did we, dwindling generation upon generation.'

'And now, both land and people will grow great again, if we but hold firm to the course the God-King has laid out.' Silus spoke confidently.

Tornus kept his doubts to himself. He had seen too much to believe victory a certainty. But without that belief, could he truly call himself one of the faithful?

He was still mulling this over when they arrived at their destination at last. They were not alone. Other Stormcasts, all wearing the silver and azure of the Hallowed Knights, were gathering there in the vast antechamber. Tornus found himself awestruck by his surroundings, and somewhat intimidated by their solemnity. Great bas-reliefs of intricate craftsmanship covered the walls, and the massive pillars that lined the path to the inner chamber were inscribed with the Canticles of Faith. Ornate lanterns hung suspended from the ceiling, each one casting a soft, blue radiance over everything.

But what caught Tornus' attention were the great ironbound books chained to the stone shelves along one wall. It was said that the mortal memories, however patchy or incomplete, of every Hallowed Knight, from Lord-Celestant to Liberator, were recorded in the Books of the Faithful. It was the responsibility of a select few Lord-Relictors to protect and add to the books, but all Hallowed Knights were allowed to read from them, to renew the wellsprings of their faith.

Tornus wondered when his memories would be added to the records. He suspected his deeds might somehow taint the purity of it all. Perhaps he would refuse, when the time came. Why burden others with his sins?

No one spoke as they filed into the inner chamber, where a group of skull-helmed Lord-Relictors awaited them with sombre patience. Clad in their baroque mortis armour, the lords of the living lightning made for an intimidating sight, even for Stormcasts. Eldritch energies crackled across their silver war-plate, illuminating the fell sigils and grim relics that decorated it. They stood arrayed around an enormous pillar of pale stone, larger than the others, erected at the chamber's heart.

Said to have been carved from purest celestine by the claws of Dracothian himself, and chiselled into its present shape by the ancestral tools of the greatest masons of the Dispossessed, the pillar shone like starlight. It was bare of all decoration, save for a scattering of what appeared to be sigmarite spikes hammered into its surface.

Tornus looked around, studying the Stormcasts around him, searching for familiar faces amongst the sea of silver. It appeared that the commanders and officers of every chamber of the fourth Stormhost were here at the ceremony. He recognised a few of them. Iorek Ironheart, Cassandora Stormforged, even Gardus of the Steel Soul were all in attendance.

The sight of the latter made his heart clench. The Steel Souls had been a persistent thorn in Torglug's bloated paw. It was said by some that Gardus had hurled himself into the Garden of Nurgle, and escaped unsullied. Tornus could almost believe it, for the Lord-Celestant's broad form shone with a faint, eerie radiance that reminded him of the purifying energies of the Celestant-Prime. The tribulations the Steel Soul had endured had changed him in undeniable ways.

Tornus knew those changes had come about after Gardus had perished in the battle for the Athelwyrd. While Torglug had not struck the fatal blow, it had been by his hand that the situation came about. Tornus could still feel the echo of his own laughter as he watched a daemon summoned by his command crush the struggling, silver form.

A Lord-Relictor thumped the floor with the ferrule of his staff, startling him. Tornus recognised Cerberac Darkfane, the Lord-Relictor of the Ironhearts warrior chamber. When he spoke, his voice was a hollow rasp. 'The Bell of Lamentation rings. The stars weep. Who shall stand, when the foundations of the heavens crumble?'

'Only the faithful,' the assembled Lord-Relictors intoned.

'Only the faithful,' Cerberac repeated. 'Come forth, Ramus of the Shadowed Soul. Come forth and perform your duty.'

One of the other Lord-Relictors stepped forwards. His armour showed signs of wear, its silver sheen dulled in places, the azure trim stripped and patchy. A great crack ran down one side of his skull-helm, allowing a thin glimpse at the pale features beneath. His dark cloak was singed and tattered. Like all Lord-Relictors, his armour was decorated with sigils of faith, death and the storm. A shield of mirrored silver, carrying a relief of a twin-tailed comet, hung from one shoulder. He carried no reliquary staff like the others, instead clutching his relic hammer in one hand, and a sigmarite spike in the other.

He raised the spike. 'How many times?' he asked, his sepulchral voice echoing through the chamber. 'How many times have we faithful few stood here since the Gates of Azyr opened, and Sigmar's storm was unleashed upon the Mortal Realms?' Without waiting for an answer, he continued, 'How many times will we gather here, in days yet to come?'

The Lord-Relictor looked around, his gaze lingering upon some faces longer than others. Tornus felt the weight of his gaze, and found himself wondering what trials Ramus of the Shadowed Soul had endured. 'I cannot say, for on this matter, the spirits are silent. Whatever the number, we endure it gladly. Much is demanded...'

'Of those to whom much is given,' Tornus and the others said in response. The Hallowed Knights spoke as one, their voices soft and low.

'This spike of precious sigmarite I bless in the name of him who is lost to us. Tarsus Bull Heart, Lord-Celestant of the Bull Hearts. Hero of the Cerulean Shore.' The Lord-Relictor placed the spike against the pillar, and raised his hammer. 'Let... let his name join those of the others who are now gone, never to be Reforged.' Tornus noticed the slight hesitation, and from the faces of some of the others, he knew he was not alone in that.

For a Stormcast Eternal, death was not the end. But there were fates worse than death, and there were endings even for immortals. There was not a single Stormhost that had not suffered such casualties over the course of the war. Tornus resisted the urge to count the spikes that studded the pillar. One was too many.

Lightning flashed as the relic hammer struck the flat head

of the spike, driving it into the pillar. It took but a single blow, and the reverberations filled the chamber, drowning out all sound for a brief instant. The Lord-Relictor stepped back, hammer dangling loosely from his hand. 'It is done,' he said. He sounded almost defeated.

Cerberac Darkfane thumped the ground again. 'It is done. Another soul lost. But while one remains, we will hold true. Who will preserve the light, to its last gleaming?'

'Only the faithful,' the Hallowed Knights answered, in unison.

'Louder, brothers and sisters,' Cerberac chided. 'Let Sigmar hear your voices, in this, our hour of grief. Who will defend all that is, even unto oblivion?'

'*Only the faithful,*' came the reply, thunderous in its intensity.

As the echoes of the mantra faded, the pillar began to glow with a harsh radiance. Sparks of lightning leapt from spike to spike, limning each in an azure radiance, if only briefly. As the light and sound faded, Tornus bowed his head, mourning a warrior he had never met, and now, never would.

'Only the faithful,' he murmured.

CHAPTER TWO

THE BAY OF FLIES

Lord-Castellant Lorrus Grymn braced himself and swept his halberd out in a wide arc. The beastman's bray of challenge was cut short as the halberd bit into its hairy neck and tore its goatish head from its shoulders. Grymn spun the weapon, sluicing the blade clean of gore, before planting it on the ground. His stern gaze passed over the surviving beastmen as they edged back from him. 'Well?' he said, his voice mild. 'Which of you wishes to die next?'

One of the gors tossed its horned head and pawed the wet earth. It extended its notched and rust-bitten blade and spat something in the dark tongue. Maggots writhed in its eye sockets, and large, fat fleas danced in its hair. Though the rest of the brute's herd snarled and gibbered in response, none of them were eager to meet the same fate as their fellow. Grymn had little patience for such antics. He reached down to the warding lantern hanging from his belt and flipped it open.

Gold light washed out over the closest beastmen, searing

their unnatural flesh to the bone the instant it touched them. Bestial screams filled the air, and several of the creatures stumbled away, eyes boiling, hairy bodies alight. The few who were unaffected lunged for him as a group, snorting and stamping, desperate to douse his light.

Grymn smiled in satisfaction. 'Tallon.'

The gryph-hound gave a shriek of joy and sprang out from behind him, hurling himself at the foe. He was a heavy-bodied creature, with the limbs and loyalty of a hunting hound, and the head of a bird of prey. Tallon knocked one of the beastmen to the ground and began to savage the brute with his beak. Grymn faced the others.

It was no contest. A moment later, he jerked his halberd free of a twitching body and allowed himself to take stock of the current situation. The battle among the salt grasses had ended almost before it had begun. The beasts had been all but beaten before the first warblade had been drawn. Which was only as it should be.

Grymn had led his Hallowed Knights in pursuit of the warherd for weeks, driving them back across the Plains of Vo and down to the mosquito-haunted coasts of the Verdant Bay, burning their filthy camps and toppling their maggot-infested herdstones. It had been the largest herd of beasts in the region, and the best organised, in the wake of the closing of the Genesis Gate. Now it was nothing more than a trail of dead, stretching across the mud flats, tidal shallows and salt marshes of the embayment.

The beasts had made their final stand in the reed banks, amongst the high salt grasses and toppled stones of a long vanished harbour. In better times, port cities had clustered like barnacles along the coastline, and ironwood galleys had plied the waters. Now nothing occupied the coasts of the Verdant Bay save ruins and monsters.

The Lord-Castellant looked out over the turgid waters, towards the distant sargasso-citadels that ringed the mouth of the bay like sores. The sea wind carried with it the monotonous thud of distant drums, and the screams of the dying. The sky was thick with noxious clouds, which occasionally wept an acidic rain that could mar even the silvery finish of the Stormcasts' armour. The clouds, like the beasts he'd just slain, had their origin in the citadels. And, like the beasts, the citadels and clouds would soon be cast down. He'd sworn as much, during the siege of the Living City.

He closed his eyes, wishing that he stood once more amid the bulwarks of ironoak and thornwood. He could still recall the warm scent of the sunfire blossoms as they stirred in Alarielle's wake, that final day at the Twelve-Thorn Gate. He could feel the deep, basso war-chant of the duardin root-kings resonating through him, as they marched to war. Sylvaneth, duardin and Hallowed Knight had fought as one, driving back the Rotbringers and casting down their flyblown standards. Alarielle had given full vent to her fury in that final hour, and the enemy had been throttled, torn and impaled from every side by thorny creepers and jagged boughs. She had been a sight to behold, and, though he would never admit it to another soul, he felt honoured to have witnessed it.

Afterwards, they had marched out, to harry the foe and bring them to heel. He opened his eyes and cast a cool gaze over the battlefield. They had forced the beasts back, into the reed beds and the shallows of the bay, even as he'd planned. The creatures had sought to flee across the three massive viaducts of boil-encrusted stone and fossilised sargassum, which connected the distant citadels to the shore, but found their way barred by closed gatehouses and sealed portcullises. Their masters had deserted them. Or perhaps they'd sacrificed their servants to buy the time they needed to ready themselves for the storm to come.

'They are wise in their wickedness,' he murmured. Tallon chirped and leaned against his leg. He stroked the gryph-hound's neck as he studied the three great gatehouses, which loomed above the shallows. They were crude bastions of stone, balanced on pylons of bone and cankerous wood. The structures were functional, almost utilitarian compared to some he'd seen since arriving in the Jade Kingdoms. Monstrous, but more so in conception than appearance. Then, that was the nature of the enemy they faced.

He nudged one of the dead beastmen over with the toe of his boot. Like the others, it wore a crude hauberk marked with a fly-shaped emblem. Bits and pieces of rusty armour, culled from a dozen battlefields, decorated its twisted frame. It was as if it had been trying to ape the appearance of something greater than itself.

'Like master, like beast,' Grymn murmured. The monsters who ruled these lands claimed membership in a knightly order, and boasted of honour and glory. But their honour was built on the bones of the innocent, and their glory was a lie. It offended him, in a way few things did, though he could not say why. Some half-forgotten memory of who he had been, perhaps, rising up like the ache of an old wound.

'My lord?'

Grymn turned. Aetius, one of the chamber's Liberator-Primes, saluted briskly. Known to his warriors as the Shield-born, Aetius was a stolid sort, a born fulcrum, able to anchor any battle line by dint of plain stubbornness. His silver war-plate was scratched and begrimed, as was his shield. The warhammer in his hand was coated in gore.

'Idle musing, Aetius, nothing more,' Grymn said. He peered

past Aetius, where a retinue of Liberators saw to the merciful dispatch of wounded enemies. Beyond them, Judicators took up positions along the shore to watch for any movement from the citadels, and a retinue of Retributors set to breaking open the closest of the gatehouses. The monstrous structure shuddered like a wounded animal with every strike of their lightning hammers. The few guards who had manned the gatehouses were dead, picked off by Judicators and Prosecutors, or fled. Grymn looked at Aetius. 'Speak, Shieldborn. Tell me a tale.'

'We have driven them into the sea, Lord-Castellant. Some few chose to drown rather than face us.' Aetius gestured to the body. 'I saw the same sigils in the reed-city of Gramin, before it sank. Have we truly found their redoubt, then?'

'One of them, certainly,' Grymn said. 'But after today, the Order of the Fly will have one less.' He spat as he said it, the taste of the enemy's name foul in his mouth. Even that was a corruption of sorts, a twisted shadow of a once fine thing.

In the days of myth and legend, the Jade Kingdoms had been defended not just by the sylvaneth, but by mortal armies as well. And the greatest warriors of these armies had been the knights of the chivalric orders, whose names were now all but forgotten. Lost to time and tide, as so many things were in this broken age.

It was possible that the Order of the Fly had once been counted among those ancient brotherhoods, before its warriors had become twisted, pestilential mockeries that now sought to drown these lands in filth. And that was the saddest thought of all, that such men might have fallen, trading hope for despair and honour for cruelty. Perhaps that was why they offended him so. The true victory of Chaos was not measured in battles won, but in the hearts and souls of their enemies.

To twist and break all things out of shape. When they convinced the righteous that they were wicked, and stole faith from the faithful, the Dark Gods rejoiced as never before.

Whatever their origins, the Order had rapidly spread its miasma across Ghyran, declaring pox-crusades on the few remaining free peoples, and conquering many lands in Nurgle's name. But now, at last, they were in retreat, their holdings smashed, many of their blightmasters slain. Grymn's grip on his halberd tightened as he thought of battles past, and the hard-fought victories that had led to this point.

But, more than that, he thought of the savageries the retreating Rotbringers had inflicted on the land and its peoples. Tribes, long in hiding, were rooted out and put to the sword or enslaved. Groves of slumbering sylvaneth, chopped and burnt to make siege weapons and hasty fortifications. They had left a scar across the face of the Jade Kingdoms. A black path, leading from the gates of the Living City to this very shore.

The sargasso-citadels, with their immense balefire cauldrons, were the last of the enemy's holdings in this region. Like a boil fit to burst. If he could break them here, the southern kingdoms might at last be freed of Nurgle's contagion.

A shadow passed overhead, and he looked up to see a familiar armoured shape swooping low. The Prosecutor-Prime called down a friendly greeting to Aetius, who raised his hammer in reply.

'Tegrus,' Grymn called, signalling the winged warrior. 'Gather Lord-Relictor Morbus and the others. Your fellow Primes as well. There are matters to be discussed before we push forwards.'

The Prosecutor-Prime gave a lazy salute as he circled once overhead and then shot off to do as he had been ordered. Grymn watched him go. Tegrus of the Sainted Eye, hero of the Nihiliad Mountains. One of the first of their number to return to battle after being Reforged. Like many of their brethren, he had perished in the Athelwyrd. But his death had been a merciful one, at the hands of Alarielle herself, after he had suffered a horrific transformation brought about by their foes.

Tegrus Reforged was not much changed from the bold warrior Grymn knew. A trifle slower in employing what he considered wit, and quicker to follow orders. It could almost be considered an improvement. Even so, it was a change. And Grymn did not care for change. He glanced at his hand, and then away quickly. He had lost the original in battle with the Rotbringers. But the sylvaneth known as the Lady of Vines had grown him a new one. The alien sensation of new-grown flesh and bone had faded over time, as had the green tinge, but even so he sometimes found himself studying it for any irregularities.

'It is not going to sprout blossoms, you know. Or, in your case, thorns.'

The voice was a rasping rumble, like the promise of thunder. Grymn turned. 'And how do you know this, Morbus? Some spiritual insight, forbidden to the rest of us?'

'Common sense,' Morbus said. The Lord-Relictor resembled nothing so much as death made flesh. His mortis armour was streaked with muck, and the runic plates steamed with fading heat. Pale eyes fixed on Grymn, and the Lord-Relictor wondered if there was a smile beneath that grisly skull-helm. 'If it was planning on it, it would have done so by now.'

Grymn made a fist. 'Possibly. Maybe it's biding its time.'

Morbus gave a hollow chuckle. 'Perhaps.' His amusement faded as he studied the waters of the bay. He leaned against his reliquary staff, fingers tapping against the sigils of faith and death that marked the haft. 'We have come far.'

'And farther yet to go.' Grymn looked at him. 'What do the spirits say, brother?'

'They say much, little of it of any use to us,' Morbus sighed. 'The very aether is in upheaval, and all that is balances upon a knife edge.' He gestured, motes of crackling energy dancing upon his fingertips. 'Possibilities sprout like saplings, spreading and branching as never before.'

'That is a good thing, surely.'

Morbus looked at him. 'Only if we nurture the right ones.' He fell silent.

Grymn shook his head, annoyed. Morbus had always taken a certain pleasure in playing the cryptic seer. He cherished his portents of doom the way a duardin cherished ur-gold. Grymn released a breath he hadn't realised he'd been holding and turned to greet several newcomers.

Tegrus swooped overhead, accompanied by the Knight-Venator, Enyo. Aetius' fellow Liberator-Primes, Osric and Justinian, splashed heavily through the low waters, accompanied by the Judicator-Prime Solus, the Retributor-Primes Feros and Markius, and the Decimator-Prime Diocletian. Last came the Knight-Heraldor Kurunta, his heavy sigmarite broadsword balanced on one shoulder. The self-proclaimed Lion of the Hyaketes was singing loudly as he splashed through the reeds. A battle hymn, as usual.

Grymn greeted them with a nod. His command had shrunk and flourished with the seasons of this realm, as the war for the Jade Kingdoms dragged on. The dead vanished with a crackle, only to return, Reforged and renewed, days or months later. Even so, a grinding attrition had set in, as the fortunes of war turned and the scope of things widened.

By the time of the assault on the Genesis Gate, the Steel Souls numbered just a hardy few. But those few had been honed into a lethal blade, capable of piercing even the most resilient battle line. Now, in the aftermath of the Allpoints Campaign, and the Great Reforging, the chamber was set to expand again. And, most importantly of all, its long-absent Lord-Celestant would once more take command.

The thought of Gardus' return brought a brief smile to Grymn's face. It was a day that had been long in coming, and one he had anticipated greatly. Grymn was satisfied with the part he had played in recent events. He had built something here that could not be easily toppled, and the Steel Souls had become an engine of war second to none in the entirety of Ghyran. But he was growing tired of the march, of the unceasing advance and the burden of over-all command. That was not his duty, not truly. He was the shield, not the sword. And his skills could be put to better use elsewhere.

But for now, he would lead.

He observed his auxiliary commanders for a moment, noting the condition of their armour, the faint signs of fatigue in some of them. Part of him considered waiting for reinforcements to arrive. But that would only serve to give the enemy time to strengthen their defences. No, best to strike now, before they'd made ready.

'Who stands before me, clad in silver and blood?' he asked.

'Only the faithful,' Kurunta said, his deep voice booming out. A flock of saltwater stabberbeaks hurtled skyward, startled. Several of the others chuckled, until Grymn's stern gaze silenced them.

'Only the faithful,' Grymn said. 'Only the faithful could have come this far. But we have farther still to go before our journey's end.' He extended his halberd towards the distant sargasso-citadels. 'There. Those stones offend me, brothers.

I would see them pulled down and something better erected in their place.'

'And how shall we get there?' Kurunta asked.

Grymn shook his head. 'You have eyes, surely – look, see… The three great viaducts that stretch out over the bay. We shall smash the gatehouses asunder and use the enemy's own roads against them.'

'The viaducts will be defended,' Morbus said. 'Or worse, destroyed.'

'No. I believe they will destroy all but one.' Grymn used the ferrule of his halberd to draw an image in the dirt. 'Forcing us onto a path to their liking, which they will then defend to the utmost. So, we must choose our own path, and swiftly.' He glanced at the Knight-Venator. 'That task shall fall to you, Enyo.'

The Knight-Venator nodded, her eyes alight with eagerness behind the false calm of her war-helm. 'You have but to name a target, brother, and I shall pierce it through.'

Grymn tapped the ground with his halberd. 'Take your sky-host and destroy the two lateral crossings. If I have judged them right, they will attempt to guide us to one of the outer citadels, where they can contain us. We shall deny them that option, and force them to meet us on the central viaduct.' He looked at Aetius and the other Primes. 'We shall push forwards down the centre, crushing any opposition.'

'And what of the slaves?' Morbus rumbled. The Lord-Relictor looked out over the bay, rather than at the map. 'I can feel the emanations of their despair from here. Thousands of mortal souls, trapped on those false islands. Will we leave them to their fates?' The beastherd they had just crushed had taken many captives during its rampages. As the Stormcasts harried the herd they'd discovered that the captives were being sent to the sargasso-citadels, though they had yet to discover the reason why.

Grymn frowned. The thought of freeing the captives had occurred to him, but he had dismissed it. There was no time and their numbers were too few. Perhaps when Gardus arrived with reinforcements, but not before. He cleared his throat. 'We have no warriors to spare, brother. Not if we wish to achieve victory here, at last.'

'And what good is victory, if it is built on the bones of those we seek to win it for?' There was no judgement in Morbus' voice. No displeasure. Or at least it was not evident. Grymn's frown became thunderous, and he felt a flush of guilt. The Lord-Relictor was right, as ever. Morbus nodded slightly, as if aware of Grymn's thoughts.

Grymn looked at Enyo. 'Sister?'

The Knight-Venator thumped her chest-plate with a fist. 'We shall shatter their chains, brother. And the bones of their enslavers besides.'

'Good. See to the viaducts first, however. And go swiftly. Speed is our only ally here.' Grymn looked around. 'Markius, you will oversee the destruction of the gatehouses. Spread your warriors equally. Favour no single point. For the moment, I wish to keep our foes wondering. Solus, post Judicator retinues along the shoreline. Harry any foe who tries to cross. They may attempt a breakout when they realise what we're up to.'

Grymn turned, studying the distant citadels. Black, noxious smoke spewed upwards from behind their high, sloped walls, filling the sky, blotting out the suns. There was sickness in that smoke. A sickness that had afflicted these lands for far too long, but which would now be cured. 'Our Lord-Celestant returns to us soon, brothers and sisters. I wish to present those citadels to him upon his arrival.' Grymn raised his halberd. 'Who shall be triumphant?'

'Only the faithful,' the Steel Souls roared in reply.

'They're at it again,' Gatrog said, his voice a liquid rumble. He leaned his armoured bulk against the rampart of the fortress known as Third Circle, his thick fingers splayed out over the fossilised sargassum. His maggoty war-plate creaked thinly as he shifted his weight, the blistered plates seeping sacred pus. Their sickly sweet perfume enveloped him and he sighed. 'That chanting is enough to drive a fellow mad.'

'Lucky for us you're already mad, eh?' his shield bearer, Agak, said, picking at his ever-increasing collection of boils and scabs. Gatrog glanced at the little Rotbringer. Agak was a starveling, bloat-bellied and thin limbed. He wore an oozing hauberk, made from the hide of a toad-dragon, and a rusted sallet helm, as was his right as a chosen armsman of the Most Suppurating and Blightsome Order of the Fly. He leaned against Gatrog's massive kite-shield. Occasionally, he would hawk and spit on its rugose surface, helpfully adding to its lustre with his nasal discharge.

'What was that?'

'I said, we're lucky you're here with us, my lord.'

Gatrog chuckled. 'One of us is lucky, anyway.' He patted the Rotbringer heavily on the head, nearly flattening him. Agak had served him faithfully, if not always wisely, since the day Gatrog had ascended to the dukedom of Festerfane. Like the other armsmen who crouched on the ramparts of the sargasso-citadel, Agak had been among the levy drawn from the heartlands of the Blighted Duchies, and brought south to garrison these lands. An honest serf, bound to the King of all Flies and the Duchy of Festerfane.

Gatrog, too, had flourished in the damp shadow of the Lord of All Things. Like a mushroom, he had grown strong and wide with Nurgle's noisome blessings. He had quested for and won a taste of the sour syrup of the most holy Flyblown Chalice, and knelt at the cloven feet of the Lady of Canker-wall to receive it. He had made the seven times seventy-seven oaths to the King of all Flies, and now rode for the glory and honour of Nurgle, as a true knight of the Realm Desolate.

And now he would fight to defend that realm, against the greatest of enemies. He turned. The ramparts of the Third Circle stretched away to either side of him, curling up and away from the thick sludge of the sea like the petals of some putrid flower. Jagged turrets, decorated with the ragged banners of the Order, rose over the ramparts. The banners, crafted from filthy rags and diseased flesh, flapped loudly in the sea breeze.

The citadel itself was shaped like a bubo, with high, thick walls composed of fossilised sargassum and the bones of the great sea beasts which had once hunted these waters. Within the walls, a crude, if enormous, web of gantries and clapboard bridges stretched in all directions, leading to a variety of inter-nal portcullises and inner walkways. These walkways, as well as the courtyard below, were a hive of activity.

Besides a few high-ranked Chaos knights like Gatrog, each citadel was garrisoned by a substantial force of Rotbringers. Many of these were mortal, though some were not. Most were ill-trained zealots, clad in tattered robes and bearing the mark of the fly on what scraps of armour they had been able to scavenge. They beat drums and rang bells with carnival exu-berance as they went about their duties in disorderly mobs.

Others, like Agak and the armsmen on the ramparts, were of a more professional disposition. Armed and armoured ade-quately, they were led into battle by putrid blightkings, obese, god-touched warriors, their bodies swollen with holy corruption. Unlike mortal warriors, the blightkings were slabs of unnatural fat and muscle, bound in straining skin, and clad in rust-pitted war-plate.

Agak peeled away a scab and stuck the wet lump on the kite-shield, adding it to the others. 'Will we sally out to meet them, my lord?' he asked.

Gatrog didn't answer for a moment, instead listening to the gentle drone of the rot flies which swarmed about the rampart. He found the sound of insects soothing. Occasionally, he fancied he could even make out words amongst the droning. Onogal the troubadour sang that Nurgle spoke through the flies, to any who had the wit to hear. Gatrog dearly wished to hear the voice of the King of all Flies, even if just once.

'My lord?' Agak pressed, hesitantly.

Gatrog shook himself and said, 'No, I suspect not, though I dearly wish it were otherwise.' He clenched his fists, enjoying the sensation of his boils splitting beneath the corroded metal of his gauntlets. 'Would that I might meet a worthy foe before this day is done. How else am I to show Grandfather my merit, save in battle?' He'd missed his chance to come to grips with the storm-warriors at the Living City, and it galled him.

'Perhaps prayer?' Agak suggested.

Gatrog stared at him. The little Rotbringer looked away hurriedly. 'No, Agak,' Gatrog said, heavily. 'Not prayer.' Frustrated now, he thumped the rampart. It cracked beneath his fist, oozing pus.

Third Circle, like the other sargasso-citadels, had not been constructed so much as grown. Its foundations had been dredged from the depths of the water by the magics of the Order's hireling witches centuries earlier. Day by day, it had grown larger, spreading across the water like a fungus, until it had become connected to the other citadels by a latticework of hardened pus, sargassum and bone. Troops could move easily and swiftly from one Circle to the other as needed. And looking at the forces arrayed on shore, Gatrog suspected they'd be needed sooner, rather than later.

The storm-warriors were fierce foes. They carried themselves as knights, though they fought on foot. Gatrog snorted in contempt. No true knight would lower himself so. Just as no true knight would vanish in a crackle of lightning when slain, rather than leaving his body to lie, so that it might fertilise the soil. In death was new life spread. Such was the will of the King of all Flies.

But the storm-warriors had their own king. Instinctively, Gatrog made the sign of the fly as he glanced skyward. Nothing good resided in that starlit void. That, he was certain of. Whatever creed originated there, it was an unwholesome one. A thing of harsh purity, scoured free of all traces of life. Like the storm-warriors themselves, lacking even honest bile in their veins. He spat over the side of the rampart.

'Would that I could slaughter them all, Agak.'

Agak nodded obsequiously. 'Aye, my lord. Would that you could.'

'Are you saying I can't?'

'No, no,' Agak said hurriedly. 'Merely that... that the moment is not yet upon us, yes. Yes. That's what I meant, oh most glopsome one.'

Gatrog nodded. 'Yes. I assumed that was what you meant.'

He ignored Agak's sigh of relief, and turned his attention to the viaducts. Festering mantlets had been erected across the width of each of the viaducts, and Rotbringers waited behind them, making a joyful noise with their drums and pipes. Like the beastmen, or the mortal guards of the shore-line gatehouses, they were a sacrifice on the altar of time. He frowned. He had not cared for the creatures, but to see them die so ingloriously pricked his sense of chivalry. Nonetheless, in dying they had served the Order better than they ever had alive. That was the black truth of it.

Clarity was Nurgle's gift to his servants. To see the world as it was, stripped bare of the tattered masks of yearning and expectation, leaving only a beautiful desolation. There was comfort in surrender, and joy in acceptance. There was love there, as well. A great serenity at the end of all things. And it was that bleak serenity that the Order of the Fly served. It was that serenity which they sought to impart to all equally, be they lowborn or high. For were not all lives of equal worth, in the eyes of Nurgle?

Goral had taught him that. He had served his cousin as a squire, before the time came for him to earn his own spurs. Goral had trained him, teaching him all there was to know about being a knight. About being worthy to serve the King of all Flies.

'Ah, cousin, what I would not give to fight beside you once more,' Gatrog murmured. But Goral had perished in the depths of Writhing Weald with his entire muster, and the responsibilities of the duchy had passed to Gatrog. 'Would that you were here to see this day, and stand with me, against such foes.'

'Would that all of our lost brothers were here this day, Gatrog,' a deep, hollow voice intoned. 'Your brave cousin, and Count Dolorugus the devoted, or even brawny Sir Culgus, who held the Bridge of Scabs alongside Blightmaster Wolgus in the days before the storm's coming. We fight as much in their name as our own.'

Agak fell to his hands and knees, bumping his head against the stones. The other armsmen did the same. Gatrog looked up into the leering, daemon-shaped war-helm of his brother-knight and commander, and bowed shallowly. 'Blight-master Bubonicus, you honour me with your presence.'

'And you honour me with your service, Lord-Duke of Festerfane.'

Bubonicus was swollen with the raw stuff of Nurgle. He was almost twice Gatrog's height, and easily three times his width, clad in thick war-plate the colour of gangrenous flesh, and draped in a mouldering cloak and tabard of dull brown. He carried a monstrous halberd in one hand, its rusted blades surmounted with the chains of a deadly flail.

The plates of his armour vibrated slightly, and Gatrog heard a faint buzzing from within it. Bubonicus had not been seen without his armour for centuries, and some whispered that the King of all Flies had bestowed the best of his blessings on one avowed to be one of, if not the greatest of the Blightmasters.

While Bubonicus was in overall command of the sargasso-citadels, he had delegated the defensive preparations to three hand-picked champions, Gatrog among them. Gatrog didn't begrudge his new-found responsibilities. Bubonicus had other, worthier concerns. That he was even up here was a surprise. Gatrog felt a flicker of unease as Bubonicus raised his great tri-headed flail. 'Do you see this flail, Gatrog?'

'Yes, my lord.' It was hard to miss it. The flail-halberd was old, older even than the Mortal Realms, some claimed. The troubadours sang that it had floated through the void for mil-lennia, only to become caught up in the birth of the realms like a bit of grit. And that even then it had thrummed with the feculent power of Nurgle.

'It is called the Gatherer of Souls,' Bubonicus said. 'Once, in another world, in a distant time, it was wielded by the greatest of Grandfather's champions.'

'It still is, my lord,' Gatrog said quickly.

Bubonicus chuckled. 'How perspicacious of you, Gatrog. Yes. With it, I have reaped a steady yield. But out there stands the greatest harvest of all.' He extended the flail out, towards the distant gleaming of the enemy. The silvery shimmer hurt to look at, even from this distance. And their chanting beat at the air like the growl of some great beast. 'Look at them, the enemies who have pressed us so fiercely. They who have cast down the banners of our allies. Where now valiant Torglug, or the Brothers Glott? We stand alone, perhaps the last defenders of the Realm Desolate.'

'But not for long, my lord,' Gatrog said, caught up in Bubonicus' stirring misery. The blightmaster had a tendency to become worryingly grandiloquent at times like this. 'What of the Gate of Weeds, and our allies beyond?'

'It remains closed as yet, my friend. Shuttered and barred against our rightful passage.' Bubonicus' massive shoulders sagged. The Gate of Weeds was an ancient realmgate, located deep in the heart of the sargassum from which Third Circle had been formed. Its luminescent surface had remained inviolate, despite the best efforts of the Order's sages and seers, including the Lady of Cankerwall, Nurgle bless her name. Thus had begun the long, arduous task of making the land bend to Nurgle's will.

Gatrog glanced at the titanic balefire cauldron that occupied the heart of the citadel. There was one like it in each citadel. Its massive circumference filled the courtyard, and many bridges and walkways crossed around it and over its smoking rim. For all intents and purposes, the citadel was but the hard outer shell for the cauldron. Flames roared deep within the stone plinth that supported the cauldron. The broken shapes of still-living sylvaneth were fed into the fire, bit by screaming bit, through grotesquely shaped openings.

Thick clouds of effluvium spewed upwards from the cauldron, filling the air with pox-smoke. The smoke crept across land and sea alike, spreading Nurgle's influence wherever its poisonous rains fell. The cauldrons were kept bubbling day and night by gangs of slaves. When slaves fell, they were hacked free of their chains by an overseer and fed into the fire by their fellows. Nothing was to be wasted. And with every passing day, the land and waters grew sicker. A slow process, to be sure, but Nurgle was nothing if not patient.

'The Gate of Weeds will open in time,' Bubonicus continued. 'But that time is not now. This land, these waters, the people yet resist our blessed contagion.' He shook his head sadly, pus dripping from the antlers that rose from either side of his helmet.

Gatrog cast a disdainful glare at the slaves below. 'Brute savages. They know nothing of life, only persistence. Hope blinds them to the serenity of despair.'

Bubonicus shook his head. 'Nay, Gatrog. Do not blame them for their ignorance. Hope is the weed in Nurgle's garden. It spreads swiftly, though we uproot it with every moment. Left unchecked, it would strangle Grandfather's blossoms in their beds.' He raised a finger in admonishment. 'Remember, hope is but the foundation stone of everlasting regret...'

'And today's palace is tomorrow's ruin. Yes, my lord.' Gatrog spat a wad of phlegm over the edge of the rampart. 'Even so, they irk me.'

'You must grasp the nettle, my friend, and find clarity in the pain. That is why we are here, in these untamed lands. We will free these gentle folk from the tyranny of hope, and teach them the peace of desolation.' Bubonicus gestured to the slaves. 'Only when all know their place in the garden can true harmony be attained. Only when they learn what men such as this already know.' He clapped a heavy hand on Agak's shoulder, nearly driving the little Rotbringer to his knees. 'Then, and only then, shall the soil of their souls be made fertile and welcoming for the attention of the Lord of All Things.'

Gatrog bowed his head, suddenly ashamed. Part of him had hoped never to return to the Verdant Bay, after their pox-crusade had ridden forth to bring battle to the Living City. He was no armsman, to spend his eternities watching over a fortress. Let others tend the garden. He'd thought himself the smile of Grandfather's scythe. 'I had almost forgotten, my lord. Our duty is a sacred one, and I am honoured to be a part of it.'

'That is good. For you play a most vital part.' Bubonicus sounded amused. 'Especially given what comes next.' He gestured loosely to the shoreline, and the gathered silvery shapes arrayed there.

'So it is to be battle, then.' Gatrog felt a thrill of anticipation. He had fought storm-warriors before, but not for some time, and never in such numbers.

'Eventually,' Bubonicus said. 'For now, we shall shatter the central and leftmost viaducts. I have already given the order to your fellow knights. The honour of meeting and holding the enemy shall fall to Count Pustulix and the garrison of the First Circle.'

Gatrog felt a flush of disappointment. He had hoped to meet the foe in open battle himself. As if reading his thoughts, Bubonicus chuckled wetly and said, 'Fear not, sir knight, for I doubt that the enemy will spare us his attention. We cannot avoid battle, but we must delay it. With the Gate of Weeds open, these bastions will serve as Nurgle's new antechamber in Ghyran. Through here shall seven times seven blighted legions pour forth, and take back what the false goddess and her allies have stolen.'

'Dark god blight her roots,' Gatrog said fervently, making the sign of the fly. Alarielle, the Queen of Weeds, who forced life itself to bow to her whims. She was no true goddess, for what sort of divinity would seek to set limits on the act of creation?

Bubonicus nodded approvingly. 'Even so.' He caught Gatrog by the shoulder and squeezed, causing the tarnished metal to creak. 'With warriors like you, the Order of the Fly cannot fail. Hold fast to your oaths, Duke Gatrog. Third Circle is in your hands.' He turned and clomped away, armsmen scattering from his path. He would be heading below, Gatrog knew, to oversee the continued unbinding of the Gate of Weeds.

'So, no fighting?' Agak said, after a moment. He sounded pleased.

Annoyed, Gatrog waved him to silence. Agak was no coward, but he was lazy – battle was too much like work for him. He turned to watch as a group of chosen slaves was herded across a high walkway, towards the rim of the vast cauldron. They wailed and wept, and their despair was sweet to hear. Despair was Nurgle's gift to his children, and one they freely shared. To know such beautiful desolation was to be freed of the cruel burdens of life. To be released from a most insidious slavery.

That was the Order's remit. They were not conquerors, but liberators, freeing the innocent from the chains of hope. Hope was a grievous lie, whispered into the skulls of men by treacherous spirits. Only when all hope was extinguished from the realms would mortal men be truly free. It was a heavy burden, but one all true knights bore willingly. Such was their oath to the King of all Flies.

One by one, the slaves were sent screaming into the noxious stew, and Gatrog chuckled. Such sounds they made! As if they had something to fear. He glanced at his shield bearer. Agak always enjoyed watching slaves fall into the cauldron. But the little Rotbringer was frowning out at the bay. 'What troubles you, Agak?'

'Why aren't they moving yet?'

Gatrog grunted and turned his attention to the enemy. Agak was right. Going by all previous experience, the storm-warriors should have been advancing by now, attempting to take the viaducts from the paltry forces stationed on them. The invaders did not normally hesitate when it came to seizing the initiative. 'Perhaps they are frightened...'

Agak looked at him. Gatrog frowned. 'Perhaps not.'

Somewhere high above, from one of the turrets, a horn sounded. Gatrog spun, hand slapping against the hilt of his blade. Out of the corner of his eye, he saw the far right viaduct crack and splinter on its foundations. A thunderous groan filled the air as the immense bridge shuddered, and its middle span abruptly collapsed into the steamy waters. He felt the reverberations of its fall through the stones beneath his feet.

He caught sight of silvery winged shapes, hurtling through the noxious clouds above, and cursed virulently. Of course. He'd forgotten. Some of them could fly. 'Well, there goes that plan,' he rumbled, unable to hide his growing excitement.

Agak sighed and lifted Gatrog's shield.

'Guess we're going to have to fight after all.'

CHAPTER THREE

THE WORD
OF THE GOD-KING

Gardus studied the bas-reliefs that marked the walls of the antechamber. The scenes depicted there were somehow familiar. While they were mostly battles, some were of gentler pursuits. He saw reapers harvesting wheat, and shepherds tending their flock. His eyes strayed most often to the image of what could only be a hospice, where a robed figure tended the sick and the lame.

Garradan... help us... Garradan... healer, help me...

He closed his eyes, banishing the ghostly whispers. Not forever. They inevitably crept back, to remind him of what had been lost. By now, they were almost like old friends.

'The dead can be persistent.'

Gardus opened his eyes to find Ramus of the Shadowed Soul watching him. 'You would know better than I, Lord-Relictor.' Around them, the gathered commanders of the Hallowed Knights spoke quietly to one another. It was rare that so many of them were all gathered in one place, and they took advantage of the opportunity, renewing old friendships and arguments alike. A Stormhost was, first and foremost, a brotherhood, united by bonds stronger than sigmarite. And it was only amongst their brothers and sisters in arms that a Stormcast Eternal truly felt at ease.

Ramus nodded. 'To my sorrow. He is not truly dead, you know.'

'Who?'

'Tarsus.'

Gardus frowned. 'Then why have we gathered here?'

'It was not of my doing,' Ramus said, his tone faintly bitter. He glanced over his shoulder. Gardus followed his gaze. The other Lord-Relictors stood in quiet conversation with Lord-Celestants Iorek and Silus. The latter raised a hand in silent greeting. Gardus returned the gesture, wondering what they were discussing.

'Why would they declare him dead, if he lives?' he asked, as he turned back.

'Because it suits the God-King's purposes,' Ramus said. Gardus gave him a sharp look. Ramus glanced away, as if ashamed of his bitterness.

'I have heard that you petitioned Sigmar for the chance to return to Shyish.'

'And you also heard that he did not grant my request, I'd wager.'

'I did.'

Gardus understood the God-King's decision. What Ramus had asked for was nothing less than leave to invade the realms of a nominal ally. Or at the very least one who was not yet an open enemy. Sigmar did not wish to provoke open war with the Undying King, until there was no other option. 'I am sorry,' he said.

Ramus gave a hollow laugh. 'That is good to hear. I had hoped you might lend a sympathetic ear, and listen to what I propose.'

Gardus blinked. 'What do you mean?'

'I will not – I cannot allow Tarsus' soul to remain in Nagash's possession. It goes against every oath I swore in the Temple of Ages, and all bonds of brotherhood. I… I failed him, both in Shyish, and in the wilds of Ghur.'

'No,' Gardus said firmly. 'You achieved your mission, whatever else. That is all that Sigmar asks of us, brother.'

Ramus gave an irritated twitch. 'And what about what we ask of ourselves, Steel Soul? Whatever our loyalties, are our wills not our own?' He hunched forwards, the haft of his hammer creaking as his grip on it tightened. 'Tarsus died for us. As you died for your warriors. And I would not have it be for nothing.'

'And you think it was?' Gardus asked, softly. 'Because it seems to me that your presence here contradicts that.' Tarsus had made the ultimate sacrifice for his chamber, and Ramus seemed determined to throw it all away, out of the same sense of devotion.

Ramus ignored him. 'I hoped, in the aftermath of Gothizzar, that Sigmar might grant my request. Nagash has proven himself as much our enemy as the Ruinous Powers.' He shook his head. 'Instead, I was told that Tarsus was lost to us, and that command of the Bull Hearts would fall to me.'

'As Sigmar commands, so must we obey,' Gardus said.

'So we must,' Ramus said, his voice harsh. 'But that does not mean I will give up. I will not fail Tarsus a third time. No matter the cost, I will see him freed.' He straightened. 'And so, I ask you, Gardus of the Steel Soul, if you will lend your voice to mine in this petition. Together, we might make Sigmar hear us.'

'To what end?'

Ramus hesitated. 'What do you mean? Have you not been listening?'

'Gardus always listens, Shadow Soul, even when he shouldn't,' Cassandora interjected, as she joined them. She fixed Ramus with a steady gaze. 'You know better than anyone that our brother is lost to us, Lord-Relictor. How many must be sacrificed before you admit it?' Her words were sharp, but her voice calm.

Ramus grunted, as if she'd struck him, and Gardus was forced to catch him by the shoulder as he wheeled about angrily. Ramus glanced at Gardus, and visibly composed himself before replying. 'What would you have of me, sister?' he asked, his voice almost a whisper. 'Why can none of you *see*?'

'We do see,' Gardus said, trading looks with Cassandora. 'I see your pain, brother, and, more than anything, I wish I could take the burden from you.' He felt the light stir within him and crushed it down, stifling it. 'But I cannot. Sigmar has made his decision. It is not for us to question it. Much is demanded...'

Ramus bowed his head. 'Of those to whom much is given,' he finished. He shook off Gardus' hand and turned away. 'But how much must we give, until we are allowed to say enough?' With that, he walked away, head held high, back straight.

'I see I am not the only one whose aid Ramus sought,' Silus the Untarnished said, as he strode towards Gardus and Cassandora, trailed by an unfamiliar Knight-Venator. Gardus was studying the Knight-Venator when Silus' words registered.

'He asked for your support as well?'

'He's making the rounds,' Cassandora said, glaring after the departed Lord-Relictor. 'Ever since the God-King recalled him from the Realm of Beasts. He approached me earlier, and the Ironheart a day ago. The others as well.'

'And after all of you turned him down, he came to me,' Gardus said, bleakly amused. 'I suppose I should feel insulted.'

'I wouldn't,' Silus said. He looked at Gardus. 'You suffered a similar fate to the Bull Heart, lost to Sigmar's sight in a harsh realm. But unlike Tarsus, you came back. Ramus is probably wondering how you managed it.'

'He's not the only one,' Gardus said. He noticed Lord-Celestant Iorek watching him. The commander of the Iron-hearts leaned towards his Lord-Relictor and murmured something. Gardus sighed. There were some among the Hallowed Knights who feared he was tainted by his wanderings in the realm of Nurgle. It was a fear he'd shared, before his second Reforging. But any stain that might have existed would have been blasted from him on the Anvil of Apotheosis. Or so he hoped. He shook his head. 'Perhaps we should–'

'What? Go to the God-King and demand his leave to invade the Realm of Death, to start a second war before the first is finished?' Cassandora gestured sharply. 'I am all for taking a hammer to Nagash's bones, but now is not the time.'

'Our sister is right, I fear,' Silus said. 'In any event, we all have our responsibilities. Some more pressing than others.' He knocked his knuckles against Gardus' shoulder-plate. 'And speaking of them, might I ask a boon of you, brother?'

'If it is in my power,' Gardus said.

'You are returning to the Realm of Life, are you not? To rejoin your chamber in the Jade Kingdoms?'

Gardus nodded. 'I am.'

'I ask that you allow one of my warriors to accompany you. He has knowledge which may be of use, for he knows those lands intimately.' Silus motioned to the silent form of the Knight-Venator. The warrior twitched, as if in surprise. 'Tornus, step forward.'

'Tornus?' Cassandora said, eyes widening. 'The Redeemed One.'

'The who?' Gardus said, looking back and forth. The Knight-Venator glanced at his Lord-Celestant before he sank to one knee, head bowed.

'I am being Tornus the Redeemed, Lord-Celestant. And we are having met before.'

Gardus stared down at him. He recognised the warrior now, though he had only seen him at a distance, loosing his deadly arrows into the ranks of the foe during the battle for the Great Green Torc. 'Have we, brother?'

'Yes. In battle.' Tornus looked up. 'But we are being on opposite sides.'

Gardus paused, wondering what he meant. Then it hit him. 'The Athelwyrd.' This, then, was the warrior who'd once been known as Torglug the Despised. The first to feel the purifying touch of the enigmatic Celestant-Prime, and the first servant of the Dark Gods to be Reforged. Bemused, he gestured. 'Up, brother. On your feet. There is no need to kneel before me. I am not the God-King.'

Tornus rose smoothly. Gardus studied him. 'I heard that you pursued one of the Maggoth Lords for thirty days and nights across the Scabrous Sprawl. Such dedication is impressive.' Then, given how tenaciously Torglug had hunted Alarielle, perhaps that wasn't surprising. 'I would welcome your company,' he said. He glanced at Silus. 'If it is your Lord-Celestant's wish that you join me.'

Silus frowned. But before he could reply, someone did so for him.

'It was not his wish, Steel Soul. It was mine.'

The voice reverberated through the antechamber like the

pealing of some great bell. It echoed through every heart and shook the marrow in every bone. One by one, the gathered Hallowed Knights sank to their knees. Gardus was the last, and as he dropped to one knee, he gazed up at the towering presence of the God-King.

Sigmar stood only a little taller than his warriors but, even so, he loomed over them, a giant made of starlight and the sound of clashing steel. He seemed more real than the world around him, as if all of the light and heat of the universe had been poured into him. His golden armour shone like a beacon, and his broad features were like new-carved marble. He carried no weapon, but needed none, such was the power he radiated. Here were the hands that had drawn up mountains and drained seas. Here, the arms that had wielded Ghal Maraz in the age before time, and cracked loose the pillars of the heavens, so that life might begin. And the eyes, which had seen the black rim of eternity and the birth of suns. The air crackled about him, as if his merest gesture might set it alight.

Sigmar Heldenhammer. Sigmar Stormlord. Sigmar, the God-King.

As he surveyed the ranks of kneeling Stormcasts, a slow, sad smile split his features. Like a man who knew the end of the story, and found it bittersweet. 'Rise, sons and daughters of the storm. I would not keep you from your appointed rounds. There is much work yet to be done.' He looked down at Gardus. 'You stay. You as well, Tornus. I would speak to you both.'

Gardus remained kneeling. So, too, did Tornus. Cassandora, Silus and the others rose and departed. Ramus was the last to leave. He stared steadily at Sigmar, as if preparing to confront him. Gardus felt a surge of relief when the Lord-Relictor left without speaking. When he had gone, Sigmar turned his attention to the bas-reliefs and said, 'On your feet, Gardus.'

Gardus rose, feeling somewhat apprehensive. 'What is it you wished to speak of, my lord?' he asked. He glanced at Tornus, who still knelt, head bowed.

'Do you know why I wish for Tornus to accompany you?' Sigmar rumbled, still studying the bas-reliefs. Gardus shook his head.

'I do not.'

'Do you object?'

'I do not.'

'That is the reason,' Sigmar said. He turned. 'Even now, there are some who doubt him, who see the echo of his former self in him. They see a shadow where there is none, and I grow weary of it.' For a moment, lightning flashed in the God-King's gaze, and the Sepulchre trembled, as thunder boomed somewhere overhead. 'So weary that I must remind myself I am not a tyrant. That I cannot force them to see sense. I can only show them the way, and hope that they follow the path I have set them on.'

'I have endeavoured to do so, always,' Gardus began. Sigmar smiled, and the burgeoning rage of a moment before was gone, dispersed like a fading storm.

'If you had not, we would not be having this discussion, Gardus.' He placed a hand on the wall. Lightning crackled, limning the carvings, each in its turn. 'The story of your Stormhost is writ on these walls, as well as in the pages of the great, ironbound books your Lord-Relictors hide here from me, as if ashamed.' He caught Gardus' frown of consternation. 'Do you truly think that such a thing would anger me?'

'It is not that, my lord. But they are ours. Our memories, however scattered and fragmentary. All that we might once have been, before we were chosen to serve you.' Gardus looked at the books. Which one contained his story? There was no way of knowing. 'In those pages are the last remnants of vanished peoples and cultures, the vestiges of better worlds, and the people who inhabited them.' His hands clenched, as he smelled again the faint whiff of smoke and saw white robes, gone red. 'Without these memories, what are we but shadows clad in sigmarite?'

Sigmar was silent. Gardus turned. Sigmar smiled. It was not a gentle smile, but neither was it wrathful. A smile of satisfaction, perhaps. 'Shadows have their purpose, Gardus. Even if it is only to make the light shine all the brighter.'

Gardus bowed his head. 'As you say, my lord.'

Sigmar looked at Tornus. 'You're still kneeling. Why?'

'I am not being worthy of standing, my lord.'

'Are you not? Well, we shall have to rectify that. For the moment, however, humour me. On your feet.' Sigmar gestured. Tornus rose. Sigmar nodded. 'Good.' He looked back at Gardus. 'I entrust this task to you, for the same reasons I sent you to the Everqueen, in her darkest hour. I have many weapons, Gardus of the Steel Soul, and not all of them are used to break things.' He pointed to the tempestos hammer dangling from Gardus' belt. 'The Stormcast Eternals are my hammer, and a hammer may be used to build as well as destroy. I think you, above all others, recognise that.'

Gardus said nothing. Sigmar continued. 'Among all the lights of the faithful, yours shines the brightest, I think. Your brothers and sisters in arms look to you, to see what path they should follow. That is why Ramus came to you last, for if you had denied him, the others would not have even listened.'

'You know, then?'

'Very little occurs in this citadel that I am not aware of, Gardus.' Sigmar tapped him on the chest-plate. It was the gentlest of touches, and even so, it rocked him slightly. 'Each of you bears a bit of me, and the same lightning courses through our veins.'

'Do not be angry with him,' Gardus said, quickly. 'He suffers a pain of the soul. One only time will heal.'

'Still the physician,' Sigmar said. 'Ramus is not alone in his pain. Others suffer from similar ailments, even as you once did. Doubt, anger, uncertainty. These things can weaken the bonds of faith that bind us all. That is why I ask you to guide him.' He indicated Tornus. 'Guide them all, by example. Build the foundations of what is to come.'

'I will do my best, my lord,' Gardus said.

Sigmar studied the Lord-Celestant, his gaze unreadable. Then he nodded, and somewhere high above, thunder rumbled. 'Good. Now, it is time for you to return to your warrior chamber at last, Gardus of the Steel Soul. There is much work to be done, and I would see it done well.'

Tornus followed Gardus at a respectful distance as they made their way to the Basilica of the Storm, where the Reforged Steel Souls waited. The meeting with Sigmar had left him shaken. He could still feel the reverberations of the God-King's voice in his bones. Sigmar was akin to a storm caged in iron, ever pulsing and crackling with repressed fury. How Gardus had been able to meet the Heldenhammer's gaze, Tornus couldn't fathom. Perhaps the stories he'd heard about the Steel Soul were true.

Even so, it made him feel no better about being passed around like a burden. Lord-Celestant Silus had departed without a word, all but abandoning him. No, that was unfair. This arrangement had not been by Silus' choice, that much was clear.

Tornus felt broken. He had hoped that feeling would fade, after he had achieved some measure of revenge. He had struck down the followers of Nurgle in the Scabrous Sprawl with a fury second only to that of the storm itself. But the fire inside had burned hot, and left nothing but ashes in its wake.

Part of him wondered if he ought to seek death, and thus be Reforged anew. Would it purify him of his doubts? Or would they grow worse, as his sense of self frayed even further? It would be better to be an automaton, he thought. A weapon did not question its purpose. It merely fulfilled it. Doubt had brought him low in the Pit of Filth. He could not afford to sink into that ever-waiting mire again, for he knew he would not escape it a second time.

'Where are we to be going?' he asked, more to fill the silence than out of curiosity. 'Lord-Celestant Silus said it was being the Jade Kingdoms...'

'Yes. The Plains of Vo.' Gardus slowed his pace, forcing Tornus to walk beside him. 'You know of them?'

'I am being there, in the long ago,' Tornus said. 'Before I am being changed.' Ospheonis chirped, and he reached up to stroke the star-eagle's beak. 'Many cities. Many people.' He hesitated, sifting through faded memories. 'Fancy hats.'

'Hats?'

'Big hats.' Tornus looked at him. 'And many boats. Is that being helpful?'

Gardus chuckled. 'Possibly. I'm more interested in the sargasso-citadels.'

Tornus grunted. 'The Order of the Fly.' He recalled few interactions with the Order. He – Torglug – had found them annoying and frustrating in equal measure. Their cheerful despair and adherence to a frankly ridiculous martial code had made them burdensome allies at best and nuisances at worst. Even the Glottkin hadn't been able to stand them. 'They are being dangerous. True fanatics. Strong warriors.'

'You almost sound as if you admire them.'

Tornus shook his head. 'They are being foolish and strange.'

'But dangerous.'

'Yes, very much so.' Ahead of them, a set of massive doors swung inwards on groaning hinges, pushed open by a retinue of Liberators. Beyond them, the Basilica of the Storm waited. The huge chamber jutted out from the edge of Sigmaron, extending over the sea of stars. Hallowed Knights stood within the chamber, standing in disciplined ranks. Thick pillars rose from the floor towards a high aether dome, composed of blue-tinted glass, set into a golden framework. Lightning crawled across the glass, twisting and crackling into strange, unsettling shapes.

As they entered the chamber, the Hallowed Knights turned as one, with a crash of sigmarite. Members of every conclave were represented among the Reforged: Liberators with warblade and shield; Retributors in their heavy armour, lightning hammers sparking with barely restrained power; Decimators, gleaming thunderaxes ready to hack a path through any foe; and Protectors, their silvery bulk distorted by the mystic shimmer of their stormstrike glaives. Above them all, Prosecutors swooped and glided, ready to launch themselves into the warm air of Ghyran.

Gardus stopped. He raised his tempestos hammer. 'Who stands ready?'

'Only the faithful,' came the thunderous reply.

'Who will be victorious?' His voice boomed out across the chamber.

'Only the faithful!'

Gardus lowered his hammer. 'Only the faithful. It is good to see you, my brothers and sisters. That you stand here, ready to return to the fires of war, is testament to your faith. And I am humbled by it.'

'It is we who are humbled by you, Steel Soul,' a voice called out from overhead. A heavy shape dropped to the ground with a snap of crackling wings. 'Though some among us would not admit it.' The warrior rose to his full height, celestial beacon shimmering in his grasp. 'Not me, though. I admit it freely.'

'I doubt there is anyone short of Sigmar himself who could humble you, Cadoc,' Gardus said, smiling. 'Though I recall making the attempt several times in the Gladitorium.' He extended his hand, and the Knight-Azyros took it.

Tornus studied the other warrior. He knew Cadoc Kel by reputation. Cadoc was often the tip of the Steel Souls' spear, speeding into battle alone, or accompanied only by the swiftest of the Angelos Conclave. His armour was decorated with prayer scrolls and reliquary sigils, and words in a tight, curling script had been etched into every flat surface. Cadoc noticed Tornus' gaze and tapped his armour. 'Canticles. I add a new one for every victory, and with every one added, the strength of my faith grows.'

'Is being the truth?' Tornus asked.

'He seems to think so,' Gardus said. 'Cadoc, this is Tornus of the Gleaming Host. He will be accompanying us into battle.'

'Can he keep up?' Cadoc asked.

'I am being quite swift.'

Cadoc burst into laughter and slapped Tornus on the shoulder. 'I have no doubt.' He swept out a hand, indicating the silver ranks of the Hallowed Knights. 'Your warriors await you, my lord. We stand ready to make war.'

'He has eyes, Cadoc,' a deep voice growled. The heavy shape of the Steel Souls' Knight-Vexillor stepped from the ranks, his meteoric standard clutched in one hand, and a warhammer in the other. 'He knew we would be ready before he ever entered this chamber.' He nodded to Gardus. 'It is good to see you again, my lord.'

'And you, Angstun,' Gardus said. 'Are you ready to return to the fields of war? Lorrus must miss your council.'

'Lord-Castellant Grymn is more than capable of making up for my absence,' Angstun said. He glanced at Tornus, and then again, staring. 'You,' he said, flatly.

'I am remembering you,' Tornus said, softly.

'I hope so,' Angstun growled, eyes flashing. His hammer twitched in his hand. 'You... you sent many of my brothers back to the Anvil of Apotheosis. And now, here you stand, clad in silver.' Behind him, a murmur swept through the Stormcasts' ranks. Tornus was suddenly very aware that many of these warriors had likely fallen due to Torglug's axe. Ospheonis screeched a warning, and Angstun stepped back. Tornus reached up to silence the star-eagle, stroking his feathers.

'I am not being the one who was killing you, not anymore,' he said.

'Are you sure of that? Because you sound like him.' Angstun leaned forwards, dark eyes fixed on him. 'If you were truly one of the faithful, you would not have fallen.'

'Faith is only tested in the falling, Angstun,' Gardus said, firmly and loudly. He stepped between them, frowning. 'It can only be forged in the fire of misfortune. And even then, the most stalwart soul can succumb to those flames. Else, how have all things come to this? Would we stand here now, our veins filled with lightning, if faith alone were enough?'

He raised his head, looking at the assembled Stormcasts. 'No. We are the faithful, and we know the limits of faith. But as with steel, strength comes from the testing of those limits. Steel may break, but it has the potential to be forged anew.

If it is but *given the chance*.' He caught Tornus by the shoulder and said, 'See! Here stands a blade Reforged. Proof that a spark of light exists even in the darkest soul.'

He looked at Angstun. 'Your anger is understandable, brother. But you must put it aside. For he is but the first of the Redeemed, Sigmar willing. Would you turn them all away, out of anger and spite? Or will you call them brother, and welcome them?' He reached out, caught hold of the Knight-Vexillor's helm and gently pressed his bare brow to Angstun's armoured one. 'Much is demanded, of those to whom much is given.'

As one, the assembled Hallowed Knights repeated the mantra, Tornus included. Gardus' words echoed through his head. He thought he understood now why Sigmar had chosen to place him here. Lord-Celestant Silus was a great warrior, and fair commander, but he had never called Tornus 'brother'. Only Gardus had, and done so without hesitation. The Steel Soul shone with an inner light that was all but blinding. As if his faith were a tangible thing. Then and there, Tornus knew that whatever Gardus asked of him, he would do.

Gardus unhooked his helmet from his belt and pulled it on. He met Tornus' gaze and tapped the Knight-Venator on the chest with his hammer.

'Gird yourself, brother. It is time for us to go to war.'

CHAPTER FOUR

THE BRIDGE OF MAGGOTS

Water hissed away to vapour as Enyo sped just above the surface of the Verdant Bay. She moved so swiftly that her Prosecutors lagged behind, unable to match her speed. Only Periphas, her star-eagle, could keep pace with her. The Knight-Venator rolled through the air, letting the edge of one shimmering wing strike the water. A gout of steam burst upwards, trailing after her as she swooped towards the underside of the viaduct. She reached for an arrow as she rose past the lip of the bridge. Without slowing, she nocked and loosed, quicker than mortal eye could follow, quicker even than thought.

On the bridge, a blightking whirled as the arrow sprouted from his helm's visor. The great bulk flopped to the ground, dead before he hit. All eyes on the bridge rose, following Enyo as she continued her ascent. Even as she'd intended. Arrows from the Rotbringer ranks clattered uselessly in her wake.

She banked, twisting in mid-air, loosing another arrow of her own. And then a second and a third.

Each found its mark, each removed another blighted soul from the world-weave. Her wings snapped downwards, propelling her to even greater height. The viaduct shrank away, and its defenders were reduced to ants. The bridge was larger than it had any right to be, given the shoddiness of its construction. It was wide enough for a hundred warriors to walk abreast along its length. But it was not a straight path; instead it was a twisting, curving morass of bone and sargassum. It more resembled a mountain trail than the gleaming platinum viaducts her folk had once constructed.

For an instant, she was again sailing through the red-veined clouds above the great scholariums of Cypria, wings of clockwork clicking and humming. Those had been good days. Or so she hoped. Her memories of that time were but the basest of elements, unmingled and inert. She brushed the sigil of the twin-tailed comet engraved upon her chest-plate. She had worn another like it, before Sigmar had drawn her up into the sea of stars, Cypria burning beneath her. Though the City of Scholars was dead, it yet lived on in her.

'And that is the heaviest burden of all,' Enyo murmured. When she fell for the last time, would any still remember Cypria, and its clockwork legions? Or would they too pass into dim legend, as so many kingdoms had? If that was Sigmar's will, so be it. Much was demanded of those to whom much had been given, and she would not balk at the debt.

She spun lazily, knowing that those below could easily make out the gleam of her armour amid the dark clouds. 'That's right, keep looking at me. Here I am, death on high...' She drew an arrow from her quiver and nocked it. Her wings thrummed, pushing at the air to keep her steady. 'Quite a distance, this. What do you think, Periphas?'

The star-eagle shrieked, impatient. Enyo laughed. 'Yes, I suppose you're right, my friend. One must have faith. Sigmar will guide it to its target.' She released the arrow, and it streaked downwards like a blazing comet.

Below, a Rotbringer died. And then, so too did the viaduct. Enyo smiled in satisfaction as her Prosecutors did their work. She had held the eyes of the foe, allowing her warriors to complete their task unhindered. She folded her wings and fell, following the same course as her arrow.

The viaduct twisted up on itself like a wounded animal. Prosecutors swooped beneath and around it, hurling their celestial hammers with precise aim. They struck at the viaduct's weak points, reducing whole sections of the bridge to smoking slag.

Enyo swooped over the bridge, pursuing the Rotbringers as they fled back towards the citadel gates. Prosecutors fell in behind her. Hammers slammed down among the fleeing enemy, pulping many. Broken bodies hurtled into the air and tumbled away into the sea. 'The bridge falls,' one of the Prosecutors called out. Tegrus of the Sainted Eye. Once, he would have spoken with levity, but now, there was only grim satisfaction in his voice. 'What of the other?'

'That I leave to you, Tegrus. Take your retinue and see to it,' Enyo shouted. 'I and the others shall remind the enemy of the true extent of what they face.'

Tegrus saluted and banked, hurtling away, out over the water. Half a dozen Prosecutors followed him. Enyo continued on her course, followed by the remaining warriors.

From the high ramparts of the citadel, war-engines sang a brutal song. Catapults groaned, hurling gobbets of fly-ridden sargassum at the darting Prosecutors. Creaking ballistae loosed iron-headed bolts that bit only empty air, as the winged Stormcasts banked, rolled and dropped, easily avoiding them.

'I will take the war-machines,' Enyo called, as she sped up the incline of the walls. 'Galatus, Carva, smash open those gates. The rest of you, follow me.'

Explosions tore at the reeking walls as she rose. She shot past the ramparts. The armsmen of the Order of the Fly scurried like insects. More disciplined than the Rotbringers on the viaduct, they were nonetheless mortal. She drew a crackling arrow from her quiver and loosed, knocking a blightking from the ramparts. Without their officers, the armsmen would break. She loosed a flurry of arrows, aiming at random. Behind her, Prosecutors rose into the sky. Celestial hammers tore divots from the rampart, filling the air with smoke and death.

A ballista bolt tore through the smoke, and hummed past her, dangerously close. She folded her wings and dropped from the air. The wooden platform of the rampart squealed beneath her weight. Revulsion welled up in her as she realised that it had been crafted from still-living sylvaneth. Bonded together by pox-hardened sap and iron bolts, the tree-kin had been forced to grow into one another, and form the internal structure of the citadel – every walkway, every platform, all of one eternally suffering piece.

A blightking thudded towards her across the whimpering planks, his notched and blunted blade raised for a killing blow. He chortled as she ducked aside. Her bow smashed into the blightking's side, the force of it cracking the corroded armour. The blightking staggered, choking on his laughter. She leapt into the air and drove both feet into his chest, kicking him off the rampart.

An arrow spanged off her helm as she landed. She spun, drawing and loosing one of her own in a single, smooth motion. Armsmen boiled out of the smoke, rusty blades hacking at her. She backed away, loosing an arrow with every step. Only one made it within striking distance of her. She caught the blow on her bow and twisted the weapon out of its wielder's grip. The armsman gaped at her. He turned to flee, and ran into Periphas. The star-eagle fell screeching upon the Rotbringer, and knocked him flat.

Ignoring his cries, Enyo looked out over the interior of the sargasso-citadel. Pox-smoke billowed up from a central structure that reminded her of nothing so much as a vast cauldron. Warriors ran to and fro, as Prosecutors rained down hammer strike after hammer strike, destroying ramparts, walkways and bridges. Where the celestial hammers struck, sargassum burned with a cleansing fire.

It wasn't enough. They couldn't destroy this place, not on their own. There were too many of the foe, and the citadel was too large. But they weren't here for that. They were here to remind both the enemy and their fell gods that there was nothing they could claim that Sigmar could not take away.

A scream pierced the din. Human. Enyo turned, seeking out its source. She caught sight of the cages through a gap in the smoke – heavy things, made from wood and iron. And inside, the sickly, wasted figures of mortal captives. 'Periphas,' she said, as she dashed to the edge of the rampart and hurled herself into the air. The star-eagle shot after her, beak and talons wet with blood.

There were hundreds of slaves, crammed cheek to jowl in the pens. Olive-skinned and dark eyed, they reminded her somewhat of her own lost folk. They reached out through the rusty bars towards her, screaming and crying. Desperate to escape the heat of the rising flames and the agitated brutality of the overseers who lashed at them with barbed whips, trying to silence them. She descended in a snarl of lightning, scattering the overseers. One, a bloat-bellied brute clad in mouldering rags and rusty mail, snapped his whip at her, spitting curses.

She caught the coils of the whip around a forearm and jerked it taut, nearly pulling him off his feet. Periphas streaked down, talons slicing through the whip. The Rotbringer staggered back against a cage, and pale hands caught at him. He bellowed in anger and tore himself loose. Enyo sent an arrow into his throat before he had staggered more than a few paces. More overseers raced towards her. She waited patiently, letting them draw close.

Hammers spiralled down, striking with meteoric force. The overseers were pulped and broken. She glanced up. 'My thanks, Galatus. Now, free the mortals.'

The Prosecutors swooped to obey. She made her way towards the closest cage, wondering what she would say. The mortals shrank back from her Prosecutors, afraid of the strange, winged beings. She could not blame them. Their armour, their height, all of it was frightening, by design.

She heard a roar of lightning and turned. Above, on a low platform, one of her warriors vanished in a blaze of azure energy. A heavy form, clad in thick armour and wearing a helm topped by what appeared to be the head of a stylised toad-dragon, stepped into view. Quickly, she loosed an arrow, splitting one of the platform supports. The structure shifted and began to sag, threatening to dump the newcomer to the ground.

'I am Count Pustulix, and I claim the right of combat,' the warrior roared, leaping from the sagging platform. He dropped down with a crash, baroque armour weeping smoke. A Chaos knight, she realised. Larger and stronger than any blightking. 'Come, face a true knight and champion of the King of all Flies.' Streamers of filthy silk snapped about his helm. He extended the heavy splitting maul he clutched towards her. 'Face me, warrior, for the honour and glory of–'

Enyo drew an arrow and loosed. The star-fated projectile left behind a bright, iridescent trail as it leapt towards its target. When it struck, it did so in a clap of thunder. Pustulix's head snapped back as it pierced his helm and entered whatever passed for his brain. The Chaos knight tottered, limbs twitching. Then, with a sigh, he toppled backwards to land with a thud of finality.

'There is no honour in battle, only in victory,' Enyo said, as she stepped over the body and continued on her way to the cages. 'And victory belongs to the faithful.'

As the lateral viaducts fell, the full might of the Steel Souls pressed forward down the remaining bridge. The Rotbringers there had been working to destroy the central supports for the viaduct, obviously hoping to collapse those sections closest to shore. The assault had interrupted their labours, and now they retreated in disarray, or else fought like cornered animals. Most were retreating to make a stand at the line of mantlets stretching across the centre of the viaducts. That was where the real battle would be.

Aetius Shieldborn led his Liberators towards the enemy, moving forwards at a steady pace. There was no need for haste, for they were not the hammer, but the anvil. Across the bay, he caught sight of the leftmost viaduct finishing its slow collapse, thanks to the efforts of Tegrus and his Prosecutors. The enemy would have no choice now but to face them head-on. Unless they destroyed the remaining bridge out of spite.

No, he thought. No, that was not the Order's way. He had fought such enemies before, in the winding streets of the reed-city of Gramin, and the Chaos knights had a twisted sense of martial honour. They wanted – *needed* – battle in a way that few other servants of the Plague God did. He suspected that whatever forces awaited them in the citadel were eager to greet them. A roar of lightning from up ahead caught his attention. Feros had met the enemy, and found them wanting.

'Make way, make way, for Feros of the Heavy Hand has come,' the Retributor-Prime roared. His lightning hammer smashed down through an upraised shield and the cowering figure beneath. 'Where I walk, no gate, no wall, shall bar the way.' His voice boomed out over the viaduct, as loud as thunder. 'Come and set your shields, I shall crack them and make a bonfire of your bones. Make way, make way!'

'Do you think they heard him?' Solus asked, as he loosed another arrow. The Judicator-Prime spoke calmly, displaying none of the excitement one might expect. His Judicators marched in the lee of their brethren's shieldwall, trusting in the Liberators to see them safely through the press of battle. It was an old tactic, but reliable. The Judicators drew and loosed with drilled precision, following their commander's example.

'I think Nurgle in his garden heard him,' Aetius said, glancing at the Judicator-Prime. 'But he's clearing us a path, and that's all that matters.'

'So he is. How thoughtful of him.' Solus loosed an arrow as he spoke, sending it high, so that it might arc down on the enemy. His aim was second only to that of the Steel Souls'

Knight-Venator, Enyo. 'We should probably catch up to him, before he gets himself in trouble,' he added mildly.

Aetius nodded. He envied Solus his serenity, especially in battle. Sometimes he fancied that the other warrior was the eye of the storm made manifest. Solus had no doubts as to his place in the world, or his purpose.

In contrast, Aetius felt as if he had nothing but questions. Unlike some Stormcasts, Aetius recalled nothing of his mortal life. Where the fragments of memory should have been was only an emptiness, an absence secreted behind a wall of faith. For him, there was nothing in the world save his duty.

Perhaps that was for the best. Memories seemed to bring only pain.

A war-horn sounded, somewhere ahead. Knight-Heraldor Kurunta fought in the vanguard alongside the Devastation Brotherhoods. The other auxiliary commanders were scattered throughout the chamber, where they could be of the most use. Lord-Castellant Grymn marched at the centre of the advance, the aleph around which the assault would pivot. Lord-Relictor Morbus had command of the far flank, on the other side of the viaduct from Aetius and his warriors.

Aetius turned to bellow at two nearby Liberators. 'Serena, Berkut... keep your shields locked. If a single Judicator falls because of your inattention, I shall send you back to Azyr myself.' He gestured to another. 'Taya, five paces to the left. Bolster the flank.'

Ahead of them, Feros and his retinue maintained their momentum. The Retributors moved as one, without speed, but steadily. A millstone of silver and azure, lightning hammers slamming down to crush bone and pulp flesh as the heavily armoured warriors ground forwards. The Retributors fought in the vanguard, clearing a path for those who followed.

The Steel Souls fought not as a single battle line, but as independent formations of Thunderhead Brotherhoods, composed of Liberators and Judicators. They marched in the wake of the Devastation Brotherhoods, consisting of Retributors and Decimators, capitalising on the carnage wreaked by the Paladin Conclaves. The Devastation Brotherhoods were a scythe, cutting through the field of foes. In contrast, the Thunderhead Brotherhoods fought as tight squares, grinding apart any enemy caught between them.

It was not a subtle stratagem, but it was certainly effective. The Rotbringers collapsed inwards, like a lanced boil. The mortal servants of Nurgle could not hope to match the sheer, destructive fury of warriors like Feros. Even the blightkings hesitated to put themselves in the Heavy Hand's path. And those that did inevitably found themselves broken, and left to the mercies of Aetius and his Liberators.

Aetius cursed as a streak of blue lightning speared upwards from the thick of battle. Another one lost, returned to the heavens to be Reforged. How many had they lost in these past weeks? How many since they'd first set foot in the Jade Kingdoms? Whatever the total, it was too many.

Infuriated, he slammed his shield into the skull of a blightking as the obese warrior heaved himself to his feet, suppurating coils of intestine tangling his legs. The blightking sank to one knee with a phlegmatic cough. Aetius hit him with the shield again, knocking him backwards. Before the blightking could rise, he brought his hammer down, crushing the rust-riddled helm and the rotten skull within. A swarm of biting flies exploded from the ruptured helmet, forcing him to take a step back. The insects dispersed swiftly.

'I hate when they do that,' he snarled.

'So you insist on reminding me,' Solus said. He turned, loosing an arrow into a charging Rotbringer. 'Dispersed volley,' he said. His Judicators turned, breaking ranks to send their arrows flying in all directions. 'There seem to be more of them than there were a few moments ago.'

'Feros is getting sloppy,' Aetius said. A rust-edged axe slammed down against his shield, gouging the sigmarite. He swept the weapon aside and pulped the blightking's exposed knee. The Rotbringer staggered, and an arrow sprouted from the visor of his helm, pitching him backwards. 'I had him,' Aetius growled.

'There's plenty more where he came from, brother. Have your pick.'

Aetius shook his head, annoyed. The battle for the bridge was becoming confused. The Rotbringers squeezed between the Thunderhead formations were fighting back, trying to win through, or else form up in ranks. They would fail, but it was a hindrance nonetheless. Spears skittered off his shield, as a trio of hauberk-clad armsmen tried to make a stand. The mortal warriors were tough and strong, but not enough of either. Aetius crashed his shield into theirs, driving the three men back step by step. They continued to stab at him, cursing and shouting prayers to their foul god.

He swept his arm out, sending them sprawling. His hammer caught the first in the head, spilling his brains across the faces of his fellows. Out of the corner of his eye, he caught sight of a heavy shape surging towards him. He turned at the last moment, only just avoiding a blow that would have sent him back to the forges of Azyr.

The Rotbringer was no blightking, but something far worse – a Chaos knight, clad in thick war-plate, decorated with eye-searing sigils, and wearing a tabard marked with the ruinous symbol of his patron god. He wore a helmet decorated with grotesquely wrought flies, and a cloak of toad-dragon hide. 'Have at thee,' the creature intoned, its voice a hollow moan. A festering blade, twice as wide as a normal sword, marked with notches, slashed out. It carved a scar across Aetius' chest-plate, staggering him.

He bulled forwards, crashing into the Chaos knight, driving him back a step. The warrior caught the edge of his shield and checked Aetius' rush. The sword swept down, hacking into the rim of his shield and driving him to one knee. 'I shall give thee a beautiful death, interloper,' the Chaos knight groaned, wrenching his sword free of the shield and raising it. Before the blow could fall, an arrow sank into a gap in his armour. The knight stumbled, turning instinctively. A second arrow followed the first, piercing his cuirass.

Aetius rose to his feet and slammed his hammer into the back of the knight's knees, dropping him to the ground. The warrior tried to turn, but too late. The hammer sang down and the knight slumped, skull crushed. Aetius looked up. 'Now who's being sloppy?' Solus said. Before Aetius could reply, the Judicator-Prime pointed. 'Look, we've reached the mantlets.' Aetius turned.

Ahead of them, Feros and his Retributors had slowed their advance. The mantlets were massive shields, arrayed across the width of the viaduct, and held in place by iron spikes and heavy chains. Behind them, more enemy warriors crouched, these clutching bows. As the broken remnants of the Rotbringer advance streamed between the mantlets, seeking refuge, the archers rose, arrows nocked. The broad heads of their arrows glowed with sickly green fire. 'Balefire arrows,' Solus said.

'Reform the line, shields up,' Aetius shouted, even as the

first volley of arrows streaked into the air, leaving trails of pestilential smoke in their wake.

The viaduct shuddered as the balefire ripsawed across it, reducing fossilised sargassum to bubbling liquidity. Ancient bones tore loose from the structure and surfaced explosively, scattering Stormcasts and Rotbringers alike. Where the green flames touched, cohesion gave way to chaos. And, amidst the crackling hellstorm, immense maggots rose into sight, burrowing up through the surface of the bridge. They launched themselves at the Stormcasts, mandibles clicking wetly.

Lord-Relictor Morbus Stormwarden slammed the ferrule of his reliquary staff down. It struck the surface of the bridge with a loud crack. Lightning thrummed through the bridge, spitting and clawing at the maggots. One of the creatures burst, and where its foul ichor fell, more flames blazed up, adding to the conflagration. The heat washed down the length of the bridge, driving nearby retinues of Stormcast Eternals back in momentary disorder.

'Back,' he called out, gesturing with his hammer. 'Do not let the flames touch you.' Liberators and Judicators fell back, pursued by the squirming maggot-beasts.

Morbus found himself facing one of the creatures. It reared up over him, mouth-parts clicking, its body pulsing with unnatural energies. Whether these creatures had been created by the balefires, or simply awakened by them, was immaterial. Only the method and surety of their dispatch mattered. The maggot-thing lunged, and he struck it with his hammer, knocking it aside. It squealed and thrashed, body undulating in repellent fashion. Another came at him, its slobbery maw fastening on his arm, swallowing both hand and hammer whole.

Its acidic bile began to eat into his vambrace and gauntlet. A gleaming blade swept down suddenly, separating its head from its body. Kurunta kicked the squirming carcass aside, taking care to avoid the balefire that sprang up. The Knight-Heraldor helped Morbus extricate his arm. 'Where in the name of the Great Bear did these things come from?' he said. 'They're all over the bridge.'

'It doesn't matter. Join the advance. Let nothing stand in your path.' Morbus raised his staff and intoned a prayer to the celestial storm, as Kurunta hurried to join his warriors. His words echoed out over the clangour of battle, rising up to the skies. Far above, the clouds contracted and twisted in on themselves. In moments, the thick pox-clouds were pierced through by a shimmering rain. Where it fell, the maggots screamed. Their flesh steamed and blistered as the cleansing waters washed them away to nothing.

The flames too seemed to struggle against the falling rain, flaring eerily in places. While parts of the conflagration were snuffed, in other places the balefires grew fiercer and continued to spread. Nearby, an unlucky Liberator was caught in one such expanding blaze. Morbus turned as he heard the warrior's scream of pain.

The Hallowed Knight's silver armour turned black almost instantly. The sigmarite plates began to blister and slough away from his frame as he screamed in agony. His limbs bulged with unnatural growth, sprouting pustules that wailed like newborn infants. His intestines swelled, splitting his body open from within. The groaning mass collapsed, convulsed and lay still. No lightning speared upwards, no spark escaped. Morbus took a step towards the steaming mass. If the soul of the warrior had not escaped, it was his duty to reclaim it, whatever the cost.

The mass heaved up. A gash split down the middle, expelling dagger-like fangs from within the roiling meat. Awkward arms, thick with infected muscle and splintered bone, thudded down, pulling the newborn monstrosity forwards, useless hind limbs dragging behind it. It shrieked in agony as it lunged with crippled ferocity towards the closest Stormcasts. New-grown teeth shattered on a sigmarite shield, only for the splinters to sprout anew. The Liberators struck at the creature. Every blow released sprays of reeking pus, which sizzled where it struck their armour.

A tendril-like arm whipped out, sending warriors flying. A Liberator slammed into the side of the viaduct and vanished over the edge. Another crunched down at an awkward angle, neck clearly broken. Blue lightning shot upwards and Morbus stepped through it, drawing strength from its connection to Azyr. He struck the bridge with his staff again, catching the attention of his warriors. 'Back, all of you back. This is my duty.'

Liberators pulled back warily, shields raised in case the abomination decided to ignore the Lord-Relictor. The monstrous bulk heaved itself towards Morbus as he approached, its limbs rupturing and expelling thick, root-like shoots as it did so. It was becoming a part of the bridge, a living bulwark, formed of pox-ridden meat and sorcery. 'Brother, can you hear me?' Morbus said.

A bony limb slashed at him, and he deftly avoided it. As it tried to retract, he pinned it in place with his staff. The creature shuddered and screamed again, its voice distorted into a bestial wail. Pustules formed and burst on its bulk, and he could hear the cracking of bones within it. With every moment that passed, it lost more of its shape. It tried to yank its limb free of him, but failed.

'Brother,' he said again, trying to pierce the fog of agony he knew was clouding the creature's mind. 'You will listen.' He twisted his staff, grinding the ferrule into the suppurating flesh. It roared and thrashed, but soon subsided.

'Kuh-kuhlmeee,' the thing gurgled from its gash-like mouth. An eye rolled in a shrunken socket, only to burst as it fixed on him. He could still make out part of the Liberator's face, taut with agony, within the altered hulk. That he was still alive was testament to the durability of the God-King's design. But in this case, it was more curse than blessing. Morbus nodded slowly, and raised his hammer.

'By the bones that I bear and call my own, I bid ye heed now, brother. Heed only the call of the God-King, and accept his blessing.' It was a poor sort of prayer, but he had little time for anything better. An urgency he could not explain gripped him.

The hammer fell. Thunder rolled. Lightning flared upwards, freed at last from a tormented husk. Morbus watched it ascend, and then turned his attention back to the battle. He started forwards. He gave no orders. None were necessary. Behind him, Liberators and Judicators followed his example.

The last few of the giant maggots squirmed towards the advancing Stormcasts, their vile flesh bubbling from the touch of the cleansing rain. Morbus met them with lightning. They had no time to waste, fighting mindless beasts. The charred husks were crushed and scattered by the warriors in his wake.

He could feel the ebb and flow of the storm above him. It was growing stronger, its rains washing the pox-clouds from the air. Sigmar – or some aspect of him – was watching and aiding his faithful. But there was something else in the air as well... a twisting, churning sensation. His stomach roiled, and he could feel the strange magics percolating through the hardened sargassum of the bridge. It was a resonance, of sorts. Like called to like, and whatever was happening, it had its origins in the same sort of corrupt sorcery that had originally formed the bridges and citadels.

Ahead of him, a shieldwall of Rotbringers were readying themselves to make a stand. He saw the corpulent shapes of blightkings among them, steadying the line with hoarse shouts of encouragement. Kurunta had shattered the mantlets and driven the Rotbringers back across to this point. They had likely expected the balefires to hold the Stormcasts at bay while they retreated. Morbus smiled thinly. The storm could not be held back so easily.

Kurunta fell into step beside him, followed by a retinue of Retributors. The Knight-Heraldor's armour was blackened in places, and marked by weapon strikes. 'Your rain was well-timed, Lord-Relictor.'

Morbus inclined his head in acknowledgement, but didn't reply. Lightning writhed over his armour and weapons as he marched towards the enemy. It sparked and snarled around him like a gryph-hound straining at the leash. 'Who will be redeemed?' Morbus said, his voice like a peal of a funerary bell.

'Only the faithful,' Kurunta and the others responded, their voices a low growl.

'Who will stand until the last stone is dust?'

'Only the faithful.' As one, the Liberators began to strike the flats of their shields with their hammers and warblades. Kurunta raised his war-horn to his lips and blew a single, sterling note, which shivered out across the air.

Morbus could feel the song of the storm building within him. It yearned to be free, to rage across all the worlds, to drown and burn all that was not pure. 'Who will rise, when all others fall?' he called out. He could make out the faces of the enemy now, frightened and pale beneath their corroded helms. The line of spears wavered, brittle and hesitant.

'Only the faithful.' A roar now, a crash of thunder.

Morbus thudded forwards, Kurunta and his Retributors following close behind. Lightning ricocheted from the Lord-Relictor, leaping towards the Rotbringers. It ripped through their ranks, killing dozens. A blightking, either brave or desperate, pushed towards him, sword raised. 'Who will know victory?' Morbus roared, as his hammer descended with all the fury of the celestial storm.

'*Only the faithful!*'

CHAPTER FIVE

THE SARGASSO-CITADEL

'You have come this far only to be mulch for Grandfather's garden, silver-skin,' the blightking burbled as he stomped forwards. Gelid rolls of fat quivered on bowed limbs, and air wheezed from between its folds. Crumbling armour squealed in protest as the blightking raised his pitted axe and gave a joyful bellow.

Lord-Castellant Grymn ignored his opponent's taunts and swung his halberd out in a narrow arc. The blightking fell in two directions, bile pumping. Grymn shook the foulness from his blade and surveyed his surroundings. The advance had almost ground to a halt. The air smelled of burning flesh and lightning. Balefire arrows shrieked out from murder holes, and greenish fire roared up, only to be snuffed by the cool wind and clean rain that filled the passageway. Lord-Relictor Morbus' healing storm soothed the hurts of the Stormcasts and kept the fell magics of the enemy at bay.

Ahead of Grymn, Order armsmen held the line against

the Hallowed Knights, amid the smoking ruins of the citadel gatehouse. The front of the gatehouse had once been the jaws of some ancient leviathan, now twisted out of shape and stretched into a monstrous parody of a portcullis. A jungle of rotting flesh and sargassum stretched beyond, and more Rotbringers lumbered to join the battle line. It was as if every able-bodied warrior were being funnelled into the gatehouse to stall their entrance.

Tallon chirruped, and Grymn scratched the gryph-hound's angular skull. The animal paced beside him as he advanced behind the front ranks of Liberators. 'Yes, I know. Too slow. We need room to manoeuvre. But they're determined not to give it to us.'

The mortals were disciplined, great iron-rimmed shields locked in a wall, spears lowered, blocking all ingress. When one fell, another stepped into his place. They were exhorted on by the blubbery champions who lurked in the rear ranks, only to squirm forth at the least opportune moment. The blight-kings fought only long enough to buy their mortal followers breathing room, and then retreated back behind their shields. Unless someone killed them first. Grymn glanced at the body of the one he'd just killed and then back at the enemy shield-wall. He could not help but admire such discipline, even as he sought to destroy those who displayed it. They knew what they were doing, these fly-worshippers.

The gatehouse wasn't wide enough to accommodate more than a few dozen Stormcasts moving forwards at a time. They were still advancing, but slowly, more slowly than he liked. At times, hidden passages sluiced open in the boggy walls of the gatehouse, releasing fly-ridden fanatics and beastmen to hurl themselves into the fray. Outside the gatehouse, those Stormcasts arrayed on the viaduct fought to smash handholds and steps in the glutinous surface of the walls. If they couldn't get through, they would have to go over.

Grymn heard Kurunta's war-horn sound, and felt the rumble of collapsing masonry. He'd left the Knight-Heraldor in charge of the forces still outside. If anyone could punch a hole in those walls, it was Kurunta. 'Best be there to greet him when he does,' he said.

He reached down and flipped open his warding lantern, letting the holy light swell and fill the passageway. He took the lantern from his belt and hung it from the blade of his halberd. He lifted the weapon high, like a standard.

Mortal Rotbringers screamed and clawed at their eyes as the light struck them, and blightkings stumbled back, altered flesh bubbling. Liberators seized the moment, tramping forwards to close the gap. Sigmarite shields crashed into the wavering line, and men fell screaming, to be trampled underfoot. There could be no stopping, no mercy. Distasteful as it was, if the only way to their objective was over the crushed bodies of these corrupt mortals, then so be it. Grymn followed the front rank of Liberators, keeping his halberd high.

Behind him, Feros and his Retributors fell in, moving to protect him should any enemy get close. Tallon was more than enough protection, but he saw no need to insult Feros or the others. It was a sign of respect, if nothing else. Given that it was Feros of the Heavy Hand, it was something of a surprise as well.

The Retributor-Prime had never been what one could call especially respectful. The Hero of the Celestine Glacier had always been the wrath of the heavens made flesh, with a personality to match. At times, Grymn had suspected that Feros cared about the opinions of only one man. Irksome, but understandable. Gardus was Lord-Celestant, and his was the hand that wielded the Steel Souls in battle.

But Feros, like Tegrus and various others, was not the same bellicose warrior who had once stalked the Celestine Ice, lightning hammer in hand. He had been Reforged, crafted anew after his death in the Ghyrtract Fen. The warrior who had come back was as fierce as ever, yet more biddable, less prone to the battle lust that had once afflicted him.

Grymn was not entirely certain that he liked the implications. For if Feros could become more obedient, and if Tegrus could lose his wit, then so too could Gardus change. Would he even recognise the Lord-Celestant when he stood before him once more? Or would he face a stranger, stripped of all familiarity? He had heard stories of the transformations of Thostos Bladestorm and Gaius Greel. Of mighty warriors, *reduced* somehow. Lessened. He smelled the tang of scorched metal, and felt a chill. 'We could use a bit of divine intervention,' he said.

'A bit more, you mean,' Morbus said. He leaned against his reliquary staff, visibly weary. He'd taken part in the initial assault, and his mortis armour had been marked and scored by enemy blades. 'It is all I can do to keep the balefires from spreading.'

Grymn glanced at him. 'Are you injured?' he asked gruffly. 'If so, you are only a burden here. One I do not need.' The words came out more harshly than he'd intended, but Morbus only chuckled.

'Simply weary.' Morbus straightened. 'Can you feel it?'

'Feel what?' Grymn asked, but he knew the answer. He'd been feeling it since they'd pushed through the outer gates. The air felt heavy, as if a storm were brewing somewhere. 'Reinforcements?'

Morbus nodded. 'Gardus is coming. We must make ready to greet him.'

Grymn frowned, though his heart leapt. He'd hoped to have this battle done with by the time the Steel Soul arrived, but it seemed not to be. 'We need to break their lines for good. Give them no chance to recover.' He glanced around, and then slammed the ferrule of his halberd down. 'Hold,' he roared, his voice carrying easily above the din. Liberators clattered to a halt, hunkered behind their shields. 'Highwall formation.'

The front rank of Liberators knelt, planting the rims of their shields on the ground. The second rank moved in behind them, slamming the bottoms of their shields atop those in the front rank, until a wall of sigmarite filled the passageway. The third rank raised their shields over their heads, parallel to the ground, and formed a narrow column. Those at the back knelt, creating an improvised ramp to the top of the wall.

The Lord-Castellant nodded in satisfaction. He was proud of this particular formation. It had never failed to win him victory on the fields of the Gladitorium. It made use of all available space in the most efficient manner possible, and his warriors could hold their position for hours, if need be. 'Solus,' he called out. Beyond the wall, he could hear the muffled cries of the Rotbringers as they regrouped. Not much time, now.

The Judicator-Prime hurried to join him. Grymn pointed to the rampart. 'I need your lightning, Solus. We have tarried in these cramped confines too long.'

'Not much room,' Solus said, eyeing the ceiling of the passageway. He turned and signalled to his Judicators. 'Enough, though. Gatius, Parnas, bring your warriors up.' Judicators carrying heavy skybolt bows and thunderbolt crossbows moved quickly up through the ranks, and then began to climb the makeshift ramp of shields.

When they'd reached the top, they sank to their knees and waited, balancing perfectly on the raised shields of their fellow Stormcasts. Grymn struck the ground with his halberd again. 'Steel Souls, make your judgement.'

With a snarl of thunder, the Judicators unleashed a devastating volley on the packed ranks of Rotbringers below. The raised shields of the Liberators acted akin to the embrasures of a battlement, protecting the archers from harm. Blasts of celestial energy were followed by bursts of chained lightning, and soon the air was thick with the stink of charred meat.

'Feros, Markius,' Grymn said, as another volley thundered into the enemy. 'Ready yourselves. Whatever is left out there, I want it ground into mulch.'

'As you command, Lord-Castellant,' Feros said, raising his hammer in salute. The Retributors arrayed themselves in two queues behind the shieldwall, ready to stream out when the order was given. Grymn waited, eyes closed, counting volleys. The second would alert the Rotbringers to the change in tactics. The third would knock them back on their heels. The fourth and fifth would set the rear ranks to flight. The sixth would sweep the immediate area of survivors. There would be eight volleys in all. No more, no less.

There was a certain amount of peace to be found in contemplating the machinery of war. Individual warriors, retinues, all parts of the machine. Machine against machine, and the first to break, lost. Keep the machine moving, and you win. For Grymn, war was all about calculation. It was a thing of minute variables, observed and processed by a mind trained in the mathematics of battle. For others, he knew, war was a more instinctive thing.

Gardus, for instance. Defensive by nature, he simply endured, until the enemy made a mistake. And then exploited that moment of weakness. The Steel Soul did not lack for courage or skill, but he had a distinct absence of aggression. More than once, that absence had caused Grymn worry, and to question his Lord-Celestant. Some small part of him, an unworthy part, wondered if perhaps Sigmar had not made a mistake in assigning them their separate roles. He shook his head, banishing the thought.

'He, the sword, and I, the shield,' he muttered.

'What was that?' Morbus asked.

'Nothing. That's eight volleys. Open the gates.' He slashed a hand down, signalling for a section of the shieldwall to disengage and fall back. They left a wide gap in the line, through which Feros and Markius led their warriors. For long moments, the only sound was the tromp of the Retributors' advance. Then came the crack of a lightning hammer. Another. A third. Grymn struck the ground with his halberd.

'Bulwark formation – quickly now!'

The shieldwall broke apart and reformed in moments, with a rattle of war-plate. The bulwark formation was simple, similar to the highwall. It was a shieldwall two ranks high, with the uppermost rank angled so as to prevent arrows, javelins or stones from crashing down immediately behind. Slowly, but surely, the bulwark advanced, moving over the bodies of the dead. Judicators dispersed along the bulwark as it moved, loosing crackling arrows through gaps in the shieldwall.

Morbus grunted. Grymn turned in time to see a shudder run through the Lord-Relictor. 'What is it?' Grymn asked, catching hold of Morbus' arm as he stumbled.

'Something…' Morbus shook his head, as if to clear it. 'I can feel something…'

'So you said.'

'Not that,' Morbus snapped. Grymn blinked. It was a rare

thing for the Lord-Relictor to raise his voice, even in the most stressful of moments. 'There's something stirring now. Below us. In the roots of this place.' He looked at Grymn. 'Something sick. It feels like a… a wound going septic. As if the waters, the very air, are crying out in sudden pain, Lorrus.'

Grymn hesitated at the Lord-Relictor's use of his given name. Whatever Morbus felt, it was bad. He pushed himself away from Grymn. 'I have felt something akin to this before, when we first arrived in the Jade Kingdoms. At the Gates of Dawn.'

A sudden chill ran through the Lord-Castellant. The Gates of Dawn had been the reason they'd come to the Realm of Life in the first place. The ancient realmgate had supposedly led from Ghyran to Aqshy. But in actuality, it had been twisted out of joint and corrupted, as so many things in these lands had been. Instead of revealing a path to the red sands of Aqshy, the Gates of Dawn had opened up into the sour heart of Chaos itself. The gate had vomited forth daemons devoted to Nurgle. The horrors that followed had set the tone for all that was to come.

The Gates of Dawn had been destroyed, thanks to Gardus. But a noisome taint yet lingered over those crippled stones. Nothing could feel the touch of the Ruinous Powers and not be changed in some way. 'Could there be a realmgate here?' he asked, one eye on the advancing Liberators.

'I would stake my soul on it,' Morbus said.

'Then it's best we finish this now.' Grymn paused, taking stock of the Lord-Relictor. Morbus appeared on the verge of exhaustion. Decision made, he continued, 'When we clear the gatehouse, I will seek it out. You maintain our lines, and wait for Gardus. When he arrives, tell him what he needs to know.'

Morbus shook his head. 'But–'

Grymn gripped Morbus' shoulder, briefly. 'We all have our parts to play, Morbus. This is mine. After all, am I not a Guardian of the Gateway and Keeper of the Keys? The spirits and their ways are your responsibility. Realmgates are mine.'

'You cannot go alone,' Morbus insisted. 'You will need me.'

'The Steel Souls need you,' Grymn said. 'Gardus will need you. And I need only myself.' Tallon screeched, and Grymn laughed.

'Well, myself and one other.'

When the first of the storm-warriors advanced out of the barbican, they did so in a deluge of rain and serpentine lightning. They were heavily armoured, their ornate panoply shining silver and gold. They wielded their great two-handed hammers as if they weighed no more than feathers, and set to work with grim purpose.

Duke Gatrog watched them from an overhanging platform, studying them with interest. It was rare that he could watch his foe in action from a safe remove, and he did not intend to waste the opportunity. A foe studied was a foe defeated, as Blightmaster Wolgus supposedly said, upon the commencement of the Second Pox-Crusade into the northern wilds of Shyish. That Wolgus had perished soon after did not take away from the sentiment.

If ever there was an enemy that required study, it was these storm-warriors. The destruction of the outer viaducts had been unexpected. The storm-warriors had reacted more swiftly than expected. Runners from the other two citadels reported confusion and devastation. Freed slaves running amok, walls torn down. Count Pustulix was dead, slain in a most dishonourable fashion. And poor Baron Feculast had been buried beneath his own walls by the relentless hammer-strikes of the enemy's winged harbingers. Gatrog shivered. That was no sort of end for a knight.

Things weren't going well at all. Gatrog couldn't help but wonder if the King of all Flies had removed his guiding hand from their shoulders. A defeat here would cripple the Order of the Fly for centuries to come. They might even be forced to abandon their holdings outside the Blighted Duchies. And all because of these silver-skinned invaders. He growled low in his throat, incensed at the mere thought of it.

'They fight like ghyrlions,' Agak said. The shieldbearer crouched nearby, eyes wide. Gatrog's great shield was strapped to his back, and he was almost bent double beneath the weight. 'How can any mortal man hope to stand against that?'

'He who holds Grandfather in his heart shall live forever-more,' Gatrog said piously. The first wave of armsmen to reach the storm-warriors died. As did the second wave. And the third. By the fourth, they were leaving some alive, though only by accident, and mostly because the smarter armsmen were using the corpses for cover.

'I guess Grandfather must not be in their hearts,' Agak mused. Gatrog looked at him, and the shieldbearer cringed. The Chaos knight turned his attention back to the enemy. Each one was an island, a silver blaze shining in a night-dark sea. They defended the inner portcullis, preventing anyone from lowering it and sealing off the barbican.

From within the depths of the gatehouse came the clangour of metal-shod boots, and the rattle of weapons. The outer walls shook from the assault of those storm-warriors still outside. Above him, the ramparts echoed with the creak of war-engines as their crews tried to guide them into new positions. It was unlikely to do any good, but there was strength in despair, and that was all any warrior could ask for.

Well, that and the high ground.

Gatrog raised his hand. 'Ready,' he said. Behind him, fifty of the best bowmen in the Order raised their wormbows. The corroded tips of the arrows glistened with the sweetest of effluvia. A man struck by one would sicken and die in moments. He was curious to see whether the same could be said of the storm-warriors.

He dropped his hand. 'Loose.'

The arrows hissed overhead, arcing above the courtyard before plummeting downwards with impressive accuracy. A single silver warrior staggered. Slumped. Fell. His body exploded into a writhing nest of lightning. It surged upwards, knocking several armsmen from their feet, and setting their jerkins alight. They rolled in the muck, howling in pain. The other storm-warriors fought on, despite the arrows bristling from their war-plate. Gatrog hissed in frustration. 'Make ready,' he snapped.

If they could not close the barbican in time, the enemy would enter the citadel, endangering all that the Order of the Fly had worked so long and hard for. He could not allow that to happen. The King of all Flies had tasked them, and Gatrog would see it done, upon his honour as a true and faithful knight. 'Loose–'

His command was interrupted as a gleaming arrow pierced the skull of the archer closest to him. The bowman collapsed in a heap. Gatrog looked up. A winged shape circled high overhead. More arrows thudded down, faster than Gatrog thought possible. He scrambled for cover in the lee of the wall. The bowmen weren't so lucky, and soon the platform was clogged with bodies. Cursing, Gatrog plucked an arrow from his forearm. It hurt, but pain was a gift from Grandfather, reminding one of the sweet brevity of life.

The arrow turned to motes of stinging light before his eyes. Such was the nature of their foe. Nothing but starlight and lightning. Where was the blood? The crunch of bone? Could these creatures even feel, or were they simply ghosts, stirred from maggotless graves by a jealous godling?

In a way, he almost pitied them. They would never know Grandfather's love, or the glory of service to the King of all Flies. But they would die in his name, all the same. He sought out Agak, who hunkered nearby, hiding beneath his master's shield. He gestured brusquely. 'Agak! Shield.'

'Keep forgetting they can fly, don't you, my lord?' Agak puffed as he carried the heavy, iron-banded shield across the platform. The winged bowmen had found other targets. Shimmering arrows pierced the murk, sending armsmen and blightkings tumbling from the ramparts and platforms. Down below, the battle continued. The storm-warriors held doggedly to their position, beating back every attempt to shift them.

'Silence, Agak. Save your breath for issuing my challenge to yon poltroon. I would have words with them.'

'Which poltroon would that be, my lord? The one with the wings, or…?'

Gatrog caught Agak by the throat, and dragged him close. 'I don't care. Pick one.'

'Yes, my lord,' Agak gurgled, eyes bulging. 'Right away, my lord.'

Gatrog tossed him aside and hefted his shield. It had been made from the faceted scale of one of the great water-drakes of the southern reach, and reinforced with iron and bone. Ruinous sigils had been etched into every flat surface, however small. The shield had been a gift from the great Lady of Cankerwall herself, and had carried him safely through fire and war for a century. He drew his sword and slammed the flat against the surface of the shield. 'Send forth my challenge, Agak. I go to confront the foe.'

Agak screamed.

Gatrog turned to chastise him, and saw the shadow. He raised his shield just in time, absorbing the brunt of the hammer's impact. Lightning snapped out, clawing at him around the edges of the shield. His bones trembled in their envelope of flesh and he staggered back, shoulder aching. He swept the shield aside, dispersing the smoke of the strike. A gleaming form arrowed towards him, crackling wings extended to their limits.

He raised his shield and set his feet, bracing himself against the imminent impact. The storm-warrior banked at the last moment, sweeping past him. The crackling feathers of one wing brushed against him, tearing through his armour and searing the flesh beneath. Gatrog bellowed and spun. His sword thudded down, narrowly missing his attacker.

'My lord, beware,' Agak shouted, moments before he leapt from the platform. Gatrog looked up and saw a deluge of blazing hammers spinning down towards him. An instant before they struck, he followed Agak's example. He hit the ground as the platform exploded into fiery splinters. Rivets popped and plates shifted as he rolled heavily to his feet. He was a knight, not an acrobat. Something inside him was broken, and he tasted blood. It would heal soon enough, if he survived the next few moments.

The courtyard was in chaos. Things were going wrong very quickly. Someone had smashed open the slave-cages, and the dim-witted savages fell upon armsmen and overseer alike with unbridled fury. It was as if the storm had driven them berserk. But storms eventually blew over, and when it was done, they would go back in their cages. Gatrog would see to it personally. For now, he needed to rally those he could and drive the enemy back.

He hunted for Agak. He caught sight of the shieldbearer rising to his feet nearby. He felt what might have been relief at his servant's survival. 'Agak, come here, man,' he called out, waving his sword. 'Quickly! There is work to be done.'

'Bloody work,' Agak said.

'But not for you,' Gatrog said, ignoring Agak's sigh of relief. 'Go below. Inform Blightmaster Bubonicus of the situation. Return to me if you can.'

'And if I cannot, my lord?'

Gatrog caught the back of Agak's head. 'Then I will assume you are dead. For that is the only reason you should not return.' He squeezed gently, eliciting a whimper. Then he shoved Agak back. 'Go, thou, my faithful servant. Do as I have bid.'

Gatrog turned, already dismissing the little Rotbringer from his thoughts. Agak would do as he had been commanded, or he would die in the attempt. Gatrog had his own duties to attend to. He bellowed at nearby armsmen, gesturing towards the storm-warriors. Before he could join them, however, he heard the crack of shimmering wings. His opponent from earlier had decided to continue their duel.

He ducked aside as a hammer swept down, wielded by a silver-clad arm. The blow would have crushed his skull. The winged storm-warrior dropped lightly to the ground and spun, one wing slicing out. Gatrog lifted his shield and, for a moment, lightning clawed at him. Then he was moving through it, sword extended. His blade carried no sigils or ruinous markings. It was merely a sword, forged in balefire and cooled in the sour waters of the Murklands. But, driven by his arm, it punched easily enough through the silver chest-plate of his opponent. The storm-warrior exploded in a blaze of celestial energy.

Gatrog heard a whirr of wings and pivoted, driving his shield into the face of a second winged warrior, with a loud clang. The storm-warrior dropped like a stone, glowing hammers fading into motes of light. He shook his head, trying to clear it. Gatrog saved him the effort and removed his head entirely. Another searing burst of lightning came and went.

When it cleared, Gatrog saw silver shapes marching from the barbican to join their fellows. And more winged storm-warriors glided overhead. Enemies everywhere he looked, and a stinking, clear rain falling from hideously clear skies. He cursed.

Overhead, thunder rumbled. Lightning flashed.

But this time it did not rise to the heavens. Instead, it descended. Gatrog looked up as the coruscating bolt speared downwards towards the balefire cauldron. It dropped from impossible, invisible heights, growing louder as it drew closer. Like a blade cutting through the substance of Ghyran itself. The light and noise of its coming swelled outwards, filling the courtyard. Gatrog raised his shield and hunkered behind it, deaf and blind. For long moments, the world was reduced to nothing but light and sound.

Then the ground bucked savagely as the immense cauldron exploded into a million fiery fragments. Gatrog fell, but managed to hold on to his shield. He rolled awkwardly away as talons of fire reached out for him. The air was drawn forcibly from his lungs as his tabard blackened and his armour warped around him. Burning slivers of cauldron struck him, piercing his war-plate. The heat scooped him up, and flung him back. His spine connected with the support beam of a platform. The wood splintered. He dropped to the ground.

The beam creaked. Through pain-blurred eyes, Gatrog saw the platform totter, and then collapse. As several tonnes of wood and sargassum crashed down atop him, all he could think to do was raise his shield.

CHAPTER SIX

THE THUNDER OF AZYR

The booming echo faded, taking with it the after glare of Sigmar's thunderbolt. Lord-Celestant Gardus' vision cleared instantly. Those forged in the storm suffered little from its attention. He took a step forwards, lightning crawling across his war-plate. Broken shards of something crunched beneath him. He felt invigorated. The feeling would fade, but for now he would put it to use. He raised his tempestos hammer. 'Who rides the lightning?' he roared.

'Only the faithful,' came the reply from a hundred throats.

Wind whipped aside the curtain of smoke, revealing the battlefield. They were in the courtyard of some colossal, unnatural fortification. A battle was in progress. He spotted a group of Stormcasts in familiar silver and azure war-plate. They fought doggedly against twice their number of blight-kings. The bulky Rotbringers paid no heed to the new arrivals, more intent on the foe in front of them.

The same story was being played out throughout the

fortress. Hallowed Knights, alone or in small groups, fighting against a tide of filth greater than any he'd yet seen. Blight-kings, beastmen and Rotbringers poured into the courtyard from high scaffolding or through crude apertures set into the walls. The rhythmic war cries of the Hallowed Knights duelled with the droning chants of the Rotbringers, as words of faith collided like blades in the smoky air above the fray.

Gardus saw at once that Sigmar had sent them when and where they were most needed. But the rest was up to them. Gardus clashed runeblade and hammer together and started forwards, followed closely by the retinue of Retributors who had designated themselves his bodyguards. 'Who will be victorious?' he shouted.

'Only the faithful,' his warriors bellowed, as they advanced in his wake. The thunder of their charge shook the ground. He gave no orders. Angstun, Cadoc and the others knew their roles and would fulfil them, or die trying. The citadel was to be taken, and the enemy crushed. All else could wait. He caught a glimpse of Tornus hurtling past, wings spread. The Redeemed One seemed especially eager to come to grips with the foe.

For his part, Gardus sought out the tell-tale signs of Lord-Relictor Morbus' presence, the shriek of lightning and that familiar, hollow cry of challenge. Morbus would be where the fighting was the thickest. Or else... ah. There. Through the pall of smoke, he spotted Morbus' gleaming reliquary standard. It rose over the fray like a beacon. The Lord-Relictor appeared to be fighting alone. Gardus signalled to the leader of his bodyguards. 'Hamu, we go to aid the Stormwarden.'

'We shall help you clear a path, Lord-Celestant,' Hamu said, hefting his starsoul mace meaningfully. He and his warriors fanned out in an arrowhead formation, with Gardus at its head. They struck the enemy ranks like a hammer blow. Hamu's mace crashed down, the shockwaves of its descent tearing the ragged souls from the Rotbringers' broken bodies. Gardus struck out left and right, crushing skulls and severing limbs. Rotbringers scrambled from his path as he surged forwards.

As the press of bodies thinned, Gardus saw Morbus standing between the Rotbringers and several cages of wood and iron. Inside the cages, mortal men and women lay curled in foetal positions or else hunkered in corners. Some few leaned against the bars, their bandaged hands catching at Morbus' cloak and armour as he swept his staff out, driving his foes back. Gardus felt an echo of familiarity. He smelled the stink of open wounds and the astringent odour of poultices prepared by his own hands. He heard the voices of the sick, the lame, calling out to him from across an ocean of forgotten moments.

He shook his head, clearing it, and saw that the Lord-Relictor had begun to smash open the cages. But the prisoners seemed unwilling, or unable, to escape. Too sick, too weak. It didn't matter. All that mattered was that they were there, and they needed to be protected. 'Hamu – the cages,' Gardus said.

The Retributor-Prime gestured, showing he'd heard, and directed two of his men to protect the cages.

Gardus ducked beneath a charging beastman, and rose quickly, throwing the creature over his back. He pinned it to the ground with his foot and, before it could rise, quickly buried his runeblade in its chest. More of the filthy creatures swirled about him. They were rank and covered in waste. Most wore ragged robes and blistered armour over their starveling forms, while others capered in clinking mail. Biting flies swarmed about them as they attacked. Huma's mace claimed the souls of two, while the lightning hammer of a Retributor accounted for another. Gardus met the charge and, as he fought, light began to seep through the joins of his armour.

As the light swelled up, the beastmen cowered back. Where the radiance touched them, their flesh sizzled audibly. Gardus hesitated, at a loss as to why his light had affected them so. They took advantage of his hesitation and scrambled away, grunting and whining in fear. He turned back towards Morbus and the cages, but a snarling, foam-jawed beastman, clad in rusty mail and a rotting tabard, sought to bar his path. Unlike its fellows, it showed no fear of the light that emanated from him.

The creature was easily twice Gardus' height, and heavy with muscle. It had a stag's head, and its mouldy antlers rose to impressive heights. It brayed something in its own dark tongue, and swung its two-handed sword down. Gardus caught the blow on his runeblade, and drove his hammer into the beastman's side. Bone crunched, and the creature gasped out a cloud of pestilential breath. With surprising speed, it whipped its sword up in a tight arc. The blackened blade scraped a thin line of sparks across Gardus' chest-plate, knocking him back a step. He backed away as it rose to its hooves.

They circled one another. The creature was more disciplined than other beasts he'd fought. Someone had trained it, taught it to wield a blade. Its nostrils flared, and the stag's jaws widened, revealing a predator's teeth. Slowly, it brought the flat of its blade up in a crude salute. Instinctively, Gardus returned the gesture.

'Who?' the beast growled.

'I am Gardus,' he said, without knowing why.

'Pusjaw. Pusjaw is knight.' The beastman straightened,

shaking its antlers in obvious pride. 'Fight for honour. Good fight. Come. We fight.'

Gardus extended his runeblade. 'We fight,' he said.

Honour satisfied, the creature resumed its attack. It was stronger than he was, but not by much. And it was slowed down by the weight of its blade. Nonetheless, it kept him at bay for long moments, and he was forced to dodge or counter its attacks, rather than make any of his own. But gradually, surely, it began to slow. Foam gathered at the corners of its jaws, and its yellow gaze burned with frustration and fatigue.

The two-handed blade swept down. As before, Gardus caught it on his own. But this time, rather than simply blocking it, he guided it point first into the ground. As it sank home, he brought his hammer down on its length, shattering it. Then, more quickly than Pusjaw could react, he drove his hammer across its jaw, snapping its neck. It fell backwards, hooves drumming the ground in its death throes. He studied it for a moment.

For a beast, it had almost been a man. He wondered if it, like Tornus, might have been capable of redemption. Was there a spark of humanity in even such brute flesh, some ineffable mote, which could be plucked free and made wondrous? If so, its death was a waste.

Metal clanged. He spun, and drove his runeblade into the swollen belly of a blightking. The corrupted warrior's own blow, meant for the back of Gardus' head, had been caught on the length of a reliquary staff. As the blightking sagged back, the staff's wielder finished him with a precise strike from a warhammer.

'I see your time on the Anvil has not rendered you more observant,' Lord-Relictor Morbus said. 'To have arrived and departed so soon would be a ridiculous thing, don't you think? What would Lorrus say?'

'I bow to your wisdom, brother,' Gardus said. 'My thanks.'

Around them, Retributor and Rotbringer still fought. But an island of calm was being cleared, slowly but steadily. Hamu and his warriors were efficient in their brutality, and the resounding claps of thunder that rose from every blow signalled another fallen foe.

'Thanks are unnecessary.' Morbus hesitated. 'It is good to see you again.'

The Lord-Relictor sounded tired, though Gardus could not see his face. He slumped against his staff, his armour covered in dents and scratches. Gardus realised that Morbus was keeping the storm overhead in place by sheer force of will, and likely had been doing so since the battle began. The healing rains fell steadily, burning away the blight of Nurgle and lending strength to the Hallowed Knights.

'And you,' Gardus said, as a blightking bulled past Hamu and charged him, roaring guttural oaths. He ducked beneath the brute's swing and let his runeblade pass through a bulging thicket of intestines, muscle and, finally, bone. The blade hissed as it bit into the corrupted meat, burning its way clear of the body. The blightking slid in two different directions and plopped wetly to the ground.

Morbus kicked the top half aside. 'Unobservant you may be, but it's good to see that your skills with a blade haven't dulled.' With the last blightking's death, the remaining Rotbringers lost their stomach for the fight. Those who could, fled, in a clatter of funerary bells and chains. The rest died. Hamu and his Retributors made short work of them, and then arrayed themselves in a cordon about Gardus and Morbus.

Gardus took the opportunity to examine the cages and

their inhabitants. 'There are hundreds like them, scattered about these citadels,' Morbus said. 'The Lord-Castellant sent Enyo and Tegrus to see to their shattering.' Gardus gave him a sharp look.

'And will they stay to defend them, as well?'

Morbus looked away. 'We have given them the chance. We can do no more, until we hold these walls.'

'Yet here you stand,' Gardus said. He knelt. A prisoner stared at him in glassy-eyed fascination, her face crawling with flies. He reached out to her, and his light caused the insects to curl up and drop from the air. She reached for his hand, her mouth working silently. He looked up, and found Morbus staring at him.

'You are glowing.'

Gardus stood, and tried to tamp down on the light, to force it back down inside him. 'A gift, from the Anvil of Apotheosis.'

'And what was the price?'

'As I said, a gift.' Gardus met the Lord-Relictor's gaze and didn't look away. There was no judgement there. Morbus, as ever, kept his true thoughts to himself. 'Besides, if I were changed, would I know?'

Morbus grunted. Feeling as if he'd scored a victory of sorts, Gardus asked, 'Where's Lorrus?' He surveyed the field as he did so, noting areas where the Stormcasts held firm, and areas where they would need reinforcement. From the sound of it, Kurunta had taken the walls. The Knight-Heraldor's war-horn blared out challenge after challenge, and shook the vast network of scaffolding that caged the courtyard.

Morbus shook his head. 'He's taken several retinues into the warrens beneath this place. There might be more to the fortresses than we thought.'

Something in the way he said it caught Gardus' attention.

'A realmgate, you mean?' he asked, voice pitched low. 'Is that possible?'

Morbus looked at him. 'We stand in a fortress made from hardened seaweed and the bones of long-drowned leviathans, and you ask that?'

Gardus frowned. 'Whether it is or not, he shall have to take care of it himself. We have no one to spare to send after him. Why didn't he *wait*?'

'Would you have waited?'

Gardus looked away. He watched as Hamu's mace crumpled a blightking's helm, causing it to jet pus from its visor. 'That's not the point.'

'Perhaps not,' Morbus said. He sagged slightly. Gardus reached for him, but the Lord-Relictor waved him off. 'Calling to the storm... fatigued me. But there is no time for rest. Not until this place is secure.'

'It will be, soon enough.' Then he would lead warriors into the depths, in search of the Lord-Castellant. If there was a realmgate here, he intended to either secure it or destroy it, by whatever means necessary.

Morbus looked up, eyes narrowing within the sockets of his skull-helm. 'Who is that?' Gardus followed his gaze, and saw Tornus swoop overhead. The Knight-Venator loosed a swift volley, felling half a dozen Rotbringers in as many moments. 'He wears our colours, but I do not recognise him.'

'You have met him before. At the Blackstone Summit.'

Morbus hissed in recognition. 'Him.' Then, 'He has changed somewhat.'

'A great deal,' Gardus said. 'Whatever he was, he is our brother now. And an asset to our cause.'

'As my Lord-Celestant says,' Morbus murmured. 'He made for a fierce foe. Even took Lorrus' hand. Nearly killed him.'

Gardus peered at him. 'He's going to be unhappy about it, isn't he?'

'Has he ever been happy?'

Gardus smiled. 'Once, I think. Just after he'd knocked me off my feet during a training bout.' His smile faded as hunting horns brayed, signalling the arrival of enemy reinforcements. Loping beastmen appeared, pouring through one of the inner gates. Tell-tale lightning flared upwards as they crashed into a retinue of Hallowed Knights.

Gardus looked at Morbus. 'Come. There is red work yet to be done, and I would have it finished quickly.'

Tornus the Redeemed sped upwards through the fly-ridden air, following Cadoc Kel. He trailed after the Steel Souls' Knight-Azyros as the other warrior hurtled towards the wooden bridges that connected the upper levels of the citadel to its neighbours. Silver-clad Hallowed Knights fought fiercely to take possession of the uneven ramparts and turrets. Tornus helped where he could as he ascended, loosing arrow after arrow.

He and Cadoc had been dispatched by Knight-Vexillor Angstun to see to the Rotbringer reinforcements spilling over from one of the other citadels. If they could not be checked, the Hallowed Knights might be overwhelmed.

It felt strange, fighting against warriors he might once have commanded. He looked into the featureless helms of blight-kings, and saw a reflection of who he had been. As he had been twisted into Torglug, so too had these warriors been corrupted. The mortal Rotbringers had been similarly broken. Their hope had been replaced with despair, and their faith stretched all out of joint. Could they be saved, as he had been? Or had there been something different about him?

Even if they could have been redeemed, Cadoc seemed to

have no interest in doing so. The Knight-Azyros fought like a maddened ghyrlion, jade in fang and claw. Cadoc burst through walkways and severed the ropes binding the rickety bridges, spilling enemies to the ground far below. He shattered bones and hacked through limbs, leaving a trail of bodies to mark his ascent. Hallowed Knights cheered wherever he passed, though the tenor of those cries was different to those Gardus received. The Steel Souls loved Gardus. But there could be no loving a warrior like Cadoc.

Tornus watched in uncomfortable fascination as Cadoc caught up a pox-monk, wrapped in stinking robes and an antiquated breastplate, and carried him high into the air. 'Look, Tornus, I have caught a mouse,' Cadoc called out, gripping the struggling, screaming Rotbringer by his throat. 'Would your eagle like a snack?'

'I am thinking such meat would be disagreeing with him,' Tornus said.

'You're probably right. Back you go, little mouse.' Cadoc opened his hand, and the monk plummeted downwards, trailing a despairing scream. Cadoc chuckled. 'You'd think their fly-god would gift them with wings.'

Tornus shook his head, somewhat taken aback. Following Cadoc was proving to be a valuable lesson. Thus far, the other Stormcasts he'd met had been stern, or even savage. But none so cruel as Cadoc Kel. The Dark Gods must have wept in rage to see his soul ascend to Azyr, for such a warrior might have risen high in their ranks. Then, perhaps not. Cadoc was zealously devoted to Sigmar. His faith pulsed in him the way Gardus' did. But it was not the same sort of faith at all. For Gardus, war was a grim necessity. A thing to be done well, but swiftly. For Cadoc, war was a celebration, and every foe slain was another sacrifice in Sigmar's name.

Indeed, he'd come to discover that few of the Hallowed Knights shared the same tenets of faith. They had all called upon Sigmar in their final moments, but not the same Sigmar. Some had called upon Zig'mar Thundercracker, or Sehgmar the Benevolent, or any one of a thousand other iterations of the God-King.

Did they still see him that way? Or had they traded one Sigmar for another, once they met him face to face? Tornus had called upon Sigmar the Builder, and there seemed to be little difference in the being he'd worshipped and the one who'd redeemed him. But he could not believe that the wise God-King he had knelt before would countenance the brutal worship of a being like Cadoc.

The Knight-Azyros dropped down onto the edge of the largest walkway. It had been carved from a single, massive bone, and was suspended in a web of chains from a framework of rotting wood, which extended across the gap between citadel walls. Far below, the sea slapped at the foundations of the sargasso-citadels. The dark waters heaved and swelled as strange, vast shapes fought over the bodies that fell from above.

Rotbringers, led by a phalanx of blightkings, were flooding across the walkway towards the citadel. They rang plague-bells and sang bilious songs, as the blightkings chanted dolorously. More groups pressed forwards behind them, eager to make their own crossing. The leading blightkings slowed as they caught sight of Cadoc, standing in their path. The Knight-Azyros laughed. 'Look at them, Tornus. Are they not ridiculous, in their tatters and rust?'

Tornus said nothing. Cadoc was speaking for his own benefit. A common occurrence, he was coming to learn. Cadoc drew his starblade and set it point first into the walkway.

'None here can stop me,' he said, raising his celestial beacon. 'I am a Prince of Ekran. You are like worms fighting an eagle, with as much hope of survival.' The light washed across the walkways, boiling the advancing Rotbringers in their own skins. The blightkings pressed forwards, despite the smoke rising from their ruined frames. None got close. One by one, they sank down, wreathed in azure flames.

Tornus winced in sympathy. He well recalled that light, and what it felt like to be caught up in it. A scalding pain, heaped upon agony. A pain so unbearable that even death was preferable to enduring it for more than a moment. Even the Dark Gods themselves could not conceive of such a pain. It was the pain of negation, of obliteration. Of the complete and utter dissolution of being. Only the strongest could survive its touch.

Cadoc shuttered his beacon and chuckled. 'See, Tornus, the mercy of Azyr.'

'This is being a mercy?'

Cadoc laughed. 'Of course! Now they do not have to suffer beneath the lashes of their false gods.' He hung the beacon from his belt. 'In another life, I would have bound them in cages of iron and hung them over the fire pits, to sweat away their sins in Sigmar's name.' He shook his head. 'Oh well.'

'Enough reminiscing. There is being more of them.' Tornus nocked an arrow and let it fly, pinning a Rotbringer to the walkway frame. The servants of Nurgle were nothing if not fearless. Pain was a gift, and one eagerly sought. Mostly, at any rate.

'Ah, good!' Cadoc spread his wings with a shrieking crackle. 'More souls for Sigmar's fires.' The Rotbringers stumbled to a halt, those at the back falling over those in front. 'Best get ready to die, friends,' he called out. 'I will be along in just a moment.'

Tornus stared in consternation at his fellow Stormcast. Cadoc slapped the flat of his blade against his chest as he strode along the smoke-wreathed walkway. 'Come on, don't be scared. I bring you peace, friends. I bring you absolution.' He spread his arms. 'But I grow impatient. Come. Hurry! You were so eager before. Are you scared?'

A blightking shoved his way to the fore and bellowed a gurgling challenge. Cadoc inclined his head in acknowledgement. 'There we are,' he said. He took a step, and then another, and then, with a single flap of his wings, he was airborne.

'Come see how a Kel fights, maggots,' Cadoc roared. His starblade looped out, removing the blightking's head. 'Cadoc Kel, last Prince of the Ekran, demands your attention.' The air boomed as he surged forwards with a snap of his crackling wings. He tore through the Rotbringer ranks, leaving a path of severed limbs and headless necks in his wake. Few of the foe sought to stand against him, preferring instead to take their chances against less swift-moving opponents. They turned and fled back across the walkway, Cadoc in pursuit, roaring out a song in praise of Sigmar.

Tornus swooped in his wake, realmhunter's bow humming as he loosed arrow after arrow at the Rotbringers trapped on the walkway, caught between Cadoc and their fellows behind. As quickly as he could grasp an arrow from his quiver, he sent it flying. Ospheonis flew at his side, talons tearing at any Rotbringer who sought to grab him. Cadoc ploughed on, hurling Rotbringers from the walkway as he sought to tear the heart out of them.

Prosecutors swooped towards the mass of Rotbringers from behind. The chamber's Angelos Conclave had been dispatched to distract the forces occupying the other two citadels. To that end, they'd freed the captives from the slave-cages in all three citadels. Now, reinforced by the newly arrived Reforged Prosecutors, they could help those freed slaves do more than just escape. A part of Tornus was sickened at the thought of using mortals in such a fashion. Another, wiser part knew that it was a sad necessity.

The Stormcast Eternals were too few to do more than pierce the dark. For their light to flourish, they needed to rally the mortal inhabitants of the realms. From the lowliest grot to the greatest gargant, and everyone in between. Every arm that could wield a sword would be needed, before the Varanspire was toppled and Archaon Everchosen, the Grand Marshal of Chaos, was cast from his throne.

As Torglug, he had feared Archaon. The thought of that volcanic presence, of the harsh weight of that three-eyed gaze, had been one of the few things capable of shaking the Despised One's certainty. Archaon was the end made flesh. The null point, where all light and courage was reduced to memory. Few Chaos lords would even consider openly defying Archaon, and those that would were either mad or foolish. Torglug had been neither.

Tornus pushed the thought aside. He didn't like to think on those days. Torglug was gone, and good riddance. As Lord-Celestant Silus had said, he was Tornus now, and forevermore. He loosed an arrow, pinning a blightking's arm to the walkway before the warrior could land a blow on Cadoc. The Knight-Azyros' wing sliced out, burning through the trapped blightking's neck and sending his head tumbling into the waters below.

'A fine shot. Cadoc would have been angry if you'd stolen his kill.'

Tornus glanced around and saw another Knight-Venator perched on a nearby buttress, her bow lying across her knees.

Her star-eagle swooped towards Ospheonis, and the two birds circled one another in a graceful dance.

'I am thinking the same,' he said. He glided towards her.

'I see you walk the Realmhunter's Path,' she said. 'And you bear the colours of the faithful. But you are not of our chamber.'

'Silus the Untarnished is being my commander.'

'Have the Gleaming Host come to aid us, then?' She sounded almost disappointed. Tornus shook his head.

'It is only being me.'

'Ah, well, you are welcome.' She spread her arms. 'Stay, and shoot, if you like.' She gestured to the walkway. 'Plenty of targets.' She rose to her feet.

'Is that how you are thinking of them?'

'How would you refer to them?' She eyed him. 'I am Enyo.'

'Tornus.'

'Well, Tornus, if they are targets, they have chosen to make themselves such. We held true to our faith, and suffered for it. Let them now do the same.' She drew an arrow, sighted, loosed. 'I will not pity them their choices.'

Tornus drew an arrow of his own. 'They are possibly not having one.'

She did not reply, simply sent a second arrow after the first. For a moment, they loosed in silent harmony, peppering the Rotbringers with arrow after arrow. There was a strange sort of peace in the rhythm of it. Tornus let his thoughts fall away, his worries and doubts. The only thing that mattered was the crackle-snap of the bowstring, and the vibration of an arrow leaving his hand.

All too soon, it was over. Rotbringers fled back the way they'd come, seeking the dubious safety of the citadel below. On the ramparts, retinues of Liberators and Judicators began to follow them. Thunderhead Brotherhoods, supported by Prosecutors, had been dispatched to see to the taking of the ramparts of the other two citadels. They would take control of the upper levels and dig in, awaiting reinforcements. Once the central fortress had fallen, and the various routes between the three were under control, the Stormcasts would be free to concentrate the full might of the chamber on the others, each in turn.

'They flee,' Enyo murmured, lowering her bow. She glanced at Tornus. 'I know who you are now. Not at first, but there is only one Tornus.'

He did not look at her. 'And so?'

'So nothing,' she said. 'You wear our symbol. You are bonded to a celestial bird. That is enough, I think. I have faith.'

Tornus nodded, and perched beside her on the buttress. 'I am glad to be hearing you saying that.' He flexed his hand, watching the sigmarite plates of his gauntlet move. 'There are not many who are being so forgiving.'

'No. I expect not. Nor should you.' She looked away. 'We were not forged with forgiveness in mind. We are the storm, and like the storm, we do only as we must, not as we might wish. A good thing, I think. Otherwise, Cadoc would be more unbearable than he already is.' She looked up. 'Speaking of whom...'

'Ha, Enyo,' Cadoc called, swooping about them. 'My tally stands at seven and thirty souls sent to Sigmar's fires.'

'You must be pleased,' the Knight-Venator said.

'What is yours?' he demanded.

'I do not count my kills, Prince of Ekran.'

Cadoc laughed. 'That means I'm winning.'

Enyo gestured. 'You see? A savage. Faith is his only saving grace.'

'My faith is shown in victory,' Cadoc said. Tornus couldn't tell whether he was angry or pleased at the insult. He swatted his beacon with the flat of his blade. 'By my light are the faithful guided to their triumph. And the false burnt to ashes.'

'I'd like to think the rest of us had a little something to do with it,' Enyo said.

'A bit, perhaps,' Cadoc admitted. 'But I shine the brightest in His eyes. Come, Tornus, join me! I go to spread my light to the darkest corners of the far citadel. Let them know the glory and terror that comes of standing against a Prince of Ekran.' He swooped upwards, without waiting for a reply.

Tornus watched the Knight-Azyros soar away. 'He is seeming to remember much of his life from before.'

On the ramparts, a few remaining Rotbringers were attempting to drive back the shieldwall of Liberators advancing on them. They shouted out praises to Nurgle with hysterical abandon, as if begging their god to intervene and save them.

'It would take more than a single forging on the Anvil of Apotheosis to dent that ego.' Enyo sighted along an arrow. She let it fly, and a Rotbringer fell. 'From what little I know of the Ekran, they were a fierce folk. And proud.'

'Pride is being a weakness,' Tornus said. Enyo glanced at him.

'You sound as if you know that from experience,' she said.

'Cadoc is not being alone in his memories,' Tornus said. He tracked a lumbering blightking along a lower scaffold. 'I am also remembering where I am coming from. And I am remembering how I got there.' He loosed the arrow. The blightking shot backwards, striking the wall, then toppled forwards through the rail of the scaffold, and down.

Tornus watched him fall.

CHAPTER SEVEN

THE GATE OF WEEDS

Blightmaster Bubonicus sighed as he felt the marshy floor of the vaulted chamber tremble beneath his feet. The battle above was not going as well as he might have hoped. He considered joining the fray himself, but then discarded the idea. One more or less warrior would change the situation little, even if that warrior was himself. The die had been cast, and a doom set in motion. Either his or theirs, it didn't matter. All that mattered was his duty to protect the Gate of Weeds until it could be opened.

The chamber was a large, hollowed-out cavern, dripping with slimes and moulds. It was damp and humid, and clouds of flies undulated through the air, dancing in time to a tune only they could hear. The walls were slick and wet, and skeletal shapes swam slowly through the hardened sargassum, moving inches across centuries. Support pillars made from dredged bones and basalt held up the ceiling, and the sevenfold rune of Nurgle had been carved into every flat surface.

Balefire torches had been thrust through holes carved in pro-truding bones, and they cast their sickly glow over the space.

The chamber was a holy place, a sacred tumour. But not for much longer, Bubonicus feared. The chamber shuddered. Water bubbled up from within the cracks in the sargassum, and the weeds, which sprouted like a carpet, rustled. 'It was inevitable, I suppose. All great quests encounter hardship. It is the price of a good song, as the troubadours say.' He could smell lightning on the air. Smell was the wrong word. Taste? Yes, that sounded right.

It all tasted of lightning. Harsh and sharp. An unpleasant taste, lacking in even the most basic of subtleties. The enemy possessed little in the way of subtlety. What could one expect of such garish creatures? But perhaps that was the point. That very lack of subtlety was what made them so fearsome an enemy, as evidenced by the armsmen scattered around the chamber, muttering nervously amongst themselves.

More than two dozen of the strongest and most disciplined of the Order's warriors were about him. Each and every one of them was blooded, and experienced in the ways of war. They were veterans of the Spindlewood War and the con-quest of the Rothorn. They had faced Bloodbound, Arcanites and orruks without a backwards step. And yet now they were afraid. Afraid of implacable silver shapes with unmoving faces. Afraid of the storm.

'Be not fearful, friends,' Bubonicus said as he walked among them, reminding them of the power he wielded. He caught one by the shoulder. The armsman yelped. 'You, Cutchuk, your grandfather stood with me at the Black Cistern, I recall.'

The armsman gave him a hesitant, gap-toothed grimace. 'Aye, my lord. He passed there, and watered the ground with his blood.'

'A worthy death. And you, Galnag, isn't it? You and your shield-sisters helped strike down the Unsung Champion in the Spindlewood, did you not?' Galnag nodded jerkily, her ratty locks slipping from beneath her helm. 'A good day, that. A fine day. As this day will be.' Bubonicus looked around. 'Death is not the end, for any of us. Fall here, and an eternity of blissful servitude awaits you in the gardens of the King of all Flies. That I swear to you.'

The armsmen cheered, their mucus-roughened voices resounding through the chamber. Bubonicus nodded in satisfaction. They would likely not survive this day. But all deaths served Grandfather's will, for only in death could new life flourish. So long as they died bravely, and in service to a righteous cause, the garden would be waiting for them.

'They come,' a voice croaked, as the armsmen continued to cheer. Bubonicus turned. The hag was blind, her eyes lost beneath pus-filled growths. She had carved the sign of Nurgle into her own skull with a rusty spoon, and it still wept an oily discharge. The witch was blessed of the King of all Flies, and nursed maggots in her pouchy flesh.

The other members of her coven echoed her, their voices like the rustling of dry leaves. They were all broken things, with bloat-bellies and withered limbs beneath their ragged robes. They squatted in the weeds, turning the clean waters that burbled up from below blessedly foul with their magics. It was only by their attention that the spells holding the sargassum to its current shape were maintained. Without it, the citadels would slowly, but surely, crumble back into patches of gulfweed and rock roses.

'They come, Sir Knight,' the witch said again. Her voice scraped the air like a knife.

'I have ears,' Bubonicus said mildly. He didn't, really. Not for a long time. In fact, there wasn't much flesh left beneath his armour at all. He had sacrificed it strip by strip in service to the King of all Flies. He felt neither pride nor dismay at this. It was simply a fact. One more milestone in his five centuries of service.

He was now the oldest of the surviving blightmasters. Gentle Wolgus was dead these long centuries, his bones fertilising the dry soil of Shyish. Gaspax Gahool had vanished into the depths of Ulgu, leading the fifth pox-crusade. Even Ephraim Bollos, Lord Rotskull himself, was gone, lost to the fires of fate. Of the others, they had been but seedlings when the Lady had first come to Cankerwall and brought Nurgle's blessings with her. It had not been Cankerwall then, but he could not recall its original name. Like so many of his memories, it was lost in the morass of time.

'You are thinking of her, not them,' the witch said. 'Your thoughts smell of moss and rotting flowers. A lover's bouquet.' Her coven fell into stuttering, nervous silence. To speak of the Lady was to draw her eye, and few save Bubonicus and his fellow knights were eager to do that. It was only right that the lower orders fear her, for she was Nurgle's daughter, and a goddess in all but name.

'I am always thinking of her,' Bubonicus said. 'The very moment we met is engraved upon my heart like a scar. She was beautiful then, in her slow decay. The beauty of despair, of new life waxing strong in dying flesh. The eternal dance.' His voice tolled out, echoing through the chamber. 'How we danced that night, around and around, as all about us the world was falling down.'

'Falling down,' the witch echoed, and her coven with her.

Bubonicus glanced at them, annoyed. A scribe crouched at her feet, recording all of Bubonicus' words on his flesh with a sharpened stylus. The scribe moaned as the stylus cut through a scab. Such was the way of the Order. The words and deeds of its blightmasters must be captured and recorded for those who came after. Else how would any know of their heroism? The deeds of the Order of the Fly were an inspiration for all who despaired in Nurgle's shadow, for in them was the true glory of desolation made flesh. They were the fly that laid the egg, which would become the maggot.

At that thought, the Gatherer of Souls grumbled in agreement. He lifted the flail-halberd. Power rippled through it. A mighty strength, such as only the gods could bestow. The Gatherer of Souls had once belonged to another. A greater champion by far than Bubonicus. He sought each day to ensure his worthiness to wield it, in Grandfather's name. Its rusted blades bit more than bone, hooking and consuming the souls of its victims, and lending their strength to Bubonicus himself. The more he killed, the stronger he grew. And the stronger he grew, the more he could kill.

'But only with purpose,' he murmured. He was no frenzied Bloodbound, to kill without thought. No, like a reaper, he took only what was owed. The souls he harvested were sent to Nurgle's garden, there to toil for all time beneath the beneficent eye of the Lord of All Things. A good afterlife, and better than most deserved.

The more souls he sent to the garden, the greater it grew. Soon, if the Order were successful, it might even spill into Ghyran itself. That would be a great day, if it ever came. The culmination of all their efforts, since the beginning.

He held out no hope for it, however. Hope was the enemy. Despair was his armour, and misery his shield. His strength waxed as that of the world waned. Whatever the outcome, the Blighted Duchies would hold to the oaths they'd made the day the Lady had come to Cankerwall. They could do no less, for a knight without honour was nothing more than a brigand.

Though it had to be said that honour had not been enough to win the day at the siege of the Living City. The Order of the Fly had fought in the vanguard, as was their right, but they had been cruelly rebuffed, time and again. At the Twelve-Thorn Gate, their standards had been cast down, and heroes had fallen. Gatrog had been there, Bubonicus recalled. The Lord-Duke of Festerfane had fought with all the courage of one of Grandfather's own beasts, but to no avail. Courage and honour meant little to the foes they faced.

The floor cracked as the enemy's thunder reverberated again through the chamber. Clean water steamed as it pattered across his armour. He glanced down at the Gate of Weeds. The realmgate had risen up through the muck of the sargassum like a pearl from an oyster. It was round and flat, a pool of crystalline water rising from within a flattened circle of bent weeds, glowing with a pleasant light that left him feeling uncomfortably ill.

Where the glow fell, the waters remained clear of all contagion. Once, that glow had filled the entire chamber. Slowly, but surely, thanks to the efforts of his witches, it had dwindled. Patience and persistence. These were a gardener's greatest tools, and Grandfather had gifted them to him in abundance. But there were all kinds of tools.

Besides the witches and armsmen, seven times seven poxmonks occupied the chamber floor, arrayed in three interlocking rings about the shimmering circumference of the Gate of Weeds. While the witches saw to the befouling of the waters, the Blessed Brothers of the Blistered Sepulchre had been droning prayers to Nurgle for as long as the sargasso-citadels had stood. Each prayer was another brick in the garden wall, bending the Gate of Weeds from its former path to another. What Sigmar had abandoned, Nurgle would claim, through the labours of his most devoted servants.

It was the most sacred of duties, and one any pox-monk worth his tattered cowl would kill for. Indeed, some of them *had* killed for it. Such devotion to the Lord of All Things was truly humbling, and Bubonicus had felt honoured to even witness it. But the time for such pleasures was fast vanishing. Now was the moment of ultimate desolation. All that remained was triumph or tragedy.

He found himself gazing into the realmgate, hoping to spot some speck of blessed filth or murk. But all that he could see were the strange, indistinct shapes that haunted the depths. Vast shapes, like clouds, or nebulae of distant stars. Slaves they had taken from Gramin and the other reed-cities believed that, once, the sylvaneth of the Verdant Bay had used the gate to swim between Ghyran and Azyr, before Sigmar had sealed all routes to his high realm. Another false god. What sort of god fled honourable combat? What sort of god stole the harvest of another? The King of all Flies was no thief, whatever else. And what he claimed, he held.

The sylvaneth who'd inhabited the bay were gone now, fed to the first balefires, or else broken and bent into servitude as scaffolding and bridges. Bubonicus sometimes regretted that. There were better uses for such creatures, and their screams had gone silent all too swiftly. But necessity had left little time for creativity.

The chamber shook again. More cracks appeared in the floor and walls. More clean water spewed up, eliciting a squeal from one of the witches. The coven-mistress shushed her follower with a clout on the side of the head. The storm-warriors were drawing close. Perhaps that was why he sought comfort in memories of better times. He tightened his grip on his flail. 'Will it open soon, do you think?' he asked, looking down at one of the pox-monks seated on the floor. The leprous fanatic continued his droning hum, eyes closed, bandaged fingers tight on his bony knees. 'No, I suppose not.' Bubonicus sighed ponderously.

'Will she think of me, should I fall?' he asked. 'Will she sing sweetly of me, or will I be a lesson to those who come after?' He shook his head. He had died before. Many times. But like Grandfather's flowers, he always blossomed anew, in fertile soil. But each time was shorter than the last. Such was the will of the King of all Flies.

Soon, another would take his place as blightmaster. Gatrog, perhaps. There was one destined to rise high in the esteem of the Lord of All Things. His cousin had been much the same, and he had perished before his time. 'Nurgle's will,' Bubonicus said. What would be, would be, and no sense in worrying.

'Nurgle's will,' the witch said, bowing. Her head snapped up, and her nostrils flared. 'Someone comes.'

'So you've said.' Nonetheless, Bubonicus gestured to the armsmen. Those closest to the only entrance to the chamber snapped to attention. The aperture was not a proper portal. Instead, it was a great crack in the sargassum, smoothed and widened by years of use. Water slithered through it, and soon enough, the sound of splashing could be heard.

A familiar form burst through the crack, slipping and sliding towards Bubonicus. The armsman stumbled to a halt and fell to his hands and knees. 'M... my lord, Duke Gatrog sends word, the enemy–'

'Are here, yes,' Bubonicus said, looking down at the little Rotbringer. Agak. That was his name. Gatrog's servant. 'So I gathered. It is even as Gaspax Gahool said, in his seminal treatise on siege-craft. No ploy survives contact with a moti-vated enemy.' Bubonicus sighed and gestured. 'Up, gentle Agak, up. There is no time for kneeling.'

The witch moaned. 'They are coming, Sir Knight. Silver and fire.'

Bubonicus grunted. He looked down at Agak. 'You were followed.'

Agak fell back, cowering in the filthy water. 'No, no!'

Bubonicus reached down and hauled him to his feet. 'Yes.' He swatted the armsman in the chest, nearly knocking him back down. 'Do not cower so, fool.' He looked at the witch. 'Close, are they?'

'Getting closer,' she said, squeezing her pustules. 'The blessed miasma recoils from them. They stink of fresh water and starlight.'

Agak stumbled back. 'I... I must go. Duke Gatrog needs me.'

Bubonicus fixed him in place with a glare. 'If the enemy has descended, he is likely beyond needing any aid you can provide. But I may yet make use of you. Draw your sword, Agak of Festerfane.'

Agak paled, but did as Bubonicus commanded. The blight-master reached down and unhooked a wormy, rust-edged chalice from his belt. One of seven, the chalice was a sign of his rank and the esteem in which he was held by the King of all Flies. The bowl of the chalice quivered with pus-filled veins, and somnolent flies clustered about its rim. The seventy-seven verses of the Feverish Oath had been etched into its circum-ference by the delicate blade of the Lady of Cankerwall on the very day she had gifted it to him.

Normally, the ritual he was about to undertake was meant only for chosen knights of the Order. It was a commun-ion with Nurgle himself, and only the worthy were fit to participate. But in some rare cases, exceptions could be made. Needs must, when daemons drove. He looked at the witch. He realised that he did not know her name. Too late to ask now. 'Bend your magics to the realmgate, help the holy brothers. I would see the garden, before I pass from this world and into the next.'

'It will not open in time,' she said.

'So long as it opens, my oaths are fulfilled. Do it.' He gestured sharply, and she bowed her head. Her coven shuffled towards the shimmering realmgate, already adding their voices to those of the pox-monks. Without the witches, the chamber would grow unstable. A price worth paying, if Nurgle's will were done.

Awkwardly, Bubonicus knelt and dragged the chalice through the murky waters. The liquid frothed and fumed, turning as black as tar. When the cup was full, he rose and said, 'Come, gentles. Come ye true servants of the King, and drink from the Flyblown Chalice. Taste the blood of Nurgle, and rejoice.'

Agak and the other armsmen gathered around, eyes wide. It was a rare thing for a commoner to be given a sip from a blightmaster's chalice. It spoke to the necessity of the moment, rather than any worthiness on their part, but no one would complain. One by one, the armsmen took a sip and passed it along, until all of them had done so. When they had finished, their flesh steamed, and their eyes were alight with the febrile strength of Nurgle. They would fight to the last now.

Bubonicus nodded in satisfaction. 'It is good. Those of you who survive shall rise up and be made true knights of the Most Blightsome Order of the Fly. Those who fall shall fertilise this ground in Nurgle's name.'

He lifted the chalice high, and poured what was left over

the gaps in his visor. The frothy brew inundated what was left of him, filling him with Nurgle's blessing. He felt stronger. Invigorated by the touch of his god. All too soon, it would fade, bringing weakness and sweet despair. The anticipation was a gift in and of itself.

'By our life or our death, we shall serve the King of all Flies.'

'Keep moving. Through the gap. Quickly now.' Lord-Castellant Grymn's voice echoed oddly in the twisting passage, as he braced the shifting sargassum with his halberd. The lintel of the gap had cracked, and had begun to sink until he'd interposed his weapon. His warriors squeezed past, moving as quickly as they were able.

Grymn was accompanied by two retinues of Liberators and a group of Protectors, a force he was confident could face anything lurking in these depths. Already, they had dispatched beastmen and Rotbringers alike, leaving a trail of burnt and twisted corpses in their wake. Once the last Liberator was through, Grymn ripped his halberd free and joined them. The lintel collapsed, and the passageway sealed itself behind them. Stinking dust billowed, enveloping them for a moment. Grymn had pushed his way to the front before it had settled. 'Come. This is neither the time nor the place to dawdle.'

The depths of the citadel were a warren of ill-shaped chambers and narrow passageways that curved and twisted in random fashion. Oily balefire torches flickered in crudely scooped alcoves, casting a sickening green haze over everything. It reminded Grymn of maggots chewing through the carcass of a dead animal, or termites boring through wood. The Rotbringers had carved routes through the fossilised sargassum, and worn them smooth with constant use. Luckily, most of their forces were above, fighting. Those left below were of little threat to either he or his warriors.

It had been a lucky thing, spotting that Rotbringer as he descended. Without him, Grymn might have searched for a way down for hours without finding it. Certainly too late to halt whatever he felt building in the air even now. Morbus' senses had not misled him. The air was thick with a growing miasma, and the deeper they went, the stronger it became. This place was like the root of a rotten tooth. One he intended to pluck out, before it was too late.

At his side, Tallon growled softly. The gryph-hound's hackles were stiff, and his feathers ruffled in agitation. Grymn ran his fingers over the beast's skull. 'You have the scent? Good. Lead the way.'

The gryph-hound broke into a lope. Grymn followed. There was no need for silence, even if he had been so inclined. Better to let the enemy hear the oncoming storm, and know fear. A frightened enemy was as good as defeated.

As the Stormcasts hurried after the gryph-hound, the passageway bucked and shuddered. Cracks grew along the walls and soon they were splashing through murky waters that bubbled up between gaps in the floor. Tallon led them unerringly through the twisting labyrinth, following the stink of the magics brewing at its corrupt heart.

The portal, when they found it, was less an entrance than an open scab in the surface of a wall. An oily light oozed from within, and flies clogged the air. There were no guards, no sentinels or sentries. Just the light and the flies. Water pulsed through the gap, trickling towards them. Tallon raked the entrance with his claws and slunk back to sit beside Grymn. It was wide enough for a single Stormcast to pass through. Grymn gestured, impatiently.

HALLOWED KNIGHTS: PLAGUE GARDEN

'Osric, liberate the path.'

The Liberator-Prime stepped forward, two-handed grand-hammer raised. He struck the wall with all of his might. Cracks spider-webbed from the point of impact. He spun the grandhammer, striking a second point, and then a third. His Liberators moved to join him, their hammers thumping against the areas he'd weakened. In moments, the whole wall gave way and collapsed. A cloud of flies erupted through the curtain of dust. Grymn lifted his warding lantern and let its light spear out, eradicating the swarm of insects.

The gap had been enlarged significantly. Now it was large enough for at least five Stormcasts to march through it abreast. Without waiting for Grymn's command, Osric led his retinue through and into the chamber beyond. Grymn and the others followed.

The chamber stank of rot and age, and was clearly not man-made, despite the pillars that studded its circumference. It resembled the hulled shell of a nut, and bones cluttered the walls. Balefire torches cast a greenish glow across the recesses of the chamber, and weird shadows danced on the scabrous walls. Reeds and water covered the floor, making it resemble a marsh more than anything else.

Grymn's eyes were immediately drawn to the realmgate. For it could be nothing else, glowing as it did. He recognised that light, felt it in his marrow, its warmth in his veins. 'Azyr,' he whispered. A guttural, echoing laugh caught his attention, snapping him from his reverie. He turned, scanning the weirdly lit chamber.

A group of Rotbringers carrying heavy shields, spears and swords, advanced across the chamber. They did so at the direction of the massive Chaos knight who stalked unhurriedly in their wake, his form bloated with fell power. He held a heavy halberd-like weapon in one hand, and a bale-fire torch in the other. The creature laughed again. 'I expected an army.' The words boomed out, bouncing from pillar to pillar. 'If this is the best you can muster, perhaps my doubts are unfounded.'

Grymn slammed the ferrule of his halberd down, splitting the dull cacophony that rose from the robed figures kneeling around the realmgate. 'Osric. Pallas. Single rank. Lock shields.' The Liberators moved up, arraying themselves in a square centred on Grymn and the Protectors. The Rotbringers charged, droning obscene chants to their blighted god. 'Kahya, clear this filth from our path,' Grymn said.

The Protector-Prime nodded and stepped through the shieldwall, her warriors spreading out to either side. As one, they began to advance across the chamber to meet the foe. Grymn and the Liberators followed at a distance.

Stormstrike glaives lanced out in sweeping rhythm, and Rotbringers fell, their chants silenced. Kahya's warriors were the image of martial perfection, every blow synchronised and efficiently timed. But the Rotbringers did not break as Grymn expected. Instead, they fought all the harder. The wounded and dying clutched at the Stormcasts' legs and arms, trying to bog them down so that their fellows could strike. The Protectors' heavy sigmarite armour absorbed most of these blows, but some few got through.

Grymn saw a Protector stagger and sink to one knee. A Rotbringer clubbed him with an axe. The blade shattered on his armour, but even so, he was knocked sprawling. Grymn extended his halberd. 'Tallon!' The gryph-hound sprang forward, winnowing through the melee. He leapt on the Rotbringer, beak piercing the mortal's throat as they fell backwards in a tangle. The Protector got to his feet, using his weapon for leverage. As he rose, he swept the glaive out, slicing through a Rotbringer's midsection.

The Chaos knight continued to chuckle as his followers spent their lives in useless battle. 'Inevitability in silver,' the creature rumbled, his voice carrying easily over the noise. 'One might even call you knights. But you serve a lie, and your honour is built upon falsehood. You must be burned to ash, before anything of worth can grow in you.' He lifted the torch he held. 'These fires were lit by the King of all Flies himself. They guide us in our quest for ruination. And now they shall light the path to your doom, invader.'

With that, the bloated warrior tossed the torch into the murky waters. Green flame erupted, spreading across the water as if it were oil. The surviving Rotbringers screamed joyfully as the flames consumed them, reducing them to the basest of elements. The water began to boil and froth. Grymn felt the semi-solid sludge of the floor shift beneath his feet. As on the viaduct, the flames were warping the substance of their surroundings.

'Guard yourselves,' he shouted, as the first burning tendril of sargassum rose, serpent-like, from the burning waters. It shot forward, and punched through an unlucky Liberator's shield and armour. The Stormcast was driven backwards and pinned to a pillar with bone-cracking force. He groaned and slumped. Grymn lashed out with his halberd and hacked through the twisting vine, freeing the wounded warrior. More tendrils burst from the water and sought their prey. 'Kahya, defensive cordon,' Grymn said, dragging the Liberator to his feet. Bloody craters marked the Stormcast's chest and arm.

At his command, the Protectors fell back, slicing tendrils as they did so. Where their stormstrike glaives passed, the air rippled with celestial energies. Sargassum vines struck the burgeoning arcane veil, and exploded into fiery bits. But not all of them. Some darted past the Protectors, and slammed into the shieldwall. Shields buckled, and Liberators perished. As the flames spread, more tendrils burst from the water beneath the Protectors to coil about them. Several of the warriors were dragged beneath the water, still struggling. The defensive cordon came apart, and soon every Stormcast was battling for their life, all but isolated from their fellows by the weaving thicket of barbed vines.

Grymn whirled his halberd about, defending himself. There were too many tendrils, darting in from every direction. Despite their discipline, and the strength of their armour, he and his warriors would soon be overwhelmed. Thinking quickly, he opened his lantern and thrust it beneath the water. Azure light swelled, stretching beneath the churning murk. Steam rose from the surface as filth bubbled away, and the closest tendrils stiffened and dried. They cracked and fell apart as the waters were cleansed of the balefire's curse. As he bent to retrieve his lantern, Tallon screeched in warning. Grymn twisted aside as the skull-shaped ball of a flail slammed down, narrowly missing him. He jerked back, halberd extended.

The Chaos knight loomed over him. 'I am Bubonicus, Blightmaster of the Order of the Fly, and Knight of the Feverish Oath. Give me your name, so that I might know who it is I have sent to the garden.'

'My name is no concern of yours,' Grymn spat. He saw his lantern, rolling beneath the water. But there was no way to reach it without opening himself up to his enemy. The Chaos knight laughed.

'So be it. Die nameless and forgotten. I salute you nonetheless.' He swept back his flail, ready to strike. A shout distracted him. One of the remaining Liberators charged, hammer raised. Bubonicus spun his weapon, so that the halberd blade extended towards this new threat. With an impossible smoothness, he lunged. The blade scraped past the rim of the Liberator's shield and struck his armour. Momentum did the rest. The Liberator stumbled back, cursing. A moment later, he screamed, clutching at his head.

Maggots erupted from the visor of his war-helm, spilling from the mouth and eye-slits. The Liberator gave out a piteous groan and sank to one knee. More maggots squirmed from the joins of his armour, plopping into the water. A moment later, he collapsed, and lightning flashed upwards.

'Fie,' Bubonicus rumbled, as the glare faded. 'Fie on all cowards. That soul was owed to the King of all Flies, even as yours is. The Gatherer of Souls must have its due.' He lifted his flail meaningfully.

Grymn set his feet. 'Come and take it, then.'

Bubonicus threw back his head and gave a hollow laugh. 'I will, friend. Of that, have no doubts.' He started forward, flail clattering. The remaining Stormcasts moved to intercept, but Grymn waved them off.

'This one is mine. Take care of the others. Whatever happens, that gate must not open.' He raised his halberd, deflecting a blow that might have crushed his skull. Bubonicus was strong, and faster than he looked. Grymn circled him, searching for a weak point. There was always a weak point. An old wound, a gap in the armour, something. The creature's plate rattled as he moved, as if it were full of metal flinders.

Grymn's eyes fastened on his opponent's joints. They were baroque monstrosities, shaped like fluted buboes or grimacing faces, and far larger than they needed to be. All of Bubonicus' armour was of similar style. Ornamental, rather than functional. Sturdy, but with obvious flaws to the trained eye.

Grymn pivoted, avoiding a sweeping blow, and jabbed with the spike-tip of his halberd like a spear. It punched into a buckle strap, tearing it away. Bubonicus clapped a hand to it and spun.

Grymn dropped to one knee. The Gatherer of Souls smashed through the column of bone. Splinters pattered across Grymn's visor as he rose up, driving the ferrule of his halberd into Bubonicus' chest. Bubonicus staggered back with a grumble of protest, and Grymn gave him no time to recover. The blade of his halberd carved a deep gouge across his opponent's chest-plate. 'You're too slow,' Grymn said, circling the off-balance Chaos warrior. 'Your armour is ornate to the point of impracticality, hindering your range of motion. And that flail is unwieldy and badly balanced.'

'It was a gift,' Bubonicus said, chuckling.

Grymn tensed, and slid forward, letting the halberd extend ahead of him. The head of the blade punched into his opponent's elbow joint, buckling it. With a twist of his wrists, Grymn jerked Bubonicus off balance and sent him to the floor. The flail hummed out, faster than he'd expected, and he threw himself backwards. Bubonicus was on his feet in moments. It lashed out again and Grymn awkwardly rolled aside. The floor cracked.

Grymn shoved himself to his feet, and was suddenly flying backwards, his world spinning. He struck a column and bounced off, falling to his hands and knees. He groped for his halberd, but he'd lost it. His chest-plate was cracked and smoking from where the flail had touched it. Vision blurring, he clawed for his warding lantern. He heard Tallon shriek in rage, and Bubonicus roar in frustration. The gryph-hound hurtled overhead, and struck a pillar before flopping limply into the water.

The floor shuddered beneath him as Bubonicus charged towards him. 'You send a dog to face me?' the Chaos knight roared, all trace of humour gone from his voice. 'Have you no honour, son of Azyr?'

Honour. They were always yelling about honour, these monsters. As if honour excused their actions. As if honour explained their crimes. Grymn caught hold of the warding lantern and surged to his feet. The flail hissed down, barely scraping his armour, as he slammed the warding lantern across Bubonicus' head. There was a sound of tearing metal and bursting rivets, and the helm popped loose and went spinning away. Bubonicus staggered. Grymn hit him again, and again, bludgeoning his opponent with the lantern.

'Honour, is it? What honour is there in befouling the land? In enslaving its people? You say my honour is a lie? Then what does that make yours?' Every question was punctuated with a blow. Bubonicus sank to his knees with a groan. 'Answer me,' Grymn snarled. '*Answer me!*'

The lantern swung down again. It smacked into Bubonicus' palm. Smoke bloomed from his gauntlet as the holy light burned the corroded metal. More burns scarred his armour; it had been reduced to slag in places. Bubonicus lifted his head. Grymn bit back an oath. The Chaos knight had no face. Indeed, his head was nothing more than a rotten skull, permeated with maggots and larvae. His blows had cracked the skull in places, and shattered its jaw, but Bubonicus still spoke. 'My answer is ever thus... *for the Lady.*' With that, he shoved Grymn back and crashed into him, knocking him backwards. They slewed through the water, struggling for control of the lantern.

'I recognise you now, friend,' Bubonicus hissed. 'I saw your stand at the Twelve-Thorn Gate, and marked you then for a brave warrior. I am pleased to see that I was right.' His jaw sagged and maggots spilled out, splattering across Grymn's visor.

Grymn cried out in disgust and drove his fist into Bubonicus' skull. Bone crumpled and burst. Maggots spilled over him, squirming through the slits in his visor and the cracks in his armour, carried by the splattering ichors. Grymn fumbled for the lantern and flipped it all of the way open, allowing the full power of the light to beam forth. The maggots shrivelled and the ichors steamed, as his stomach heaved. He forced the twitching body away from him.

He couldn't say whether any of them had got into his mouth. He clawed at the clasps on his helmet and pulled it off. He pounded on his chest and coughed, letting the light of his lantern wash over him. Tallon limped towards him, favouring one paw. The gryph-hound chirruped in concern, and Grymn leaned against his flank, breathing heavily.

Several of his warriors started towards what was left of Bubonicus, weapons raised. Grymn waved them off, still coughing. 'Stay... stay back. Don't get near it.' He heaved himself to his feet and snatched up the warding lantern. 'Only the light of Azyr can purify such a creature,' he rasped. His throat felt as if he had swallowed jagged shards of metal. He swept the light over Bubonicus' body until the baroque armour collapsed in on itself and was reduced to a scum of rust, floating on the water.

Only when the last of it had dispersed did he turn his attention to the realmgate. Bodies lay scattered about it. Kahya and Osric had done as he asked, with brutal efficiency. 'All of them?' he asked, glancing at the Protector-Prime. She nodded.

'They continued to chant, even as we cut them down.' By her tone, he could tell she was sickened both by their foes and what she had been forced to do. 'Why did they not resist us?' she asked, shaking her head.

'I don't think they even knew we were here,' Osric said, peering into the depths of the realmgate. 'As if there were weightier matters that better held their attention.' He stepped back. 'Something's wrong. The water...'

'Get back, Osric,' Grymn said as he pulled on his helmet. The air throbbed with the buzzing of innumerable flies. The abominable runes marked on the walls began to glow with a faint radiance. The balefire torches whipped, as if caught in a strong wind. The surface of the realmgate began to bubble and foam, and the compacted reeds writhed in place, as if in agony. The clear waters turned an iridescent black, before suddenly spewing upwards in an unending flood. From out of the dark came a sound. Deep and dolorous.

As the black waters swept towards him, Grymn thought that it might have been the tolling of some vast funerary bell.

CHAPTER EIGHT

POX-WATERS

The sounds of battle had faded. Now, only its echoes remained. The moans of the wounded, the soft susurrus of a healing rain, the sizzle of the last embers of balefire as they were snuffed. The great cauldron had been shattered, and its contents reduced to stinking clouds by Gardus' arrival. Throughout the citadel, Stormcasts worked diligently to stack and burn the corpses of their slain foes in clean fires set by the lightning strikes.

Lord-Celestant Gardus knew it was much the same in the other two citadels. The Steel Souls had dispersed upon arrival, moving to take control of the walkways and glistening paths of sargassum that connected the trio of floating fortresses. They had been met there by enemies, and by newly freed captives as well. Hundreds of them.

He looked around at the faces of those who crowded about him. They were silent and hollow-eyed, sullen with fear and resignation. They had suffered much in their short, brutal lives, and his heart twisted in his chest, convulsing in sympathy.

But not pity. Pity was what one felt for a lesser thing, like a wounded animal or a dying foe. These folk were neither animals nor foes. They might as well have been his own people, his kith and kin, at a remove of many centuries and generations. It pained him to see them, to see any being brought to such ruin. But, Sigmar willing, it was but a temporary thing.

Already, great cities were being constructed in the wild places of Ghyran. And not all of them with the blessings of the Everqueen, if the rumours he'd heard about the Greywater Fastness were true. But others, such as the Living City, were constructed from the very bedrock of Ghyran, by the magics of Alarielle herself. The Steel Souls had bled on the ironoak bulwarks of that place, and Grymn had held the Twelve-Thorn Gate against the Rotbringer forces besieging it. The same forces they had pursued here, to the Verdant Bay, in the aftermath of the war.

Morbus had told him of the trail of devastation they had followed south, of the burned forests and desecrated groves. Of the gallows raised on every hill and peak, and the bodies swinging in the breeze. And of the slave-caravans, many miles long. The Order of the Fly had much to answer for, and Gardus intended to see to it that they did so. The destruction of the sargasso-citadels was but the first step on that road. Gardus would not rest until he had restored all that Nurgle had taken from this realm. Including hope.

That was the heart of their campaign here, the reason for their presence. Other Stormhosts brought vengeance or freedom. Some inspired the downtrodden to take up the fight anew. But the Hallowed Knights brought hope. For hope was the seed of faith, and once planted, it could not be easily destroyed.

And the beginnings of hope were what he saw in the faces of those gathered about him. Beneath the pain and fear, the first flickers of belief in something better. And that was why he allowed them to gather about him, and followed them where they led. Though they refused to look at him, or answer his questions, he had faith that they meant him no harm, and had bid his warriors to leave him to discover the reason for himself.

The crowd that encompassed him was made up of men and women and children, all ages and descriptions. Many were thin with privation, bones visible beneath grimy skin. The sickly sweet smell of gangrene hung thick over the crowd, and there were too many gaps where legs and arms ought to be. Too many faces sagged with clusters of boils or leprous encrustation. All were sick. Broken. But at least these could stand.

The cages were full of those too weak to do so, as Morbus had shown him. Those too sick to rise, or too crippled. The worst of it was, they had not been brutalised. Their state was due to negligence and proximity, rather than harsh treatment. His stomach clenched as a nearby child plucked at the sores on her cheek. She led her mother by the hand. The woman was blind, the sockets of her eyes scabbed over. A hunched form scraped past him, hands braced on wooden blocks, the stumps of useless legs dragging in the dirt. Everywhere Gardus looked, there was decay and ruin. And he had the feeling there were worse things yet to be discovered.

A few hundred enemy warriors remained at large, having retreated into the tunnels below or else escaped on slow moving, barnacle-ridden barges for the far shore. Even now, his Steel Souls hunted them, under the direction of his auxiliary commanders. The citadels were not yet fully conquered, but they soon would be. Even so, he felt uneasy. As if… something was wrong. As if the battle were not yet won, but only just beginning.

He'd felt this way once before, in the Ghyrtract Fen. A Rotbringer tribe, dead at his feet, and the Gates of Dawn pulsing with corrupt life. He felt again the sudden sense of nausea, as the realmgate had convulsed and gaped, vomiting forth a thing out of nightmare. Bolathrax. He closed his eyes, banishing the image from his mind. Bolathrax was gone, sent back to the realm of its master in tatters, thanks to the Everqueen.

He heard a gasp, and realised that his light had grown bright as his mind had wandered. It shone as fiercely as the glow of Grymn's warding lantern, washing aside all shadows. The mortals huddled closer, murmuring in awe. Grimy bandages steamed in the glow, and infected wounds began to bubble and leak. Without thinking, Gardus reached out to them. Where his hands touched, open wounds began to scab over and buboes shrank. Men and women wept in mingled fear and joy as his light blazed ever more vibrantly.

Gardus looked around in confusion, uncertain as to what was happening. How was this possible? All around him, the mortals sank to their knees. 'No,' he said. Then, more loudly, 'No. Up. I am not the one to whom you should kneel.' Gently, he pulled those closest to him to their feet. 'In fact, it is I who should kneel before you.'

'And why is that?'

Gardus turned. The old man was blind. His eye sockets were a ruin of faded scars, and his face was worse still. His nose had been partially eaten away by some disease, and his brown teeth showed through gaps in his lips and cheeks. A halo of stringy white hair framed the wreckage. He sat cross-legged in the lee of a makeshift tent made from a tattered cloak, stretched over a quartet of broken spears. What was left of the old man's mouth twisted in a faint smile. 'I can smell the storm on you. You smell of spring rains and clean water. I remember those things, though not well.'

Gardus allowed the crowd to carry him towards the old man. 'You speak for these people?' he said. The old man chuckled. The laugh degenerated into a racking cough, and he bent forward, wheezing. Gardus reached for him, but the old man waved him back.

'I speak only for myself.' He coughed. 'That they choose to listen is more a sign of our desperation than any wisdom I might possess. I am Yare of Demesnus.'

Demesnus. The name rang through Gardus' mind like a bell. 'I am Gardus.'

'You are not a mortal man, Gardus. I can hear the echoes of your voice in what remains of my marrow, and feel the heat of your armour on my face.'

'No,' Gardus said. 'I am not mortal.'

Yare nodded weakly. 'That is good. The days of mortal men are drawing to a close, I think. We are too fragile to survive what these lands have become. We pass into myth, and leave the ruins of the world to gods and monsters.'

'Do not leave on my account,' Gardus said.

The old man laughed again. 'I'm in no hurry. I merely state a belief. I was a philosopher, you know. One of the last, I suspect. Not much use for philosophers, these days.'

'You are wrong.'

Yare cocked his head. 'Am I? That would be a welcome thing. Come closer. You said you should kneel before us, Gardus, and I asked why. You have not answered my question.'

Gardus sank to one knee before the old man. 'I want to ask your forgiveness. And to make a promise.'

'Promise?' the old man said, searching blindly for a face he would never see. Gardus removed his helmet and set it aside. He caught the old man's groping hand, and guided it to his face. Yare hissed in surprise. Gardus wondered what he had been expecting.

'Yes. You are the faithful. And we shall not abandon you again.'

'A fine sentiment,' Yare said quietly. 'But is it the truth?'

Gardus hesitated, uncertain how to answer such a question. Despite the kinship he felt with them, these people were no longer his, not truly. There was an ocean of time between them, and the realm Garradan of Demesnus had left was not this one, not any more. Things had changed, and the healer was now the warrior. Demesnus, a ruin. And philosophers made slaves. He was spared having to articulate any of this by a sudden rumbling from below. He rose swiftly to his feet, and the mortals drew back, their adoration turning to fright.

'What?' Yare asked. 'What is it?'

'Something has happened.'

The ground trembled. Gardus heard a great cracking sound, as of rock shearing from a cliff-face. The ground split, and murky water spewed upwards. Mortals were knocked sprawling as liquid spilled across the ground, slopping against the walls. Scaffolding tore away from the inner walls of the citadel as the destructive vibration rose. It crashed down, filling the air with dust and jagged splinters. Gardus interposed himself, shielding Yare and several others from the worst of it. He turned, scanning the courtyard. He spotted Morbus hurrying towards him, accompanied by Aetius and a retinue of Liberators.

'Aetius, get these people to safety,' Gardus said. 'Morbus, what is this? What's going on?' The Lord-Relictor staggered as another tremor shook the ground. Gardus steadied him. 'Is this some new trick of the enemy?'

'I do not think so. At least, not an intentional one.' Morbus braced himself with his staff as the citadel juddered again. 'Lord-Castellant Grymn has not yet returned. I fear the two are connected.'

'Lorrus…?' Gardus pulled on his helmet. 'We must find him. And swiftly.'

Tornus swooped low as the citadel continued to shudder. Already, pox-waters had filled the lower courtyard and extinguished many of the funeral pyres. He wondered if the fortress were dying. Sometimes, the bastions of Nurgle possessed a crude life of their own. If that were the case, the entire edifice might soon sink into the sea. The thought gave him no pleasure. There were too many mortals yet to be freed, too many sick, too many wounded. They would not be able to save them all.

Already, hundreds were being shepherded across the remaining viaduct by Liberators and Judicators. But not quickly enough. Prosecutors swooped overhead, carrying those too weak to move on their own. While much of the chamber was engaged in the evacuation, a substantial portion of its strength, led by Lord-Celestant Gardus, had descended into the depths, seeking the source of the pox-waters that threatened to drown them all.

Tornus banked sharply, his keen gaze searching the rubble below, seeking any signs of life. The task of searching for any survivors not yet gathered with the others had fallen to he, Cadoc and Enyo. While many of the mortals had turned on the Rotbringers as soon as they were given the opportunity, others had fled, seeking a safe place to wait out the fighting.

Further, the surviving Rotbringers were mustering. Those who hadn't fled in their ironwood barges across the bay would be readying themselves to counterattack. In their madness, they would see the death of this place not as a threat, but as an opportunity.

His wings dipped, and he swooped beneath a tilting scaffold. Loose ropes and chains slapped against his armour like vines as he drew close to the ground. Ospheonis screeched from somewhere above. 'Yes,' he said. 'I saw it as well.'

Movement. Below a mound of fallen timbers. A steady stream of murky water curled through it, threatening to drown anyone who might be trapped beneath it. He dropped to the ground with a splash, slung his bow across his chest, and caught hold of a heavy timber. While not so strong as he once had been, he was still far more powerful than a mortal. The timber shifted with a creak and he got his shoulder under it, forcing it up. 'Whoever you are, if you can hear me, try to crawl out.'

Something moved beneath the rubble. A noxious odour enveloped him. 'My thanks, friend. Without your aid, I might have mouldered in the dark o'er long.' The voice was a deep rasp, like a dull knife across burnt flesh. Tornus hurled the timber aside as something foul and dripping rose out of the dark to clutch at him with thick, wet fingers. He fell backwards, his attacker on top of him. A strong grip fastened onto the sides of his helmet and slung him to the ground, hard enough to smash the air from his lungs.

'My apologies, friend. I dislike attacking one who has done me a good turn, but we are enemies, after all. Now, lie there and I shall crush your skull quickly, by way of thanks.' The Chaos knight caught up another timber, this one not quite as large as himself, and lifted it like a club. Tornus rolled aside as the timber crashed down. One of his wings extended, and its shimmering length sawed across his opponent's arm, raising a burst of sparks. The Chaos knight staggered back, clutching at his arm. The timber dropped to the ground, forgotten.

'I almost felt that. Perhaps I spoke too soon.' He inclined his head. Ragged strands of silk hung from the crown of his enclosed great helm, woven among a circlet of stubby horns. The tusks of an orruk decorated the front of the helm and his oversized gorget. His armour was dark and plain, save for the clumps of blisters that marked its plates. He wore a threadbare tabard, marked by the sign of the fly, and a belt of broken skulls around his waist. He spread his arms and said, 'I have no weapon, as you can see. Will you permit me to recover my sword?'

Tornus unslung his bow and reached for an arrow. 'No.'

'Fie, sir, fie! Will you shoot me down like a cur?'

'It is being more than you are deserving, pox-knight.'

The Chaos knight cocked his head. 'Those mangled words seem overly familiar. Only one other have I ever heard speak in such a barbaric manner, and he is dead. Perished in honourable combat.'

'Not honourable,' Tornus said. Did this creature know him? Or who he had been? He could not recall, though he had fought alongside the knights of the Order more than once. Compelled by some dark curiosity, he said, 'Be speaking your name.'

'I am Gatrog, Duke of Festerfane.'

'Is Goral being dead then?' Tornus asked, despite himself. Torglug had met Goral, though only once. Torglug had found Goral infuriating, he recalled.

'Aye, and these many months. I suppose the duchy shall fall to our cousin now.' Gatrog took a step forwards. 'Whatever happens, Festerfane shall always have a duke. So we were promised, and upon that promise we made our oaths.'

'False promises, false oaths,' Tornus said, stepping back. He pulled on the glimmering drawstring, arrow nocked and ready. But he did not fire. Something stayed his hand. 'You are being a living falsehood.'

'You speak as if you know me,' Gatrog said. He took another step forwards, fingers flexing. 'I'd heard that Torglug died in battle with the storm-warriors...'

Tornus shook his head. He felt as if he were in a thick fug, as if his lungs were constricting in his chest. 'Torglug is being dead,' he said, his voice hollow.

Why could he not loose his arrow? He had killed number-less Rotbringers since his apotheosis. Why did he hesitate with this one?

'Is he?' Gatrog asked. 'No. I can see the shadow of his blighted hand on you, whatever you call yourself. Hidden in starlight and silver, but it's there nonetheless. Nurgle's seeds are tough things, and life always finds a way.' He reached out. 'Is it you, Torglug?'

Tornus lurched back and loosed his arrow. Gatrog grunted, but lunged forwards regardless, hands spread. He drove Tornus back, clutching at his throat. 'It *is* you, isn't it? You've been enchanted. Ripped from Grandfather's bower by some Azyrite curse.' One big fist slammed down on Tornus' shoulder-plate, driving him to his knees. A second blow sent him sprawling in the water.

Dazed, he lashed out with his bow. Gatrog reeled back, curs-ing. Ospheonis shrieked and darted about the Chaos knight. Gatrog's curses grew in volume as he swatted at the star-eagle, until they were cut short by an arrow hammering into his chest. Three more arrows sprouted from his chest-plate and pauldrons, staggering him.

Tornus looked up. Cadoc crashed to the ground with a splash, starblade flashing as he removed one of Gatrog's hands at the wrist. He kicked the stunned Chaos knight in the chest, knocking him back into the pile of broken timbers. Gatrog roared in protest and shoved himself to his feet.

Cadoc laughed. 'Some fight in this one, eh, sister?'

'Finish him, Cadoc,' Enyo said, as she dropped to the ground beside Tornus. 'Are you injured, Tornus?'

Tornus shook his head. 'It is only being my pride.' He felt like a fool, allowing a creature like Gatrog to get so close. And more so for requiring aid. Enyo nodded, as if reading his thoughts.

'Better your pride than your body,' she said, extending a hand. He caught it, and allowed her to pull him to his feet. 'Surprisingly durable, some of these pox-knights.'

'Knight or slave, they all burn the same,' Cadoc said, flipping open his beacon. 'Look, abomination, look upon the light of Azyr one time before you perish. A gift to you, from the last Prince of Ekran.'

The azure radiance spilled forth, and Gatrog screamed. He stumbled forward against the light. His armour blackened and warped. Smoke rose from between its plates, and his tabard smouldered. Nonetheless, he groped blindly for Cadoc. One step. Then two. Three. Cadoc cursed and lifted his beacon higher. 'Fall, filth,' he snarled. 'Yield to the light.'

'A true knight… never yields,' Gatrog said, his voice little more than a hoarse rattle. His remaining hand fumbled towards the beacon, as if to snatch it from the Knight-Azyros' grip. Instead, he sank to one knee, with a groan. Cadoc, incensed, kicked him onto his back and set a foot on his chest, pinning him to the ground. He raised his starblade.

'No,' Tornus said.

Cadoc glanced at him. 'What?'

'Be staying your sword.' Tornus extended his bow, forcing Cadoc to step back.

'Tornus, he is an enemy, a slave of the Dark Gods,' Enyo said.

'Even as I was being once.' Tornus looked at them. 'And now, I am standing before you, being clad in silver and bearing a realmhunter's bow.' He gestured to Gatrog. 'Who is to be saying that he could not be doing the same?'

'Did that last blow to the head addle your wits?' Cadoc demanded. 'He is an enemy! His sort must be purged in the holy fires of Azyr.' He took a step towards the fallen Rotbringer. Tornus interposed himself. Cadoc extended his blade. 'Do not think that because you wear silver, you are safe from my judgement.'

'Enough, the pair of you.' Enyo thrust her bow between them. She tapped an arrow against Cadoc's chest-plate. 'You speak of judgement as if you were Sigmar himself, rather than his servant.' She looked at Tornus. 'And you have chosen an inopportune moment to come to these conclusions, worthy though they may be.' As if to emphasize her point, the citadel gave another shudder. Chunks of rotting sargassum tumbled down from above, raining across the courtyard.

Tornus lowered his head. 'I am bowing to your wisdom, Enyo.' He reached down and snatched up a length of rusty chain from the rising waters. 'We shall be binding him and taking him before Lord-Celestant Gardus. Let him be deciding what we are to be doing, yes?' He looked at Cadoc, waiting to see if the Knight-Azyros protested.

Cadoc snorted and hung his beacon from his belt. 'I await his judgement with interest.' He pointed at Tornus. 'Know this, though, do not seek to come between the Prince of Ekran and his prey again, Redeemed One. Else we shall see which of us Sigmar truly favours.' He laughed. The sound was decidedly lacking in mirth.

Tornus turned to Enyo. 'I am to be thanking you, huntress.'

Enyo nodded. 'Well you should. Now, let us chain this blubbersome creature before he recovers his strength. Having gone to the trouble to spare him, I would rather not be forced to kill him now.' Swiftly, they bound Gatrog in the chains, melting the links together with the heat of their arrows. Injured as the Rotbringer was, he gave them little trouble.

'What sorcery is this, that can transform a great warrior so?' Gatrog croaked, as they stepped back, task complete. His body still smouldered from Cadoc's beacon, but his wrist stump had begun to scab over. He would heal, Tornus knew, but not soon. 'What fell curse has reduced you to this base treachery, Torglug?'

'No curse,' Tornus said. 'Hope. There was being one last spark of hope in me, one last ember of faith.' He looked down at his foe. 'There is being a spark of hope in you as well, Gatrog.' Even as he said the words, he knew they were true. He believed that hope, that faith, was what had allowed him – had allowed Torglug – to endure the celestial beacons of the Stormcast Eternals. Where his followers had been reduced to ash, Torglug had stumbled on. As Gatrog had. Somewhere, deep inside the pox-knight, was a spark of the man he might have been, before Nurgle had corrupted him.

Gatrog slumped. 'Hope is the weed in Grandfather's garden.'

'Yes,' Tornus said. 'That is being the truth of the thing.'

Morbus Stormwarden felt old. Fingers locked about his reliquary staff, he bent mind and will against the rushing pox-waters that sought to flood the depths of the sargasso-citadel. A force of nature, even a corrupted one, was not an enemy to be attacked. Instead, it had to be redirected, its fury purged. Behind him, Stormcasts advanced, protected from the rising deluge by his magics. Ahead of him, the storm raged, and he let the leash slip, matching wind and lightning against water.

It was no easy thing to carry the storm, and this campaign had all but worn him to a nub. Cleansing the skies, the waters, the land itself was no simple task. Added to his burden was the constant threat of Nurgle's shadow. Here, in Ghyran, the Plague God held more sway than he ought, and every Stormcast who fell in battle with the Rotbringers risked having his or her soul devoured by the daemons capering unseen just behind the veil of reality. It took a great deal of concentration to guide the souls of the fallen back to Azyr, and he'd spent many restless nights in communion with the dead.

Morbus had never spoken of these difficulties to anyone. They were his burden, as Bearer of the Bones of Heroes, and he endured them gladly. Even as he had centuries past, as Ar-Morr of Baran-Ulut. He could not recall much about his mortal life, but he remembered his title, and the smell of incense. The weight of his ceremonial armour, and the stiff, scratchy fabric of his robes of office. The feel of the scythe in his hands, as he harvested the souls of the soon-to-be dead. He had been old then, as well. And though his body was young now, his mind and soul still bowed beneath an accumulation of years. Age brought wisdom, and only the wise could endure the Twelve Rites.

However, he didn't feel particularly wise at this moment. Tired, angry, but not wise. Something had gone wrong. Or perhaps right. It was hard to tell. The spirits of the air and water were in an uproar, screaming of a black wound in the belly of the sea. A wound that spat bilious water and shook the foundations of the citadel. He could feel the rawness of it at the edge of his perceptions. A phantom pain, impinging on his ability to focus. Then, that had been the way of it since he'd first set foot in the Jade Kingdoms.

An infernal miasma clung to the ghost-winds here, choking the skeins of fate and death with life unbound. Life without purpose or place in the heavenly mechanism, life that could only grow, stagnate and rot eternally on the vine. All things had their season, but now those seasons were in disarray. Even now, despite the victories they'd won, Ghyran was still in upheaval. The spirits of the land screamed, and it was all Morbus could do to ignore them and forge on. Just as he'd ignored the obvious flaw in the Lord-Castellant's plan.

The realmgates were a Lord-Castellant's responsibility, true enough... but purging them of corruption was a Lord-Relictor's. He'd allowed Grymn to divert him, and now they would pay the price for his failure. He tightened his grip on his staff, drawing strength from the whispers of the dead. Spirits clung to him like a second cloak. Fallen heroes, spared Reforging by some whim of Sigmar's. They added their potency to his.

But that potency came with a price. Beneath the comforting whispers was the echo of another voice. A darker one by far, and as vast and deep as the sea itself. Morbus knew that voice intimately, as all Lord-Relictors did. It rode the night winds and spoke in the language of the charnel fields. It gnawed their very being like a jackal with a bone, and demanded obedience. Of the Twelve Rites, four, in their entirety, were devoted to resisting that demand, and enduring the wrath of the one who'd made it. Failure in either case was unthinkable. There were worse fates than death.

Sigmarite-hard mantras slid into place, drifting in tight whispers from parched lips. The dark voice grew faint, and was soon drowned out entirely by the crash of the storm. Morbus' head rang with the crash of blades and the music of the spheres, as his limbs began to tremble from the fury of the forces at his command. He knew that he had to unleash it, or risk being torn apart by his own magics. But to do so too soon would only add to the destruction the pox-waters had already caused. Gardus wanted the citadel to remain intact until it could be fully evacuated.

That sense of mercy was both the Steel Soul's greatest weakness and his greatest strength. Other Lord-Celestants burned with a desire for vengeance or justice. Gardus shone with compassion. For him, war was but the difficult first step. It was what came after that was the most important task. If Gardus survived the battles to come, he might rebuild the Mortal Realms singlehandedly. Morbus hoped he would be there to witness it.

Behind him, he could hear the firm rumble of Gardus' voice, and Kurunta's roaring bellow, but ignored both. They knew better than to speak to him at such a moment. A small, brief smile cracked his composure. Well, perhaps not Kurunta.

The passageway bucked around him as he channelled the storm winds through its narrow coil. The waters surged forward and back, their strength blunted and tamed by his winds. Lightning surged, spreading through the noxious liquid, reducing much of its volume to steam. Not all of it, but enough to lessen the risk of flooding. He'd drawn more and more of the wind to him as they'd descended, using it to contain the waters, or else force them back. Behind him, Liberators smashed crude drainage points into the walls and floor, bleeding off the remaining liquid a bit at a time.

They had employed the same tactics to good effect in the storming of Quagmire Keep, much to the detriment of its semi-amphibious masters. If it worked as well here as there, the citadel might not sink into the Verdant Bay. At least not yet.

Morbus stumbled as another convulsion shook the passageway. Hardened sargassum ground against itself. Ochre dust sifted down in thick clouds. Behind him, Gardus barked an order, and shields rose with a rattle, forming an improvised roof over the heads of the Stormcasts. 'Enough,' Morbus murmured. He raised a hand, and the others halted. He kept moving, until he was some distance ahead of them.

He raised his staff, channelling the power of the storm into its sigmarite core. The reliquary at the top of the staff began to clatter. Lightning crawled across the skull, licking out to scorch the walls to either side. The air in the passageway thickened and his breath congealed in his lungs. He closed his eyes and slammed the staff down. The moment the ferrule struck the floor, the water evaporated. Steam swelled up, filling the corridor. It billowed away from him, spilling outwards in all directions. Where the steam passed, the water boiled away to nothing. The passageway shook as the echoes of his unspoken prayer reverberated through it.

A moment later, he felt the first ebbing of the pox-waters, though not solely through any effort of his. Some power worked at them from their source, choking it off, even as he weakened them. He suspected he knew the source of it, however. He took a step, and staggered. Without the fury of the storm keeping him upright, he felt barely able to stand. Gardus caught his arm. 'Lord-Relictor...?'

'I am fine, Gardus. I endure, as ever.'

'Like the stones of the mountains?'

'Like the faithful,' Morbus corrected. He stepped away from the Lord-Celestant. Gardus was glowing again. The light shone out between the plates of his armour, casting its soft glow over everything. It felt similar to the light of Grymn's warding lantern. Invigorating and comforting, all at once. As if Gardus had become a living beacon. Did blood still course through his veins, or was it all just starlight now?

Morbus had heard the stories. Every Lord-Relictor had. The souls of their fellow Stormcasts were their responsibility, and when the souls came back changed, so too did their responsibilities change. To watch, to judge. Sigmar was a wise god, and left little to chance. If something happened, if a Reforged soul displayed a flaw, it needed to be dealt with. And swiftly. Before that flaw spread. But was this light of Gardus' a flaw – or a blessing?

As if noticing Morbus' unease, Gardus tensed. His light flickered, dimmed, faded. 'I forget, sometimes,' he said softly.

'Unobservant, as I said,' Morbus chided. He turned and gestured. 'That way.' He could feel the pulse of celestial energies somewhere close by. It spoke to him in a way few things did, in the language of the stars themselves. That the stars spoke to one another had not come as a surprise to him, when he'd learned of it. All things spoke, if one but had the wit to listen. And sometimes what they said was important.

This particular strand of energy spoke to him of desperation. Of loss and determination. It flickered, growing weaker by the moment. Tired as he was, he quickened his pace. The passageway echoed with the crash of sigmarite as the others followed his example. When they found the entrance to the chamber, Gardus laughed. 'Lorrus has definitely been this way,' he said.

Morbus eyed the devastation, noting the black scarring

and scattered chunks of hardened sargassum. Grymn had his faults, but vacillation wasn't among them. Upon finding a wall, he'd made a door. 'Through here,' he said. The Stormcasts warily picked their way through the rubble.

The chamber beyond was waterlogged. The floor was lower than the passage, its expanse interrupted by fallen support pillars. Muddy filth rose in miniature mountain ranges, before dwindling into valleys and dog-leg canyons. There were bodies entombed in the mud, their pale faces peering out from beneath folds of rotting sargassum.

Morbus ignored all of this. His eyes were drawn to the black, bubbling lake at the chamber's heart, and the half-formed things that floundered in its shallows. Cyclopean eyes rolled in sagging sockets, glaring blearily at the Stormcasts. Faces caught in a constant cycle of death and rebirth twisted into mocking smiles, as shapeless mouths droned out a dull razor of sound. The closest of the daemons struggled up out of the muck, leaving bits of itself behind. It made as if to speak.

'Kurunta,' Gardus said, his voice flat.

Kurunta moved swiftly, his broadsword looping out in a wide arc. The daemon's head plopped into the water, dissolving even as it did so. Its body followed suit, collapsing in on itself, until nothing remained but a thick scum on the surface of the water.

More daemons crawled towards them, hauling themselves half out of the muck, their bodies crumbling with every second. Morbus stepped back with a grunt of disgust. 'They cannot sustain themselves here. They are already being pulled back to their master's realm.'

'Then let us hurry them along. Solus, pass a fitting judgement.' Gardus' hand flashed down. A moment later, the wasp-hum of skybolt bows echoed through the chamber.

Daemons burst like rotten fruit. Those that survived the volley were dealt with by blade and hammer. Long moments passed, as the Stormcasts fought in grim silence. Only when the last had subsided with a disgruntled sigh, was Morbus free to seek the reason for their abortive manifestation.

'Where are they, Morbus? I see no sign of our brothers and sisters.' Gardus gestured. 'Kurunta, Aetius, I want this chamber searched. If they're here, I want them found.'

Morbus was only half listening to the Lord-Celestant. He stepped to the edge of the dark water and sank down to one knee. Heedless of the bubbling daemonic detritus nearby, he let his hand sink into the mire. It resonated with the echo of foul magics, and his skin crawled. But there was something else. A mote of light, deep in the dark.

He concentrated on it, probing it. His submerged fingers bent and curled into a fist. The tainted water began to bubble. Cries of alarm sounded from behind him, but Morbus ignored them. It was taking all of his focus to reclaim that which the dark had sought to claim. Slowly, he drew it towards him. As it rose, its light grew bright, stretching through the water, until it seemed as if a star were shining beneath the surface.

Morbus stood, drawing his hand up, water streaming between his fingers. As he did so, the light broke the surface in a cloud of steam. He heard Kurunta curse, and couldn't fault the Knight-Heraldor his reaction. The light bled from the shattered casing of a Lord-Castellant's warding lantern.

'Morbus, what does this mean?' Gardus asked.

Morbus bowed his head.

'It means we are too late.' He looked at Gardus. 'Lord-Castellant Grymn is gone.'

CHAPTER NINE

IN THE GARDEN

Grymn floated in darkness. No. Not floated. *Drowned.* He came to awareness, wrapped in sargassum. He pawed at the shroud of decaying plants, spinning in place, end over end, unable to see anything save a cloud of rippling, oily bubbles. He tore the weeds aside, searching for something, anything, he could use to orient himself. His lungs strained, and black clouds clung to the edge of his perceptions. The foulness of the waters permeated his armour, mouth and lungs. It clawed at his insides like poison. He forced aside the pain, trying to find a way out of his predicament.

As he ripped the thickest fold of sargassum away, he caught sight of the corpses. Innumerable and spreading out away from him in all directions. An infinity of the dead. Bodies bloated with rot and blackened with disease floated together, a reef of decaying meat. Blind eyes met his everywhere he looked, and he pushed them aside. Limp fingers flopped against his helmet and war-plate.

For a moment, the reef broke apart, revealing the dark beyond. He glimpsed something vast and squamous undulating away into the black. Hints of impossible shapes, mighty in their foulness, teased him, drawing his eyes this way and that. Beyond the corpses, he saw forests of splintered teeth, clashing together in silent ferocity, and rolling waves of blistered scales as immense leviathans tore at one another in elemental fury. A tail the size of a mountain range whipped out of sight. Its movement stirred the waters and the dead. The force of it pummelled him like the blow of a gargant's fist. He felt like a sailor adrift in a sea of monsters, and knew that should one of those shapes turn its attention to him, he would be lost, without hope of ever seeing Azyr again.

He tried to swim away from the distant shapes, but his armour was dragging him down. No, up. Dead hands tangled themselves in his cloak and the straps of his war-plate. He gritted his teeth, trying to ignore the growing ache of oxygen deprivation through sheer force of will. Far below him, he glimpsed something, like a twist of smoke rising from a chimney flue. But it was not smoke, nor even sargassum. It seemed to grow larger, even as he was pulled away from it. He twisted, seeking some sign of Sigmar's grace in the roiling darkness. He couldn't believe that it was his destiny to die here, drowned in an ocean of corpses.

And then there was light. Not a bright light. A weak, watery shimmer. But it was better than the dark. Lungs burning, he groped towards the light above, no, *below* him, dragging his armoured bulk free of the entangling weeds and corpses. The dead seemed to follow him, and the waters turned thick as their buboes and boils burst. He had to fight the urge to gag, and concentrated on swimming.

Grymn's head split the water, and he inhaled a lungful of

dense, caustic air. Flies buzzed around his head as he dragged himself to a weed-covered shore. Strange lumpen trees rose above him, partially obscured by a yellowish mist. Patches of soft mould turned to spore clouds as he floundered through them. He felt semi-solid earth beneath his hands and feet and pushed himself upright. Water poured off his begrimed armour as he staggered to shore.

He turned, taking in his surroundings. He appeared to be on the edge of a mere. Strange, unnatural plants loomed on all sides, jostling with the gnarled arthritic trees for space. He could hear heavy shapes floundering in the distance, and the croaking roars of things best left unseen. A vile rain streaked down and, where the droplets cascaded across his war-plate, patches of mould sprouted.

He scraped a patch of the newly grown mould from his armour. A moment later, it began to creep back. He hissed in disgust. The canopy overhead dripped constantly, and, besides the rain, the air was alive with stinging flies and drifting spores. Empty hands clenched uselessly. He'd lost his halberd and his lantern both. He was weaponless and seemingly alone. But where was he?

No. He shook his head, chiding himself. To pretend ignorance served no purpose. He knew where he was, at all times, in all ways. Every Stormcast did. Whatever the realm, they knew. They could feel the distinct power of it, deep in their bones. And they could feel when they were elsewhere. Outside the realms. Out of reach of Azyr's light.

There was no light here. Not really.

Only the soft sheen of infected flesh, reflected and refracted a million times.

Above him, the clouds of murk briefly parted and revealed a grin as wide as a chasm, and two pus-cream eyes like infant moons. The rains dripped from those titanic eyes like tears. Then the apparition was gone, leaving behind only the ghost of a single, thunderous, sardonic chuckle. Nothing occurred in the garden that its master was not aware of, in some fashion. He felt cold and feverish all at once.

Water splashed. Grymn whirled, and saw a silver gauntlet pierce the skin of the water. Without hesitating, Grymn waded back into the waters, hoping to reach whoever it was before they were drawn back down into the depths.

Even as he clasped the groping hand and hauled back, he saw more flashes of silver. And, among them, a flurry of spotted limbs, followed by a shrill cry of disapproval. Tallon burst to the surface, feathers and fur slick with foulness. The gryph-hound floundered to shore, issuing sharp shrieks of discontent as he did so. Grymn laughed in relief as he dragged a Liberator out of the water. Osric coughed up yellow liquid as Grymn helped him to shore. Kahya had survived as well, and one of her Protectors. Grymn took a head count. Only six Stormcast in all, counting himself. And Tallon.

'I suppose misery loves company,' he said, as he stroked the gryph-hound's head. Tallon's tail lashed in agitation and he trembled, as if ready to bolt. Grymn understood the feeling. The air here was wrong. Every inhalation was an effort, and it seared the lungs. Though he had the strength of the storm in his limbs, he could feel it ebbing. They were far from Sigmar's light. Too far.

'Where are we?' Osric growled, fumbling with his grandhammer. The weapon looked as if it had been put to use recently, and Grymn wondered what the Liberator-Prime had encountered in the depths.

'Use your senses,' Grymn said. 'Smell the air. Where do you think?'

'It can't be,' Osric said. But they could all hear the lie in his words. A murmur ran through the group. Fear, Grymn knew. Stormcast were courageous, filled with righteous fury, but there were some things even courage and fury weren't enough to overcome.

'Of course it can. The realmgate twisted in upon itself, and was corrupted.' Grymn let a harsh edge creep into his voice, startling his warriors from their worries. If they faltered now, they were lost. Those final few moments came back to him. He recalled a frantic struggle to open his warding lantern, to release its light and hopefully purge the gate of its taint. That they were here now, implied that he had failed.

Something chuckled.

Grymn turned, searching. The sky was obscured again, in roiling, sickly clouds. The others appeared to have heard nothing. He shook his head. A trick of this place. The dangers here would not simply be physical. He would have to be wary. They all would, if they were to survive. 'I require a weapon,' he said.

Osric unsheathed his gladius. 'Here, take my blade, Lord-Castellant.'

'My thanks, Osric.' Grymn took it and sighted down the length of the sword. 'Have you been caring for this properly?'

'Every day,' Osric said.

'Only it feels a bit off.' Grymn flipped the blade and caught the hilt as it came down. 'No matter. I shall soon have it gleaming like new.'

Kahya laughed, though there was little humour in the sound. 'Even here, he seeks to teach us a lesson,' she said, leaning on her stormstrike glaive. 'Lecture on, Lord-Castellant. Shall we practise our drills?'

'You should have thought of that earlier,' Grymn snapped. 'Then, perhaps we would not be here.' Kahya fell silent, as did

Osric. Grymn took a breath. 'My apologies, Protector-Prime. The fault is that of our foes.' Kahya nodded after a moment's hesitation. Grymn looked around, taking in the trees and bubo-like hummocks of soft mud. He could hear sad, soft moans on the wind, and there were things that might have been faces in the vegetation. Creeping fronds groped for him like the fingers of penitents. 'We must stay together. To become separated here, now, even if only in spirit, will be the death of us.'

No. Not death. There is no death here, friend.

Grymn stiffened. The voice had slipped in, as if on the wind. It was familiar. He looked around, grip tightening on the hilt of his gladius. Soft lights swooped through the dark, just at the edge of his vision. Something, a voice, a song, tugged at his hearing, trying to draw him away, and deeper into the swamp. He ignored it. 'What was that?'

'What was what, Lord-Castellant?' Osric asked.

Kahya held up her hand. 'Hsst. I hear it as well. It sounds like… oars.'

Tallon hissed. The gryph-hound stood stiff, tail lashing. The feathers on his neck flared out, and he snapped his beak. A moment later, they heard the drum beat. Slow and sonorous, like the heartbeat of a dying gargant. 'Defensive positions,' Grymn said. The two Liberators moved into a line, shields locked tight. Osric took up position behind them. Kahya and her remaining warrior moved to flank Grymn.

A pitiful force. But brave.

Grymn shook his head. Kahya glanced at him. 'Lord-Castellant?'

'I'm fine,' he said. 'Look to yourself.' It came out more harshly than he'd intended, but perhaps that was good. He was not known for his consideration, and if they doubted him it could be fatal. The rhythmic sound of oars striking sludgy water grew louder. And with it came the groaning chants of mortals in pain, their voices rising and falling with the drum beat. The water rippled, and the sound of trees creaking and crashing rose up to join the rest of the noise. Something heavy was coming towards them.

It stopped.

Silence fell, broken only by the shrill cries of things that were not birds. Then, a heavy splash, as of something weighty being shoved into the water. A moment later, a squashy, moist sound, like fat raindrops slapping metal. It was joined by the sound of rustling reeds, and a droning dirge that rose up from all directions.

Tallon turned in a circle, clacking his beak in obvious agitation. 'They're all around us,' Grymn said. 'They must not be allowed to reach the realmgate.' Forms moved in the murk, indistinct, but growing more solid with every passing moment. Dozens of them. No, twice that. More. More than they had any hope of seeing off. Inhuman voices rose from the stinking mists, joined together in a malignant song. The sound of it curdled Grymn's soul.

The first plaguebearer burst out of the murk, jaws lolling in an almost cheerful expression. Bloat-bellied and thin limbed, the daemon was covered in mottled, scabrous flesh, through which decaying bone and rotting muscle showed. A single, curving horn rose from its shapeless head, and its lone, bulging eye fixed on the Liberators with a merry gleam. The blade it clasped in its knotted fingers was designed for cleaving, and its edge was pockmarked with rust and other, less respectable substances.

The festering blade slapped down against a shield, rocking the unsteady Liberator on his feet. Osric's grandhammer looped out and smashed in whatever passed for the daemon's skull. It slumped back with a disgruntled sigh. A second dae-mon slid from the tree line. Then a third. A fourth. More. Until the Stormcasts were surrounded by more than three times their number. Grymn turned, trying to count them. Had the creatures been waiting for them, or was this merely happenstance?

It didn't matter. If they wanted a fight, he would be happy to oblige. 'Who are the unluckiest souls in creation?' he asked, a crooked smile on his lips.

'Only the faithful,' Kahya said, laughing.

'Who will teach these creatures what it means to dare Sig-mar's wrath?'

'Only the faithful,' Osric growled.

'Only the faithful,' Grymn echoed. He extended his gla-dius towards the closest daemon. 'Well? Get to it. We don't have all day.'

The plaguebearers jerked into motion, and loped through the reed-choked waters, chuckling darkly. Osric's Liberators fought back to back, making themselves an obstruction in the tide. Osric sent daemons sprawling with precise blows from his grandhammer, displaying an impressive skill with the bulky weapon. Kahya and her remaining warrior wove a wall of shimmering energy between their opponents and the other Stormcasts, protecting them. Grymn and Tallon fought on the edge of the fray, forcing the daemons to split their attention.

But even Stormcasts had their limits, and they couldn't be everywhere at once. The first to fall was the last Protector. The heavily armoured warrior lost his footing in the muck and slid to one knee. The daemons were quick to capitalise and they swarmed him. Kahya noticed his predicament, but too late. The warrior fell, and was buried beneath a heap of hacking, slashing forms.

Grymn shoved himself around, borrowed gladius whirling in a tight circle, as he opened a daemon's throat and popped the eye of a second. 'Kahya, Osric, guard yourselves,' he roared.

Osric spun, his grandhammer snapping out to crush a daemon's skull. But two more of the creatures bore him to the water, their festering blades stabbing. Osric's shout of anger became a scream of pain, before fading to silence. The two Liberators fell, each in their turn, joining their Prime in death.

But, to Grymn's horror, their souls did not burst free, did not rise to Azyr as they should have. Instead, the bodies lay where they had fallen, broken and bleeding. At once, he knew the reason. Somehow, this place was caging their souls, preventing them from fleeing. Enraged, he removed a plaguebearer's head. He spun his blade and drove it into a bloated belly, bursting it like a pimple. He slung the deflating plaguebearer aside and turned to see Kahya sink down, a daemon-blade in her back. He was alone.

Tallon squalled and pounced on a daemon, driving the creature face first into the murk. The gryph-hound snapped the chortling plaguebearer's spine and silenced its laughter with a vicious snap of his beak. Grymn splashed towards the animal as more plaguebearers plunged nearer. He caught hold of a horn and ripped it free of its skull, before jabbing it into a grinning maw. A plaguebearer hurled itself at him, hoping to tangle his limbs, and he caught it by the throat. He dashed its maggoty brains out against the bole of a tree, and removed the sword hand of another.

Tallon caught the wounded daemon by the leg and jerked it off its feet. As it flailed in the water, Grymn trod on its head, squashing it. Breathing heavily, he looked around. No daemon remained standing. 'Only the faithful,' he muttered.

What good faith, in a place like this?

Grymn closed his eyes, trying to block out the voice. It was just a trick. A whisper of ill wind, trying to undermine his certitude. Gardus had spoken rarely of his time in this place, but Grymn remembered his warnings well enough. He'd spoken of weeping trees, and accusing ghosts. Of a swamp that extended forever, and every breath made fouler than the last. 'I am not Gardus,' Grymn said. His lungs ached, and his limbs felt heavy. He looked at Tallon. 'I am the shield, and I will endure whatever this place can throw at me.'

But he would need more than a gladius. He belted the short blade about his waist and lifted a warblade from the mud. The longer sword would give him the reach he needed. He caught up a shield. It was dented and cracked, but still serviceable. He slung it over his back. They weren't the weapons he preferred, but they would serve. He heard the winding of a horn, and realised more daemons were on the way.

The sounds they'd heard earlier had been some sort of conveyance. A vessel. That meant a crew. Perhaps even an army, looking to enter the realmgate. He glanced back at the dark waters they'd emerged from. Alone, he could not mount a proper defence, of either the gate or the bodies of the fallen. If their souls were caught here, they needed protecting as much as the path to Ghyran itself.

When defence was impossible, offence was the only option. He would build a rampart out of motion, and make himself a fortress to be conquered. He would lead the enemy away for as long as he could.

As he started towards the sound of the approaching daemons, Tallon splashed after him, chirruping. Grymn waved the animal back with a sharp gesture. 'No. Stay. Guard.' Grymn caught Tallon's beak and bent, so that their heads touched. 'Guard them until I return. Let nothing touch them.'

The words came harsh and swift and, even as he said them, he knew they were a lie. He would not return, and Tallon too would perish, eventually. Either from starvation, or an enemy's blade. He wanted to apologise to the beast, to say something, anything, but knew the animal wouldn't understand. But he would fight. He would protect the souls of the dead until there was no strength left in his spotted frame.

The sounds of approaching daemons drove Grymn to his feet. His hand ached for his lantern, but he would have to make do with what he had. Taking a tighter grip on his warblade, he started towards the daemons, picking up speed as he went. A single charge ought to carry him through and past them. They would turn and follow. He would lead them a merry chase for as long as he was able. And when he wasn't, he would die.

But not easily.

He burst through a patch of fungus-trees, shield raised, and slid to a stop. Plaguebearers lurched towards him from all directions, chuckling. Grymn slammed the flat of his blade against his shield. 'Who will face the dark and cast it back?' he said. 'Only the faithful.' Another crash of sigmarite against sigmarite. 'Who will walk the world's black rim and fear no shadow?' Slam. 'Only the faithful.'

He backhanded a plaguebearer with the shield. As it tried to climb to its feet, he drove the warblade down, bursting its single eye. Another lunged from the side, and he ducked beneath its blow, driving his shoulder into its sunken chest. It stumbled and he bisected its horned skull, crown to jaw. 'Only the faithful. That is who stands before you. *Only the faithful!*' Grymn cried, as he surged into their ranks, chopping and slashing. 'Come and get me, you bastards.'

He pressed forward without stopping, absorbing blows on

his battered shield. The plaguebearers seemed perturbed by his enthusiasm, and their chuckles had faded to dark mutterings. They got in one another's way in their haste to attack, and he made the most of it. 'Lazy. No tactical acumen. I am one, you are many. For shame.' He booted a daemon in the face and trod on it until its swollen belly burst, releasing a cloud of flies.

He whipped away from them, barrelling on. He swept aside any creature that sought to bar his path. His heavy war-plate turned aside those blows that landed. But he remained in motion, never halting unless he had no choice. Daemons splashed in his wake, their chants devolving to incoherent snarls of frustration.

Several times, he caught sight of great, low-slung shapes slipping through the mangrove-like depths of the swamp. Galleys, he thought. Though like no galley he'd ever seen, with sails of billowing mould and creaking, fungus-spotted hulls. He couldn't tell which way they were sailing, in the murk. It grew thick about him, and soon he couldn't even tell which way he was going. But he kept moving, regardless, until his breath burned in his lungs and sweat stung his eyes. His muscles cramped, but he shook it off.

Time stretched strangely. Minutes passed, or perhaps hours. Trees rose up and fell away like agonised figures. And still, Grymn pressed on. The attacks came less often, as if the creatures had grown tired of him. But still, they followed. Still, he could hear the slap of oars and the creak of rigging. Stinging flies swarmed about him, rising in clouds from the muck beneath him. Strange, half-familiar faces swam to the surface of the loathly water, mouthing silent imprecations.

Grymn shook it all off. He ignored the murk, the ghosts, the sounds, all of it, and concentrated on putting one foot after the other. Another Stormcast might have faltered, but Grymn would not. Could not. The same strength of will that had carried him through the Rotwater Blight would sustain him here. It had to. Exhaustion clawed at him, but he pressed on. Until, finally, he stumbled. A root, perhaps, or something more sinister. It caught his ankle, wrenching it painfully. He sagged, catching himself with the edge of the shield.

All at once, the daemons swarmed towards him. They came from every direction, chortling in satisfaction. He snarled in frustration and slashed out with his warblade. A daemon folded over, its chortles cut short. A blow crashed against his shield, rocking him. Another caromed off his helmet, making sparks dance before his eyes. He needed to clear some space. He swung the shield out, driving several of his attackers back. But even as he rose to his feet, a blade skidded off his side. Acidic grime ate away at the sigmarite. He pivoted and brought his warblade down on the creature's skull, splitting it.

They pressed in around him, an unceasing tide of filth and degradation. Blades stabbed at him, and the droning chant filled his mind, drowning out all coherent thought. Still he fought on, his body moving by instinct. He was not merely a wielder of weapons, but a weapon himself. Honed to a lethal, killing edge.

But even the strongest blade eventually breaks.

'Only the faithful,' Grymn hissed, between clenched teeth. There was blood in his eyes, but he didn't need to see this enemy to fight them. 'Only the faithful.'

You fight well, for an Azyrite. But this battle is done.

The voice echoed through him, and he stumbled, momentarily disorientated. He recovered quickly, removing a plaguebearer's hands as it tried to hack at him. He slammed the rim of his shield into its throat, silencing its droning cry.

You are strong. Quick. You'd have made a fine knight, were your soul your own. Instead, you are chained by lightning to Sigmar's throne.

Grymn shook his head, trying to clear it. But the hateful words resonated like the boom of a drum, shaking him to his core. A blade caught him in the back of the head, shattering on his helmet, but knocking him from his feet. He rolled over and tried to rise, but more blows came, hammering him down. The shield was smashed from his grip. A blade sawed across his forearm, and the warblade fell away, lost to the mire. He lashed out with a fist, pulping a cancerous jaw, and clawed for the gladius. His stomach churned. He felt as if something were reaching up from within him to grasp at his heart. A dreadful weight settled on his lungs, and he began to cough.

Do you feel it, Azyrite? My hand, on your heart. Will you tell me your name, now?

'W... who?' Grymn spat. Bile filled his mouth. More than bile. Wriggling shapes. He pitched forward, spitting an oily discharge. Fat maggots plopped to the water. Vision wavering, he found he could no longer rise.

Am I so quickly forgotten, then? Fie on thee, Azyrite. Fie and fie again. Ah. The captain of this merry crew approaches.

The plaguebearers retreated as the sound of heavy, splashing footsteps sounded. As the daemons parted ranks, a broad figure strode through them. The creature was taller than any daemon, and twice as broad, with a bulk that would have put an ogor to shame. Clad in broken war-plate and filthy leathers, the monstrosity wore a featureless helm, dominated by a sharp-edged horn, and carried a heavy, single-bladed axe in his one human hand. Fully half of the being's body was rent asunder, and from the gaping wound emerged the snapping beak and twisting tentacles of some vile sea-beast.

'Well, there's a familiar face,' the bloated creature said, in a voice like water spilling over barnacles. He extended his axe and caught Grymn's chin with the flat of it. 'Insofar as all of you shiny-skins have the same one.'

'You,' Grymn said, as he was overcome by a wracking cough. He recognised the creature well enough, for they'd fought before, atop the vile peak known as Profane Tor. The abhorrent thing had almost killed him then, and would have, if Tallon hadn't intervened.

'Aye, me,' Gutrot Spume, the Lord of Tentacles, said. 'And I'm thinking that I know ye, don't I, shiny-skin? Have we traded blows, then? Who won?' Spume sank to his haunches with a grunt. The seven writhing tendrils wrapped tightly around Grymn's head and arms, dragging him closer. 'Must've been a draw, if we're both still alive, then. Though, with your sort, maybe not.' Dark laughter rippled through the daemonic ranks.

'Still, you're a pretty prize, and no mistake. I don't think you'll be dying today, either.' Spume rose to his feet and rested his axe on one flabby shoulder. 'Get him up. And be gentle with him, my lads. He's worth more than any blighted soul in this garden.'

CHAPTER TEN

AN OATH AND A PROMISE

The warding lantern, or what was left of it, shone with a steady light. It sat amid the filth of the corrupted realmgate, its silvery frame bent and twisted out of shape. Even now, damaged beyond belief, it shone with the light of Azyr. The Six Smiths had no equal, save the duardin god Grungni, when it came to the crafting of weapons and tools.

'The Rotbringers succeeded in opening the realmgate, but only briefly,' Morbus said. 'For which we should be thankful. If it had stayed open any longer, it would have vomited forth more than just filthy water and a few half-made daemons.'

'Why only briefly?' Gardus asked, circling the black waters of the realmgate. Where once it might have glowed with the reflected light of the heavens, it was now opaque and reeking. Turgid waves lapped at the crumbling sargassum, expanding the circumference of the lake with every undulation. 'Did Lorrus interrupt them?'

'Yes, but I doubt that's the whole of it.' Morbus indicated the softly glowing lantern. 'The warding lantern. Its light keeps the pox-waters at bay, so long as Grymn lives.' He sank to his haunches and poked at the muck-encrusted beacon. 'In time, it might even cleanse this place. Unfortunately, time is a luxury we cannot afford. If this gate has been corrupted, it must be closed forever.' He looked at Gardus, his gaze unreadable. 'Nurgle cannot be allowed another foothold in this realm.'

'And what of Lorrus, then? Or Kahya, or Osric? What of our brothers and sisters?' Gardus gestured to the lantern. 'If it still glows, they must still live.'

'He is gone. They are gone. Lost to the garden.' Morbus shook his head. 'Nothing not of Chaos could survive that for long.'

'I did,' Gardus said.

Morbus looked at him. 'Yes.'

'So too might they.'

Morbus looked down at the bubbling froth. 'Grymn is not Gardus. The others are not Gardus. They cannot survive.'

'I was not Gardus, once.' Gardus let his hand rest on the hilt of his runeblade. 'And perhaps Gardus might vanish entirely, come some future calamity. But I am here now, and I say that they might yet live.'

'And what of it?' Angstun asked. The Knight-Vexillor shook his head. 'Their survival might be measured in moments, or eternities. The realms of Chaos are madness manifest. You might arrive before they do, or centuries after they've perished.' He looked at Gardus. 'You have only just returned to us, and the Lord-Castellant will not thank you for throwing your life away merely to save his.'

Gardus said nothing. Angstun was right. Grymn would not thank him. He would berate him, instead. Call him a fool. And it was foolish. To even contemplate such an act was a thing of hubris, greater than any he knew of. And yet... the thought of leaving the souls of his warriors in such a place was equally unbearable.

'Is the realmgate stable?' Gardus asked.

Morbus nodded, after a moment's hesitation. 'Whatever was done to it has stabilised it. It will remain open, unless I close it. But the longer it does so, the harder it will be to close. In time, it will be beyond even my abilities.'

'How much time?'

Morbus shrugged. 'Hours. Days. Years. Such things are impossible to predict.'

Kurunta laughed. 'It is Chaos. That's its nature.' The Knight-Heraldor shook his head. 'So long as it's quiescent, it shouldn't be much of a problem.' He stepped back as the gelid waters stirred, lapping lazily at the floor. He lifted his war-horn. 'One good tune will bring this chamber down, and destroy the portal with it. But say the word, Lord-Celestant, and I shall play a merry refrain.'

'No.' Gardus gestured sharply. 'Not yet.'

He found himself casting back to Sigmaron and the Sepulchre of the Faithful. To Ramus of the Shadowed Soul and the burden he carried. To know that his Lord-Celestant might yet persist, suffering in captivity, while he could do nothing. Much was demanded of those to whom much had been given. But when the demands began to outweigh the gifts, what was one to do? Ramus had asked him the same question, and Gardus had had no answer then, either.

A shout from the entrance to the chamber drew his attention. He turned and saw a chained Rotbringer stumble and sink to his knees in the muck. Three winged figures surrounded him, their hands on their weapons. 'What is this?' Gardus said. 'Cadoc? I have warned you about your... offerings, Knight-Azyros.'

'Not mine, Steel Soul, not this time,' Cadoc Kel said, sinking to one knee before him. 'This foolishness is his.' He gestured sharply to Tornus. The Knight-Venator bowed his head.

'He is being speaking true, Lord-Celestant.' He caught the back of the Rotbringer's twisted helmet and dragged his head back. Gardus knew a warrior of Chaos when he saw one. This one appeared to be on his last legs, given the state of him. 'This is being my burden and request, to be sparing the life of this wretched creature.'

'I don't understand,' Gardus said. He looked at Enyo, wondering if she could shed some light on whatever this was about. The Steel Souls' Knight-Venator shook her head. Gardus turned back to Tornus. 'Explain. And quickly.'

'He is surviving the light of Azyr,' Tornus said, simply.

Gardus stared at him, wondering if he'd misheard. 'That is not possible.'

'I am surviving the light of Azyr. Before.' Tornus met Gardus' gaze. 'Before I am being Tornus again, I am being a greater monster than this one, I am thinking. And I am surviving. Light calls to light, yes? Is that not being the way of it?'

Gardus shook his head and looked to Morbus, hoping he had an answer. But the Lord-Relictor stared silently at Tornus in what might have been consternation. Gardus turned back to the Knight-Venator. 'I don't know,' he said, finally. 'You were cleansed, but that is no guarantee…' He trailed off, wondering at his own words. He gestured to Cadoc. 'He survived your beacon's gaze?'

Cadoc shrugged. 'Evidently. Myself, I would burn him again, until it takes. But the Redeemed One refused that mercy on his behalf.' He glanced at the Knight-Venator. 'Perhaps he still feels some kinship with such creatures. Who can say?'

Tornus visibly bristled, but held his tongue. Gardus waved

Cadoc to silence as Morbus stepped forward. The Lord-Relictor extended his staff. 'Your soul was freed when Torglug's body was destroyed by the touch of Ghal Maraz, wielded by the hand of the Celestant-Prime.'

Gardus felt, rather than heard, the intake of breath from the assembled Stormcasts at the mention of the first, and greatest, of their kind. He was nothing less than the Storm of Sigmar itself, Bearer of the World-Hammer, and the Light of Azyr, carried into the darkness. Resplendent in the first, and finest, suit of sigmarite war-plate to be forged, he hurtled forth on blazing wings, wrapped in chains of lightning and purpose.

From what he knew of the battle of the Blackstone Summit, it was only the arrival of the Celestant-Prime that had turned the tide in favour of the Stormcasts and sylvaneth. Torglug had nearly claimed Alarielle's soulpod when the first Stormcast fell upon him like a thunderbolt. Torglug had perished in that moment, and what was left of him had ascended to Azyr, to be Reforged on the Anvil of Apotheosis.

He looked at Tornus. What changes had his Reforging wrought upon him? Could he, in some way, sense the embers of humanity in a fallen foe? Or was this merely wishful thinking? He hesitated. Was this what Sigmar had meant, when he'd mentioned the foundations of what was to come? Tornus was the first. There would be others. Was this creature one such? Was it a brother to be?

'What is he called?' he asked.

'I am Gatrog,' the Rotbringer croaked. 'Lord-Duke of Festerfane, and true knight of the Most Blightsome Order of the Fly. Release me. Give me a sword. If you mean my death, let it be an honourable one.'

'Festerfane,' Morbus said. 'One of the seven Blighted Duchies. A tumour in the body of the Jade Kingdoms.'

'Aye, and an old and respected tumour we are. We have always fought, and will do so until the last flower withers. For Nurgle, and the Realm Desolate.' Gatrog tried to get to his feet, but Cadoc forced him back down. 'Give me a sword, even one of these flimsy ones you carry will do. I will fight you all, one at a time, or all at once, it makes no difference. I will show you how a lord of Festerfane dies.'

He was brave. That much, Gardus would admit. But bravery by itself was no sign that one was capable of redemption. Gardus had fought many servants of the Dark Gods, and few of them could be called cowards. Yet, if this creature had endured the light, it might mean that there was more to his valour than simple animal courage.

'Remove his helmet,' Gardus said. 'I wish to see the face of our enemy.'

Tornus stooped and pried the filth-encrusted helmet loose. The ancient scabs lining the gorget burst, weeping clear pus and oily blood as the helmet slid upwards. The face within had clearly once been a man's, but not for some time. Blisters and leaking sores rose out of mounds of scabbed-over flesh, and what hair was in evidence was colourless and lank. One eye was as opaque as the waters of the realmgate, while the other looked as if it had been boiled. Yet Gardus knew that the warrior could see him clearly. A ruined slash of a mouth twisted up into a smile.

'Aye, I am handsome, am I not?'

'No,' Gardus said.

Gatrog gave a gurgling laugh. 'Then I am in good company.' Cadoc growled and drove a boot into the Rotbringer's side. Gatrog wheezed and nearly toppled over.

Gardus gestured sharply.

'Leave him, Cadoc.' His tone brooked no argument, and the

Knight-Azyros stepped back, head bent in contrition. Gardus looked down at Gatrog. 'Look at me.' Gatrog did, a sneer on his malformed features. That sneer faded as Gardus let the light within him blaze forth. Gatrog winced. Yellowish tears streamed from his eyes as he twisted away.

Gardus reached up and removed his own helmet. He hung the helmet from his belt, and then caught Gatrog's chin. He forced the Rotbringer's face up. 'Look at me, I said.'

'No,' Gatrog snarled, trying to twist away from him. Thin wisps of smoke rose from his scabrous features as Gardus gazed down at him. 'Get your filthy hands off me.'

Gardus looked into the Rotbringer's eyes, seeking a sign. Gatrog tried to meet his gaze and failed. He made again to pull away. He was afraid. Not of death, but something else. Gardus didn't know how he knew, but he did. Gatrog was afraid.

'I will give you a sword,' Gardus said, softly.

Gatrog's eyes widened.

'But first, you will swear an oath,' Gardus said.

Gatrog blinked back tears. 'I'll swear no oath to a silver-skinned lubberwort.'

Gardus reached down and gripped the chains that bound the Rotbringer. He jerked the bloated warrior to his feet with no sign of effort. 'You will, or I will strike your head from your shoulders here and now.'

'Better death than bondage,' Gatrog spluttered. But the undercurrent of fear was still there. Gardus wondered at that. What did such creatures see in the light that he did not? Tornus might know, but he hesitated to pose such a question.

'Says the slave to the free soul.' Gardus pulled him close. 'An oath. Your life, for the oath of but a moment. You will serve us, until such time as I grant you your freedom. And then you will be free to die as you choose.'

'And what is this service that you require?' Gatrog grunted, squinting against the glare. 'Shall I best some foe for you, or hunt a questing beast? For those are my only skills.' He twisted away, blinking. 'What do you want?'

'You have the look of one who has been to the garden.'

'A… Aye,' Gatrog said. 'I won my spurs fairly, in its noisome glens.'

'Good. I require a guide.'

'A guide?' Gatrog stared at him through slitted eyes. 'You would go into the garden. You are either especially brave or mad.'

'Neither,' Gardus said. 'Merely determined.'

'You actually want me to lead you through the garden?' Gatrog threw back his head and laughed. 'Give me a sword, and bare your neck, if you're so eager to die.'

'Do you swear?' Gardus said. His light swelled. The water bubbled around him, and a rivet on Gatrog's armour burst as if from a sudden heat.

'I… I swear,' Gatrog said, turning away.

'On your honour as a knight,' Gardus continued, relentless.

Gatrog's head snapped around, eyes narrowed. 'Yes. Fie on thee, yes. On my honour as a true knight, I'll guide you where you wish to go.'

Tornus watched in astonishment as Gardus let the Rotbringer slump to his knees. 'You are to be sparing him, then?' he asked.

'That is what you wished,' Gardus said. His aura had faded somewhat, dwindling to a soft glow. He looked at Tornus, his expression calm. 'Isn't it?'

Tornus nodded. 'I am to be thanking you, Lord-Celestant.'

'Do not thank me, Tornus. This may yet prove to be a

mistake on both our parts.' He gripped Tornus' shoulder. 'I leave him in your hands for the moment.' He turned away to speak to Angstun and the others, leaving Tornus looking down at the kneeling Rotbringer. Gatrog's bravado had melted away beneath Gardus' attention. His head was bowed, and he mumbled what might have been prayers. Tornus shivered, knowing well who the Chaos knight was praying to.

Morbus joined him. Tornus glanced sidelong at the Lord-Relictor, wondering what he wanted. Morbus studied him for long moments. 'Your soul was fractured. Now it is whole. Truly, a blessing from Sigmar.'

'Yes,' Tornus said, uncertain as to what the other Storm-cast meant.

'You hope to see lightning strike twice.' Morbus looked down at Gatrog.

'Is it being so impossible?'

'No. But we lack a crucial element.' Morbus gestured. 'I do not see the Celestant-Prime in evidence, do you?'

Tornus turned away. 'The Rotbringer is being frightened,' he said, avoiding the question.

'Compassion can be as terrible in its own way as cruelty,' Morbus said. 'And Gardus' compassion even more so. Like the light of Azyr, it burns without judgement or hatred. But it burns all the same. And few can bear its light.'

'He still lives,' Tornus said.

'No. He persists.' Morbus looked at Tornus. 'As you per-sisted. A perversion of the natural order, skewed all out of joint and made monstrous.' He shook his head. 'There is a point where resignation and stoicism are warped into an unholy perseverance. A refusal to accept what must come, while at the same time losing all hope as to a worthy end-ing. That is the point where our enemy raises his walls and erects his towers. You fell to it, as this one did. Your refusal to die, when all hope fled, brought you to ruin.'

Tornus, confused, shook his head. 'You are saying we are to be surrendering?'

'No. Only that we must recognise the difference between acceptance and surrender. All things have their season. All things have a beginning and an ending. To cast that aside is to deny the natural order.'

'I was once knowing much of seasons,' Tornus said. He realised that he could recall the Lifewells, but only dimly. As if they had been seen by someone else, in another place and time. He was Tornus again, but not the same. 'I was once feeling the turning of the leaves in my heart. Now, I am feeling only the storm.'

Morbus looked at him. 'And this too shall pass. Storms have their ending, as all things do. The stars burn out, suns go dark and storms pass. Only death does not die.'

'So long as there is being life,' Tornus said, looking at the Lord-Relictor. For a moment, Morbus' voice had had an odd resonance. One that chilled him to the marrow. But the feeling passed quickly, as Morbus looked away. Tornus cleared his throat. 'I am being sorry. For when I am trying to be killing you.'

Morbus gave a dry, hoarse laugh. 'You will forgive me if I do not tender my own apologies.' He looked at the Knight-Venator, and Tornus was relieved to see the humour in his gaze. 'Still, that was in another kingdom, and Torglug is dead.' He bent his staff, so that its charms and prayer scrolls thumped against Tornus' armour. 'You are who you are, and Sigmar would not have sent you to us if there was not reason.'

The ferrule of Angstun's standard striking the ground filled the chamber. The Knight-Vexillor struck the ground twice more, drawing all eyes. 'The Lord-Celestant wishes to speak,' he said. Given his tone, Tornus suspected he didn't approve of what Gardus was about to say. Gardus, helmet tucked under one arm, shot a bemused glance at his subordinate.

'Thank you, Angstun.' The Lord-Celestant looked around. 'I intend to enter the realmgate, and follow its path wherever it leads. Our brethren are somewhere on the other side, and I would find them and bring them back.' He spoke softly. Nonetheless, his voice carried, echoing through the chamber.

'I will not command you to follow me,' he continued. 'I would not sacrifice us all on the altar of my hubris. But I will not abandon Lorrus and the others to the horrors of that place. Not while even the slightest hope yet remains.' He looked around at the gathered warriors. 'Without hope, we are no better than the enemy.'

'You cannot go alone,' Morbus said.

'No. I go to make war on a god. It would be preferable if I did so in good company.' Gardus' smile was crooked. 'I will not command you. But I will ask you. Those who wish to join me may do so. No shame will fall upon those who do not. This is, as Angstun and Morbus have so respectfully reminded me, a fool's errand. It is thus fitting that only the foolish should attempt it.'

A small ripple of laughter greeted these words. Tornus wondered at it. Among the Gleaming Host, humour was often seen as a sign of a lack of discipline. Laughter wasn't proper equipment for the battlefield. But for the Steel Souls, it seemed to function almost as a shield against the dark. Humour, like faith, was their armour. The laughter faded soon enough, as the import of Gardus' words sank in. Stormcast looked at one another, waiting to see who would go first.

'I will go,' Cadoc Kel growled, pushing his way through

the throng. 'What better soul to feed to the fire than that of a false god? My beacon shall light your way, Lord-Celestant.'

'And I,' Enyo said. 'You will need my bow.'

'My thanks to you both,' Gardus said.

Aetius Shieldborn cleared his throat. 'We have decided. We shall accompany you. And our retinues as well.' The Liberator-Prime gestured to Solus and Feros. Tegrus of the Sainted Eye landed behind the Liberator-Prime and set a hand on his shoulder.

'And I, also. You will need eyes in whatever passes for the sky there.'

'We stood beside you at the Gates of Dawn, Steel Soul, and we shall not abandon you here,' Feros rumbled. The Retributor-Prime leaned on the haft of his lightning hammer. 'Besides, it sounds as if it'll be a fight worth the name, and I'd not miss it. What say you, Solus?' He glanced at the Judicator-Prime.

Solus shrugged. 'Someone has to keep these three out of trouble.'

Gardus laughed. 'Well said.'

A deluge of voices followed. Individual warriors, pledging warblade and hammer to their Lord-Celestant's service. Gardus seemed at once pleased and saddened, Tornus thought. 'What about you, Redeemed One? Will you test your new-forged soul in good cause?' Cadoc said, startling him. The Knight-Azyros glared at him challengingly. And he wasn't alone in his challenge. Tornus looked around, feeling suddenly very isolated.

Before he could reply, Gardus held up a hand. 'That was in poor spirit, Cadoc.' He looked at Tornus. 'I would not ask you to come, Tornus. Further proof of your worthiness is not required, brother.'

'You do not have to be asking,' Tornus said, haltingly. He gazed at the slick surface of the water beyond the Lord-Celestant, and felt something inside him twist painfully. But he met Gardus' eyes and nodded. 'Two bows are being better than one. And you are putting this one in my responsibility.' He gestured to Gatrog, who still knelt in silence. 'Someone is having to be watching him, yes?'

Gardus smiled. 'Yes. And I am glad to have you.' He extended his hand, and Tornus caught it firmly. He felt Cadoc's eyes burning into him, but ignored the Knight-Azyros.

'As touching as this is, the likelihood of any of you returning is slim,' Morbus said. 'If we die on the other side of that realmgate, we will not return to the forges of Azyr. We will be lost, or worse.'

Gardus looked at him. 'Perhaps you should stay. The chamber still needs a commander.'

'It has two,' Morbus said, gesturing to Angstun and Kurunta. Both began to protest, but he silenced them with a glare. 'Kurunta must stay, in order to seal this chamber, should the worst happen. And Angstun must stay, to obliterate this citadel and everything in it, in the event Kurunta fails.'

The Lord-Relictor looked at them. 'Do you understand? If we fail, you will know, for every rot-bellied daemon in that realm will attempt to repay our insult a hundredfold. They will not stop.' He thumped the ground with his reliquary staff. 'With the fall of the Genesis Gate, Nurgle's grasp on this realm has been weakened. This portal, if left unchecked, would see him in control once more. It must be destroyed.'

'But not by you,' Gardus said. Morbus looked at him.

'My first duty is to safeguard the souls of every warrior in this chamber. And I will do so, even if they are intent on walking into the maw of Chaos itself.' He straightened, his skull-helm gleaming eerily in the watery light of the realmgate.

'May Sigmar preserve us, faithful and fools alike.'

186

CHAPTER ELEVEN

ABOARD
THE BLACK GALLEY

The black galley pushed through the dull waters with relentless pace. Neither fast nor slow, it moved steadily, a hundred oars rising and falling to a monotonous drumbeat. Its porous hull, crafted from black blightwood and slathered in pitch, cut the scummy waters like a knife. The masts creaked in sympathy with the drum, and the sails were sewn from fungus-riddled skins, which wept blood and pus with every foul gust of wind.

It was a ship with a thousand brothers, all plying the feculent swamps of Nurgle's realm. Lost souls wandered in the dark, drawn into the garden, but not yet a part of it. The masters of the galleys sought them out and brought them into the light of despair.

'Or so those with ideas above their station like to claim,' Gutrot Spume said. 'In reality, it's because the work must be done. A garden must be tended, and loose souls, such as yours, are things that need gathering.' He sat on a barrel of maggoty meat, boots crossed over the scarred back of a galley slave. The mortal trembled in silence, head and hands pressed tight to the deck. 'Happenstance and coincidence are the tides of the divine sea,' Spume continued, as he slurped noisily from a leaky goblet. 'They cast a soul where the gods wish it to go, don't you agree?'

Grymn stared at Spume, willing his death. The Lord-Castellant hung from rusty chains draped along the interior of the galley's hull, the weight of his war-plate dragging him down. His arms had pulled to their fullest extension, at the very point of dislocation, and he'd lost most of the feeling in them. Filthy water dripped onto his head and shoulders, leaving black streaks across the begrimed silver. Hanging as he was, it was hard to breathe, and the extension of his arms prevented him from simply bursting his fetters, freeing himself and smashing in the bloated creature's skull with his chains.

Spume chuckled, as if he knew what his captive was thinking, and leaned forward to dip his goblet into the open cask sitting beside him. 'Silence is the same as agreement, aye.' He extended the goblet. 'Care for a drink? Captain's prerogative.'

Grymn spat on the deck.

Spume gave a gurgling laugh. 'Oh, it's a hard one, ye are. Tough as rusty nails. But even nails bend.' He leaned back, shifting his weight. The barrel beneath him creaked, and the galley slave whimpered. 'Did ye think me dead, then, after the dirgehorn blew its last note?' Grymn said nothing. Spume nodded as if he had. 'Almost was. But I'm made of sterner stuff than that. Blessed of Nurgle, I am.' His tentacles undulated in the watery light of the balefire lanterns strung about the hold. 'And more blessed will I be, once I rip your secrets from ye and offer up your carcass to Grandfather.'

Still, Grymn did not reply. He was determined not to indulge the creature.

Spume grunted and refilled his goblet. 'I've thought much on our last encounter,' he said. 'It tasks me. I've never met a warrior I couldn't grind into mulch. Yet, here ye are, bold as buboes.' A tentacle stiffened, as if pointing. 'And I want to know why.'

'Faith,' Grymn said. He hadn't meant to speak. The word hung on the air.

Spume emptied his goblet. 'Maybe so.' He shook his head. 'Or maybe there's some trick to it. There's always a trick to it, I've found.'

'No trick, monster. Only faith.'

Spume dipped his goblet and held it up, swirling it gently. Then he booted the slave aside and heaved himself to his feet. A tentacle shot out and wrapped tight about Grymn's throat. Sigmarite creaked in the monstrous appendage's grip. Spume leaned close. He stank of bilgewater and rotten sargassum. 'Have a drink. I insist.' He emptied the goblet over Grymn's face-plate. The sour liquid stung his eyes and mouth, and he thrashed in his chains. Spume laughed. 'Want another?'

'I'd rather die of thirst,' Grymn croaked, glaring at the Rot-bringer. That only made Spume laugh all the harder. He flung the goblet aside. The galley slave scrambled towards it, and Grymn frowned in disgust as the mortal desperately licked at the dregs as they seeped into the deck. Spume ignored the whimpering slave.

'You won't. Your sort don't die easily.' Spume poked a blunt finger against Grymn's chest-plate. 'And you come back.

Life without living. Grandfather has a special pity for you, shiny-skin. You're like a field left fallow, or unfished waters.'

'Pure, you mean,' Grymn said.

'If you like.' Spume shrugged his single shoulder. 'Not for much longer, though. Ye'll be writhing in worms, soon enough. I can smell them, percolating in your gut.' The finger trailed down and stabbed against Grymn's abdomen. 'Something got into you, out in the mire. And now it's eating you hollow, though ye don't feel it yet.'

Earlier than that, I confess.

Grymn stiffened, causing his chains to rattle. Spume stepped back, his gaze sharpening. 'Hunh. I hear something. Like flies buzzing about my head. Is someone in there with you, shiny-skin?'

'No,' Grymn said, through clenched teeth.

Fie, sir. I am no delusion. I yet live.

Spume chuckled. His fingers curled into a fist and he drove a piston-like blow into Grymn's abdomen, slamming him back against the hull painfully. 'Two for the price of one, is it? Well, I'll not have some grubby soul pilfer my hard-bought plunder.' He caught hold of Grymn's head again and leaned forward, sour breath issuing from the holes in his helmet. 'I shall go a-grubbing, little worm. And ye'll scream as mightily as the shiny-skin.' He slammed Grymn's head back, causing the sigmarite to ring.

Spume caught the slave by the scruff of the neck and jerked him to his feet. 'Up, dog. Back to your bench. We have leagues to go, and every man at his oar.' He tromped back above decks, leaving Grymn hanging alone in the weak light.

No, not alone.

'Who are you?' Grymn said, softly. If Spume had heard the voice then he wasn't going mad, which came as little relief. If he wasn't mad, then something was inside him. Something unspeakable.

You know me. We traded blows, you and I. Am I so easily forgotten?

It squirmed in his gut, and he grimaced. 'The pox-knight,' he said. 'Bubonicus.'

Aye, you know me. You killed me, and I will be reborn in you. A fair exchange, don't you agree? Bubonicus' voice echoed through him.

'No,' Grymn said.

No, they rarely do. A shame. It is a high honour, I assure you. I choose only worthy souls to make my home in. It is not happenstance.

Grymn ignored the voice and began to test his chains. His legs were bound tight at the ankles, but his knees were free. He set his feet against the hull and dragged them up through the mould. A few moments later they slipped down. His chains jerked taut, and he groaned as new pain flashed through his shoulders.

A valiant effort.

'Shut up,' Grymn snapped. He looked around. The hold was larger than it ought to have been, given the size of the galley. It was packed with supplies, all rotting and stinking. Broken bodies were stacked like cordwood at the far end, their suppurating flesh crawling with maggots and rot flies. Coils of mouldering rope and rusty chain lay slumped beneath folds of moth-eaten sail.

A moan drew his attention down. An iron crosshatch was set in the deck. Pale fingers reached up through it. More slaves. Broken souls, bound for unknown torments.

Harsh words, from the ignorant.

'I thought I told you to shut up,' Grymn growled.

These souls are in captivity now, aye, but they are meant for better things. They will know the freedom of despair, and be freed from the chains of hope and want. Is that not a better fate than what might have awaited them otherwise?

'That is not up to creatures such as you to decide,' Grymn said. He studied the hold, trying to find something, anything he could use to free himself. 'Why am I even arguing with you? You're nothing. The voice of a dead thing.'

Dead? No. I cannot die... Lorrus. That is your name, isn't it? Lorrus. Grymn.

The sound of his own name rang through Grymn's head like the trump of doom. Words of defiance died unspoken on his lips. He felt as if something cold had crawled inside him and was now seeking to make room.

We have much to talk about, in the time left to us, Lorrus Grymn...

Gutrot Spume stood on the foredeck of his galley. He leaned on the head of his axe and watched the waters part before the prow of his vessel. The galley was a poor sort of ship, compared to others he'd captained, but fast. He closed his eyes and listened to the hiss-crack of the whips, as his crew encouraged the rowers to greater efforts. The sooner the slaves learned what was expected of them, the sooner they would be fit to crew a proper ship. One that sailed fiercer seas than these moribund waters.

Grandfather's garden was a pleasant place, and no denying it. Its storms were swift, like Grandfather's wrath, and its waters gentle. Idly, Spume scraped a tentacle's worth of sputum from the rail and cast it into the wet air. The mass swirled and congealed, taking the shape of an inverted pyramid, or of a spreading plume of smoke. The current shape of the garden, though that could change at any moment. It split into seven flat planes, dwindling to the reverse apex. Grandfather's manse sat there, holding up the garden on its creaking foundations. The mass dripped back to the rail.

Spume chuckled, thinking of the first time he'd sailed into the garden, quite by accident. He'd been harrying an Abak treasure ship bound for Sartos. Only it hadn't been treasure they'd been carrying – at least, not the kind he'd been hoping for. And when he'd boarded them at last, their captain had proven to be more capable than he seemed. Spume had killed the poxy harem-born princeling regardless, but by then it had been too late.

His chuckles faded as those final moments came back to him, as strong as ever. Bad, black moments, etched forever on what was left of his worm-eaten soul. The waters rushing suddenly and swiftly in the wrong direction; the wind, screaming and stinking of offal; and those rotting hands, leagues across and so big as to blot out the sun and stars, reaching up out of the maelstrom and pushing aside the waters as if they were sand. Reaching up to draw the spinning vessels down into the vast deep.

There had been things down there, in the dark. Shapes greater than any leviathan, and hungry. Men had been plucked screaming from the decks as the ships sank, drawn upwards into the crashing curtain of displaced water. But not Spume. He'd ridden the carcass of his ship into the garden and, when they'd surfaced, he'd set about exploring.

He ran a wide thumb along the edge of his axe. He'd almost worn the blade to splinters in those first few months on the plague-yellow seas. His crew had died around him, their bodies fruiting and spoiling in the sickly glare of the sun. But he'd only grown stronger, determined to conquer these new, squirming waters as he'd conquered the Wolftooth Fjords and the Breakwater. He'd swelled, basking in Grandfather's attention, though he'd known it not. And when he'd at last reached the headwaters of the garden, he'd knelt at Nurgle's feet, as if that was what he'd been born to do.

But Grandfather was a jolly sort, and profligate with his favour. Spume had soon realised that he was not the only maggot in the meal, nor even the biggest. But that was good. What was life without challenge? Let the flydandies and bilefops mutter about the art of surrender and write odes to sweet despair. Gutrot Spume fought, as he'd always fought. Let the storm close over him, if it would. Hope was a tattered sail, a cracked hull, a shattered rudder. He embraced the misery of it all, and fed on it. Or, at least, he had.

Spume sighed, thinking of what had been lost. He had been trapped on the wrong side of the Genesis Gate when it had closed, his vessel shattered by Alarielle's wrath. He could still recall his consternation as those pillar-thick vines had skewered his hull and cracked his masts. His crew had died screaming, even as Spume hacked himself an escape route. He'd fallen into the flowing rotwaters, and been carried by the current into the garden with the rest of the detritus. Separated from what remained of his flotilla. The thought brought him a rare moment of pain, and he cherished it.

His ships, vast galleons of rotten wood and putrid caulk, which could sail upon the waters and pox-clouds with equal ease, were the pride of Nurgle's plague-fleets. And none more so than his flagship, *Lurska*. The titanic rot-kraken was an old friend, and the citadel built upon her back was a mighty thing indeed, studded with black iron cannons and balefire throwers. Her tentacles could uproot elder oaks like saplings, and shatter even the strongest hulls. She was a true companion, a pirate to her noisome core. He missed her dearly, and looked forward to treading her barnacled decks once more.

No, the garden was not for him. Once he'd secured suitable replacements for his lost crew, he'd find the nearest path back to Ghyran and the Rotwater. Beautiful as they were, the seas here were soft things, gentle, tamed and lacking in true excitement.

A monstrous, serpentine head broke the gelid surface and arrowed towards him, jaws agape. The poxwyrm's scales gleamed with an oily hue, and its milky eyes fixed on him with greedy intensity. Spume pivoted, letting his axe rise and fall as he avoided the poxwyrm's snapping jaws. Its head flopped to the deck, and its long neck reeled away like a fallen tree. As it struck the water, he spotted the threadbare fins of more of the creatures, closing in to feed on their fallen kin.

Spume ran a tentacle along the notched edge of his blade, wiping it clean of steaming ichors. His tentacle bent and snapped, scattering droplets across the closest bench of rowers. The galley slaves screamed as the poisonous bile stung their afflicted flesh. Whether in pleasure, or in pain, Spume didn't know, nor did he care. That they reacted was enough. He glanced at Durg, his first mate. 'They need toughening up. Whip them until their scabs get scabs.' The plaguebearer grinned, displaying erratically spaced teeth.

'Aye, captain,' the daemon grunted. He snarled phlegmatically, and the crew snapped to, plying their whips with gusto. Spume nodded in satisfaction. Daemons made for poor crew on long journeys. They got bored too quickly to make proper sailors. But, for these shorter jaunts, they served well enough.

Only the toughest souls were worthy of serving aboard his galleons. Bodies and spirits hardened by drowning and disease, made strong by Grandfather's blessings. And the strongest souls were those plucked from the soil of the garden. But no soul was quite like the one now languishing in his hold. Tougher than any he'd ever encountered. He needed answers. At the very least, he might be able to use his captive to barter passage back to the Mortal Realms. Decision made, he gestured to his first mate.

'Durg! Bring me a soul.'

Durg dutifully dragged a whimpering soul up onto the foredeck, depositing the pale thing at Spume's feet. The soul was an indistinct thing, covered in yellowish barnacles and clumps of fungus. It had been here long enough that its origins, even its gender, had been lost to the mire. It cowered away from Spume, babbling inarticulate prayers to gods whose names it had long since forgotten. They always forgot, eventually. Only one god held sway in these waters, and he weighed heavily on the mind.

Spume planted his axe in the deck and grasped the soul with his mortal hand. 'Up,' he said. 'I be needing your assistance.' His tentacles writhed and stiffened, spearing into the soul like daggers. They undulated through the open wounds on the soul's body, and into its open mouth and eyes. The soul gurgled shrieks, writhing in pain. Spume chuckled, forcing his tendrils deeper into its putty-like form. When he judged that they'd inundated the squirming form thoroughly, he tore it apart in a welter of gore.

Gobbets of steaming meat fell to the deck. Spume uprooted his axe and used the blade to shift and smear the bloody spray. He began to murmur as he did so, speaking the seven words taught to him by the one he was trying to reach. As he did so, the gore began to bubble and burst. Rot flies squirmed out of the smeared redness and flew lazily upwards, circling about Spume's head like a halo. The flies joined together in a cloud, bunching and roiling until they formed what might have been monstrous features. The vaguely mouth-shaped clump of flies undulated, humming.

'*What do you want, pirate?*'

'Careful there, Urslaug,' Spume chided. 'I'm not the sort to endure disrespect. Especially from a thin-shank mollyboggle such as ye.'

The flies hummed for a moment. Then, '*My question stands.*'

Spume snorted. 'I have a gift for ye.'

If a cloud of flies could look suspicious, this one did. The swarm convulsed, and the flies hummed, '*What sort of gift?*'

Spume laid his axe over his shoulder and chuckled.

'One that'll benefit us both mightily.'

CHAPTER TWELVE

INTO THE DARK

At the centre of the chamber, Morbus knelt before the frothing, black waters of the corrupted realmgate. The Lord-Relictor's head was bowed in prayer, and the purity runes etched into his mortis armour shone harshly. He held his staff out before him, and the reliquary mounted atop it burned with a blue light. All around him, the sargassum smouldered in its purifying glow, and thin streamers of smoke danced about his kneeling form, as if alive. And perhaps they were, or had been, once upon a time.

Gardus had seen Morbus commune with spirits before. Once, in the Nihiliad Mountains, he had witnessed the Lord-Relictor sit and speak with the desiccated inhabitants of a long forgotten barrow. And later, he had drawn up the ghosts of the drowned, to lead them safely through the Canker Cascade. Despite this, Gardus still felt a frisson of elemental unease as he watched more smoky shapes rise up to join the rest in their silent dance.

Kurunta, Lion of the Hyaketes, seemed to share his opinions. He growled softly as he watched the Lord-Relictor at his task. 'I hate when he does that.' He shifted the weight of his broadsword from one shoulder to the other.

The Knight-Heraldor wasn't tall, but he was big, with a chest and shoulders thicker by half than any other warrior in the chamber. His silver war-plate strained to contain him, as if the force of his mighty voice were threatening to burst his frame. The profusion of amethyst plumes that sprouted from his helm like a mane were threaded through with silver coins. These clinked softly as he glanced at Gardus. 'I still say you should let me cap this wretched hole, Steel Soul,' he said, indicating the war-horn slung across his back.

Gardus looked at him. 'Admit it – you want to come with me.'

Kurunta shook his head. 'Of course I do. We should still bury it, though.'

Gardus nodded. 'So we should. And yet we cannot.'

'No,' Kurunta said. He toyed idly with one of the prayer scrolls hanging from his armour. 'I don't like being left behind. You might need me.'

'To announce my coming to Nurgle, you mean?'

'Well… yes.' Kurunta shook his head. 'It's only polite. Not honourable, invading in secret.' The look in his eyes was disapproving. 'How will they know who defeated them, if we don't announce ourselves?'

Gardus laughed. 'I don't think that's something we have to worry about, my friend.' No, he had no doubt that their arrival would not go unnoticed. A snarl of hoarse laughter made him turn. He looked at their prisoner, crouched before Tornus. The Rotbringer had remained on the ground since their confrontation, but he seemed to have regained some of his courage, despite the situation. Or, perhaps, because of it.

'The King of all Flies sees all,' the creature croaked. 'If you invade his demesnes, he will respond in kind.' He sounded pleased.

'You are being silent,' Tornus said, catching a handful of the Rotbringer's sparse hair. Gardus raised his hand, and Tornus released his hold. Gardus looked down at the creature.

'What is waiting for us on the other side of that gate?'

Gatrog grinned, displaying rotten teeth. 'Nothing you wish to meet, I assure you. The garden is fit only for the courageous.'

Kurunta let the blade of his sword swing down to rest on the Rotbringer's shoulder. 'Have a care with your words, filth,' he said darkly. 'I am inclined to take offence.'

The Rotbringer looked up at him, eyes narrowed. 'Give me a sword, and I will attempt a proper apology.'

Gardus waved Kurunta back. 'I asked you a question. By your oath, give me a clear answer. What waits for us beyond the gate?'

Gatrog hawked and spat. 'By my oath, I will answer. The garden is sevenfold, and has been for seven centuries. Seven gardens, which are nonetheless one, each atop the next. Some say the King of all Flies saw the hanging gardens of the Lantic Empire and did admire them. And so he shaped his realm in similar, though inverted, fashion.' His chains rattled as he tried to gesture with his newly grown hand.

'And no doubt each tier is more dangerous than the last,' a new voice interjected. Gardus turned to see Angstun making his way towards them. 'Morbus is soon finished,' Angstun said. Like Kurunta, the Knight-Vexillor didn't sound pleased about it. 'Are you sure it is wise to depart so soon?'

'Soonest begun is soonest done,' Gardus said. 'Foolish as I

am, I would rather spend no more time than I have to in that foul realm.' He hoped that Grymn would be close by. That this assault would be swift. But in his heart, he knew that it wasn't likely. Time travelled strangely beyond the Mortal Realms. Centuries passed in seconds, and moments stretched into days. They might return moments after they'd left, or not at all.

Gatrog seemed to have similar thoughts. The Rotbringer gave a gurgling laugh. 'An eternity awaits you, storm-warrior. Deny it all you like, but no soul leaves the garden, save by Nurgle's will.'

'I have,' Gardus said solemnly. 'I walked in willingly, and left in the same fashion.' His solemnity seemed to unsettle the Rotbringer, and the creature looked away. A crackle of lightning caught his attention, and Gardus saw Morbus push himself to his feet.

'The way is as safe as I can make it,' the Lord-Relictor intoned. He held up a hand wreathed in snarling bands of lightning. 'My prayers will bind us together, so that none are lost in the under-realms, and will serve to abate the horrors there somewhat. Kneel, oh sons and daughters of Azyr.'

Stormcasts sank to their knees, heads bowed, hands clasped about their weapons. Gardus moved through the rows, hammer on his shoulder. 'Who kneels here, to receive the blessings of the heavens?' he asked, as he walked towards Morbus.

'Only the faithful.'

Gardus looked at Morbus. 'We are the faithful, Lord-Relictor. Say your prayers.'

Morbus nodded. He spoke, softly at first, and then more loudly. His words were lost the moment he said them, carried away in the roar of the lightning as it speared from his hand. The shimmering bolt caromed from Stormcast to Stormcast, striking each in turn and binding them to one another. Gardus was last and, when the lightning struck him, he staggered slightly. Heat rushed through him, flooding his limbs and driving out all the aches and pains he'd accrued. His head swam as, for an instant, he heard the dim echoes of his warriors' thoughts, fears and hopes. More than that, he felt their faith in him, in their mission, and in Sigmar.

Faith was the torch in the dark of the cave. Only faith had led him safely out of Nurgle's realm. Now he trusted it to lead him into the garden once more. To lead them all. Gardus straightened and turned towards the black waters. 'It is time,' he said.

'Why are we doing this?' Morbus asked, as he stepped up beside Gardus.

'A bit late to be asking that,' Gardus said.

'Answer the question.'

'For Lorrus, and the others.'

Morbus nodded. 'Perhaps. Partially, at least. But that's not the whole of it. Why?'

Gardus paused. 'I don't know.' He looked up, wishing with all his heart that he could see the stars. His conscience would have to make do, in their absence. He drew his runeblade. 'Perhaps simply to prove that it can be done, and that we are the ones to do it. We are the faithful. Who better to march into this green hell than us?'

'You know that if Sigmar were here, he would command us otherwise.'

'Would he? Or would he lead us himself?' Gardus looked around. His warriors were ready. But was he? He felt the familiar weight of doubt curled up inside him and waiting for its moment. Was this the right thing to do? He wished that the God-King were here to tell him whether he was on the correct path, but Sigmar could not be everywhere.

Or perhaps he simply had faith in Gardus, as Gardus had in him.

He turned and surveyed his warriors. 'Who is this I see before me?' he said, his voice carrying throughout the chamber. As one, the Steel Souls rose to their feet, heads held up, weapons at the ready. 'Who will dare the darkest road at my side?'

'Only the faithful,' Morbus intoned. The others echoed him, the steady growl of their voices rising to fill the chamber. Gatrog twitched in his chains, as if the sound of those words pained him. And maybe they did.

'We are the faithful,' Gardus said. 'And we shall carry the light and Storm of Sigmar into the heart of darkness, as only we can. Who will be remembered?'

'Only the faithful,' came the response.

'Who will the darkness fear?'

'Only the faithful!'

Weapons thumped against shields or the floor, until voice and sound merged into a single roar of challenge. It echoed throughout the chamber, throughout the citadel itself. The waters of the realmgate rippled from the fury of it. Gardus turned away from the silvered ranks and started into the water. 'Pray us a path, Lord-Relictor. Open the way to the garden.'

The waters began to bubble and froth. Gardus felt unseen hands clawing at his legs, trying to pull him down into the depths. He smiled as he allowed them to draw him down. They would take him where he wanted to go.

It was time that the Dark Gods knew the true strength of the faithful.

Tornus cringed inwardly as he waited his turn to follow Gardus into the dark waters of the realmgate. He could feel the evil radiating from them. No, not evil. Evil implied malice. There was precious little malice in the workings of Nurgle. Cruelty, yes, as life was cruel. Rapaciousness, even. But the horror of Nurgle was one of cosmic consideration. Khorne cared not from whence the blood flowed, but Nurgle cared for every life, no matter how tiny. Nurgle *noticed* every life. Every soul that crossed the threshold of the Lord of All Things received a splinter of his attention, and suffered for it.

Even those souls that had escaped his clutches once already. The water surged up about him as he watched Enyo wade out into the oily lake. It slopped against his armour, tarnishing the silver. He longed to spread his wings and fly away, to leave this place, with its reeking odour and hazy glow. Ospheonis, perched on his shoulder, gave an interrogative screech and he reached up to ruffle the star-eagle's feathers.

'The others might be blind, but your bird and I see the truth well enough. You are scared,' Cadoc said, from just behind him. The Knight-Azyros leaned forwards. 'Have you no faith, Tornus?'

'I am being faithful,' Tornus said. Cadoc's friendship had quickly turned to spite. But then, princes were known to be mercurial in temperament.

Cadoc chuckled. 'We'll see about that. And if that proves a lie, I'll set your soul alight and purge it once more.' He clasped Tornus' shoulder with mock-friendliness, and pushed past him. The Knight-Azyros waded into the waters, beacon raised.

'He's a foul one, and no mistake,' Gatrog said, from beside him. The Rotbringer stood nearby, waiting to follow Tornus into the realmgate. In contrast to the Stormcasts around him, the pox-knight displayed little evident nervousness at the thought of entering the black waters. 'Your taste in friends has become poor, Torglug.'

Tornus jerked the Rotbringer's chains, nearly pulling him off his feet. 'You are being silent, monster.' He looped the chain about his forearm, so that there was no chance of the Rotbringer slipping free during their journey. Though there was small chance of that, a treacherous part of him whispered. The knights of the Order of the Fly were honourable, if nothing else. Gatrog could no more break an oath than he could burst his chains.

Gatrog stumbled, but steadied himself. 'I am no more a monster than you yourself once were, Torglug.' He spoke slowly, almost pleadingly.

'Torglug is being dead. I am being Tornus.'

Gatrog chuckled thickly. 'Not so, not so.' He bowed his head. Tornus followed his gaze and saw his reflection, wavering on the dark surface of the water. Only it wasn't him. Not as he was. But as he had been. A bloated thing, swollen with unholy power. Eyes like rotten pomegranates met his, but only for an instant. A moment later, Torglug was gone, leaving only Tornus.

'No,' Tornus murmured. 'It is not being so.' He stumbled into the water, splashing heedlessly, dragging Gatrog in his wake. 'It is being a trick of this place.'

'Is it? Or is the silver you wear the trick? A trick played on a noble hero, by a deceitful godling.' Gatrog grimaced. 'A warrior such as the one I knew would not so easily be twisted out of shape as this. Some speck of blessed cancer yet clings to your soul, Torglug. Pray to the King of all Flies, that he might nourish it until it blossoms once more.'

Tornus wrenched Gatrog around to face him, and lifted the Rotbringer from his feet. The pox-knight thrashed helplessly as Tornus heaved his bulk up. Stormcasts drew back as the Knight-Venator shook his prisoner the way a gryph-hound shook a rat. 'My soul is being my own, creature. And the sooner you are to be learning that, the better it is being.'

Gatrog began to rasp a reply, but Tornus flung him into the water. The pox-knight swiftly sank out of sight, drawn down by the magic of the realmgate. A moment later, Tornus followed.

He plunged into the water, Ospheonis behind him. There was no flash of light, no radiant coruscation. Instead, it was like sinking into mud, at once constricting and irresistible. It pulled him down, even as it sought to suffocate him. He felt as if he had fallen into a grave, thick with worms. His war-plate creaked as things slithered about it, testing its strength. Then, with a sluicing sensation, he was through and tumbling between realms.

The dark yawned beneath him, broken at first only by a dwindling silver chain of glowing figures. The water surged, drawing him down. He spread his wings and dived deeper, pursuing the tumbling form of Gatrog. Bruised lights flickered all about him as the dark bled into distinct and familiar greens, browns and greys. The colours of rot and mulch, of fertilised soil and stagnant water. Holy colours, he'd thought, once upon a time.

Eerie shapes writhed about him: pale wyrms and dark, batrachian forms, as vast as sunken islands or as tiny as dust-motes. Entities of all shape and no shape at all passed over and through the sinking Stormcasts, without noticing them or being noticed in turn. Tornus had seen such malignancies before, though he could not recall where, and had no wish to do so. Horrors without name sprang from the soil of Nurgle's garden.

Morbus' rites kept the waters, and what lurked within them, from penetrating his armour or interfering with his descent.

Even so, Tornus shuddered as a curving pillar of iridescent scales shot past him, rising up and away. He caught glimpses of fangs and milky eyes, heard the roar of passing leviathans. And something more, besides.

A voice. So great as to be almost unperceivable. It rumbled up out of the depths, speaking to him. Calling to him. He could not make out the words, but he knew what it was saying. It was welcoming him home. Worse, it forgave him his mistakes. His failures. He tried to ignore it, to block it out, but it was omnipresent. A bell, tolling him on.

Below him and opposite him a shadow swam. It kept pace with him easily, despite its bulk. *I am still being here, fool,* it said, in a voice like the creaking of a coffin lid. *I am being a weed which is not so easy to pluck.*

Light, sickly and grey, swelled up below. He dived towards the weak, watery shimmer, following the others, trying to ignore the mocking shadow. It clutched at him, but almost playfully. As if there would be other, better opportunities to catch him. He broke free with a desperate convulsion, leaving it laughing in the dark.

He felt the soul-deep ache of its grip all the way down.

Angstun Drahn stepped into the open, and took a deep breath. The murk had not faded from the air yet, but the crisp sting of the sea breeze was growing stronger. Kurunta had offered to take the first watch on the bubbling pool, and Angstun had readily agreed.

He had little patience for such things, since his death and Reforging. He closed his eyes and leaned against his standard, trying to recall the moment Sigmar's voice had called him up out of the black. A strange moment, balanced on the precipice of agony and peace. Between death and life.

Of late, he had begun to wonder whether the one was not preferable to the other. In death, there was peace. To drift, at one with Azyr itself, would be a fine thing. In life, there was only another death to look forward to. He shook his head, banishing the thought, and looked up at the comet sigil that topped his battle standard. 'To be a part of the eternal tempest,' he murmured. 'That is the reward I shall claim, when the storm rolls on.' A selfish desire, perhaps, but it was his, and he held to it.

Others had their own dreams for when the war was done and the darkness was cast back for the last time. Kurunta intended to return to his people, on the Felstone Plains of Aqshy, and unite the clans of the Caldera once more. Enyo desired time to explore the vast, celestial sea. And Gardus – it was whispered, in the corridors of the Sigmarabulum, that the Steel Soul wished only to rebuild that which he had lost. That the war-leader of their chamber desired to set aside runeblade and hammer and once more tend to the sick.

Angstun found much to admire in that, even as he suspected that it would never occur. The war would never end, and they would march beneath the banners of heaven until the stars burned out and the suns became cold. While Sigmar still fought, so too would the Hallowed Knights. They were the faithful, and could do no less.

For now, his duty was to secure this place against the enemy, lest the Steel Souls lose whatever ground they had gained. Part of him was tempted to summon aid – there were other Stormhosts abroad in Ghyran, and those Prosecutors left to him could seek them out swiftly enough. But there was no need, as of yet. He snapped orders at a passing retinue of Judicators, and felt somewhat better. This place was corrupted, and required cleansing. That much, at least, they could do, while they awaited Gardus' return.

He heard a voice call out and saw Yare, hand raised. The old man had been moved by his followers from the wet ground to the top of a massive, reptilian skull. The skull had once been part of the wall, but the sound of Kurunta's horn had shaken it loose from the sargassum. Now it lay in a nest of splintered timbers, glaring sightlessly out at the courtyard. Much like Yare himself. Another prisoner crouched by the old man, whispering into his ear. Blind eyes sought out Angstun. 'He has gone, hasn't he?' the old man called.

'Our fellows were swallowed up by dark magics,' Angstun said, after a moment. He made his way towards the skull. Mortals scattered from his path. 'The Steel Soul goes to free them.' He forced himself to relax. Gardus had ordered him to stay, and so he would stay. But he didn't have to like it.

'You fear for him.'

Angstun frowned and looked up at Yare. 'I know neither fear nor doubt, old man. They have long since been burned out of me, in the forges of Azyr.'

'A shame,' Yare said. He winced and rubbed his face. Angstun wondered if his wounds pained him. Yare had refused to be escorted to the shore, declaring that he would leave last, or not at all. His followers had remained as well, and now those healthy enough to do so were helping in the rescue efforts, or else standing sentry, watching for the foe.

Angstun admired their grit, but couldn't help but feel that they'd made themselves an unnecessary burden to the Stormcasts still stationed in the citadels. The Hallowed Knights couldn't both hunt down the remaining Rotbringers and guard the mortals. Yare sighed. 'Doubts are the currency of discourse.' He leaned forward, coughing. Wheezing, he added, 'I have not engaged in proper debate for many years.'

Angstun's frown faded. 'Nor I,' he said softly. His mind had been scoured free of unimportant things on the Anvil. But some brief memories yet clung to the blade of his soul. He remembered columns of marble, and mirrored domes. The sound of voices, raised in heated discussion on the properties of reflected light. Shaken, he reached up and unlatched his helmet, wishing to feel the sea breeze on his face. 'But it seems we both have time on our hands, old man. Would you care to cross blades with one who is equally out of practice?'

Yare smiled. 'I would like that, I think.'

CHAPTER THIRTEEN

BOTTLED LIGHTNING

Gardus opened his eyes. Ghosts surrounded him, wispy fingers clutching at his war-plate. Indistinct faces pressed close as a wave of whispers washed over him. *Garradan... help us... Garradan... it hurts...* He swept his runeblade out, as gently as he could, and dispersed them. As ever, the voices were the last thing to fade.

Oily rain fell across a leprous glen. Nurgle's garden was much as he remembered, down to the sickly stink of the air as it scoured his lungs. He tensed and, for a moment, he was lost once more, fleeing for his life across the endless mire, sustained only by faith and desperation. He forced himself to relax. Now was not then, and Bolathrax was dead, or as good as. Slain by a goddess. Gardus wished he had been there to see it.

'It's like breathing soup,' Aetius muttered. The Liberator-Prime stood nearby, scraping at the brownish-grey mould growing patchily on his armour. It was the rain that brought it. Rain

created by the clouds, which were fed by the smoke from Nurgle's cauldrons. Or so their unwilling guide swore. He glanced
at the Rotbringer crouched in the mud.

'It gets worse,' Gardus said. His own armour, while grimy,
was free of mould. The rain sizzled when it struck him, puri-
fied by the nimbus of light seeping from his pores. Where
he strode, the water bubbled and the flabby vegetation withered and blackened. He wondered if Sigmar had foreseen
this moment during his Reforging, and welded the light to
his renewed soul for this very purpose. If so, to what end?
Was he merely another weapon, to be employed on corrupted
battlefields? Or was there some deeper meaning?

He shook his head, annoyed with himself. 'Only the faithful,'
he murmured. Whatever Sigmar's purpose, Gardus would see
it through. He had faith in the God-King's design. He pushed
his doubts aside and moved among his warriors, speaking
quiet words of comfort and encouragement to those who
needed it. And there were more of those than he liked.

The pox-rain did not simply stain armour; it tarnished mind
and soul as well. He was not the only one seeing ghosts, or
hearing the voices of those they'd failed. One Judicator leaned
slumped against a tree, breathing heavily. Gardus could smell
the acidic stink of vomit on the warrior's breath. He set a hand
on the Stormcast's shoulder. 'Breathe easy, brother. And shal-
low. It helps, somewhat.'

'I... I did not think it would be this way,' the Judicator
said. He fumbled at the clasps of his helmet. 'I can't breathe.
There... there are flies in my armour. I can hear them. *Feel*
them.' His voice cracked.

'Cadoc,' Gardus barked, as he caught the warrior's hands.
'I require your beacon, Knight-Azyros.' Cadoc dropped like
a stone from the sky. He unhooked his beacon from his belt

and opened it wide. The radiance within washed over the struggling Judicator. He stiffened and then, gradually, relaxed. Gardus turned. 'Solus, Aetius. Check your men. This place affects some more strongly than others, even with the protection of Morbus' prayers. I would not lose anyone else.'

He left the afflicted Judicator in the care of his Prime, and splashed towards Morbus. 'Any sign of them?' Overhead, Tegrus led his Prosecutors in an ever-widening circle. The winged Stormcast flew lower than normal, hampered by the thick air and the poisonous clouds above. Morbus shook his head.

'No, but they are close. I can feel something. Like heat from newly stirred ashes.' He turned. 'And something else as well. Hotter. Brighter.'

He was interrupted by a long, ululating shriek. Stormcasts whirled, groping for weapons or nocking arrows. Overhead, Enyo called out something. The Knight-Venator dived into the tree line, moving so swiftly that she was no more than a blur of silver. As Gardus hurried towards where she'd vanished, he heard the hiss-crack of her bow. 'Tornus,' he roared, extending his hammer. Tornus shot past him, drawing an arrow from his quiver as he did so, his star-eagle at his side.

Gardus burst through a clump of trees and slid to a halt in the slippery mud. The clearing was alive with savage movement. A serpentine length of scaly flesh thrashed, seeking to coil about a spotted shape, which screeched and snapped in a frenzy. The two Knight-Venators peppered the scaly coils with arrows, but the crackling missiles seemed to have little effect on the monster, whatever it was.

'Poxwyrm,' Gatrog said from behind Gardus. The Rotbringer stood within a phalanx of Liberators, and Aetius held his chains. 'Ugly brutes. Always hungry. And venomous.' He looked around. 'Give me a blade, and I'll soon have its head off, if you like.'

'Keep him back,' Gardus said. He splashed towards the battle, drawing his runeblade as he did so. A wedge-shaped head, marked by tattered fins and bloody wounds, shot forwards to meet him, jaws wide. A blow from his hammer shattered the blackened fangs as they tried to close about him. His blade carved apart the wormy tongue, filling the air with poisonous ichors. He ignored its shriek of agony and lunged, carving through the muscles of its mouth. Unnatural flesh split and tore as he bulled forwards, chopping away at its maw and throat.

Finally, it swayed back from him, shattering trees in its death throes. As the coils settled into the water, the poxwyrm's opponent was revealed. 'Tallon,' Gardus said, dropping to one knee. 'That is you, isn't it?'

The gryph-hound stood shakily, his spotted form scored by bloody wounds. He favoured one paw, and chunks of fur and feathers were missing from his hide. Flanks heaving, the creature stared at Gardus suspiciously, as if unable to believe the evidence of his senses. The Lord-Celestant set aside his hammer and extended a hand, murmuring soothingly. A wounded gryph-hound was a dangerous thing, as the poxwyrm had discovered. They had even been known to turn on their handlers, on occasion.

Tallon leaned forwards, beak scraping down his palm. After a moment, the animal stumbled against him, chirping softly. Gardus stroked the beast's neck. 'Easy,' he murmured. 'Easy. You're among friends.'

The gryph-hound pushed away from him and growled. Gardus rose as the animal limped away, casting backward glances every few steps. He splashed after the beast. Morbus was waiting on them nearby. The Lord-Relictor crouched beside something shrouded in moss and mud. 'Tallon was protecting them,' Morbus said, scraping a chunk of mud away to reveal a swathe of silver.

Gardus' mouth was dry. 'How many?'

'Five. All dead.' Morbus stood. 'Lorrus is not among them.'

Gardus felt a flash of relief. 'Then he might still live.' He hesitated. 'But if they're dead, why are they here?'

'Their souls are trapped in their flesh. Caught fast by the baleful magics of this place. Like lightning in a bottle.'

'Is there anything to be done?' Gardus said, looking down at the corpse.

'One thing.' Morbus extended his staff, and Gardus took it. The Lord-Relictor raised his hands over the body and began to murmur a prayer. The body started to shimmer, and twitch. A thin web of lightning crackled between Morbus' fingers. He uttered a single, hammer-stroke word, and slammed his hands down. The body bucked, and Morbus wrenched his hands up, drawing out the energies trapped in the body. He lurched to his feet, forcing Gardus to step back. Lightning crawled over Morbus' arms and chest as the body was reduced to swirling ash. He clenched his fists and bent double. The lightning faded until only a faint glow remained.

'Now, the others,' Morbus hissed. He shoved past Gardus and stumbled towards the other bodies, where they lay shrouded in filth. Morbus repeated the ceremony, drawing the lightning of the fallen Stormcasts, their very essences, into himself. His eyes sparked as he reclaimed his staff. 'I have their souls. They are safe, in my keeping.'

'And what of you?' Gardus said. 'I have never seen this rite. Never even heard a whisper of it. What is it?'

'It has no name, and you have not seen it because it has

not yet been necessary,' Morbus said. He leaned against his staff. 'The rites of the Temple of Ages are manifold. This is but one.' He fixed Gardus with a burning gaze. 'Would you see the others? Shall I draw down the full fury of the celestial storm here and burn this garden to its roots? It would mean our deaths, but better a quick death than what I fear is to come.'

'No,' Gardus said, shaken. Morbus was among the most powerful of the Storm Summoners. Some said that he was second in wisdom only to Ionus Cryptborn, though Morbus kept his opinions in that regard to himself. 'No. We go forward.'

'Whatever the cost?'

Again, Gardus paused. 'We must do this, Morbus.'

Morbus nodded. 'So we must. Lead on, Lord-Celestant.' He gestured briskly, and Gardus almost smiled. He turned to where their unwilling guide knelt in the mire under the watchful eyes of Tornus. He waved his hand, and the Knight-Venator roughly dragged the Rotbringer to his feet.

'Which direction?' Gardus said.

'There are no directions,' Gatrog said with a laugh. 'Not here.' He gagged as Gardus caught him by the throat. 'But we should definitely go that way,' he gurgled, jerking his head to indicate a path. Gardus released him.

'Why?'

'Because that's where the current goes, and where the galleys will be.' Gatrog hawked and spat. 'This is but the first tier of the garden. The antechamber, if you will. The place where souls drift into the garden, and become lost. The servants of the King of all Flies haunt these waters and capture any they come across.'

'And take them where?'

'Despair. Despondency. Desolation.'

'He talks nonsense,' Cadoc said, reaching for his starblade.

'No. They are being places,' Tornus said. He clutched his

head, as if trying to pry the information free. 'At least, I am thinking they are.' The Knight-Venator sounded shaken. Worried. Gardus wondered if it had been a mistake to bring him; not because he doubted Tornus' loyalty, but because of the obvious strain the situation was placing on him.

'Then that is where we must go,' Morbus said. 'I can sense the Lord-Castellant's soulfire, but it is growing faint.' He shook his head. 'We may not be able to catch up in time. Lorrus might well be lost to us, Gardus.'

Before Gardus could reply, a whistle from above caught his attention. Tegrus swooped low, and gestured. 'Something approaches, Steel Soul. A vessel of some sort.'

Gardus glanced at Morbus. 'Sigmar provides,' the Lord-Relictor said with a shrug, as they followed Tegrus to the edge of the dripping glade. Through a curtain of fungal trees, Gardus spotted a wedge-shaped prow nosing through the miasma, and heard the thump of drums. Great oars struck the water, and dragged the bottom of the galley across the more solid areas. He heard croaking voices raised in an abominable song, and the rattle of rusty weapons. The flies swarming about them seemed to grow more agitated, and Gardus swept out his hand in a futile attempt to disperse them.

He signalled and Tornus dragged Gatrog forward. Gardus stared down at the pox-knight. 'What is it?'

'As I said, a galley. Soul-slavers. They gather up the lost spirits who wander aimlessly in these swamps and sell them into useful servitude, deeper in the garden.' Gatrog spat. 'Sometimes honest travellers, as well, it must be said.' He frowned. 'I was almost taken by such an opportunistic crew of malcontents as I sought to win my spurs.' He shook his head, as if in disappointment. 'Base creatures they were, lowborn and lacking in honour.'

'Will they disembark?' Gardus asked, cutting the Rotbringer's reminiscences short.

'Aye, if they see a soul in need of capture. Like as not, they already know you're here.' Gatrog laughed. 'The flies that swarm so thickly on the air sometimes carry word to favoured captains, and lead them to their prey.'

'Tactics,' Gardus said tersely.

'None. They are rabble,' Gatrog sneered dismissively. 'Daemons too lowly to join one of the blighted legions, or half-things, unfit for any other task.' He strained slightly. 'But give me a blade, and I would defeat them myself.'

Gardus shoved him back towards a retinue of Liberators. 'Hold him safe.'

'I need no protection,' Gatrog spluttered.

'I did not mean for your sake.'

A plan was already forming in his mind. A crude one, to be sure, but subtlety required time they didn't have. They needed a vessel, and here was one, ready to be taken. But they would have to do it swiftly, and without damaging the galley. He gave his orders briskly. 'Solus, pin down those brave enough to disembark. Tegrus, keep any stragglers from retreating. Enyo, Tornus, see to any left on board. The rest of you, move in on my signal. I want that galley in one piece.'

'And what will you be doing?' Morbus said.

'I should have thought that would be obvious. I'll be getting their attention.' Without waiting for the Lord-Relictor's reply, Gardus swept aside a fungal tree with a single blow from his hammer and strode into the open. The galley had come to a halt not far away, beaching itself on a soggy hummock. In shape, it reminded Gardus of similar vessels he'd seen in his mortal years. They'd crowded the docklands of Demesnus Harbour, crewed by people from the southern coasts.

Merchants and travellers, offering up exotic spices and silks from across the Great Sea.

But no vessel such as this had ever blighted those waters. It was a shaggy thing, its stern scabbed with hairy pustules and raw blisters. Its splintery hull was daubed in pitch and studded with rusty iron sigils, which gleamed in a sickly fashion. The mast was a looming gallows, and the sails were flabby and unnatural. A ramp, made from wood and iron, thudded down from the upper deck into the muck, scattering a swarm of flies, and sending something large slithering away into the mists.

From where he stood, Gardus could just make out the crew as they swarmed across the deck, shouting to one another in deep, inhuman voices. A lean shape appeared at the bow, its single, bulbous eye narrowed in curiosity. The cyclopean daemon wore a cuirass of beaten, mouldy leather, and a cloak of what looked to be filthy silk. The plaguebearer gave a monotone cry and pointed at him with a festering blade.

Gardus clashed his weapons together. 'Come and get me,' he called.

Plaguebearers galumphed down the boarding ramp, their droning cries filling the air. There were men, or things that were almost men, among them, their bodies covered in cancerous encrustations and weeping barnacles. These half-daemons splashed ahead of their more sedate companions, closing in on Gardus with excited yelps.

The Lord-Celestant stepped back into the trees. The creatures raced after him. He killed the first with a single slash of his runeblade. The second fell with a crushed skull. The others slowed, suddenly uncertain. 'Aetius,' Gardus said.

Liberators pressed forwards from between the dripping trees. As the mortals fell, Solus gave the order, and skybolt bows hummed as the Judicators loosed a fiery rain on the approaching daemons. Gardus led Feros and his Retributors towards the creatures. The fight that followed was swift. These daemons were clearly not used to their prey fighting back. Lightning hammers crashed down, rupturing ragged bodies and reducing them to sludge. Gardus cut himself a path through the throng, and was soon pounding up the boarding ramp. Decaying daemons lay everywhere, their bodies marked by glowing arrows.

The vessel stank of rot and standing water. Everything dripped with slime, or flowered with barnacles. The captain bounded down a set of sagging steps towards him, cloak flaring about its narrow shoulders. Gardus casually beat aside the daemon's blade and ran it through. It stumbled against him, body blackening to ash. He ripped his sword free, and it dispersed on the breeze. Down below, the last of the crew was disposed of by a blow from Feros' hammer.

'A less than satisfactory fight,' Cadoc said, as he landed at the stern with a thump. 'Greedy, fair Enyo, very greedy,' he called up to the circling Knight-Venator.

'Be silent, Cadoc,' Morbus said as he climbed the ramp, ferrule thumping the wood with every step. He nodded to Gardus. 'You are right. Our journey will be easier with a ship. Even a ship in this condition.' Liberators and Judicators followed him, dispersing throughout the vessel to check for hidden foes.

'Yes.' Gardus strode down the line of rowers' benches. The creatures chained there were strange indeed. Some of them might once have been human, but now they were malformed by disease and harsh treatment. Clusters of fungi and barnacles crusted their flesh, obscuring faces and reducing limbs to formless lumps. He could smell the blight within them, and knew it was too late. Even so, he was bound to try to help, if he could. He shattered a loop of chain with a single blow from his sword. 'You are free,' he said.

The spirits stared at him in incomprehension. He broke another chain, freeing a second row. At his command, Liberators followed suit, smashing the chain loops. 'Free,' Gardus said again. 'Do you not understand?'

'They do not,' Morbus said. 'Nor, it seems, do you.'

'What do you mean?'

'Do you think that they were drawn here unwillingly? Some of them, perhaps, but not all. These souls have succumbed to Nurgle's blandishments as surely as that creature we hold in chains. They know only despair, and no light we possess can draw them out of the dark.'

'You cannot know that,' Gardus said.

'Look at them. Your light, Gardus. See how it pains them.'

Gardus looked around. The rowers cowered back from him, hiding their eyes, their faces, as if they could not bear to look upon him. Morbus was right. He could not save them. Not this way. But neither did he have to let them remain in captivity. 'Shatter all of the chains,' he said harshly. 'Free any trapped in the hold.'

When the last of the chains had clattered to the deck, the souls rose. Not in unison, but in arhythmic fits and starts. More emerged from the hold, their moans rising and falling like a winter wind. The Stormcasts stood aside and let them pass. They flooded down the ramp and spilled into the marsh, scattering into the murk.

'We cannot just let them go,' a Liberator said, her voice startling in the silence that followed. 'It is not right.'

'Nothing about this place is right,' Gardus said. He looked around. 'The vessel is ours. The question now is how to get it moving.'

'I dislike the thought of spending time on such a ship,' Aetius said. The Liberator-Prime's disgust was palpable.

'You prefer walking?' Solus said from where he sat on the rail.

'Walking is the only honourable means of travel.'

'Slow, though,' Solus said. 'And Tegrus might disagree. What say you, Sainted Eye?'

Tegrus, perched on the mast above, laughed. 'I could carry him in a sling. Like a babe in arms. And in armour.'

'Quiet,' Morbus said sternly. 'Cadoc.'

The Knight-Azyros looked towards the Lord-Relictor. 'Command me, Stormwarden.'

Morbus gestured with his hammer. 'Hang your beacon from the mast, Prince of Ekran.'

Cadoc stabbed his blade into the mast and hung his beacon from the hilt. Cerulean light spilled out, washing over every board and nail. It raced across the rails and climbed towards the flabby sails. Morbus strode amidships and thrust his staff down. Lines of cobalt fire converged on him and rose up in an eye-searing conflagration as he spoke a single word. The flames swelled, colours darkening, as the Lord-Relictor reached out and plucked something from within them. Morbus turned, offering up what appeared to be a spike made from sapphire light. 'Cadoc, you may retrieve your beacon. Gardus, place this at the centreline, and strike true.'

Gingerly, Gardus took the spike. It was the size of a gladius, but had no weight to it. He did as Morbus had requested, pacing to the midpoint of the ship. He sank down and set the spike into the deck. The boards creaked and began to blacken. Gardus stood and lifted his hammer in both hands.

When he struck, a thunderclap echoed. Strange birds took flight from the closest of the crooked trees, and the miasma thinned as a blaze of azure enveloped the galley, stem to stern. The old sails burnt away, traded for new ones of flame. The rigging was consumed and replaced by strands of lightning. Every board, every oar, every stack, was limned by a blue nimbus. Smoke rose from the waterline as the sludge was burnt momentarily pure by the touch of the vessel's hull.

The Stormcasts looked around in wonder. 'It will not last long, in this place,' Morbus said, his voice a ragged growl. 'But it will last long enough.'

Gardus nodded and looked around. 'You heard him,' he said loudly. 'Every warrior to an oar. Time runs thin, and we have leagues yet to travel.'

Clear of the trees and miasma of the swamp, Gutrot Spume could see the great cloud of pox-smoke that rose up in the distance, spilling from the hollows of the garden's heart. The smoke billowed up from Grandfather's cauldron, inundating each level with his blessed contagions. Spume inhaled deeply, drawing the wonderful stink into himself. 'Pah,' he exhaled. 'It smells like victory, eh, Durg?'

'As you say, captain,' the plaguebearer said. It prodded the ruined hole that might once have been a nose. 'Can't tell, myself.'

Spume chuckled and slapped the daemon on the shoulder. 'A shame.'

Durg's single, bleary eye narrowed. 'Land ho,' he said, pointing a knobbly finger. Spume nodded. He'd spotted the gateway. There were only seven true paths out of the swamp and into the deeper garden, and this was the largest of them. At a distance, it resembled a half-submerged range of mountains or leprous fingers reaching for the yellow sky.

Spume lifted his axe and set it across his shoulder. He

mused on his good fortune. The silver-skin chained in his hold was a prize Nurgle, indeed, all of the Ruinous Powers, had long desired. Sigmar's return had upset a balance long in the making. Chaos had held sway in the Mortal Realms for uncontested centuries, and things had, to Spume's way of thinking, fallen into a pleasing rhythm. Like the tides of the sea, Chaos had begun to wear away at the foundations of existence, and Spume had sailed those tides to power and glory. Not alone, either. Others had accompanied him in his voyages.

Urslaug was one such. She was not a friend, as such. The sorceress had once served aboard his ship, wielding the pox-winds in his favour. But she had grown tired of the seadog's life and retired to her studies, in the comfort of the garden. It had been a century or more since he'd had need of her services, and that time hadn't ended well. From the sound of things, she hadn't forgiven him yet.

'Women, eh?' he gurgled, glancing at Durg.

'Rot fly,' Durg said.

Spume blinked, momentarily confused by the plaguebearer's reply. Then he heard the tell-tale hum of wings. He looked up, shading his eyes with a tentacle. 'What's this then?'

The fly was larger than a man, and fat with strength. It bobbed through the damp air, riding the currents with an awkward inexorability. Its hairy legs were decorated with tarnished gee-gaws of gold and silver, and a saddle made from woven scalps was cinched across its abdomen. The plaguebearer that sat astride it was similarly bedecked, in a fine yellowish coat of mouldering cloth and fraying ruffles of silk. A bent rapier was sheathed on its bony hip, and its horn was polished to a pulchritudinous gleam.

The rot fly struck the deck with a thump, scattering crew.

'Ahoy,' the rider croaked. 'Step forward, Lord of Tentacles. I come bearing word from your betters, sir.'

'And who would that be?' Spume said, glaring up at the rider. 'Come to it, who are ye?' He knew this creature's sort. One of the courtiers who clung like errant motes to the disease-infested corridors of Nurgle's manse. They did not speak for the Lord of All Things. Rather, they spoke for his closest servants, and waged silent wars in their name. The Court of Ruination was infested with them.

'I am Puersillimous Blotch.' The plaguebearer snuffled noisily at a reeking handkerchief he extracted from one sleeve. 'Forgive me, I am not used to such uncultured foulness.' Blotch's eye narrowed. 'I much prefer the artisanal bouquets of Desolation. Have you ever smelled them, reaver?' The eye gleamed with malice. 'No, I expect not.'

Spume frowned. 'Aye, I have, as a matter of fact, and most pleasing they are. Though I much prefer the tang of saltwater to the soft fens of the garden. Why are you here? Who sent you?'

'One who far outstrips you in power, I assure you.' Blotch cast about condescendingly. 'Though that is not difficult. You have fallen far, admiral. Come down in the world, haven't you?'

'A setback,' Spume said. The haft of his axe creaked in his grip.

'A permanent one, if you are not careful,' the plaguebearer said. 'Things have changed, in the wake of the Glottkin's failure to hold open the doorway to Ghyran. Those who fought in those verdant fields are no more the favoured children. New bile is needed in these troubling times, don't you think?'

'No,' Spume said.

'And that is your problem, corsair,' Blotch chuckled. 'You don't think.'

'How dare ye set foot uninvited on my ship and cast insults,' Spume gargled, lifting his axe. 'I ought to split your mossy skull, flydandy.'

'And attract Grandfather's ire, captain?' the plaguebearer hissed, leaning over to bare his bulbous throat. 'If you would have it so, strike, sir. Strike then!'

Spume bristled. He swept the axe back, but could not bring himself to do it. The flydandy was right. He might be the wormy apple of Grandfather's eye, but his visitor was part of the same bunch. And perhaps an even wormier one than Spume. He let the bite of his axe thump to the deck. 'What do ye want?'

'You have something that does not belong to you, pirate.'

'Do I?' Spume gestured to the bent backs of the slaves. 'One of these wretches, perhaps? Or a keg of finest cankerwine?'

Blotch chortled. 'You know of what I speak, slug-trail.'

'Aye, mayhap I do. What concern is it of yours?'

'You will bring it to Desolation, or suffer the consequences. Father Decay would see this thing you have found, and soon.'

Spume grunted. Father Decay was the Hand of Nurgle, one of the Council of Ruination, and a name to send shudders through every soul in the garden. This Blotch had friends in low places. 'And how does his loftiness know what I've found, or not found?'

The flydandy grinned and plucked at his filthy cuffs. 'How could he not, when the very air speaks of a cleansing taint?' The plaguebearer sat back in his saddle. 'And more besides.' Black teeth clicked together in a crooked smile. 'It is not alone, this thing.'

Spume tensed. 'What do you mean?'

'Can't you smell it, reaver? The air burns. And not in the way it should. Look to the horizon. See the fires there, as Grandfather's galleys blaze.'

Spume turned, and saw that the creature spoke the truth. Something was burning out in the swamp. And he'd smelled that sort of fire before, at Profane Tor, and then later, in the Canker Cascade. That they were here, now, was deeply unsettling. Not since the Age of Blood had an enemy dared breach the sanctity of the garden. He lifted his axe. 'Shall I take their heads then, these invaders?'

'No,' Blotch said. 'They will be dealt with. Bring your plunder to Desolation, and be rewarded. Fail, and suffer as no being has yet suffered.'

Spume cocked his head. 'I'll do as ye ask. But ye won't be there to see it.' His axe looped out and smashed the flydandy from the saddle. Startled, the fly heaved itself upwards and away, buzzing loudly. The flydandy gurgled in shock as Spume planted a boot on his throat. 'No daemon threatens me on my own ship.'

'You can't,' Blotch whimpered, clawing at Spume's leg.

'Who are ye, to tell me what I can and can't do on my own vessel, eh?' Spume raised his axe. 'A fool, that's who. When Grandfather remakes you, Blotch, hold fast to this memory, and let it guide you to future wisdom.'

The axe fell, and Blotch collapsed into itself. Durg prodded the remains with a boathook. 'Father Decay won't be happy about that.'

'No,' Spume said, flicking bits of Blotch from his axe. 'He should keep his courtiers on a shorter leash next time. I'll not play the worm-belly on my own ship, by Grandfather's wormy guts.' He pointed with a tentacle. 'Make haste for the gate.'

Durg nodded and uncoiled its whip. 'Stroke,' the daemon bellowed, 'stroke!' The plaguebearer snapped its whip over the heads of the rowers, causing them to ply the oars more swiftly. The sails billowed as they caught the pox-wind, and soon they were cutting swiftly through the waters towards the gate.

Spume planted his axe and rested his forearm atop it, watching the swamp as it receded. Blue fire flickered in the murk, and he felt the kraken in his abdomen shift in agitation. Sometimes, he could feel a whisper of the thing's thoughts, dripping into his own. He felt its nervousness. An animal wariness that added to his own irritation.

The flydandy had been right. He'd been a fool. He'd given no thought as to where the shiny-skin had come from, only the possibilities he represented. And now it seemed more of them were on the way. He considered dropping anchor and waiting for them. If he dispatched them, Grandfather might be pleased. Unless...

'Ah,' he murmured. That was it. The garden was only for the willing. If the shiny-skins wanted to smash themselves a path to Desolation, Grandfather would let them. Once they got deep enough in the mire, there'd be no getting out for any of them. And he was the bait, drawing them in. 'He's a cunning old oaf, Father Decay,' Spume said.

A shadow fell across the deck, and Spume felt a shiver run along his barbed spine. He turned. They'd reached the gate, at last. He raised his axe in salute to the guardians of the gateway as the galley passed the edge of the swamp.

Broken stones of immense size marked the vast, curving rim of the abyss at the swamp's heart. They rose up in haphazard ridges, between which scummy water eddied and poured down into the depths of the garden. Grandfather brewed his pox-clouds, which rose up through the abyss and filled the swamp with rain. And that rain in turn ran back down, feeding into the lower tiers, through passages, rivers and waterfalls.

The gateway itself was a gargantuan arch of crudely carved basalt. It was longer than a dozen galleys chained prow to stern, and hung thick with yellowing vines. Hundreds of fruiting bodies swayed among those vines, caught fast either by the will of Nurgle, or that of his chosen guardians: Hope and Despair.

The guardians were two ossified daemons hunkered on the stone plinths that rose to either side of the vast archway, gazing sightlessly and eternally out over the swamps. One was a bloated Great Unclean One, its posture strained, its features twisted into an expression of savage contempt as it raised a broken blade. The other was a vulture-like monstrosity, with skeletal wings and withered limbs, leaning on a great staff, as if bracing itself against a strong wind. No servant of Nurgle, that one.

Legend had it that, in the aeons before the Mortal Realms had congealed from the cosmic sump, a servant of the Changer of Ways had slipped secretly into the garden. The daemon had whispered treacherous hopes into the ears of many of Grandfather's most loyal servants. Including one of the oldest, and mightiest, of Nurgle's sons, whose name had since been erased from the Ledger of Souls. Treachery followed, as the son sought to usurp the father and paid for his temerity. Neither had the instigator of such foolishness escaped unchastised. Now both stood watch over the antechamber of the garden, until such time as Grandfather had forgiven them.

The eyes of the Lord of Change seemed to follow Spume as the galley slid beneath the archway and into the curtain of vines. He heard a whisper of sound, like a voice calling out to him from some impossible distance. Spume laughed and made a rude gesture. 'Peddle your promises to someone else, or I'll carve my name in your scrawny neck.' The voice faded into insulted silence as the galley moved out of the shadows of the archway.

It was always the same. Some daemons never learned. Spume reached up with his axe and tapped a dangling foot. The leprous body danced and twitched in its vines, and emitted a sound like a groan. He laughed. No soul passed through the archway, save that Nurgle willed it. And those that tried regardless lived eternally to regret it.

Beyond the vines, the edges of a massive, fungus-covered aqueduct rose. The passage was the only safe way down to the next tier of the garden. Spume thumped the deck with his axe. 'Lay on some speed, Durg. I've got an appointment to keep.'

CHAPTER FOURTEEN

A TOWN CALLED DESPAIR

Aetius Shieldborn cursed and ducked away from the groping hands of the vine-snared corpse. Splintered nails clattered
against the face of his shield as stinging flies spewed from the
sagging jaws. He bashed the hanging body aside and crushed
its skull, blocking the torrent of insects. Immediately, he was
beset by another. There were too many corpses to avoid, and
possibly more than even he could handle.

The enormous, cracked archway above was thick with a
shroud of yellowing vines. The innumerable corpses trapped
within them had twitched into motion the moment the
cobalt-limned galley had swept beneath them. The flickering
starlight that danced along the rails and mast kept most of the
dead at bay but, even so, there were simply too many of them.
Bodies flopped and fell to the deck, smothering the azure radiance long enough for more of the dangling corpses to descend
and attack.

Dead hands groped and battered at unwary warriors, as the

bodies descended towards the ship like twisted spiders. More and more of them with every passing moment, attacking the Stormcasts on the deck, and those rowing as well. The galley shuddered with their weight. The decks were a riot of struggling forms, as Stormcasts fought back to back against the deluge of leprous corpses. 'This is intolerable,' Aetius said, glaring up at the clutching canopy of hands and teeth that groped for him.

'I shall pass along your complaints to the Steel Soul,' Solus said, sheltering beneath another Liberator's raised shield. The Judicator-Prime loosed a scintillating arrow, and nodded in satisfaction as it thumped into a corpse's skull, rendering it limp.

Aetius ignored Solus and concentrated on the task at hand. 'Berkut – keep that shield up,' he growled, jostling one of his warriors. 'Serena, Tomas – brace and step, make us some room. Taya, stop playing with that thing and get back into position.' He moved to help the warrior as she struggled with a particularly stubborn corpse. The diseased carcass clung to her shield with fierce tenacity, its crushed jaw flopping against her war-mask.

Aetius scraped the thing away and trod on its head, pulping it. Taya nodded her thanks. 'These things smell worse than orruks,' she said, coughing.

'Then breathe through your mouth,' Aetius said gruffly. He spotted Gardus fighting at the prow, where the dead were thickest. Tallon fought at his side, savaging corpses with his beak and claws. The Lord-Celestant blazed with an elemental radiance as he struck down corpse after corpse. Truly a sign of Sigmar's favour. Tearing his gaze from the Lord-Celestant, he slammed his shield into a corpse as it swung itself towards him, and smashed its crumbling face out of the back of its skull. A blow from his hammer caught another in the spine and dropped it to the deck.

Everywhere he looked there were vines, and bodies wriggling through them. They needed to clear this place – to purify it, all at once. Even as the thought occurred to him, he caught sight of Feros and his Retributors swatting corpses from the air. Aetius glanced at Solus. 'Solus,' he called. Solus nodded, understanding instantly. He signalled, and nearby Judicators switched their aim, covering Aetius and his retinue, as they pushed towards the Retributors.

'Heavy Hand, remember the Seeping Fen?' Aetius shouted, shouldering aside an arrow-studded corpse. Feros glanced at him in evident confusion. Then, his eyes brightened with realisation. He laughed, loud and long.

'Brothers and sisters, let us play our war-song,' Feros rumbled. 'If the dead wish to dance, we will give them reason to do so.' Retributors turned towards one another, ignoring the enemies that crowded about them. Aetius' Liberators moved to surround them, warding the paladins with their shields and hammers. Feros and his retinue began to chant, slowly and sonorously, as they clashed their hammers together rhythmically. Fat sparks of crackling sky-magic danced with every contact. The crash of hammers grew louder, and quicker. More lightning leapt up, dancing from hammer to hammer.

Aetius resolutely looked away from the burgeoning glow. To stare at it too long was to risk blinding oneself. Behind him, Feros' voice rose in a paean to Sigmar's glory. Despite himself, Aetius began to sing along. Sparks leapt up, and flitted across the plates of his armour and the runes of his hammer.

And then, with one final, echoing clash of hammers, a gout of celestial lightning snarled upwards, through the vines. Fire blossomed on the rotting vegetation, and raced from vine to vine. Twitching corpses were consumed, reduced to ash and blackened bone in moments. Aetius raised his shield and swatted aside a burning cadaver, pleased. They'd used the trick before, to cleanse the air of miasma at the Seeping Fen, and burn away the thick swarms of flies that had sought to blind them.

A rumbling groan of displeasure drowned out the final verse of the war-hymn, and punctured Aetius' self-satisfaction. He looked up, and saw the two monstrous statues crouching to either side of the archway turn, slowly, inexorably, towards the galley. The Great Unclean One twisted on its plinth, sword rising, as if to chop through the vessel. The eyes of the statue blazed with hideous life, and its face cracked and crumbled as it twisted with gloating malice.

Before it could strike, a whirling barrage of hammers slammed into its blubbery features, further cracking them. Tegrus and his Prosecutors had been, until now, grounded by the canopy of vines. Now, they had taken advantage of the canopy's incineration, and hurtled skyward to bombard the threatening statue. But even as the Great Unclean One rocked on its plinth, its companion undulated towards the flying Stormcasts, avian beak wide. The stony Lord of Change vomited a coruscating bolt of eldritch flame.

One of the Prosecutors, half a second too slow, fell twitching to the deck, his armour warping and bulging in an obscene transformation. Stormcasts scattered as the warrior crashed down. The Prosecutor screamed in agony as his own armour consumed him, using his skin and muscle to build itself a glistening, fleshy shell. Tendrils crafted from ligament lashed at any who drew too close, and a stinger made from a splintered spinal column emerged from the heaving mass.

'Sigmar preserve us,' Aetius hissed. The newborn Chaos

spawn clattered towards the closest group of Stormcasts, claws of twisted sigmarite clacking. He glanced at Feros. The Retributor-Prime nodded.

'Lead the way, Shieldborn. My hammer is at your back.'

They advanced on the creature. It spun towards them, eyeball-topped cilia sprouting from the stretched mouthpiece of a bent helmet. Something rattled, and it scuttled towards them, snapping its claws. A volley of gleaming arrows peppered its flank, drawing its attention towards Solus and his Judicators. Aetius gave a silent prayer of thanks for his friend's quick thinking. He closed with the creature, absorbing a blow from its stinger tail on his shield. Swiftly, he smashed the tail to flinders. He dodged back as the monster whirled towards him, claws snapping. 'Feros, put it out of its misery!'

'Only the faithful,' Feros roared, as his lightning hammer slammed down against its fleshy shell. The spawn was momentarily flattened by the force of the blow, and Feros finished it off before it could recover. He pinned it in place with his foot and brought his hammer down again and again, until the creature was a broken ruin.

Feros stepped back. 'Sleep now, brother, that your soul might rise again, with storms yet to come,' he said. 'Sleep the sleep of the faithful.'

Aetius heard a monstrous shriek, and saw that they'd left the statues behind. Both had endured the attention of the Prosecutors, and clouds of smoke and dust rose from them. But already they were repairing themselves. Cracks closed, debris rolled back up the hunched forms, seeking familiar divots. 'Sigmar's bones, we're going to have to fight them again, aren't we?' he said in frustration.

'Your confidence is encouraging,' Lord-Relictor Morbus said as he strode between Aetius and Feros. He sank to one knee beside the steaming remains of the Chaos spawn. Aetius looked at him, confused.

'My what?'

'To fight them again implies that we will survive to return this way,' Morbus said, as he waved a hand over the broken thing. He made a grasping gesture, and murmured softly. Sparks of light rose from the ruin of meat and bone, and danced briefly across his fist, before sinking into his hand. Morbus sagged, as if a great weight pressed down upon him. He rose and glanced at Aetius. 'That was quick thinking earlier.'

Aetius shrugged. 'It needed doing.'

Morbus chuckled. 'So it did.' He staggered, and Feros caught him.

'Are you injured, Lord-Relictor?'

'No. Merely tired.' Morbus pushed himself away from the Retributor-Prime. 'But then, so are we all.' He leaned against his staff. 'Though our bodies are fatigued, we yet advance. Thus are the faithful known.'

'Only the faithful,' Aetius said solemnly. The deck shuddered. Waves smacked at the sides of the galley as it travelled down an overflowing runnel of moss-covered stone. The walls of the aqueduct rose high over the galley, and its rim was encrusted with tumorous malformations that might have been ramparts and towers. Strange, pale faces peered out of gaping holes, watching as the galley passed by. The fungoid features retreated as the light washed over them. Aetius watched them warily. 'This place is full of horrors.'

'This is only the first level,' Morbus said. 'There are six more, according to our captive.' Aetius glanced towards the mast, where the Rotbringer sat chained. Thus far, the pox-knight had given them no cause to pitch him over the side, but Aetius itched to do so regardless. As if reading his thoughts, Morbus said, 'He has been truthful, so far.'

'It will not last.'

'And why should he lie?' Solus asked, as he joined them. His armour was streaked with ash and gore, but he seemed unharmed. Aetius was glad of that, though he'd never admit it. Solus was the closest thing he had to a friend.

'He is a thing of Chaos,' Aetius said.

Solus nodded in agreement. 'Fair enough.' He studied the Rotbringer. 'Still, one can't help but wonder...'

'One can, if one tries,' Aetius said.

Solus dropped a companionable fist on his shoulder-plate. 'Forgive me, brother. I sometimes forget who I'm talking to.'

Aetius couldn't decide whether to be insulted or not, so he remained silent. In any event, it was soon too noisy to speak. The roaring of the waters had grown deafening, and it was all they could do to hold on. The galley rose and fell, seemingly at random.

Past the edges of the aqueduct, Aetius could see more lengthy runnels, all slanting downwards along a cliff-face at wrong angles from their own monstrous gateways. Water roared between them in an unceasing torrent, tumbling into the depths. This shroud of water was only broken by a series of steep, winding paths, which cut through the thick, fungal foliage clinging to the inner curve of the cliffs. No, not cliffs – the inner rim of the great tiers that made up this place. Carved by some gargantuan stonemason in time out of mind, at the behest of a daemon-god.

Everything about this realm spoke of filth and degradation. It stained one's mind, as well as one's armour. Despite Morbus' protective incantations, and the prayers they murmured almost constantly, a fell aura surrounded the Stormcasts. It was like a piece of grit, caught between armour and flesh, all but unnoticed at first, but growing ever more uncomfortable and distracting. It was a constant battle to keep their armour scraped free of mould, made worse by the spores that floated through the damp air.

The deck shifted beneath him, timbers groaning. The angle of the aqueduct was levelling off as they neared the bottom. Water filled a swirling bay, surrounded on all sides by jagged rocks and thick-boled trees, the branches of which dipped into the waters. Flocks of things that might have been birds or bats glided through the air, their shrill cries sawing over Aetius' nerves. Moisture pattered across the deck from above. It turned to steam as it reached the blue radiance flickering from the rails and mast.

'That grinding sound is going to get on my nerves quickly,' Feros said.

Aetius was about to ask him what he was talking about, when he heard it. Like two massive stones, scraping away at one another. 'What is that?'

'This place is in constant motion,' Morbus said. 'The tiers turn at the whim of their maker, spinning slowly, but inexorably, in place.'

'Like one millstone set upon the next,' Solus said.

Aetius looked at him. 'What?'

'This place. It's like a stack of millstones.'

'How would you know what millstones look like?'

Solus shrugged. 'I was a miller.'

Feros turned. 'You were a what?' The Retributor sounded aghast.

'A miller. I worked in a mill. Grinding corn.' Solus looked at them. 'What?'

Feros and Aetius exchanged a glance. 'Nothing,' Aetius said.

'It's just...' He shook his head. 'Never mind.' It was a reminder that heroism was more a matter of moment than birth. While many Stormcasts had been warriors in their previous lives, some had been farmers, merchants, even beggars. Faith and a moment of courage had earned them their place in the Hallowed Knights.

A shout from Tegrus, circling above, drew him from his reverie. 'What in Sigmar's name is that?' he said, staring at the edifice that rose from the mist before them.

'That, I believe, is the gate to Despair,' Morbus said.

Aetius had seen similar structures, or the ruins thereof, before. Walled harbours were common, on the coast of the Verdant Bay. Most had been destroyed by the plague-fleets of the Rotbringers. Others had been twisted to new purpose, and made into a pale copy of the swollen bastion now coming into view.

The harbour gateway was constructed from haphazardly piled stones, and immense, moss-covered logs, lashed together with rusty chains and thick vines. A decaying stockade of stone and wood extended to either side, vanishing into the thick mists, which rose from the roiling waters. The gateway portcullis was open, and galleys slid beneath it into the harbour beyond. 'Should we douse these lights?' Solus asked.

Bells rang from somewhere beyond the palisade. Morbus shook his head. 'It was too late for that the moment we entered this realm. Our coming was heard all the way to Nurgle's manse.' Aetius could hear voices raised in dolorous chanting, and the thump of drums. Reeking water vapour drifted down from the titanic waterfalls, staining everything with a vile, ashen patina. And the grinding of the tiers. Always, the grinding.

Gardus turned to look down at them from the foredeck.

'Aetius, move your Liberators to the rails. Solus, form up your Judicators midships. Feros, to your warriors will fall the oars, I'm afraid.' He gestured to Tegrus. 'Tegrus, you and your warriors will accompany Enyo. Scout ahead and see if you can find the Lord-Castellant. Do not engage the enemy unless you must. Tornus, Cadoc, remain here. We may need your speed in the hours to come.' Cadoc, for once, offered no argument. Aetius wondered if the oppressiveness of this place was beginning to affect even the unruly Knight-Azyros.

As the others moved to follow their orders, Aetius looked out over the rail at what awaited them beyond the stockade. Through the noxious mist, he could see the outline of what might have been a town, or towns. As the galley passed through the gateway, he realised that the rickety structures were not all in one place, but instead encrusted the cancerous hummocks of spongy-looking fungus dotting the surface of the water. A roaring sound rose from somewhere beyond them, and the current grew stronger. Soon, the order to lay on oars was given.

Aetius glimpsed galleys drifting in the pall, and other things besides, as he ordered his Liberators into position. He saw great, undulating shapes that moved noiselessly through the water and between the half-submerged wrecks littering their path. Ghostly orbs of colourless light floated across the water's surface, drawing near, only to then dash away.

One of his warriors pointed towards a galley that had been cracked in two. 'Look,' she said. The wreck was covered in thick moss and large clumps of fungus. Makeshift tents had been erected on the drier stretches of its hull, and pale shapes huddled about flickering balefires. At the sight of the cobalt-limned galley, the inhabitants of the wreck fled into its overgrown hold.

'Can we not aid them?' a Liberator asked.

'I do not think they would welcome us,' Aetius said. 'Stay alert. There are more than daemons and lost souls in these waters.' Far above, something shrieked. Carrion birds, or something worse, circling overhead.

Aetius hoped it wasn't an omen.

Tegrus of the Sainted Eye glided through the noisome air, searching the murky waters below for a tell-tale flash of silver. The Lord-Castellant was close by. Tegrus could smell the tang of lightning on the air, clear and sharp, despite the obfuscating stench of this place. He banked, swooping low around the garret of a shaggy house leaning haphazardly over the water. Faces peered at him from within, eyes wide with fear. What little he glimpsed of their features, before they scrambled out of sight, set his stomach to turning.

Even worse was the omnipresent grinding that haunted the air. It was the slow turning of the garden's levels on an unseen axis. The air shuddered with it. Much of the miasma that clung to everything was spewed out from between the rims of the levels as they ground against one another. He could just make out the flatulent spurts of pollution in the distance, spreading over everything.

There was foulness wherever he looked. It was in the air and the water, and in the faces of every inhabitant of this twisted realm. He saw shuffling, hunched figures fishing off crooked jetties, or wandering aimlessly along the shores of the islands. Their flesh shone with an unhealthy radiance, and their movements were stiff and full of pain. What were they? Captives? Slaves? Or had they always been here, sprouting like mushrooms in the dark? Was this what awaited the inhabitants of Ghyran if the Stormcasts failed?

Sympathy warred with revulsion. It was his duty, as one of the faithful, to help those who could not help themselves, but did that extend to people such as this? Were these lost souls worthy of help? He banished the thoughts and tried to focus on the task before him, letting the heat of his crackling feathers burn him a path through the falling rain.

Once, such a hunt would have come easily to him. But in the months since his Reforging, he'd come to realise that his mind was not as sharp as it had been. It was as if part of him had been erased. His eyes were as keen as ever, but the old instincts had been blunted somehow, and replaced with... something else. Something he could not articulate. It was as if there was some strange song, just at the edge of his hearing. It taunted and teased him, drawing his mind from his duties to the contemplation of the winds, the sound of the trees, the murmur of the storm-blown grasses. Things he'd never noticed before.

Tegrus could not help but wonder if it had something to do with the circumstances of his death. Had something been planted within him by Alarielle? She had grown Lord-Castellant Grymn a new hand. Had she done something similar to him? Whatever it was, he could not feel it here, and that absence was almost as distracting. He shook his head, and checked his warriors' positions.

His Prosecutors were spread out, to either side of him, flying in a dispersed formation. Enyo, as ever, ranged far ahead. The Knight-Venator swooped low through the mists, her wings cutting the water and causing jets of steam to billow upwards. Tegrus watched her for a moment, and then let his attention drift. He banked again, cutting left. Below him, he saw what he took to be walled gardens of filth, containing quivering rows of blighted vegetation, or skull-shaped blossoms, which screamed shrilly as his shadow fell over them. Hunched shapes tended to the shrieking flowers, and stared upwards in dull-eyed curiosity asthe Prosecutors passed overhead.

'What is this foulness?' one of Tegrus' huntsmen growled, swooping close to him. 'Everywhere we look, they till the soil, as if anything of worth could grow here.'

'A death's head garden,' Tegrus said. 'I saw its like when we burnt the Rotfane. They are farmers, tending to a blighted crop.'

'We should destroy these hovels,' the Prosecutor said. His voice was strained with emotion. Tegrus glanced at him. All of them were feeling stretched thin. The air here was almost poison, and the omnipresent stench ate away at their composure like acid.

'And, like mushrooms, they would sprout anew in a few days.' Tegrus bent his head. Something had caught his eye. 'No. Such destruction would serve no purpose, save to alert the enemy and waste what little time we have.'

'I think they're already aware of us,' the warrior muttered. The dull tones of a funerary bell began to sound from a crooked bell tower. The tower's pointed roof was decorated with a plethora of fish carcasses nailed to the mossy slates, and something bloated and giggling dangled from the weathercock. More bells sounded, in response to the first, until all the air was trembling with the vibration of them.

Tegrus flinched back as an arrow cut past him to embed itself in a nearby rooftop. He turned and saw Enyo hurtling towards them as swiftly as her wings could carry her. She'd loosed the shaft to catch his attention. She signalled urgently, and he followed her gestures.

Down below, dark shapes nosed through the narrow, winding canals between islands. Though they were shrouded by the mists, he nonetheless recognised the shapes of galleys. A dozen or more, converging swiftly on the blue glow of the Stormcasts' commandeered vessel. The thump of drums echoed up, and the watery glow of balefire illuminated the decks, revealing the daemonic shapes which crowded them.

How had they got so close without him noticing? Was there some enchantment at work, or had he simply been inattentive?

'Spread out,' he said, even as he cursed his carelessness. 'Strike swiftly. Aim for the rudders and the masts, and retreat after.' Without waiting for a reply, he swooped around a ruined turret, scattering a flock of scaly pigeons, and dived down through the rain towards the closest galley. There was no time to send warning. All they could do was hope to delay the enemy, and alert the others with the crash of battle.

As his hammers shimmered into his waiting hands, Tegrus prayed that it would be enough.

'You can feel it, can't you, Torglug?' Gatrog said. The Rot-bringer stood at the farthest extension of his chains, so close Tornus could smell the stink of his armour. 'How familiar this all is?'

'Torglug is never coming here,' Tornus said. His eyes remained fixed on the islands, with their tottering towers and slumping rooftops. Strange birds, their feathers waxy with rot, watched the passing galley with flat eyes. Their cries sounded like laughter. Every mould-drenched wall and square of sloughing thatch seemed to twist itself into a leering, jovial face. His hands tightened around his bow.

'I find that hard to believe. The Woodsman was most devout.' Gatrog shuffled closer, so that he stood beside Tornus. 'It is sad to see faith twisted so.'

Tornus looked at him. 'Yes.' He wished he were anywhere

else. Even in the air, with Tegrus and the others. Instead, Gardus had tasked him with guarding their prisoner.

Gatrog smiled and nodded, acknowledging the point. 'It is even as Blightmaster Gahool said, in his thirty-second missive to the Oakdwell King. Faith, like a river, must occasionally find its course altered, for the good of the land.'

'The Oakdwell King is being dead,' Tornus said. He knew this, because Torglug had been the one to kill the ancient creature, in his robes of leaf and vine. He could still hear the snap of an antler as it broke off in his fist. Still feel the warm gush of sap, as it coursed over his hand, and the Oakdwell King gasped his last.

'And his people serve the King of all Flies to this day,' Gatrog said, solemnly. He peered at Tornus. 'They live, because they chose a new course.'

Tornus said nothing. Gatrog leaned close. 'The King of all Flies offers life, my friend. Freedom from doubt and pain. Freedom from those raw, red things that taint even the smallest of moments. To know, to understand and give oneself over to him, is to know, with unalterable certainty, that you are loved.'

'His love is being a lie.'

Gatrog looked away. 'No. The lie is that there is any hope at all. That there is something better awaiting you, in the dark and the quiet.' He shook his head. 'Hope is the chain that drags you in the wake of the universal wheel. Free yourself of it, Torglug.'

'I am not being Torglug,' Tornus said. But, even as he spoke, he heard a rasping, glottal whisper of rebuttal... *you are, you are*. Ospheonis stirred on his shoulder, talons tightening their grip. He wondered if the star-eagle could hear what he heard.

'You are, for I see the seed of holy despair in you.' Gatrog thrust a grimy finger into Tornus' chest. 'Like a corpse-blossom, buried under ash. Awaiting the rain, to draw it to the surface once more. Torglug you were, and are...'

Tornus caught Gatrog's finger and twisted it back. It popped free with a squeal of metal and a crack of bone. He stared at it in disgust, and flung it at the Rotbringer. Gatrog scrabbled to retrieve it, cursing. 'I am not being him anymore. Torglug is being dead, and only Tornus is remaining.'

'That which is not dead can forever lie, until even Death himself dies,' Gatrog said, as he tried to reattach his finger. 'Those touched by Nurgle cannot die. When the old sun goes cold and dark, we will sink beneath the ground to await the touch of the new, in millennia to come. Not even the cursed light of Azyr can sear the realms clean.'

Tornus caught Gatrog by the throat and shoved him back against the mast. 'That is being a lie. I am being cleansed. As you are being, soon.'

Gatrog's eyes widened. 'What?'

'There is being a seed in me, you are saying? Well, there is being one in you as well. I am seeing it, earlier. It is being the seed of humanity. It is being the flicker of order, amidst the chaos.' Tornus spoke softly, intently. 'Your rules, your honour, is it being playacting, or something real?'

'How dare you question my honour?' Gatrog growled. 'If I but had a blade, I would silence you.' His hands clenched uselessly, and he sagged. 'But I do not. So we must fence with words instead.' He glared at Tornus. 'You were a hero, once. What happened?'

'I am seeing the light,' Tornus said. He stepped back. 'As you will be seeing it.'

'Never. Better death than such a dishonour.' He stopped, as a glittering blade came to rest against his throat. Cadoc Kel studied the Rotbringer.

'Easily done. But say the word, and I shall feed you to whatever passes for fish in these waters.' Cadoc looked at Tornus. 'Why do you insist on talking to this... thing?'

'Every deed is having a seed which is remaining,' Tornus said. He used his bow to pull the starblade from Gatrog's throat. 'I am learning such, at the Lifewells.'

'These would be the same Lifewells you destroyed?' Cadoc sheathed his blade with a flourish. 'Yes, I can see that you must have learned much from them.'

Tornus flinched. 'That was not being me.'

'Oh, but it was.' Cadoc gestured to Gatrog. 'On this one point, I agree with this creature. It was you.' He leaned close. 'You lost your faith, and your people suffered. You have found it again, but how do we know that you will not lose it once more?'

'I am being redeemed,' Tornus said. His words sounded weak, even to him.

'There is no redemption,' Cadoc said. 'No forgiveness. There is only faith. You either have it, or you do not.' His hand slipped to the hilt of his sword. 'Do you have faith?'

Tornus' fingers curled into a fist. He wanted nothing more than to strike the Knight-Azyros. To pummel him into silence. Instead, he forced himself to relax. 'My faith is not being yours to judge.' He glanced at Gatrog. 'Or his.'

'That remains to be seen,' Cadoc said. He clapped a hand on Tornus' shoulder then strode away. Tornus watched him go. Was this a test, then? Was Sigmar judging his worthiness even now?

Ospheonis chirruped and flapped his wings. Tornus turned, scanning the waters. They gleamed greenly in the pale light of Arghus, the Plague-Moon. Something was moving out there. He heard the thud of drums and the slap of oars. Swiftly, he drew an arrow and loosed it into the mist. A scream pierced the air as the arrow struck home. Lightning flashed in the distance, revealing the outline of something drawing close. He heard the crash of thunder, and recognised the sound of a Prosecutor's hammer. A moment later, the black prow of a galley pierced the murk and surged towards them.

'To arms,' Tornus called. 'To arms!'

'Wake up, sir knight.'

Grymn stirred in his chains. Blearily, he shook his head, trying to clear it. Had he fallen asleep? A hand, small and smelling of strange unguents, stroked the cheek of his war-mask. He jerked back, alert now. Flies crawled across his helmet and chest-plate.

The woman who stood before him was beautiful and repugnant in equal measure. She was dressed as a noblewoman of the Jade Kingdoms, in a rotting gown, and her face was covered by a filth-encrusted veil. He was thankful for that, as he had no desire to see the face beneath. Her hair hung in a lank coil down her back, and trailed after her like a serpent's tail. A corroded chalice, dotted with maggots and boils in place of gemstones, hung from a corded belt about her narrow waist.

'Who...' he began. He trailed off as the smell of her hit him. She stank of damp rock and sour water, of mossy coolness and wet shadows. But beneath that was a more foetid odour, one that was hot and scalding. She reached up with pale fingers, wet with what might have been blood, and traced them across his chest.

'Seven days from never, we dance always and do not fall,' she said, drawing shapes on his chest-plate. 'History dreams of us, my knight. We are its shadow and soil, all in one. We carry his blessings on our skin, wherever we go. We shimmer with the light of black stars, so that those who know the way might dance in our wake.' She leaned close, and he could see things squirming beneath her veil. 'The burning in your blood will set you free.'

Grymn closed his eyes. 'You are not here. You are some evil dream.'

He felt warm, wet breath wash across his face. 'I am a dream,' she said. 'Your dream. Will you, won't you, dance with me?'

'Begone, witch,' Grymn snarled, twisting his head aside. A sound like dead leaves dancing across stones greeted his words. He opened his eyes, and saw that she was gone. She had never been there in the first place.

She was beautiful, was she not?

Bubonicus' voice tore through him like a spasm. Grymn's hands curled into his fists, and he relished the sensation, painful as it was. He preferred pain to numbness.

'She was not,' he said.

You have no eye for beauty, then. She is life itself, that sweet lady. Queens are as the dust beneath her gentle hooves, and goddesses even less. You should feel honoured, Lorrus.

'Do not speak my name.'

I shall. Soon it, like all that you are, will be mine.

Grymn shook his head. 'Who was she, then?'

Do you not recognise the Lady of Cankerwall, when she graces you with her presence? For shame. It is no wonder you did not bow.

'I am chained up.'

That as well. Laughter burbled up inside Grymn, threatening to burst through his lips. It was not his laughter. Grymn felt sick. He wanted nothing more than to cut himself open and drag out the cancer he felt festering in his gut. Tear it out, in red, wet gobbets, and fling it into a cleansing fire.

And you would die in the doing so.

'Better death than whatever it is you intend,' Grymn said.

Then you'd best be quick about it.

Heavy steps thumped on the stair. Spume ducked beneath the entrance, followed by a group of stunted figures. The creatures wore filthy robes over their malformed bodies, and carried a large cauldron on their shoulders. They moaned a soft, sad song as they went about their labours. Boiling liquid sloshed over the rim as they set the cauldron down, and Grymn gagged at the smell.

'Still breathing, then? Good.' Spume scratched himself, dislodging fat, black lice from beneath his armour. 'I'd hate for you to miss this.'

'Where are we?' Grymn demanded.

'The Port of Despair,' a thin, hissing voice answered. A hunched, feminine shape stepped out from behind Spume and shuffled towards him. 'Is this the one?'

'Do you see any other shiny-skins, Urslaug?' Spume drawled, dismissing the slaves. They trooped back above decks, still moaning their sad song.

'Mm.' The woman peered up at Grymn, her eyes hidden beneath a filthy blindfold. She might once have been beautiful, but centuries of neglect had left her a ruin of a woman. Her body was frail and bent, her hair lank and tangled. The faded remnants of tattoos marked her grimy skin, and Grymn wondered who she had been.

'A witch,' she said, as if reading his thoughts. She reached out as if to touch him, and then drew back. 'There's a storm in this one. Lightning in his veins and thunder in his bones.'

'Yes, and silver on his fingers. Can you divine his secrets?' Spume sounded testy. 'Or should I take you back to your garden and leave you to tend your death's heads in peace?'

'If I thought you would, I might say the latter.' Urslaug cocked her head and whistled.

Tiny, bloated shapes bounded and bounced down the steps into the hold, giggling and shrieking. Grymn felt his stomach churn as the nurglings spilled and slid across the deck. They clambered up Urslaug's robes and clawed pitifully at Spume's shins. He kicked them aside, eliciting screams of laughter. Urslaug gathered several into her arms, and stroked their bulbous heads. She turned towards Grymn. 'It's a very nice garden, I assure you.'

'They all tend gardens here. Grubbers and growers.' Spume chuckled. 'They refuse to give in, ye see,' he said. He tapped the side of his head. 'Stubborn, like you. So here they stay. Too afraid to travel deeper, or attempt escape. Too foolish to resign themselves, as they ought. So they sit, and grow moss in their gardens and on themselves.'

'We are necessary to Grandfather's great plan,' the witch said. 'Even as much as yourself, reaver.'

'Pfaugh. What use a farmer, when you can simply take the crops of another?' Spume's tentacles yanked gently on one of her wormy braids. 'I am the fire that makes the soil black and fertile. A true servant of Nurgle, and Life itself. Just as you once were.'

'And who tends the soil, when the fire burns itself out?'

Spume shrugged. 'The Lord of All Things provides.'

Urslaug shook her head. 'And that is why they say you are a fool, Gutrot Spume. Even the Woodsman, in his madness, recognised the purpose behind his actions. But you might as well serve the Blood God.'

Spume grunted, and his grip on her hair tightened, eliciting a pained hiss. 'Careful what you say to me, Urslaug. My patience runs thin these days.'

A fat spark of balefire leapt between them. Spume released her and stepped back, swatting at the flames that smouldered on his chest. 'As does mine,' Urslaug said. 'I grew tired of your bullying long ago, Spume.'

'Then you'd best be about your task, eh?' Spume wriggled a tentacle towards Grymn.

'Many have tried to divine the secrets of these half-souls,' Urslaug said, as she selected a squealing nurgling and gave it a gentle squeeze. The tiny daemon giggled in pleasure. 'They all failed.' It gave a squeak of pure delight as she tossed it into the cauldron. 'What makes you think that I'll be any more successful in my own attempt?'

'I have confidence in the quality of your cunning, witch,' Spume said, running a calloused tendril over the blade of his axe. 'The knowledge you seek would earn the pair of us much esteem in the eyes of the Lord of All Things.'

'And you'd willingly share such plunder, would you?'

'I pay my debts,' Spume said.

Urslaug laughed until she coughed. 'You lie as well as you sing, Lord of Tentacles.'

Spume thumped the deck with the haft of his axe. 'And your laughter is as shrill as ever. I can have you thrown overboard, if that is more to your liking.'

'Peace,' the witch murmured. She raised her blindfold and glanced at Grymn with a single, pus-laden orb. The eye was not that of a human, or even an animal. Instead, it was a dollop of daemonic putrescence, smoothed and shaped into a semblance of an eye. It glistened evilly in the light of the balefire lanterns, swimming with obscene shapes. Grymn turned away from its gaze, sickened to his core.

'Two souls,' she said, lowering her blindfold. 'There are two souls in that body.'

Spume nodded. 'So I suspected.' He raised his axe. 'I'll be cutting the one out, and salvaging the other. Only I need to know which is which.'

'Hard to say, hard to say,' Urslaug wheezed, stirring her cauldron with a finger. 'One thing I do know is you'll have to fight to keep either. Hark at that.' She cupped an ear.

Grymn stiffened. He'd heard it as well. The whisper-crack of whirling hammers. The growl of lightning unleashed. 'No,' he said, unable to believe his ears.

'What are you babbling about? I – by the wormy bones of Bolathrax!' Spume stumbled as something shook the ship down to its barnacles. The prisoners in the bilge-cage screamed and groaned as the hull sprouted numerous leaks.

Urslaug chuckled and tossed another nurgling in the cauldron. She hadn't stumbled at all when the ship shook. 'It'll take me some time to brew what I need. You'd best go and see to whatever that is.'

As Spume thudded back above decks, cursing with every step, Urslaug turned to Grymn. A chill ran through him as she gave a tombstone smile.

'Now… we have much to discuss, you and I.'

CHAPTER FIFTEEN

BLACK SAILS

'Think on this, my friend. The realms, as we know them, are but the echo of an echo. Iterations, extending outwards into an infinity of possibility from a singular source.' Angstun leaned forward, gesticulating for emphasis. 'Is not that source – the wellspring, if you will – the truth of the thing?'

It had been three days since Gardus had entered the realmgate. Three days with no sign of any of them. Three days of trying to bury his worry beneath arguments about truth, beauty and the nature of all things. There were worse ways to spend time.

'More true, you mean, than the air we breathe, or the sun that warms our faces?' Yare asked, frowning thoughtfully. The Stormcast and the old man sat together on the broken skull of the leviathan, sheltering in the shade of a tattered lean-to. 'Ansolm of Talbion had it that to conceive of a thing lends it a certain weight of truth. In that sense, the world around us is as true as your wellspring. An equal truth, in fact.'

Angstun shook his head. 'You cannot lend equal weight to an echo, Yare.'

'Ah, but who is to say what is an echo, and what is the voice from which it emanates?' Yare smiled widely and clapped his hands. 'Indeed, it is even as Dullas of Rhyran said.'

'And now he twists the words of the Sage of Rhyran to make his point,' Angstun said to one of the nearby Judicators who stood on guard around the skull. 'Have you ever heard such blatant sophistry?'

'He makes a good point, though,' the Judicator mused. He scratched his chin. 'Sarthe of Thyria maintained that reality was a communal effort.'

'I'm surrounded by sophists,' Angstun bawled despairingly.

'Harsh words,' Yare protested. 'My reasoning is built on the bedrock of Dullas and Ansolm. The Verdant School itself. You call that sophistry?'

'Fine, casuistry,' Angstun amended, waving a hand in surrender. Before Yare could reply, a shout brought him to his feet. He saw a Liberator hurrying towards him, mortals scattering before him like frightened birds. Despite his best efforts, there were still too many people in the fortress. Too many refused to leave Yare, and Yare refused to leave until the last of the innocents were safely gone. Angstun leapt off the skull, and crashed down with a rattle of sigmarite. 'Balogun, what is it?'

'The Knight-Heraldor requests your presence, my lord. There are… things… coming out of the realmgate.' Balogun sounded uncertain.

'Daemons?'

Balogun began to nod, but his head snapped back as a flickering balefire arrow sprouted from the eye-slit of his war-mask. Angstun spun, and saw a group of Rotbringers charging across the courtyard. He barked an order. The Judicators loosed a volley, dropping most of them, including the archers. This wasn't the first such attack the remaining Rotbringers had made. The citadel was too large, with too many nooks and crannies, to be searched effectively. Those Rotbringers who hadn't fled periodically launched suicidal raids, attempting to retake parts of the fortress.

'We should have flattened this place when we had the chance,' Angstun snarled, planting his standard. 'Yare, calm your people. We can't protect them if they're running about.' The old man began to shout, hands raised. His voice carried easily. Then, he had been an orator before he'd been caught.

The courtyard trembled, water spurting up through the cracks. Angstun gave a brief thought to Kurunta, fighting down in the dark. He would need reinforcements. But then he thought of nothing save defending himself, as a roaring blightking stumped towards him, rusty blade raised over his lumpen head.

Angstun shattered the sword, and then its owner's skull. The blightking flopped to the ground. Spears sought Angstun's life. The Order armsmen were fanatical and determined to follow their masters into death. Angstun obliged them. Soon, his hammer was wet with blood and brain matter. The remaining Rotbringers fled, scattering across the courtyard. Judicators brought down those they could.

Before he could order his warriors to hunt them down, he heard a cry from above. A Prosecutor swooped low. 'Black sails, my lord,' she called out. 'Looks like they've regained their courage.'

Angstun cursed. Many of the Rotbringers had fled in galleys and barges when the citadels had fallen. It looked as if someone had finally taken command of the rabble. 'Do what you can to sink a few. And send word to the retinues in the other citadels. I want them back here now, at the double!'

'More trouble, my friend?' Yare called down. The old man was pale, but unbent.

'It is time for you to leave, Yare,' Angstun said. He looked around at the other mortals. 'All of you.'

'We will fight,' a mortal said. The man was missing an eye and a hand, and covered in stained bandages. He held a length of iron, pulled from one of the cages. Others took up the call. Angstun looked around, chagrined.

'If you fight, you will die,' he said bluntly.

'All men die,' Yare said. Two of his followers helped him to the ground. 'Not all men die for a great purpose. Would you deny us that, my friend?'

'I would rather you not die at all,' Angstun said.

'Take it up with the gods,' Yare said. 'We will defend this place, and our peoples for so long as the gods will.' He smiled. 'Besides, we have not yet finished our discussion. Truth must be pursued at every opportunity.'

Angstun stared at him. Then he laughed. 'Yes, I suppose it must.' He looked around. His forces were sparse, but they would serve well enough. What his Judicators lacked in numbers, they more than made up for in accuracy. He turned to one. 'Falkus, make your way to the walls. I will join you, in time.' He signalled a nearby Liberator. 'Advika, gather your retinue. Reinforce Kurunta. Pass along my apologies, but I must stay here.'

She slammed the flat of her warblade against her shield. 'As you command, Knight-Vexillor,' she said. He watched her lead her warriors away, and turned back to Yare.

'I am going to the walls. Will you see to things here?'

The old man nodded. 'To the best of my humble ability.' He

cocked his head. 'Do not die, friend Angstun. That would be a poor way to end our conversation.'

'I will do my best.' Angstun uprooted his standard. As he set off, he couldn't help but wonder at the timing of it all. Daemons coming through the realmgate, and now this attack? It felt as if the jaws of a trap were closing about them all, and there was nothing they could do about it, save endure. He shook his head.

'Wherever you are, Gardus, I hope this was worth it.'

Gardus and Tallon stormed across the boarding plank, heedless of the green flames which rose to either side of them. His hammer snapped out, pulping a daemonic visage. His runeblade followed suit, its tip carving a bloody gouge across a bulbous eye. He kicked the blinded daemon from his path, and Tallon pounced upon it, beak tearing at its flesh. The gryph-hound hadn't left Gardus' side since they'd found him, and the Lord-Celestant was grateful for the animal's presence.

Gardus dropped onto the deck of the galley. The vessel, like the others floating on the plague-slick waters, was aflame. Daemons and corrupted warriors raced to intercept him as he moved towards the rowers' benches. 'Enyo,' Gardus roared, without stopping.

A rain of arrows descended from on high, punching through armour, flesh and bone. Bodies fell to the deck, twitching in their death throes. Enyo swooped low around the mast, loosing an arrow as she sped towards the stern. A plaguebearer tipped over the rail, clawing at the shaft in its skull.

Gardus' runeblade chopped through a coil of chain. The souls at the oars watched him as blankly as all the others had, unable to even conceive of freedom. He looked about him, frustration growing. Behind him, something laughed.

He turned to see a distended mountain of a beast squatting behind a rawhide drum atop the aft deck. The creature smiled widely, split lips curling away from greyish teeth. It might have been a man, once, but now it was shapeless with decay and covered in mossy scales.

'They are lost to you, silver one. Lost even to the light that seeps out of your husk.' Its voice was like boiling mud, and it had stretched, reptilian features. 'All that reside here belong to the Lord of All Things, body and soul. Even a humble musician, such as myself.' The creature rose on barrel legs and hefted a filth-encrusted flail. 'Even you, though you do not yet know it.'

'We are the faithful. And our faith protects us.'

The creature threw back its head and laughed uproariously. 'For now.' It looked around. 'We were told of your coming, and sought to claim the bounty on your souls. But we were too over-eager. Every plague-dog out for himself. Others will not be so foolish.' It waggled a fat finger at him. 'The harder you struggle, the deeper you sink, eh?'

'Unless you have wings.'

The creature stiffened, an almost comical expression of dismay passing across its reptilian features. It looked down at the tip of the blade jutting between its sagging pectorals. Then it toppled forward, crushing its drums beneath its limp frame. Cadoc held up his starblade, studying the black bile coating it. 'Why do they talk so much?' He stepped over the twitching hulk. 'It is as if they think we are so foolish as to listen to their lies.'

Gardus straightened. 'It told me one thing of use. This attack was not simply by chance.' He looked out over the harbour, scanning the wrecks that littered the waters. Most of the galleys had been destroyed at a distance, scythed clean of crew by arrows and lightning, or the hammers of the Prosecutors. Those that had managed to draw close had been boarded by his warriors and made to regret their eagerness to get to grips.

'Nothing is by chance, Steel Soul. We are the blade of Sigmar, thrust into the very heart of the Dark Gods.' Cadoc sounded ecstatic. He looked around and laughed. 'Even here, the thunder of Sigmar will be heard. We shall make the realms tremble with the strength of our faith.'

'I fear this realm trembles with the anger of its creator, rather than any display of ours.' Gardus turned and saw Morbus making his way towards him, leaning on his staff. The Lord-Relictor's armour crawled with thin strands of lightning, and his eyes shone with a faint radiance. From the way he moved, Gardus could tell he was in pain.

'Morbus, are you hurt?'

'We lost four,' Morbus said. 'Four more souls.' He pressed his hand to his chest. 'I have them all. But I do not know for how much longer.' He looked at Gardus. 'Our brethren are heavy, Gardus. And they are burning me up from the inside out.'

Gardus closed his eyes. This was his fault. He had plunged headlong into this place, attempting to save a warrior who was already lost. And now, his chamber would suffer because of it. He took a shaky breath, trying to push the sudden surge of guilt back down. Now was not the time. Later, perhaps. If he survived. But not now.

'Look upon ruin, and remember these words,' Cadoc said, as if reciting an old lesson learned long ago. Gardus glanced at him, and saw that the Knight-Azyros was watching the enslaved souls, hunched on their benches. 'Though you cut a man's spirit, he must bleed all the same.' His hand inched towards his beacon. 'Let me end their suffering, Steel Soul.

Let me set their bodies alight, so that their souls might rise like smoke.' Morbus caught his wrist.

'And where would those souls rise *to*, Cadoc?' the Lord-Relictor hissed. 'If you think they suffer now, imagine what torments await them upon dissolution. Soul stuff is the mulch of these gardens. Killing them will only serve to feed new-born horrors.'

Cadoc jerked his wrist from Morbus' grasp. 'Then what would you have us do, Stormforged? Ignore this blasphemy?'

'No. Endure it.' Morbus pointed. 'There is nothing we can do. Not here. Grymn's soulfire grows dim, and there might well be oceans of filth between us by the time you finish sacrificing these lost souls for your own grandeur.'

Cadoc spluttered, his eyes blazing with anger. Gardus extended his arm, separating the two. 'Peace, Prince of Ekran. Set aside your anger, and you will see that he is right.' Cadoc growled wordlessly, but subsided. Gardus looked at the rowers. Some were clambering over the rail, to slip soundlessly into the water. Others simply sat, staring at nothing. 'Is there anything we can do for them?'

Morbus turned away. 'They were drawn here. Their souls glow rotten with despair and the ailments that spring from it – envy, hatred and all that comes with them. And any attempt to help them will only draw Nurgle's attention to us all the more swiftly. Already, I can feel the weight of his stirring...' He trailed off, head bent.

Gardus cast a wary glance to the sky, but saw nothing save the roiling, black clouds of smoke. He stroked Tallon's bloody skull, and the gryph-hound gave a shrill, rumbling purr. 'Let us get back to the galley before this wreck sinks.'

When the Stormcasts had returned to their vessel, Gardus was met by Tegrus. 'Steel Soul, one ship escaped,' the

Prosecutor-Prime said. 'I... I did not see it in the smoke.' Tegrus seemed hesitant. Uncertain. Gardus waved his excuses aside.

'It was not your fault. Without your quick thinking, our foes might have overwhelmed us.' He looked at Morbus. 'Could this fleeing galley be the one that holds Grymn?'

Morbus nodded wearily. 'It stands to reason. I can feel his essence growing faint, as if he is moving away from us. And at all speed.' He pointed his reliquary staff. 'There. That way. Towards the heart of this realm.'

'That was the direction the galley was fleeing in,' Tegrus said.

Gardus frowned and extended his hammer towards Tornus and Gatrog. The Rotbringer had remained chained to the mast for the duration of the battle, and the Knight-Venator had stood sentinel over him, dealing death from afar. 'What is in that direction? More aqueducts?'

'Yes,' Gatrog said. 'They are crude things, and overgrown. It will be slow going. And even slower when you reach the tier below.'

'Where is the galley going? Is there some fortress or sanctuary there?'

'There is no shelter in the third level. It's a wilderness,' Gatrog said, glaring. 'They will likely be heading for the walled city of Despondency, on the fourth tier. Most captives taken in the first tier are bound for the soul-markets there.'

'Is there any way to get ahead of them?'

'Not unless you can fly,' Gatrog said. He smiled. 'But I can show you the quickest route. It will be dangerous, though. Few ships survive that journey. Most take the slow current, around the edges of the jungle, until they reach the outer rim of the Great Vent, the stone tunnel that coils around and down to the very gates of the city. But there are other ways.'

'We cannot trust him,' Cadoc said. 'He will send us to our deaths.'

Gatrog snorted. 'Aye, and so I will, but I do not lie. Upon my honour, I do not lie.' He shoved himself to his feet. 'I swore an oath, and I will fulfil it. They will be waiting for you at the Great Vent. And in greater numbers than here. Only by bypassing the obvious route do you stand any chance of reaching your goal.'

'What is this route?'

The pox-knight smiled, his expression eerie in the light cast by the flames. 'A way even daemons fear to tread.'

'Stripe their backs to the bone, Durg,' Spume roared, as another galley erupted in flame behind them. 'Get us moving. We need to get out of here.' He braced himself against the mast, glaring out at the destruction. The shiny-skins had torn through the other galleys like the Red Plague, shattering the shaggy ships and leaving them burning. In a way, it was impressive. Even Khornates couldn't have done it so quickly.

Durg uncoiled its whip and gave it a snap. 'Work, you dogs! Row, or you'll be food for the poxwyrms.' The plaguebearer stamped up and down amidships, cursing and snarling in his flat monotone. Spume nodded in satisfaction as the oars began to creak in time to the thudding of the drums. Speed was their ally today.

The black galley smashed aside a shattered wreck, spilling its remaining crew into the soupy water. Daemons clawed at the hull, trying to clamber aboard. Spume's crew pried them off with boathooks or lashed their claws with thorny whips. He had no room for the weak aboard his ship. A pall of smoke rolled across the water, momentarily obscuring the battle. Spume refused to relax. The shiny-skins could fly faster than his galley could move.

He'd underestimated them before, and paid the price. And now he'd done it again. Angry, he slammed his fist against the mast. He looked at his hand, at the splinters and the oozing blood, and felt a sense of calm settle over him. Suddenly, he understood what the flydandy's message had meant. He'd assumed the Stormcasts would be driven back, or else contained in the swampy outer ring.

But it seemed that wasn't what Grandfather wanted. A bark of laughter slipped from him. He was to be the bait, drawing them deeper into the garden, and to the walls of Desolation itself. It was a simple enough plan, he supposed.

Draw the shiny-skins in, and close off any route of escape. Tighten the noose, slowly but surely, until they finally realised that they were on the scaffold. Their despair would be all the sweeter when that realisation hit.

'And what will be my reward for bringing that about, I wonder?' The Court of Ruination was a snake pit second only to the bureaucracy of the Impossible Fortress. Many was the loyal warrior who had been ground to mulch by their machinations. Spume didn't intend to suffer the same fate.

There were places he could go to seek refuge. The Ossified Hills, even the Septic Isles. But none were certain to be there when he arrived. Parts of the garden were ever shifting and changing according to the whims of its master, and if Grandfather had decided his fate, there'd be no escaping it.

No. He'd never run from a fight before, and didn't intend to start now. He'd stay the course, and prove himself Grandfather's most favoured son.

Screams danced on the plague wind. The slave galleys of the Eternal Swamps had never been a match for the invaders. Their captains were lazy, their crews fat with easy meat. The daemons aboard those ships were unfit even for service in

Grandfather's blighted legions. It was no surprise that they'd been defeated so quickly. For too long they'd pillaged the waters of the first tier, hunting souls that couldn't fight back. But Spume was made of sterner stuff than that.

Perhaps this was the way Grandfather intended for him to prove his worth. He'd ride out this storm, lead them on, and stand tall against the winds. And, at the end, he'd claim the glory for himself. Perhaps he would even ascend to the Court of Ruin. They would name him Grand Admiral of the Plague-Fleets.

But if he intended to turn this to his advantage, he needed to know the secrets of the captive dangling in his hold. He raised his axe. 'Whip them harder, Durg. I would be gone from these waters as soon as possible.'

Order given, he started towards the hold. It was time to let Urslaug know that she'd rejoined his crew, whatever her feelings on the matter. He smiled, pleased at the thought. It had been too long since he'd sailed without a witch at his side.

'We are moving,' the witch said, peering up. 'What has that fool done now?' The balefire lanterns twisted on their hooks, casting weird shadows across the hull.

'Maybe you'd best go and see,' Grymn said. He could hear the crack of thunder and, for an instant, wondered again if someone, perhaps Sigmar himself, had come for him. As he had earlier, he dismissed the thought with a savage twitch of his head. No one was coming. Not even Gardus would be so foolish. Doubtless some sorcery was at work. The servants of Chaos warred with each other as often as they did anyone else. And Spume seemed like the sort to have plenty of enemies, even here.

Urslaug twitched an admonishing finger. 'Shame. Do you

think me so foolish as that, just because moss grows on my skull?'

Grymn didn't bother to reply. She leaned close. 'Or perhaps it's not you, eh?' She held up a giggling nurgling. 'What do you say, my pretty? Which soul so insults me?' The little daemon chortled and bounced on her palms.

'I don't know what you're talking about.'

'Another insult,' she said, tossing the nurgling over her shoulder. It struck a beam and slid to the floor with a wet plop. 'I know the stink of the Order of the Fly when I smell it. Their chivalry is like a canker, infecting all it touches. Honour. Pfaugh. What is honour, save the hope of order?'

Insulting witch! Would that I had a blade and a hand to wield it with.

'And if you had, what then, pox-knight? Remove my head?' Grymn jerked, and looked up in shock. She cackled and tugged on an ear. 'Yes, I hear him. And I suppose you would kill me if you could, pox-knight. You lot are worse at taking criticism than even fat-bellied Spume. His arrogance, at least, is tolerable in its simplicity. Yours is unearned, save in your own delusions.' The witch spat into her cauldron.

'You speak harshly of your ally,' Grymn said. 'Or is he your master?'

'He's a fool and a braggart,' the witch said, peering up at Grymn. 'Brave, but no wiser than that kraken which shares his skin.' She thrust a finger up to its knuckle into her eye, and withdrew the glistening digit with agonising slowness. With it, she painted a strange sigil on the curve of the hull. 'Else he would not have stopped here.'

'You intend treachery,' Grymn said, testing his chains. He needed to keep the creature talking, keep her from beginning whatever sorcery she intended. 'That is to be expected.'

'And what would you know of it?' she snapped.

'I know that you are a broken thing. Without hope or beauty in you.'

Urslaug stared at him, her eye expanding and contracting like a beating heart. 'Then you know nothing at all,' she said, after a moment. 'Like Spume, you are ignorant and deserve whatever fate befalls you.'

She pressed her sticky fingers to his chest. He flinched back, and she laughed. 'Scared? Good. No reason to be, though. I have no intention of doing as he wishes. No soul-carving for you this day.' She smiled, displaying brown teeth. 'No. Others will be interested in you as well, I'd wager. Ones more willing to cross my palm with something of real value... ah.' Grymn saw that the mark she'd made on the hull was glowing.

'*Why do you summon me, witch?*'

The voice shivered dully through the planks of the hull, causing Grymn to shudder in his chains. 'Not just you, Gulax,' she said. 'Wait but a moment and all will be revealed.' Swiftly, she drew a second sigil with a dripping finger, this one on the deck. Greenish vapour rose from it, twisting into the long, lean shape of a verminous, horned skull.

'*Speak-speak, hag. I have no time to waste-spend in idle talk!*'

'If you didn't, you wouldn't have answered my summoning, Rancik,' Urslaug said, sinking inelegantly to her haunches. 'I have something here that the both of you might be interested in. Something I am willing to barter, should you be of a mind.'

'*I am Filthblade of the Rotguard, witch. I do not barter,*' Gulax rumbled.

'No? Then you may leave.' The witch spoke confidently, but Grymn could see the tension in her withered form. She turned her pulsing eye on the smoking sigil on the floor. 'What about you, Bleak One? Or have the Children of the Great Corrupter also lost their taste for honest trade?'

'*I am listening-heeding, yes-yes… speak-talk, quick-fast.*'

'I have a soul for you. A soul heavy with the stuff of the storm. You know of that which I speak.' She sat back on her heels.

'*Yesss,*' both voices murmured in unison.

'I offer it up to one of you, in return for…'

'Death.'

Urslaug shot to her feet with a squawk. She whirled, hands full of balefire, but not swiftly enough. Spume's axe swept out and thudded home in a support beam. Urslaug's head tumbled into her own cauldron, as her body slumped to the deck.

Spume kicked her body and shook his head in disgust. 'This is the thanks I get for offering ye a share of the plunder.'

'*I know that voice,*' Gulax growled. '*Thief. Corsair. Liar. Reaver…*'

Spume chopped into the sigil, obliterating it, and silencing the basso voice. He whirled, ready to do the same to the second sigil, but it had already faded to a smudge of ash on the deck. He cursed. 'I should have known. Never trust a woman, or a witch, shiny-skin.'

Grymn laughed. 'It seems you are to be undone by your own kind, beast.'

Spume lifted Grymn's chin with the edge of his axe. 'Competition is a fact of life, in the garden or otherwise. And I welcome the chance to prove my superiority.'

'Let me loose, and I'll prove which of us is superior,' Grymn said, with a cough. Something wriggled from between his lips and plopped to the deck. Spume trod on the maggot. He chuckled.

'And who said that, then? Ye, or the worm that gnaws?'

'Either will serve,' Grymn said. 'For neither of us care much for you.'

Spume threw back his head and gave a hoarse laugh. 'Good. I've friends aplenty, and need no more of them. But good enemies are in short supply.' He kicked over Urslaug's cauldron, spilling the bubbling brew everywhere. Nurglings fled in every direction, warbling in dismay. The souls in the hold screamed in agony as the liquid spilled through the bars of the cage. The Rotbringer scooped up a tentacleful of the hissing stew, and slapped it across Grymn's chest-plate. The tentacle writhed, smearing the concoction. Grymn could feel the heat of it through his armour.

'It might please you to know that you're not the only one of your sort in the garden,' Spume said. 'Someone is out there, tearing apart ships. Ye must be friendlier than ye seem, if they'd come all this way to get ye.'

Grymn felt a spark of hope. Then, a rush of anger. What fool had come for him? There were easier ways to die, if they wished. Spume wrapped a tendril around his helmet and forced his head up. 'I know now why Father Decay is interested in you. And why I've been commanded to drag your carcass to Desolation. It's not just you the Court of Ruination is interested in.'

Grymn didn't know what Spume was ranting about, but he understood the implications well enough. He sagged in his chains, and Spume chortled. 'Aye, ye see it now, don't ye? The deeper ye are taken into the garden, the deeper they'll have to come to get ye. Why settle for one drink, when ye can have a cask, eh?' He stepped back. 'It's no wonder Father Decay wants ye, the fat lubber. To offer up such a prize to Grandfather is a worthy dream indeed.'

And one you will not willingly share, I'd warrant, Bubonicus murmured.

Spume twitched, and chuckled. 'No need to worry, though. I'll offer you up to Nurgle myself, even if I must chop a path to his manse and drag this ship with my teeth.' He slammed Grymn's head back against the hull. 'You're very welcome, I'm sure.'

Grymn watched the chuckling creature climb back above decks, dearly wishing he was free. Just one hand, even.

Clink.

He looked. The bilious stew was sizzling against the chains. Several links had been eaten clean through. He tested them, and found a little give. Not much, but maybe enough.

And where will you go then, Lorrus?

'Anywhere is better than here,' Grymn muttered.

I do agree, but now is not the ideal moment.

A dull pain flared through him, and he tensed, gritting his teeth. 'You're just trying to buy yourself time, monster.'

Yes. But my time is your time. I would no more have you die to that brute's axe than I would have you offered up by some wretched princeling looking to curry favour. I have set my standard in the soil of your soul, and I shall defend what I have taken.

Grymn laughed, painful as it was to do so. 'The enemy of my enemy is still my enemy. You all serve the same darkness, whatever you call it.'

Oh, aye, and your God-King is a singular being, is he?

Grymn fell silent. Sigmar had many names, it was true. And with each name, a face. All of these were equally true. Facets of a greater whole.

And so it is with us. The King of all Flies is vast and contains multitudes. Only once you accept your fate will you see his more beneficent side, Lorrus...

'Do not speak my name,' Grymn said.

And why not? We are boon companions, now. Your fight is my fight, and my fight, yours. Once you accept this, we can–

'Be silent, damn you,' Grymn thundered. His voice echoed through the hold, silencing even the whimpers of the trapped souls below. 'Be silent,' he said again, more softly. Bubonicus said nothing. Grymn sagged in his chains, and tried to ignore the feeling of worms gnawing at his innards.

'Only the faithful,' he said.

It was less a prayer than a plea.

CHAPTER SIXTEEN

ROT IN TOOTH AND CLAW

The jungle seethed.

The trees stretched to the very pox-clouds, which spewed from between the grinding tiers, and the canopy formed a crude roof over the entirety of the jungle below, blotting out the light of the Plague-Moon. Filthy waters pattered down along the trunks of twisted trees and soaked the spongy earth, or filled the raging rivers that stretched like gangrenous wounds across the body of a dying man.

There had been a city here once. Temples and avenues. All of them lost to the jungle, by the whim of Nurgle, and their inhabitants made over into new, more amusingly monstrous shapes. All that remained of their great works clung like scabs to the continent-spanning edifice known as the Great Vent. A mountainous burrow of stone and dirt, dug by the great god-worm that had once been worshipped here, before Nurgle had claimed it for his own. The Great Vent

wound about the jungle, before spilling down through its
heart, and into the depths of the garden.

As everywhere in the garden, there was no death in its
green embrace, only life. And that life was engaged solely
in wrathful predation, seeking only to devour, before being
devoured in turn. Mould-covered monsters, born from the
corpses of those who had perished before their time, hunted
one another through a green hell of hungry plants and
strange, fungal growths. The dark waters of the river that
wound through the jungle in serpentine fashion boiled with
hungry shapes, which thrashed and coiled in never-ending
battle. Things perished, only to rise anew from spores or
scat.

Life at its truest, in all its glorious fury.

At any other time, the black galley sweeping down the river
would almost certainly have been attacked. But there were
greater predators about, and they had marked the galley and
its crew for their own. And on the seventh hour of the third
day, they attacked.

Plague drones swooped low over the opalescent waters and
swarmed over the galley. Plaguebearers, clad in rust-riddled
cuirasses and grimy mail, flopped to the decks with clumsy
eagerness. They launched themselves into battle with the galley's crew. Duelling, droning chants punctured the damp air
as the two groups of daemons traded blows.

'Avast and avaunt, ye scabrous dogs,' Gutrot Spume roared,
as he swept his axe out and bisected the rot fly in mid-swoop.
Its rider tumbled to the deck with a frustrated grunt, single
eye glaring. Before the plaguebearer could find its feet, Spume
removed its head. He punted the pustulating skull over the
rail. 'This ship and all it carries is mine, and I'll not give her
over to any poxy lubberworts, whatever their purpose.'

'You speak harshly, corsair, and with an ignorant tongue,' a thunderous voice rumbled. Spume turned, axe raised. The Great Unclean One squatted among the rower's benches, crushing dozens of souls beneath his flabby weight. His vast bulk was still wet from the river's embrace. The greater daemon had hauled himself aboard even as his vanguard of blight drones had swooped down out of the miasma to attack. He'd nearly capsized the galley in his haste, which now rode dangerously low in the water.

The creature was almost the height of the galley's mast, and bulky with fat and muscle. He was clad in rusty armour plates and mail, which strained to contain his grey-green form. Where his flesh was visible, it was by turns stretched tight or else torn and oozing. Infected coils of intestine bulged between the plates of armour like ribbons of merit, and his head was nothing more than a lump set on his broad shoulders. The creature wore a dented, full-face helm, topped by a single, curved horn of pockmarked iron. He pointed a heavy, square-tipped blade, dripping with tarry poisons, at Spume. 'A dog should know its betters, even if only by instinct. I am Gulax, oldest blot-son of Bolathrax, and Filthblade of the Rotguard. What are you, but a mote in Grandfather's smallest pustule?'

'A mote serves well enough to bring down a mite such as yourself, ye overbearing moss-brained oaf,' Spume gurgled in reply. 'I bow before no one, daemon or otherwise, on the deck of my ship.'

'Not yours for much longer, mote,' Gulax rumbled. 'I knew you would not dare traverse the Great Vent. Instead, you seek a lesser waterway, more fitting for such a puling wretch. You wish to reach the Hopeless City in secret, as if the ways and means of your journey are not high entertainment for the Court of Ruination.'

'And ye think to stop me then? To take my glory for your own?' Spume wriggled a tentacle invitingly. 'Well then, come and have a dance, if you're of a mind to return to Grandfather's cauldrons. Here, let me choose the tune for us.' He broke into a sudden, lumbering charge, axe raised. The Great Unclean One reared back, murky eyes widening in shock. Gulax's blade swept down, but thudded into the deck, rather than bisecting Spume, as the creature had apparently intended.

Spume leapt onto the edge of the immense sword and swiftly scaled its length, as the daemon tried to wrench it free of the swollen wood. It was no more difficult than running along the mast in a storm. Spume's axe crashed down, splitting the rusty shoulder-plate and biting deep into rancid flesh. Gulax howled and heaved his blade free in a cloud of splinters, but Spume had already found a new perch.

One tentacle held tight to the horn on Gulax's helm, allowing Spume to tear his axe free in a welter of ichor. Gulax shrieked again, and stumbled, nearly snapping the mast in two with his weight. The galley rocked dangerously, and daemons tumbled into the river, still locked in combat. Spume chopped down at the point where Gulax's flabby neck met the fat of his shoulder. Gulax dropped his blade and clawed for his attacker, trying to pluck him from his perch. The daemon staggered towards the foredeck, heedlessly squashing his own warriors. 'Get off me,' he roared.

'Gladly,' Spume snarled. 'But I'll be taking something with me to remember ye by.' His axe rose and fell again, and Gulax's screams spiralled up, higher and higher. The Great Unclean One toppled forwards, and Spume rode him to the deck. When he landed, his tentacles tensed, stretched taut, and the daemon's head tore from his shoulders with a loud, wet squelch. Gulax continued to scream, even with his head off, but that was to be expected. The Rotguard were infamous for their stubbornness, even among Nurgle's legions.

Spume heaved the head up and sat it on the rail. 'Call your flies off, or I'll chop your skull into bits,' he growled. Gulax bellowed wheezing obscenities. Spume pressed the edge of his axe against the side of the daemon's head. 'When I dump ye, it'll be in chunks. Make it easier for the poxwyrms to digest ye.'

Gulax gnashed broken teeth in a grimace of surrender. He spat out a command, and the remaining plague drones retreated, swarming out over the jungle. The daemon eyed Spume. 'You'll pay for this indignity, mortal. Gulax shall have his just vengeance.'

'But not today,' Spume said. He jabbed the head with his axe and laughed as Gulax toppled into the swirling waters below. He'd never said he wouldn't dump Gulax, after all, just that he wouldn't chop him up first. Setting his axe over his shoulder, he turned to survey the damage.

His galley was still mostly in one piece, though the same couldn't be said for his crew. Pieces of daemons writhed on the deck, still possessed of some spark of life. Many of his rowers were in no state to continue either. Those who could no longer ply the oars were tossed into the river to feed the beasts there.

'This will earn you precious little thanks in the halls of the Plague Lord.'

Spume grunted and turned to the mast. Urslaug's head hung there, nailed to the wood by her hair, her eye pulsing with frustration. Death was not the end, in the garden. Not even for mortal souls, and Urslaug hadn't been mortal for a long, long time. 'I didn't do it for anyone but me, witch. Your warning came in handy, though. So ye have my thanks.'

'You've tied my fate to yours, pirate. What other option do I have?'

Spume laughed. The witch's body had been nailed into a cask of cankerwine, to pickle until such time as he chose to let her reattach her head. If he chose to do so. Until then, she would help him to conjure pox-winds to fill his sails, and speed their galley along. Though she could not cast the spells herself, she could guide his hand. 'None. But choices are for the hopeful, are they not?'

Urslaug grimaced. 'You taunt me.'

'And you betrayed me.'

'This wreck will never make it through the Great Vent in one piece, if what Gulax claimed is true,' Urslaug croaked. 'May as well scuttle it now, and seek safety in the jungle.'

'You'd like that, wouldn't you?' Spume stalked towards the mast. 'I'll not surrender so easily. Let the legions waiting there rot. We'll take the road less travelled.' Gulax had been correct in one assumption, at least. Spume had sought a swifter route to Despondency and the levels beyond. 'The Gape is just beyond the next twist of this river, and past it. The current will take us to the gates of Despondency, before anyone is the wiser.'

'The Gape?' Urslaug laughed. 'Trust a sneak thief like you to use that skaven-dug rathole of a path.' The Gape was a crude tunnel, barely large enough for a single vessel, carved into the soggy walls of the Great Vent. It was said by some that the skaven of the Clans Pestilens had gnawed it in secret, seeking a safer way into the soul-markets from their warrens. Only the mad and the brave dared the narrow passage these days. There were worse things than rats in the dark.

But Spume had braved its coils more than once, in his travels. So far as he knew, he was one of the only captains to do so. He'd sold a thousand souls to the ratkin for the trick of finding the path in centuries past, and he intended to get full use out of it.

Thunder rumbled in the distance. Spume turned, frowning. He'd been hearing it since they'd entered the jungle. At first, he'd thought it merely the eternal grinding of the tiers. But the flickers of silver in the distance convinced him otherwise. 'How did they find us so quickly?' he hissed.

'They follow the soulfire of your captive.' Urslaug cackled.

'What?' Spume rounded on her. 'Did ye not think to inform me of this earlier?'

'I did. I simply chose not to.'

Spume snarled and raised his axe. 'I ought to...'

'What? Cut off my head?' Urslaug cackled again. 'There is no death here, reaver, and I long ago lost the ability to feel pain. Throw my body in the river, if you like. Hack my skull into pieces. You do not frighten me.'

Spume took a threatening step towards the dangling head, but a grunt from his first mate brought him up short. 'Captain,' Durg said. The plaguebearer pointed. Massive shapes stalked through the trees on the shore, keeping pace with the galley. They were taller and thinner than Gulax had been, and more awkward in their movements. They shoved aside trees and toppled rock formations from their path.

One of the shapes broke from the jungle's edge, and stepped into the river. It had been a gargant once, like the kind that peopled the high places of Ghyran. Now, it was covered in mushrooms and jungle-moss, its hulking frame bloated with gases of decay, and strange, claw-like brands, which glowed with an unpleasant light. A spiked collar was all but embedded in the bloated flesh of its neck, and rusty chains hung from its shoulders and chest, the thick links hung with funerary bells and warpstone tokens. It clutched a stone sword in one mouldering paw, and issued a guttural challenge to the approaching galley.

'At last,' Spume said. He stumped to the prow, axe dangling from his grip. He raised his axe, drawing the gargant's eye, and issued his own challenge. The gigantic creature splashed towards the ship. Spume thumped the ferrule of his axe against the deck and spat a string of high-pitched gibberish. The gargant's brands began to smoulder, and the beast stiffened. It shook its shaggy head as if in pain, and retreated.

'I didn't know you spoke Queekish, Spume,' Urslaug said.

'There's a lot ye don't know, witch,' Spume said. He thumped the deck again. 'Ply your oars, ye dogs. They'll not let us alone for long.' The gargants had once roamed free on the Plains of Vo, before the skaven of the Clans Pestilens had brought the entire clan of behemoths low and broken their will with diseases and pestilences. Now, the last of the great brutes were scattered throughout the realms, acting as watchmen for the secret paths of their verminous masters.

These were bound by the cursed brands seared into their afflicted flesh. The words Spume had said caused the brands to grow hot, a signal for the gargants to retreat and let the speaker pass safely. But only until the brands grew cool. He'd had the secret of them from a plague monk of his acquaintance, a one-eyed frothspittle named Kruk, in return for several hundred hardy souls to labour in the gut-mines of one of the great worm-nations of the Ghurlands. That had made the going easier. Previously, he'd had to fight his way past the brutes every time.

As the galley slipped past them, one of the creatures raised its head and sniffed the air. Spume turned, and a chorus of slobbery growls and groaning howls rose from them. He tensed, readying himself. If they attacked...

'The air stiffens, corsair,' Urslaug laughed. 'It quivers at the touch of blue heat. Best whip your rowers and fill your sails with some of that hot air you like to blow.'

'What are you nattering about?' Spume began.

Lightning ripsawed through the jungle, obliterating trees and beasts both. It was followed by a sweeping blaze of cobalt fire. Monstrosities without description hurled themselves into the water, their greasy hides ablaze. Spume threw up his hand and felt the skin of his palm begin to bubble. He knew the feel of those flames. That they should be here, now, was inconceivable. And yet, there it was.

They were relentless. Impossibly, improbably relentless. Somehow, they'd caught up with him. Urslaug cackled. 'I'll bet even Grandfather didn't expect that.'

The gargants gave a roar and stumped towards the blaze, ready to do battle with the intruders. Spume wished them luck. He whirled and fixed Durg with a glare. 'What are you gawping at? Ply your whip! Row until the oars splinter. Our fortune awaits, and death follows close behind!'

'Morbus, Cadoc, cease,' Gardus bellowed. 'The way is clear. The enemy is before us. Enyo, Tegrus, to the air. Aetius, drop your chains and bring your shields to the forefront.' The Lord-Celestant's voice carried easily in the sudden silence following the hurricane of celestial energies. 'To arms, my brethren, to arms.'

For days, they had fought their way through the jungle, step by bloody step, without food or rest. The descent had been perilous enough, plagued as it was by giant rot flies and the shrieking bat-things that preyed upon them. The immense monsters had circled the glowing vessel like moths, making darting attacks, until Solus and his Judicators had sent them fleeing.

Things had not got easier when they reached the rivers below. Their guide had insisted that the quickest route was overland, through the monstrous jungle. Chains had been found in the hold, and the strongest among the Stormcasts had begun the portage, while the rest saw to clearing a path, and defending the haulers from the ever-increasing attacks by the jungle's bestial denizens. The ground was soft enough that the hull of the ship split it like a plough, and the entangling creepers which strangled the jungle floor retreated before the blazing azure glow.

Atop the prow Morbus had stood, reliquary staff raised, voice booming out in prayers. Though he could not call down Sigmar's storm here, in this daemon-realm, he could still draw on the lightning within him, as well as the celestial energies within Cadoc's beacon. The Lord-Relictor had used these to burn a path through the jungle, setting it aflame with a holy light.

Behind Gardus, Stormcasts dropped the chains with which they'd been dragging the glowing galley through the jungle. Where the chains fell, the soft ground turned cracked and dry. Trees bent away from the cobalt glow of the galley, as if seeking to flee its radiance. Aetius growled out an order and his weary warriors moved forward, pulling their shields from their backs, and unhooking hammers and warblades from their belts.

As the heat of Morbus' lightning faded, the jungle's hunger returned. And with it, the desire to devour those who had encroached upon it. Such was the intent of the half dozen fungal monsters stumbling towards the hastily forming shieldwall. They might have been gargants, once, but now they were ambulatory heaps of jungle-rot. The ground trembled beneath them as they picked up speed, heedlessly swinging about stone weapons caked in moss.

Gardus moved into the front rank, followed by Feros and his remaining Retributors. Tallon paced after them, tail lashing. 'Remember the Celestine Glaciers?' Gardus said.

Feros nodded. 'I remember that it was cold. And wet.'

The Retributor had earned his war-name on those glaciers, splitting the ice and dropping their enemies into the freezing waters below.

'One out of two isn't bad,' Gardus said. Feros laughed. 'When I give the word, split the ground. Let's see if we can't slow their charge some.' He raised his hammer. Solus' warriors would be in position by now, behind Aetius' shieldwall. 'Who will hold, though the seas rush in and the ground crumbles?' he roared.

'Only the faithful,' Feros and the others bellowed in reply. Gardus brought his hammer down. A volley of arrows hissed overhead, and the lead gargants staggered. The arrows burst into incandescent fire, leaving scorched craters in infected flesh. Feros and his warriors lunged forward, lightning hammers raised.

The ground cracked as the hammers slammed down. Poison gases spewed upwards, enveloping Retributors and gargants both, but the Stormcasts continued to pulverise the ground. As Gardus had hoped, the spongy earth deflated like a lanced boil.

Gargants stumbled, roaring in bewilderment. Some fell, sinking into the ruptured soil. Others tumbled over them. Two came on, crashing over their fallen kin. Gardus stepped aside as a stone blade thumped down, nearly bisecting him.

He thrust his runeblade into a crack, and shattered the gargant's weapon with a twist of his sword. The gargant clutched at him, but shied away as Gardus' light blazed up. The creature stumbled back, moaning. Arrows punched into its flesh, and the gargant screamed in agony, before one of Enyo's arrows silenced it. The Knight-Venator swooped past, followed by Tegrus and his Prosecutors. Celestial hammers smashed down with meteoric force, dropping wounded gargants to their knees. Enyo's arrows blinded others, making them easy prey for the Prosecutors.

The Retributors moved in, hammers swinging. The fallen gargants did not rise, and those that had not yet fallen soon joined their fellows in death. Or as good as. Even the most badly wounded of them could not truly die. Instead, they lay gasping, eyes blinded by pain and rage, wounds already festering. Gardus looked down at the beast Enyo had felled, and tried to quash the rising tide of pity. Its jaws champed mindlessly, despite the arrow jutting from its skull. As he watched, the arrow disintegrated into motes of light, leaving only a burnt wound between the gargant's eyes.

Gardus drove his sword down into the wound and the brain beyond. Only when he felt the tip bite the earth beneath did he pull it free. The gargant's eyes rolled up, and it gave a soft moan. Its body shuddered, and went still. It was not dead, but perhaps its pain was ended for a time. The other five beasts had suffered similar fates, their skulls and limbs crushed, eyes pierced through, bodies torn asunder. One, its abscessed skull studded with curling horns of bone, writhed worm-like towards the Liberators, biting at the air.

Aetius stepped forwards and drove his hammer into its cranium, splintering horns and crushing bone. The creature flopped down, its face still twisted in a grimace of effort.

'Madness,' Gardus murmured. And it was madness. All of it, even his own desire to enter this realm and retrieve those they'd lost. He was coming to see that now.

A nearby Retributor turned. 'Can you see them?' he croaked.

Gardus looked at him sharply. 'What?'

'I… I can see them,' the Retributor mumbled. His ichor-stained hammer slipped from his hands. He had been wounded in the battle, and he reeked of infection. Injuries festered immediately here, and infection was rapid. 'My kin, my family, why are they here?' The Retributor reached towards the jungle's edge, as if beckoning to someone. 'Where are they going? Wait…'

'They are not,' Gardus said intently. He stepped between the injured warrior and the trees. 'They are not here. Ignore them.'

'No, I see them. I… I–'

Gardus slugged the other Stormcast. The Retributor sank to one knee, shaking his head dully. He reached towards the trees, mumbling. Gardus struck the warrior again, flattening him. He motioned two others forwards to see to the dazed Retributor. 'Hold him. His blood is inflamed. Have Morbus see to his injuries.'

The Retributor wasn't the only one injured. To a warrior, the Stormcasts' armour was caked with mud and grime, and their limbs sagged with fatigue. They were all tired. Weary in body and soul. Worn down by this place and its horrors. Insects of all sizes and descriptions filled every scrap of space, stinging and biting one another and everything else. Through the gaps in the canopy, Gardus caught glimpses of hazy shapes in the sky above – great, crouching god-shapes, squatting on their haunches, watching the savagery below with phantasmal glee. Life was a horrid celebration in this place. Even the water was alive, filled with creatures as large as a poxwyrm, and as small as a speck of dust. And all of them trying their best to kill one another. To devour and be devoured in turn.

Suddenly frustrated, Gardus caught the edge of his war-cloak and swept it up. The enchantment woven into its threads awoke, and a barrage of gleaming hammers smashed through the remaining trees, revealing the river beyond. He stalked through the smoke, accompanied by Feros and Aetius.

'The Great Vent,' Gardus said. Past the bend, the great wall of rounded stone and packed earth rose towards the sky. Trees had grown into it, and roots the width of the galley squirmed across it like veins. Ancient guard towers, long abandoned and forgotten, clung to its highest points, and the broken shapes of forgotten temples jutted from its slopes like grave markers. Unholy sigils hung tangled in the vines – icons devoted to Khorne, Tzeentch, and a hundred other, lesser powers, now broken and given over to rust.

'It looks like a burrow,' Feros said. He craned his neck, trying to follow the edifice's convolutions. 'As if some monstrous worm passed this way.'

'It did, at least according to our guide.' Gardus had spent some time conferring with Gatrog on the journey through the nightmarish jungle. As with everything relating to Chaos, the origin of Nurgle's garden was a morass of lies, mixed with some truth. This jungle, like everything in the Plague God's realm, was all that remained of a once vibrant realm. Nurgle had encroached upon it, even as he did Ghyran, and reduced it to its current, mad, broken state. He'd remade it in his image, after slaying its previous ruler – the titanic god-worm whose spawn still roamed the Amber Steppes of Ghur, as semi-divine city states. Now, the great burrow cast up by that fallen god's final death throes acted as a conduit from this level of the garden to the next.

'A battle was fought here,' Aetius said. He kicked at the soil and dislodged a skull, overgrown with moss and fruiting toadstools. The skull was marked by the rune of Khorne. 'They say the Blood God turned on the others, when the Gates of Azyr were sealed.'

Gardus pointed with his sword. 'There. Do you see that?'

Aetius and Feros followed his gesture. 'What is it, my lord?' Feros said.

'Our way in,' Gardus said.

It was a gap in the towering span of stone. A crack, twice the height and width of the galley, but cleverly disguised with vines and packed soil. Or it had been – something had passed that way recently, to judge by the torn vines and clumps of filth floating in the water. Someone had gone to a lot of trouble to make it look as if it were nothing at all, but he could see the strange, claw-like runes that marked its edges. The same runes that had been branded on the gargants.

'Sentries,' he said. 'Those beasts were set here to guard this place.'

'By whom?' Aetius asked.

'The loathsome ratmen and their vile kin.'

Gardus turned. Tornus approached, hauling Gatrog in his wake. Cadoc and Morbus followed after. The Knight-Azyros had one hand on his sword, and appeared ready to remove Gatrog's head at the least provocation. The Rotbringer looked around with distaste. 'Poor brutes. To be enslaved so is a foul fate, and one I'd not wish on my worst enemy. The ratkin have no understanding of honour or the beauty of despair, and they twist Nurgle's blessings for their own duplicitous ends.'

'You offer up such information freely,' Gardus said.

Gatrog shrugged. 'I swore an oath.'

'Fair enough. Where does that passage lead?' Gardus swung his hammer up, to indicate the concealed aperture.

'It is called the Gape. A wound, carved in the flesh of the Great Vent. I'd heard stories, but gave them little credence.' Gatrog stared at the immense crack in fascination. 'Truly, there are yet wonders undreamed by humble knights.'

'You are having a strange definition of wonder,' Tornus said.

'And of humble,' Cadoc said.

Gatrog glared at him. 'I am humbler than thee, at least.' Cadoc reached for the hilt of his blade, but a look from Gardus stopped him from drawing it. 'Skaven carved it, after they'd diverted the river, with help from their gargant slaves. The King of all Flies was magnanimous and allowed his allies to find sanctuary in his garden. For what is a garden without vermin?'

'And where does it lead?'

'To the fourth tier, and the Hopeless City. The skaven sought to avoid the tallies rightfully collected by the guardians of the Great Vent.' Gatrog's smile spoke as to the nature of those tallies. Suddenly, Gardus was glad for the efforts they'd taken to avoid travelling via the river. 'The ratmen have a warren within. It is a deadly road, but swift.'

'Deadly or not, it is a road we must take. Aetius, Feros, see to bringing the galley to water. Tornus, restrain our guide.' For once, Gatrog went without complaint. Undoubtedly, the creature saw an opportunity for escape in their chosen course.

'We should kill it now,' Cadoc said, watching as Tornus hauled his prisoner back to the galley. The Knight-Azyros tapped the hilt of his blade for emphasis. 'We will catch up to our prey in the tunnel. We have no more need of such foulness.'

'Save that Tornus believes that he might be redeemed,' Gardus said.

Cadoc said nothing. Gardus did not press the issue, merely watched as the Knight-Azyros took to the air, to scout ahead. In truth, Cadoc was right. They should have executed Gatrog long before now, however useful he'd proven himself. But, time and again, Gardus had stayed his hand. Part of him wished to believe that Tornus was right, that some spark of humanity yet remained in their prisoner. For if that were the case, then perhaps there was hope for all that the Dark Gods had touched.

'You put much stock in the word of one we have only just met,' Morbus said.

'Who? Tornus or the Rotbringer?'

'Either.'

'Gatrog is being more helpful than I anticipated,' Gardus said. 'He seems to hold his honour sacred. Unusual for such a being.'

'The Order of the Fly were heroes once. Men of virtue. The true horror of Chaos comes not from what is warped, but from what remains the same.'

'Perhaps Tornus is right, and he can be redeemed in some fashion.'

'Perhaps.' Morbus sounded amused. 'And perhaps the light of Cadoc's beacon is having a deleterious effect on him. Being exposed to the pure light of Azyr on a constant basis… perhaps it is cleansing his soul.'

'Is that possible?'

Morbus laughed softly. 'You should know by now, Gardus, that all things are possible, for the faithful.'

Gardus hoped there was truth in what the Lord-Relictor said. He hoped that he had not doomed them all with this quest. More, he hoped that those left behind were not suffering because of his choice. 'Only the faithful,' he said.

* * *

'Only the faithful,' Kurunta, Lion of the Hyaketes, roared as he killed. His broadsword dripped with foul ichors as it rose and fell to a butcher's rhythm. The plaguebearers were no match for him – few things were. It was a sad fact that he could find little challenge in these fallen realms. He, who had once warred with demigods, was now little more than a night-soil collector. A daemon lunged up at him out of the bubbling muck. He caught its greenstick wrist and pulped it, before chopping through its chest and abdomen.

He began to sing as he kicked aside the suppurating mass of intestine and flesh. The war-songs of his people were still sung in the mountains west of the Black Grasses. The songs had changed some, in the intervening centuries, but the melody was the same. The sound of his voice rose up, drowning out the droning cries of the daemons crawling out of the half-sealed realmgate.

The retinues under his command joined him in song, their voices following his, as they had these past five days. He elbowed a plaguebearer, perforating its soft skull with the force of the blow. Something about the crackling remains of Grymn's broken lantern was weakening the daemons, draining them of vitality. Even now, Grymn was warding them. Kurunta spun, blade licking out. A cyclopean head fell to the water with a splash.

Five days. Five days since Gardus had led the others into the Garden of Nurgle. Angstun was beside himself. Kurunta wasn't worried, however. He would worry on the seventh day, no earlier. Five days was nothing. He stamped down on a knobbly claw, crushing it. He whirled his blade about and drove it down, piercing the daemon's shapeless skull. More daemons squirmed on the walls and floor, trying to drag themselves from the semi-solid sargassum. They had burst into being like hellish flowers, but found themselves trapped. Now, they clutched at the legs and arms of his warriors, trying to slow them down. More daemons, flesh sloughing from half-formed bones, stumbled out of the swirling black waters. His warriors were holding their own. If the creatures had been at full strength, the Stormcasts would have been overwhelmed and driven back.

The chamber shook. Debris fell from the ceiling. It sounded like Angstun was having his own difficulties. A Liberator had brought word that the Rotbringers were attacking again. They were determined to reclaim their citadels. But where Angstun set his standard, no enemy would pass, no matter how determined. Angstun would hold.

'Even unto his death,' Kurunta murmured. Much was demanded of those to whom much was given. Such was the first canticle of the Hallowed Knights, and the truest expression of their ethos. Kurunta had never thought of faith, either its lack or its power, in his time as a mortal. For him, faith simply was. To worship the Great Bull-Roarer was what all men did, unless they were godless and profane.

A plaguebearer's blade drew sparks from his shoulder-plate. He split it open with a single blow, and shoved what was left back into the waters. A crackle of lightning alerted him to the death of one of his warriors, and he cursed. More and more half-formed daemons were rising from the waters. Their droning chant grew louder, and the glow from the shattered lantern was growing dimmer. He gestured to the nearest Liberator. 'Advika, pull the others back. It's time our guests heard my roar.' He whirled his sword about, driving it point first into the muck, and reached for his war-horn.

The horn had been bestowed upon him by Gardus after the battle at the Celestine Glaciers. He'd had it recast in a more familiar shape by the Six Smiths, made over into a curling shape which resembled a stylised lion, crouching on four bent limbs. From between its jaws emerged the rounded bell, and the mouthpiece was set between its shoulders. Oath-ribbons and prayer scrolls, akin to those that decorated his armour, hung from its golden shape. He raised it to his lips.

Stormcasts retreated, backing away from the bubbling waters. They knew what was coming next. Kurunta relished the chance to make a joyful noise. There was power in such things. A great roaring, to break the enemy's will and send them fleeing, or to destroy them utterly. He would settle for the former. To destroy them would mean destroying this chamber, and sealing it. And that he would not do, until those who had gone were returned.

Kurunta blew a single, booming note. What emerged from the stylised lion's maw was a roar worthy of the great beasts of the Felstone Plains. It flared outward, and plaguebearers were smashed back off their feet. Their rotten forms disintegrated as the note ravaged among them, casting them back into the primordial soup from which they'd emerged.

Pillars cracked and burst as the echo bounced among them. A section of the roof plummeted down, piercing the skin of the water and casting up a shower of blighted liquid. Kurunta stepped back, lowering his horn. For the moment, the daemons had retreated. Even the ones stuck in the walls and the floor were silent. They glared at him as he strode back towards the other Stormcasts.

The others would return, and in greater numbers. He glanced at the broken lantern, its blue glow barely a flicker within the shattered casing. He estimated it would vanish entirely in two days. And then there'd be nothing to stop the servants of Nurgle from flooding the fortress, and killing all within.

'Two days left. Then I will worry.' He slung his war-horn

and looked around. Some of his warriors were wounded. Many were dead. But those who remained had no give in them. Steel, down to the soul. 'Who knows no despair, save in failure?'

'Only the faithful,' came the response.

Kurunta nodded and planted his broadsword before him, resting his hands upon the hilt. 'Aye. And we are that. Whatever else, we are that.' Even as he said it, his eyes could not help but fix on the fading light of Grymn's lantern. Some said that the light in such a lantern was tied to the soul of the one who carried it. He hoped that was not the case.

He hoped for many things.

'Two days,' he said quietly.

CHAPTER SEVENTEEN

THE RAT NEST

Tornus snarled in fury and loosed one arrow after the next, so swiftly that his movements were a blur of silver. Hunched, verminous shapes were punched backwards, nailed to the rail, or sent hurtling over it. But still the skaven came on. The diseased adherents of the Clans Pestilens were everywhere, clinging to the rigging or scurrying across the deck, swinging enormous, smoke-spewing censers.

The attack had begun mere moments after the Stormcasts' vessel had passed through the Gape. True to Gatrog's word, the tunnel had been carved by the skaven. The cavern rose above and around the river like the petals of some obscene flower. It was larger than it had appeared from the outside, as if the space within extended into some other, overlapping realm of existence. Strange lights flickered from the mouths of tunnels, and skaven wrapped in mouldering robes poured into view, pursuing the galley from the shore.

Crooked walkways and bridges made from bone and wood

stretched across the upper levels, hanging from ancient archways and crumbled walls. Skaven-sign marked every surface, and nets full of steaming warpstone hung from every surface, casting an eerie green glow through the darkness. The diverted stretch of river ran through the warren, kept on course by dams and blockages of toppled stone and packed filth. Skaven ran everywhere, ringing the great bells that hung from the highest archways. Some hurled rocks, empty cauldrons and makeshift spears down on the galley as it passed below them.

Worst of all was the trio of monstrous flying rat-beasts, which swooped low under gantries and around crumbling columns, keeping pace with the galley. Pox-smoke belched from their distended maws, and greenish ichor dripped from the brands of ownership on their flanks. Crude howdahs were strapped to the beasts' backs by slime-encrusted ropes and cruel hooks embedded in their abused flesh. Whenever one drew close, the plague monks crammed onto the howdah attempted to board the galley, or else hurled sling stones at those fighting near the rails.

A Judicator staggered as one of these stones crunched into his helmet. Skaven hurled themselves at him, crawling over him, their rusty blades seeking the joins of his armour. Tornus' arrows plucked them away, one by one, but too late. The warrior spasmed and fell, poisons leaking from every pore. Tornus looked away. Another life lost, because of him. His stomach clenched, tightened and twisted. He felt as if something were reaching up inside him to clutch at his heart. He staggered.

It almost cost him his own life. A blade sawed at his side. He stumbled, and brought his bow around like a club, smacking the skaven aside. Before it could rise, Ospheonis swooped down on it, screeching. Tornus groped for another arrow, trying to ignore the familiar, hateful whispers that echoed through his head.

'To your left!'

Tornus spun, driving his arrow into the throat of a skaven as it leapt at him. Sore-covered paws scrabbled at his forearm as he twisted the arrow in the wound, killing the ratkin. An instant later, he ripped it free, nocked and loosed it in one smooth motion, killing a second. He turned. 'You are having my thanks, sister.'

Enyo nodded as she reached into her quiver. 'You shouldn't let your attention wander during a fight, brother.'

'So I am being told,' Tornus said. He loosed an arrow and nailed a skaven's tail to the deck. The plague monk shrilled in pain, before Feros' lightning hammer tore its head from its shoulders. 'There are not being as many of them as I am expecting.'

'I think our quarry stirred them up,' Enyo said, as she sent an arrow through a censer bearer's skull. The skaven leapt up, as if stung, and then collapsed into a heap. 'With luck, they're taking a worse beating than we are.'

Tornus was about to reply when he heard a ripping sound and looked up. Skaven slid down the sails, shredding them in the process. He smacked his fist into Enyo's arm and pointed. They leapt skyward, each taking a side. Arrows hummed like wasps, and skaven fell to the deck with despairing squeals.

Tornus swooped over the deck and the heads of those Stormcasts bent over the oars. Morbus had filled the sails with a conjured wind, but it wasn't enough in these waters. The Lord-Relictor stood in his customary place at the prow, reliquary staff planted before him. His head was bent, and

Tornus felt, rather than heard, the rumble of his prayers as he tried to lend strength to the oarsmen.

Lightning crawled across Morbus' armour and flickered over the deck. The spectral shapes of fallen Stormcasts knelt in a circle about him, their forms fading or strengthening with each passing moment. Any skaven so foolish as to draw close to the Lord-Relictor and his ghostly coterie was immediately struck by flickering strands of chain lightning.

Gardus led the defence of the vessel, launching himself into battle wherever the skaven massed. Feros and his Retributors warded the Lord-Celestant, keeping the ratmen from over-whelming him. Everywhere, those Judicators and Liberators not manning the oars had formed into small phalanxes.

A searing burst of celestial radiance caught Tornus' attention. He saw Cadoc drop down onto the howdah on the back of one of the flying monstrosities, starblade flashing. Tornus banked and sped back along the length of the galley, loosing arrows as he did so. He and Enyo met near the prow and raced upwards, their wings carving shimmering trails in the miasmatic air. They split up and shot between the swooping bat-creatures.

Tornus rose up in front of one of the beasts and sent an arrow into each of its eyes. It gave a thunderous squeal and its movements became panicked. A moment later, the creature slammed into a wooden bridge and hung from it. Skaven tumbled from the howdah as the massive creature thrashed about. As he raced away from it, he saw Enyo land on the head of the second of the beasts, and loose an arrow down into the centre of its flat skull.

Ospheonis screeched and Tornus saw the last creature hurtling towards him, jaws wide. He shot upwards, narrowly avoiding the snapping portcullis of teeth. The star-eagle dived at the monster's eyes. Tornus swept down along its length, and caught sight of Cadoc wreaking havoc amongst the plague monks on its back. Then the Knight-Venator was past and plunging downwards, back towards the glowing shape of their galley.

Gatrog watched in no small amount of amusement as skaven swarmed across the deck, chanting shrilly. They wore the corroded armour and ragged robes of one of the more militant Clans Pestilens, and fought with ferocity, if little enthusiasm.

The Stormcasts, in contrast, fought with a vigour he found surprising, given the circumstances. Most, seeing the odds stacked against them, would have given up by now. The cobalt fires that had protected them were dimming as their skull-faced shaman stumbled beneath the weight of the souls that clung to him like chains.

Gatrog strained against his own chains, wishing that he were free. While he was at it, he wished that he had a sword. And some armsmen. Tornus had left him bound to the mast, able only to move a short distance. 'Release me,' he bellowed at one of the skaven. 'I am a true knight, and servant of the King of all Flies.'

The plague monk glanced in his direction. The skaven bared broken black teeth in what might have been a smile. It sidled towards him, lifting a notched and rust-splotched blade. More plague monks joined the first, closing in on him. Gatrog realised his error a moment before the first blade jabbed at his thigh. Roaring in anger, he booted the skaven in the head, snapping its neck. The skaven crowded close, sensing easy prey.

'Is this how you treat your allies?'

A blade sank between the plates of his armour, drawing

pungent ichor. He heaved himself to the side, shouldering the ratman away. A skaven leapt to the mast, a blade clamped between its leprous jaws. It crawled down towards him, its eyes lit by a feverish glow. But, before it could reach him, an arrow sprouted from its skull. The skaven flopped down to the deck. The others scattered, like the cowardly vermin they were. Gatrog kicked the corpse and looked up.

'You saved me.'

'Torglug would not have been saving you,' Tornus said, as he descended. 'Torglug would have been letting you die.'

'A lie,' Gatrog said. The Knight-Venator drew another arrow from his quiver and turned away. 'Torglug was – you are a noble warrior. A hero...' But the words sounded hollow. The Woodsman had been a mighty warrior, it was true. But honourable?

'When I am being Torglug, I am being consumed with hatred,' Tornus said. 'It is eating away at me, every moment of every day. I am hating all that lives, even myself. I am even hating Nurgle, though I am fearing him as well.'

Gatrog frowned. 'Hate is good. It is as the rain that nourishes the soil.'

'Nothing of worth is growing in that soil.'

Tornus loosed his arrow, and a skaven died. He reached for another, moving without hurry. The skaven were fleeing, hurling themselves over the rails rather than face the Stormcasts. Though the plague-bells still rang, the signal was one of retreat rather than attack.

Gatrog hauled himself to his feet. 'My home flourishes because of Nurgle's kindness. We survive only because our garden pleases him. We despaired, and in our despair, the Lady came to us and showed us the truth of the world.'

'Whose truth?' Tornus turned and held up his hand,

displaying the twin-tailed comet emblazoned on his gaunt-let. 'This is being my truth. What is being yours?'

Gatrog spat on Tornus' hand. 'That,' the Rotbringer growled.

'And yet, my truth is still being here. Beneath yours.' Tornus scraped the spittle from the silver. 'Just as I am always being beneath Torglug.' He hesitated. Then, 'Yes. Yes, I am always being within Torglug. As there is something being within you.'

'Whatever is in me was planted by the King of all Flies.'

'But in what soil is he planting it?'

Gatrog stared at him. He made to answer, but could find no words. He didn't remember much of his life before he'd sipped from the Flyblown Chalice. It had been hard. Harsh. A tem-pering, so that he was fit to serve. But when had he chosen to serve? Had he done so, or had his choice been made for him?

Once, that might have filled him with pride, but now, being here, on this vessel, burned day and night by this unrelent-ing radiance, he felt... uncertain. And he didn't like it. There was a comforting certainty in despair. The worst had come, and he was all the stronger for it. But hope was the weed in Grandfather's garden.

It always crept back when he least expected it.

'Avast, ye vermin,' Gutrot Spume bellowed as rusty blades bit into his blubbery flesh. He caught one of the frothing skaven about the throat with a tentacle and dashed the crea-ture's brains out against the deck. His axe licked out, bisecting another ratkin in mid-leap. 'I have safe passage, ye pestifer-ous brutes!'

Skaven scurried everywhere across the galley, attacking his crew with maddened savagery. Others clung to his mast, or the rail, and banged gongs as they chittered high-pitched praises to their verminous god. They'd appeared suddenly, pouring out of the tunnels and high places that marked either side of the river, and raining themselves down on his galley with berserker glee. While the ratmen of the Clans Pestilens were known to be a sight braver than their less infectious kin, this was something else again. It was almost as if something were driving them towards him.

Spume flung the twitching body he held over the rail and shook his head. 'Rats on a ship. What's the garden coming to?'

'One might say the same thing about pirates,' Urslaug said, from her spot on the mast. The witch seemed amused. Then, she was always amused. He was starting to remember why they'd parted ways. It wasn't just the treachery. Urslaug had always seemed to be laughing at him, no matter the situation.

'This is your doing, witch,' Spume said, pointing a tentacle towards Urslaug's head. 'How many foes have you put on my trail?'

'Not so many as all that,' Urslaug said. 'You did interrupt me, after all.'

Spume gave a guttural snarl, and considered pitching Urslaug's head over the side. But that was likely what she wanted. 'Silence, witch.'

The skaven warren abutted one of the immense runnels of tumour-stricken root, fossilised vegetation, and fallen trees that stretched down from the jungle into the upper levels of the Hopeless City. The river that wound through the third tier split into seven branches, each one cascading down through part of the city and into the tier below. If they could reach the runnel, and swiftly, they might yet outpace their pursuers.

A shout from one of his daemon crewmen brought him around. Heavy shapes slunk in the black galley's wake. Crude, flat-hulled vessels, driven forward by rat-powered paddle-wheels, with rickety, tower-like decks, occupied by

plagueclaw catapults or plague furnaces. Their crews numbered in the hundreds. But skaven, and plague monks in
particular, made for poor sailors. Their bulky scows could
wallow in his wake for as long as they liked. They would
never catch him.

One of the catapults launched a boiling mass of filth towards
the galley. Spume held up his axe and tentacles as the sludge
rained down. He bellowed with laughter. Trust the skaven to
think a bit of hot sludge would be enough to stop him. Ignoring the cries of the rowers who'd been struck by the sludge,
he made to turn towards the prow. A flash of silver caught
his eye, and he stopped.

One of the skaven barges cracked in two with a thunderous roar. Bits of rotting wood pattered against his helmet,
despite the distance. He cursed as a silvery figure darted over
the surface of the water. Something blazed in its hand, before
spinning out and away to strike the paddle-wheel of another
barge, shattering it.

'Closer than barnacles,' Spume snarled. He chopped through
another plague monk as the creature sought to take advantage of his distraction. His blow split the creature crown to
tail. Flicking the wreckage from his axe, he turned, seeking an
escape route. More barges were up ahead at the bend in the
river, moving to cut him off. He had to get past them before
the other shiny-skins, or the rest of the skaven, caught up.

A whisper of sound caused Spume to whirl. A curved blade
sank into his chest. A bare skull, carved with eye-searing
sigils, rose above him. Twisted, curving horns rose from
within a shaggy lice-filled mane. Eyes like glowing embers
met his. A second blade looped out, heading for his neck.
He interposed his axe, blocking the blow.

'I was wondering if one of you would show up,' Spume said.

His tentacles curled about the blade embedded in his chest. 'You're the rat Urslaug was chattering to, aye?'

The Verminlord ripped its blade free and drove a hoof into Spume's abdomen, knocking him sprawling.

'Yes-yes, reaver-fool,' the daemon growled. 'I am Rancik, most-high favoured whelp of the Great Corrupter. And you are dead-dead.'

All was sound and fury. The clangour of weapons biting iron-wood. The bone-rattling war-hymns of the root-kings as they marched into the balefires, on behalf of a lie. The servants of the Great Conspirator had duped the duardin into war against the servants of the King of all Flies. The Black Cistern glistened with the blood of the slain.

Grymn stared about him in horror. The battle had been won centuries past, but the smells and sounds of it inundated his senses, overwhelming him. He felt as if he were drowning. Everything had a watery, colourless tinge to it. He clutched at his head, trying to look away as a phalanx of blightkings, led by Torglug the Despised, lumbered towards the reeling duardin. Axes flashed. Shields, scorched by bale-fire, split and shattered. A severed head struck him in the chest, its green-dyed beard clotted with blood.

The Woodsman was magnificent that day. A hero of old, unleashed upon the enemies of all life. His axe severed the hearth-trees of fourfold clans.

Grymn looked up. Bubonicus stood beside him, arms crossed. 'This is your memory, isn't it? Get out of my head.' He made to lurch towards the Chaos knight, but found himself unable to move. He groped uselessly, willing his limbs to work. Bubonicus looked at him.

It will soon be my head. Look.

Grymn did, and wished he hadn't. Maggots squirmed between the plates of his armour, thousands of them. He wanted to rip them off, to scrape them away, but he remained frozen as they began to gnaw at him. He screamed.

Pain brings clarity. That is Nurgle's gift. Look. See. Lord Rotskull meets his foe upon the field, the Change-knight, Ompallious Zeyros.

A bloated, horned figure, wearing a fraying tabard marked with the sigil of the fly, waded through the battle towards an iridescent shape clad in multi-coloured armour. The two clashed, amid dying duardin.

Once closer than brothers, now enemies. It was from Lord Rotskull that I learned of the memory of maggots. He learned it from a sage in the Grove of Blighted Lanterns. It was said that the sage himself had been taught by the Lady or one of her sisters, but I feared to ask. Some secrets are best left to moulder.

The pain was worse now. Things moved within him, chewing away at all that made him, him. Something rose up in his throat, and he gagged. Squirming shapes filled his mouth and pressed against the backs of his eyes.

In death, I bring life. In life, I bring death. I am the eternal cycle manifest, and am honoured to bear that burden. As you will be honoured, when you become me. For as you witness my memories, I, too, see yours. You are a warrior without peer, cruelly used by your half-god. What is a man, but a collection of memories? The very things he strips from you, with each blow of his hammer.

'Get... out... of... my... head,' Grymn croaked. His limbs twitched. The maggots squirmed in agitation. Fragments of memory flashed across the surface of his mind. Pale shadows of a life once lived, and now lost to the roar of the storm.

Why do you resist me? Your death is certain. Let it be with honour. I shall not rip you asunder and torment you, as the reaver intends. I am no savage. I am a true knight, and I shall slay thee truly, with all due respect.

Bubonicus' hollow tones were almost pleading. Grymn smiled, despite the pain. 'If... I am torn asunder... you shall be as well.' There was no such thing as a good death. But that might be a tolerable one. Bubonicus snarled in frustration and reached for him.

Grymn's eyes snapped open. He smelled smoke. Heat washed down over him from somewhere above decks. In the dimness of the hold, something chittered. Skaven scurried towards him, eyes gleaming feverishly. The ratmen wore filthy robes and cowls, and what flesh was visible beneath them was lice-ridden and blotchy. They carried mattocks with hollow cores, into which shards of warpstone had been inserted. The mattocks wept an oily light that made the shadows twist and buckle.

'See-see, storm-thing is chained, yes-yes,' one of the plague monks chittered, licking its rotting snout with a black tongue. 'Helpless, yes-yes.'

'Has eyes, fool,' the other growled. One of its eyes was milky in hue, and wept a white discharge. It pawed at the afflicted orb, snuffling.

'Eye,' the other corrected, with a snigger.

For a moment, Grymn thought the one with the bad eye would strike its fellow. Then it turned its attention to him with a shrill snarl. 'Helpless, yes-yes,' it hissed, drawing close. 'Break its limbs, drag it up-up.' It reared back, readying its mattock for a blow. The warpstone glow swept down.

Chain links snapped and Grymn caught the mattock on his palm. The obscene heat of the shards scorched his gauntlet black, and made blisters rise on the flesh beneath. He ignored the pain and wrenched the weapon from its wielder's paws. The skaven fell back, bad eye twitching fit to pop. 'What-what…?'

More chains burst, and Grymn fell forwards. He caught the skaven and dragged it beneath him. The vermin squealed as his weight crushed it to the deck. As it squirmed, he smashed its throat, silencing it. The remaining skaven gave a squeal of panic and swung at him with its mattock. He caught the blow on his forearm, and the mattock came apart like so much rotten wood.

Grymn rose to his feet, dragging the broken chains with him. The skaven stared at him, snout twitching. Then it turned to flee. Grymn smashed its skull with a loop of chain. He kicked the body aside, and looked down at the souls trapped in the bilges.

There was no hope in their eyes. Nothing save the despair of broken animals on their way to the abattoir.

If you would flee, now is the time.

'No.' Swiftly, Grymn threaded the chains through the bars.

They have found peace, Lorrus. Would you steal that from them?

'Gladly,' Grymn said as he hauled back on the chains, exerting every bit of his remaining strength. 'I would spill an ocean of my blood to spare one soul the horrors you call peace, monster.'

The bars bent, buckled, burst. Grymn staggered back. No soul emerged. They squatted in the filthy bilge water, uncomprehending. Grymn cursed. 'Up, damn you – up! We must go!'

They cannot hear you, Lorrus. You speak words of hope, and these blessed ones are deaf to such foolishness.

'Shut up.' Grymn reached down. The prisoners shied

away from him. They began to chant a low dirge, their voices barely audible over the noise of the battle above. It was a prayer to Nurgle. Disgusted and horrified in equal measure, he pulled back his hand and stood. He could not save those who did not wish to be saved, but even so, he could not leave them. Whatever the state of their souls, they did not deserve this.

Deserve? And who are you to judge such things, my friend? You are but a mote in the eye of a god. That you think such stubbornness will earn you anything save death is laughable. A child's bravery, matched against the will of one who was witness to the birth of stars. Run, if you would. But do not seek to steal that which has been rightfully earned.

Grymn staggered as something struck the ship. Steaming sludge dripped from the deck above to plop into the bilge waters. The souls moved beneath the searing wetness, bathing in it, though it marked their flesh with burns. Repulsed, the Lord-Castellant turned away towards the steps. There was nothing more he could do here.

And what will you do up there, eh? Swim to shore?

'No.' Grymn pulled his chains taut. 'I intend to render this ship adrift.'

Warily, he climbed above decks. Skaven scurried everywhere, locked in battle with Spume's crew. Grymn searched for Spume amid the confusion. He spotted the pirate trading blows with a towering skaven Verminlord. The creature moved swiftly, despite its size, but so did Spume. Wherever its curved blades slashed, his axe was there to meet them.

Grymn waded into the melee, broken chains swinging in a tight circle over his head. Skaven and daemons alike were smashed from their feet or slapped aside by his charge. He thudded down the centre line towards his captor. If he could kill Spume, even if he died in the process, he would have removed a potent threat to the Mortal Realms.

A plaguebearer attempted to interpose itself, and lashed at him with a thorn-studded whip. Grymn knocked it sprawling, and split its mossy skull with a slash of the chain. 'Spume,' he roared. The pirate whirled, and the Verminlord embedded both of its blades in his back. Spume screamed and sank to one knee. The Verminlord planted a hoof against his head and tore its scythes free in a welter of gore. Spume toppled to the deck.

'There you are,' the Verminlord hissed, pointing a blade at Grymn. It bounded towards him, more quickly than he could move. He lashed out with the chain, driving it back, but only momentarily. It lunged and drove its shoulder into him, knocking him from his feet. The deck cracked beneath him as he fell, and the world spun about him.

'Rancik will claim your soul, storm-thing, yes-yes,' the Verminlord hissed as it circled Grymn. It scraped its curved blades together, forming fat sparks of green heat. 'I will gnaw-strip it of all secrets, yes-yes.'

Grymn groaned and tried to push himself to his feet. But his limbs refused to obey him. His head ached.

Surrender to me, Lorrus. Surrender, and I will dispatch this beast.

'No,' Grymn said, from between clenched teeth.

A hoof slammed down on the back of his head, driving him face first into the deck. 'Yes-yes,' the Verminlord growled, resting its full weight on the back of his head. 'Take you back, strip you to the bone, learn your secrets.'

Let me do this, fool, or we both die, Bubonicus said. Grymn didn't have the breath to answer, nor the strength to resist the claws of pain tearing at his muscles. Despite his best efforts, he couldn't muster the strength to throw the daemon off him.

'If anyone is going to peel the meat from his bones, it's going to be me.'

The Verminlord turned, and the haft of Spume's axe cracked into its fleshless muzzle. The daemon stumbled back, narrowly avoiding a blow that would have sliced it in half. The two faced each other over Grymn's crumpled form.

'Ye look to be a smart rat,' Spume said, aiming the bite of his axe at the Verminlord's shaggy throat. 'So I'll make ye and your scabrous brood an offer.' Blood dripped from his bulky form, but the wounds in his back were already healing.

'An… offer?' Rancik grunted.

'Ye want these shiny-skins, aye?' Spume motioned to Grymn with a tentacle. 'Well, there's a whole galley of them coming fast in our wake.'

'No,' Grymn croaked, trying to get up.

Spume slammed the ferrule of his axe into the back of Grymn's head, flattening him. Black spots danced before Grymn's eyes, as the world faded to a dull roar.

'Hush,' Spume said. 'Ye can keep fighting me, or have a bigger prize all to yourself, Rancik. What's it going to be?' Spume's kraken snapped its beak and his tentacles intertwined in agitation. He lifted his axe.

'Best hurry now. I'm not known for my patience.'

CHAPTER EIGHTEEN

THE HOPELESS CITY

Gardus heaved the last of the ratkin overboard, and looked up as a shadow swept over him. 'Enyo, what news? Is the path clear? Is our quarry at hand?'

'The way ahead is blocked,' Enyo said. The Knight-Venator dropped to the deck, folding her wings behind her. 'Our quarry has escaped, and the skaven seem to have turned their full attention to us.' She pointed to the vessels lurching towards the galley.

The barges were inelegant things, even in comparison to their commandeered galley. Flat and low, their motion was controlled by creaking paddle-wheels that struck the water inharmoniously. The sound of it merged with the clangour of bells that hung from their hulls and masts, and sent discordant echoes shivering through the close air.

'A trap,' Cadoc said, scraping blood from his armour. He was covered in gore, none of it his. 'They seek to drown us in rat flesh.'

The Knight-Azyros sounded eager. Gardus gave him a wary glance. Cadoc was one of the faithful, but his faith was a thing of sharp edges and searing heat. Of judgement and sentencing. And it seemed to grow worse with time. He was the tip of the God-King's spear, meant only for drawing blood.

Gardus waved him to silence. 'And our prey? Where has it gone?'

Tegrus had brought word that the galley carrying Grymn was close by, and similarly afflicted by the skaven. They now appeared to have come to some accord, which boded ill for their rescue attempt. He'd hoped their quarry would be brought to bay and unable to slip away.

'Speeding ahead, driven by a plague wind,' Enyo said. Her star-eagle circled her, shrieking in frustration. 'Some fell conjuring, by the look of it.'

'You expected something else in this place?' Morbus said. The Lord-Relictor sat slumped on the steps to the forward deck, head bowed. His armour gleamed with an azure luminosity, and the air around him stank of scorched metal and ozone. 'We are running short of time. I can feel something gathering its strength, preparing itself to strike.'

Gardus gave him a sharp look. 'The skaven?'

Morbus shook his head. 'I do not think so. They are but one piece of the whole.' He looked up. His eyes shone with a cold, eerie radiance. 'We are being baited. Drawn deeper and deeper into this place.'

'Then all of this has been a trap,' Gardus said, softly. 'And I have led us into it, like a blind fool.' He watched as Solus barked an order, forming up Judicators along the rail. They would scythe the life from one barge, maybe two, before the rest reached them. After that, it would be down to blade-work.

'It is not being a trap,' Tornus spoke up. The Knight-Venator leaned on his bow, studying the approaching enemy. 'Nurgle is not thinking like that. Nurgle is merely reacting. He is… slow, yes? Slow of thought, slow of deed. Nurgle is being patient. If we are to be coming to him, then he is to be simply laying out a welcome.' He shrugged. 'Of the Four, he is being the most content in the moment. What is being, will be.'

'That isn't exactly comforting,' Gardus said.

'I am not meaning it to be.' Tornus shook his head. 'I am feeling him watching us.' He struck his chest with a fist. 'I am feeling it in my head and in my soul. Like cold water dripping through cloth.'

'He is right,' Morbus said. 'Nurgle is watching us. And so far, we have done exactly as he wishes. We chase, and they run. We are like the child in the fable, following the singing lights into a mire. The longer we run, the thicker the mist grows and the deeper the mud. Soon, we might well be swallowed up.'

Gardus didn't reply. He let his gaze wander over those who had chosen to follow him. Liberators plied the oars in silence, their silver armour encrusted with a black patina of filth. Others sat slumped, heads bowed, weapons at their feet. The smell of blood and vomit was thick on the air. They'd lost six warriors in the attack. Six more lives added to the burden Morbus carried. Only thirty of those who'd volunteered to come were left. And of those, a third were wounded. Worse still, the enchantments that bound their weapons were fading in this place. The quivers of his archers were slow to refill, and the shields and armour of the others were cracked and damaged by the hard fighting. Soon, the magics of the Six Smiths would fade entirely and they'd be down to rocks and harsh language.

He saw a Judicator scratching at a bandage around her arm, pus leaking from beneath it. Nearby, a Retributor sat on the rail, cradling his head. One of the skaven's acidic censers had shattered too close to him, and his face was a mass of weeping burns. As if sensing Gardus' attention, he raised his head, revealing eyes made opaque and sightless. Gardus looked away. They could be healed, if Morbus were strong enough. But for how much longer could the Lord-Relictor's prayers keep them in the fight?

A Liberator stood near the rail, mumbling to someone only he could see. Aetius caught him by the arm and gently pulled him away, just in case. They'd nearly lost several warriors that way, led into the darkness by ghosts from half-remembered pasts. More and more of them were seeing things that could not be, or hearing the voices of those lost centuries past. Flies crawled over their faces, mould spread across the plates of their armour, and the smell of decay hung heavy on the air. And above it all, the distant but ever-present rumble of stone grinding against stone.

It was wearing them down. Nurgle was patient. Nurgle was slow. And Nurgle was inevitable. The longer they stayed here, the worse it would get. Their faith held firm for now, but soon even it would begin to crack. And as they pressed deeper and deeper, not even the radiance which infused their vessel would protect them.

He heard Solus' voice crackle in command, and the hiss of bowstrings. The scream of lightning as it ravaged among the enemy. In that roar, he heard the whisper of a god's voice. And knew at last what he must do. He turned back to his officers.

'I've been down this road before. I have passed through this dark garden and into the light. I have denied our foe in his very manse, and I intend to do so again, even if it means my destruction. It is time the Plague God learned that we are made of sterner stuff than he knows. We were forged in lightning and thunder, clad in starlight and carry the heat of suns in our veins.' Gardus turned, letting his light shine forth. It blazed upwards around him, casting back every shadow. 'It is time we showed him – showed all of the Ruinous Powers – not simply how the Stormcast do battle... but how the faithful wage war.'

He drove his runeblade point first into the deck and held his hand out to Morbus. 'Do you have the strength to call upon one last storm, brother?'

Morbus heaved himself to his feet. 'One more and a thousand others, if need be.'

'Good. For we will need them.' Gardus caught Cadoc by the shoulder. 'Fly ahead of us, and take word of our coming to the enemy, Prince of Ekran. Morbus...?'

'I can summon a storm for Cadoc to drag behind him. It will collapse this part of the warren and carry us down through the next tier.' The Lord-Relictor's voice crackled strangely. But he sounded certain. He set aside his staff and raised his hands. Lightning writhed between his palms. As he pulled his hands apart, the lightning formed itself into the links of a flickering chain. 'Lift your beacon once more, Knight-Azyros.'

Cadoc did so. Morbus opened it, and fed one end of the chain into the shimmering light. He turned swiftly, dragging the other end over his shoulder, causing it to spontaneously lengthen. Flickering loops pooled on the deck. Cadoc staggered, as if the chain were connected to the interior of his beacon. He extended it out over the deck, and the light crawled across the links and spread over the deck, merging with and feeding the radiance there. Morbus turned and knelt, proffering the links to Gardus. 'Take your place at the prow, Steel Soul. Your light will serve as our anchor.'

Gardus strode towards the prow, knotting the chains about his forearms and torso as he did so. The heat of the lightning was incredible, but it did not burn him. Cadoc swooped overhead, beacon extended, hauling the chain behind him. Gardus could hear Morbus beginning to chant, and the dull boom of his staff striking the deck. The heat grew more intense, as did his own radiance. He felt as if a storm were roiling within him, raging to be let free.

The skaven vessels were drawing closer, and he could make out their squeals as the light washed over them. Cadoc's wings snapped out and back, and he surged forwards, pulling the chain taut. Gardus braced himself, and held firm. 'Make a joyful noise, my brethren,' he called out. 'Sing the war-song of our Stormhost. Give them thunder and lightning.'

Feros was the first. His voice rose in a hymn of reckoning, deep and low. Aetius joined him, then Tegrus and Solus. Their warriors joined them, until every voice was raised in a song of war and judgement. Stormcasts began to stamp their feet in time to the rhythm. The hafts of hammers hit the deck, and warblades struck the rims of shields. The sounds merged, joining into a pulsing rumble. As it rose up and swept over him, Gardus felt the heat of the chain grow, and the silver of his gauntlets began to blacken.

For a moment, there was only the thud of sigmarite and the clangour of plague-bells. Then, with a deafening groan, the bow of the ship rose out of the water. Lightning raced down the chain and outwards along the rails, striking the water and turning it to steam. It lanced out, cascading across the blighted structures to either shore of the river, setting some aflame and destroying others utterly. Gardus tightened his grip on the chain. Cadoc gave a great cry and swooped towards the approaching skaven barges. From behind Gardus came the rumble of Morbus' voice as he called out, 'Who will ride the storm winds?'

'Only the faithful,' the others replied, as one.

'Who will be the light in the darkness?'

'*Only the faithful.*'

The words echoed through Gardus, giving him strength. And as he spoke them himself, his light blazed ever more brightly. The chains tightened. The links twisted in his grip like a living thing. And the galley's stern followed the bow. The water beneath bubbled away into nothing as the galley rose fully into the air and swept after Cadoc.

Their hull crashed through the forest of masts, splintering them and scattering the crews of the barges. The force of their ascent set the river heaving, and great waves slammed to either side of the tunnel, flooding the caves and warrens beyond. Skaven were swept screeching into the depths as their vessels capsized, or were reduced to fragments.

Gardus strained against the pull of the chain. Morbus' prayers and the song of the faithful rose to a fevered pitch, until their voices were lost in the roar of the galley's passage. Lightning streaked out from the galley, striking the walls of the tunnel or the barges below. Smoke filled the air, roiling in their wake. Cadoc blazed with elemental fury, and the light from his beacon speared out to pierce the gloom ahead.

The chain bowed suddenly. Gardus stiffened as a blotch of darkness swirled into being above the midpoint. It raced down towards him, gradually resolving itself into a monstrous and familiar shape. The Verminlord sped down the chain, the azure energies drawing smoke from its greasy pelt. Its monstrous form was streaked with ichor, and splinters of wood stood out from its flesh. It shrilled out a cry of challenge as it gathered itself and leapt towards him, curved blades raised.

Gardus tensed, unable to risk releasing his grip on the chain to defend himself. He ducked his head, hoping that his armour would absorb the worst of the blow.

Twin arrows shot past him, one on either side. The arrows punched into the Verminlord, knocking it sprawling to the deck. The curved scythe-blades clattered from its grip. It shrieked in pain and clawed at the arrows embedded in its flesh.

Gardus acted swiftly. He reared back and kicked it in the head, dropping it on to its back. Tornus and Enyo moved up from behind him. The Knight-Venators raised their bows, new arrows nocked and ready. Still holding tight to the chain, Gardus looked down at the injured daemon. 'Run,' he said. 'Run fast, and run far.'

The Verminlord hissed and struggled to its hooves, bifurcated tail lashing. For a moment, he thought it might attack him. Then, with a screech of frustration, it flung itself over the prow and was gone.

'You are sparing it,' Tornus said.

'Mercy is the sharpest blade there is,' Gardus said. He lifted a loop of chain and handed it to Tornus. 'Lash this about the mast.' He glanced at Enyo. 'Help Cadoc.'

Tornus flew back towards the mast, dragging the chain. Gardus turned, holding tight to both lengths of chain. He could feel the galley trembling beneath his feet, and he said a silent prayer that it would survive the next stage of their journey. It was no longer solely a vessel of wood and iron, but also one of faith. And only faith would sustain it.

A bone-deep rumble filled the air as the galley swept on. The river below was reduced to wisps of steam by the constant barrage of lightning streaking from the hull. The cavern began to crack and crumble. Sections of stone plummeted down, only to be obliterated by the talons of celestial energy emanating from the galley. A wall of dust spewed upwards as the skaven palisades collapsed in on themselves. The galley burst through the dust, and Gardus heard the roar of falling water.

A moment later, he caught sight of the immense tangled root system that led down into the next level of the garden. It was a slumped bastion of ruptured roots, broken mountains and crushed structures, pouring down into an abyss at a gentle angle. Water flowed in crooked rivers, winding through the ruins to eventually splash into the depths. Cadoc's arc took him out over the descent.

Gardus could see that the next tier began where the one above it ended. The gates of the Hopeless City were almost flush with the rim of the drop. They resembled a circular trapdoor, many leagues across and covered in enormous malformations, which resembled gigantic, leering faces. Grated apertures had been built into the immense portcullis to allow for the passage of water, and crude towers rose around them, manned by legions of daemons. Fascinated despite himself, Gardus watched as the great gates creaked open to allow for the passage of a flotilla of galleys. They swung inwards and down, casting up clouds of water vapour and startling flocks of mould-winged birds. The creatures rose in a shrieking spiral towards their galley, only to scatter as they came close.

Down below, horns began to sound and warning bells tolled. Cadoc dived towards the creaking gateway, dragging the galley behind him. Gardus fought to remain standing, and heard the shouts and curses of his warriors as they found themselves knocked from their feet by the sudden acceleration. Tegrus and his Prosecutors took to the air, swooping around the galley in a protective cordon. Their hammers spun down to pummel the watch-towers like a rain of meteors. Cadoc hurtled downwards and through the closing gates.

'Morbus,' Gardus cried.

He heard the Lord-Relictor strike the deck with his staff, and felt the galley tremble. Lightning sheared away from the vessel to rampage across the gateway. The leering faces twisted, becoming grimaces of pain and shock. Watch-towers were set aflame, and hapless vessels were reduced to smouldering wreckage as they swept by them. And then they passed the gates of Despondency and entered the Hopeless City.

Enyo swooped around the blazing length of chain. She drew an arrow from her quiver and loosed it, plucking a periwig-wearing rider from its grotesque rot fly. The daemons boiled upwards from within the round hive of the city, emerging from off-kilter apertures and upside-down portcullises in a solid cloud.

The Hopeless City was a lunatic's dream. It resembled the interior of a colossal, hollowed-out tower, many leagues across and of seemingly infinite height, with crooked streets and skeletal buildings that looped and jutted in every direction at once. The city was in constant motion, built as it was against the grindstone tiers of the garden. Its blocks and districts slowly rasped against one another, filling the air with spurting clouds of noxious dust. Water cascaded down through crazily angled aqueducts, spilling out over parts of the city in cacophonous arcs and jets. Oily vapour mingled with dust, to create a greasy pall over everything. Ships rode the jets of water to and fro, heedless of the pull of gravity. She swooped by a tri-masted galley moving vertically up a waterfall. The deformed faces of the crew were twisted in confusion, and perhaps fear, as they watched her plummet past them.

Below Enyo, Cadoc roared out prayers and imprecations as he plunged through the horde of plague drones, his starblade carving him a path. The Prince of Ekran was many things, but hesitant wasn't one of them. To him, more enemies only meant more chances to show the strength of his faith.

Enyo banked, loosing two more arrows in quick succession. These daemons were of a different sort to those they'd encountered earlier. They wore filth-encrusted, foppish uniforms beneath corroded armour, and basket helmets decorated with stylised insect mandibles. Some carried crude lances or hunting spears, while others waved serrated blades. Her arrows punched through them easily enough, however they were clad.

Periphas streaked ahead of her, clawing at the compound eyes of the rot flies. The star-eagle's hunting cry pierced the muggy air. She rolled through the air, letting the edges of her wings caress the abdomens of a pair of flies. The insects convulsed as the shimmering feathers ate through their flesh like acid. Their riders were thrown from their saddles and tumbled away, striking bridges and walkways before vanishing into the gloom below.

Enyo spun in a tight gavotte as she drew an arrow from her quiver. Her last, as it happened. She felt the electric tingle of the Six Smiths enchantments as new shafts appeared, refilling the quiver. But there were fewer arrows than there ought to have been, and they were taking longer to reform. The enchantments were fading, the longer they stayed in this place. She pushed the thought aside and loosed the arrow she held, piercing the brain of a darting rot fly. She reached for another.

Above and behind her, the galley thundered through the heart of the city, its hull wreathed in cobalt fire and lightning.

A tower of stone burst as the lightning played across it. A bridge crafted from the jawbone of some long dead monstrosity was reduced to splinters. A vessel sank into a torrent of water, a smoking wreckage. The inhabitants of the city fled in all directions as the galley passed, leaving destruction and fire in its wake. Wailing daemons danced in agony as they were caught by the strobing light of Cadoc's beacon, or consumed by lightning.

Lord-Celestant Gardus stood braced on the prow of the galley, Cadoc's chain of light wrapped about his arms and torso. She didn't understand how the magic worked, but she had faith that it did and would, until Sigmar decided otherwise. And when that moment came, they would die as the God-King willed. As only the faithful could.

Such fatalism would have once been alien to her. In lost Cypria, the inevitable was to be fought. Hope was doctrine. But Cypria was gone, and soon, she would be as well. This place would claim them all. But their deaths would have meaning. That she believed. The Stormcast Eternals were the arrows in Sigmar's quiver, to be drawn, nocked and loosed when the time came. And if this was her time, she welcomed it.

A shout from below caught her attention. Cadoc gestured downwards with his starblade. Beyond the glow of his beacon, she saw a second, smaller gateway, reminiscent of the one they'd used to enter the city. It was closing. Mechanisms of rusty iron and mushroom-covered wood clicked and stuttered as gangs of mortal Rotbringers laboured beneath lashes wielded by daemon overseers. The mortals hauled on chains, forcing ancient hinges to swing shut. Her wings folded, adding to her speed. She loosed three arrows in quick succession, dropping a Rotbringer with each. The operation stuttered to a halt as the Rotbringers panicked. Enyo sent a fourth arrow into the skull of one of the daemonic overseers as it tried to restore order.

Rot flies swarmed towards her, their riders droning curses. She banked sharply and began to ascend, as Tegrus and two of his Prosecutors swooped past, summoning their hammers. She drew the plague drones up and away as the Prosecutors sent their hammers hurtling down onto the gate mechanisms.

Smoke and fire belched from the gateway as daemons and mortals fled the destruction. The gates themselves hung half shut, and the Prosecutors slammed into them, forcing them to open. Cadoc led the galley through, and the fury of the vessel's passage finished the task the Prosecutors had begun. Lightning ricocheted through the daemonic mechanisms and set the pustulant wood aflame. Daemons squealed as they burned in the ensuing conflagration. Enyo plunged through the billowing smoke, Periphas beside her. The bird's plumage shone like the stars it had once called home.

More gates waited ahead. She lost count after the fifth. Each one sealed off a new level of horrors. Streets made from leprous tissue, and buildings crafted from screaming, infected bodies; a district built from innumerable square blocks of crimson-veined stone, the facets of which were marked with yowling, bestial faces; pleasure palaces of pus raised up from within city-sized wounds; a market full of fleshy tents and inhuman merchants whose strange wares wept and howled; a garden of singing flowers, their bulbous blossoms wet with unshed tears.

All these things and more she saw as she followed Cadoc's beacon into the darkness. Legions of daemons, some in periwigs and armour, others in hauberks of wyrm-skin, and some clad only in the filth of their creation, mobilised in the streets and alleys around the galley, racing to cut them off. Plague drones hurtled in their wake, not quite fast enough to catch up, but gaining with every obstacle. Tegrus and his Prosecutors dropped back to dissuade them, and Judicators loosed volley after volley into the streets around them.

But it wasn't simply the inhabitants who were opposed to them. The city itself seemed to be contracting around them. Walls and streets pressed close, and the omnipresent rumble drowned out all but the loudest of her thoughts. She recited the Canticles of Faith as she descended, drawing strength from the words set down by the first of the faithful.

And then she saw it. Their quarry.

The black galley sped along a concourse of water, far ahead. It sailed perpendicular to their course, moving downwards. Tattered sails plumped with an ill wind, it crested a torrent, and dropped to a parallel course. They had the lead, but she could catch them. They were sailing towards another gate, larger by far than the rest, and more ornate.

Like the others, it resembled a massive trapdoor, albeit with pimple-like watch-towers rising from its surface. It was shaped like a sneering, daemonic countenance. Bloated and toad-like, it seemed to gaze up at the approaching vessels with something akin to pleasure. The huge winches and pulleys encrusting its outer rim went into motion, and the face split in two as it began to swing open.

The black galley would be through it in moments. 'Periphas – find Tegrus,' she called. The Prosecutors would notice the gate soon, but not soon enough. She had to slow it down.

Enyo raced in pursuit. Her bowstring thrummed as she sent arrow after arrow whistling down towards the vessel. Daemons were knocked from the deck, their bodies tumbling up past her, before vanishing in the torrent of water. She caught sight of the hulking figure of the ship's captain on the aft deck. A bloated, betentacled monster, with a single-bladed axe resting on one shoulder. The creature twitched a tentacle towards her, as if in invitation. She loosed an arrow in reply.

The arrow streaked down, gathering speed as it punched through the air. At the last moment, a glistening tentacle snapped out and snared it. The shimmering tip halted, mere inches from the captain's featureless helm. The tentacle twitched, and the arrow snapped, releasing a burst of searing light. The captain tossed the pieces away with a roar audible even at such a distance.

Enyo folded her wings, adding speed to her descent. She had to reach them. She could see Lord-Castellant Grymn bound to the mast, sagging in his chains. She could not tell whether he still lived. She muttered a quiet prayer as she closed the gap. If she could just reach him, she might be able to pluck him free before his captors could stop her.

Glowing hammers whirled past her, sending up sprays of water to either side of the black galley. Prosecutors shot by. A hammer exploded against the galley's hull, rocking it in the water. One of the winged warriors sped towards the captain. A hammer snapped down, and was intercepted by the haft of the monstrous axe. For a moment, the two struggled across the heaving deck, trading blows. Then, more quickly than she thought possible, the captain whipped his axe out in a blow that tore through the Prosecutor's chest and shoulder. The Prosecutor fell back, struck the rail, and tumbled away and up.

Even now, after having seen the others who'd fallen here, she was taken aback by the lack of dissolution. The body didn't dissolve, didn't rupture into a thousand motes of lightning. Instead, it remained in one piece, his soul trapped within. To let his body vanish into the depths of this place would be to consign him to eternal torment.

The Prosecutor's body hurtled past her, trailing lightning. Instinctively, Enyo turned. She snagged the corpse's ankle and drew him to her, even as she turned to continue her descent. Below her, she saw the galley vanish through the gateway. The gateway slammed shut with an echoing crunch, and she landed atop it with a crash.

Daemons spilled from the watch-towers and lurched towards her across the steeply angled surface. Dozens of rotting, rancid bodies pressed in on her from every direction. Those first to reach her thrust barbed spears at her, as their droning chants assailed her ears. She backed away, still cradling the body of the Prosecutor.

Then came a shriek from above. Periphas swooped over her head, talons extended. A plaguebearer reeled back, wailing, as the star-eagle clawed out its single eye. A moment later, Tegrus and his remaining Prosecutors landed in a clap of thunder. Celestial hammers lashed out, pulping inhuman flesh.

'Lady Enyo, are you well?' Tegrus asked, as he swatted a plaguebearer from its feet.

'I am, but your warrior is not.' She booted a daemon in its split abdomen, doubling it over. As it staggered, she caught it in the jaw with her knee, snapping its head back. It stumbled into Tegrus' hammer, and its head burst like an overripe fruit.

'I was not quick enough. I sent them ahead, to aid you,' the Prosecutor-Prime said, his voice harsh with emotion. 'But our foe escaped again. *Again*.' He made a sound that was almost a snarl, and whirled about to fling one of his hammers towards the distant control mechanisms. The hammer gathered speed as it plunged through the daemonic ranks, and its glow grew brighter, until it shone like a falling star. When it struck the winches and pulleys, it did so with a cataclysmic roar. The gateway dropped away beneath them, and the daemons fell howling into the void.

Below them, Enyo saw a grey expanse stretching out into infinity. They'd breached the last gate of the city and passed through it. The fifth tier of Nurgle's garden awaited them. She felt a tremor go through her and, for a moment, she thought that the emptiness below twisted suddenly into an inhuman countenance, as wide as the realm itself and possessed of a malevolence far beyond the limits of her experience. Eyes like dying suns stared up at her, and she felt her soul shudder in its envelope of flesh and bone.

'Gardus was right. It is a trap,' Tegrus said, his voice hoarse with fear. She felt some relief that she wasn't alone in witnessing the apparition, but not much. 'The Plague God is waiting for us.'

The great eyes suddenly blinked, as if stung. Light swelled above them, and Enyo felt her fears diminish as the radiance spilled over her. She looked up and saw Cadoc and the galley approaching. In their wake, the capital city of Nurgle's realm burned with cobalt fire. Rot flies tumbled from the air around them, caught by lightning and arrow.

The way was clear. The Hopeless City had been conquered.

CHAPTER NINETEEN

OLD GHOSTS

The galley sped through the mist-soaked air above the feature-less mire. Grey sludge stretched in all directions, broken only by a few scraggly trees and sluggish inlets scattered about in haphazard fashion. The mist clung to everything, and stank of old, dark places and forgotten waters. Gardus felt his soul curdle as he contemplated the emptiness. This was a place where hope came to die. Nothing lived here, save that which had not yet died. There were no shrieking birds, no monstrous shapes. Only the turgid squelch of the grey waters, as they swirled slowly towards the garden's black heart.

There were no shapes to break up the monotony of the sky above. No leering faces, no ominous clouds. Only a colour-less, infinite, expanse. Everything here was grey and washed out. So oppressive was it that even the vibrant hue of their vessel had grown dull, and the distant bobbing of Cadoc's beacon was barely visible. Gardus kept to his post, anchoring the chain of light. His limbs and back had begun to ache, and he felt a soul-deep weariness within him. He wanted nothing more than to cease. To sleep.

Garradan... sleep, Garradan... sleep as we sleep... sleep and dream no more...

Gardus blinked, trying to keep his eyes open. His grip on the chain slackened.

Help us, Garradan... why don't you help us... don't leave us...

He felt the feather-light touch of hands on his war-plate. Heard the whisper of many voices in his ears, asking him to sleep, to rest. The chain grew slack.

Garradan... help us, teacher... burning up... it hurts... Garradan...

Gardus jolted awake. His fists clenched around the chain and he hauled back on it, looping it more tightly about his forearm. 'I'm sorry,' he said, softly. But he did not know who he was apologising to.

'You hear them as well, then.'

Gardus glanced over at Morbus. The Lord-Relictor had startled him. 'Yes.'

'As do the others.' Morbus spoke quietly, as if afraid of being overheard. 'Seeing things, as well as hearing them. Things that grow worse, the closer we get to...' He trailed off. Gardus knew what he meant. Their guide had been quiet since they'd left the Hopeless City behind, as if dumbstruck by their persistence. Despite this, they knew where they were going. Everything here was moving, however slowly, in the same direction.

'And you? Are you seeing things? Hearing things?'

Morbus was silent for long moments. Then, 'I hear only the voices of those whose souls are in my keeping.' He held up a hand. Light flickered between the gaps in his armour. Not the soft light that Gardus had become so familiar with, but the harsh, burning light of the storm. 'At times, their cries crowd out my own thoughts.'

'You should not have come,' Gardus said.

'If I had not, their souls would be lost.' Morbus looked at him. 'Yours as well. There are more subtle enchantments here than we have faced – lights that can draw souls into abyssal bogs, horrors stalking through the poison clouds far above. We have faced only the least of what this place has to offer, thanks to my rites, and Cadoc's lantern. Without those protections, we would have lost more warriors than we did.' He shook his head. 'Why did we really come here, Gardus?'

'You have asked me that before.'

'And you did not answer me then. Not really. You said you did not know. Do you know now?'

Gardus looked at him. 'No. It is merely a thing I must do. Back there… I heard a voice. Telling me that this must be accomplished, whatever the cost.' He held up a hand, watching the light play across the silver of his gauntlet. 'This light… it eases the pain of some, and causes injury to others. Am I like Cadoc's beacon – a tool of judgement? The souls here cower back from me, the vegetation withers. To what end?'

Morbus sighed. 'Sigmar's.' He said it as if the answer was obvious. 'This war of ours, it is not waged solely with rune-blades and hammers. And there are battlefields less tangible than even this place. The Ruinous Powers forced Sigmar back – broke his Great Peace, and shattered his allies. Thus, we were forged. Symbols and swords in one. We are the sound of the hammer, beating the world into shape. We purge the land, raise walls… Where we stand, order holds true, and Chaos is cast back.'

Gardus nodded, for Morbus' words were familiar. But the Lord-Relictor wasn't finished. 'We are also a message. A challenge, cast into the teeth of the foe.' Morbus bowed his head. 'That we stand here now, battered and weary as we are, is a sign of Sigmar's contempt for his enemies. And a warning as to his intentions.'

Gardus hesitated. 'You think he knew, then? That this would happen?'

'I think he sent us to the Plains of Vo for a reason. I think there is a purpose behind every command, whether we understand it or not.' Morbus leaned heavily on his staff. 'I think... if it was not us, it would have been someone else.' He chuckled. 'You are not alone in surviving a journey to the realm of the Dark Gods. Others have done it... Thostos Bladestorm, Orius Adamantine. None for so long as you, but it has been done.'

'And now we are doing it again.'

'But for it to mean anything, we must walk out again. And that is the true test. That is – ahgk!' Morbus bent forward, limbs twitching. The lightning crawling across him grew darker and fiercer, driving Gardus back. Morbus' staff fell from his grip, and he dropped to his hands and knees. The Lord-Relictor screamed. Lightning snapped out, carving black gouges across the deck and mast.

Gardus threw up a hand to shield his eyes. Morbus screamed again, and it was not his voice alone that cried out. His scream was echoed five, six, seven times. Gardus heard Osric and Kahya's voices among them, as well as others who had died since entering the garden. Their shapes were superimposed over that of the Lord-Relictor, mimicking his agonised movements. Their pain was his.

Worse yet, as Morbus writhed, the chain in Gardus' hand began to crumble away into flickering motes. The galley shuddered, as if caught by an unseen wave. The radiance that had protected them since they'd begun their journey was fading.

The hull creaked as the galley began to lose altitude. The sails flapped and tore as their descent grew swift. 'Hold on,' Gardus cried, as the last motes of light slipped between his fingers.

The galley did not plummet like a stone as he'd feared. Though the magic was fast fading, it did not vanish all at once. But the descent was not gentle in the least. The vessel spun through the air like a leaf caught in a downdraft. It rolled end over end, losing pieces of itself as it fell. The hull cracked, spilling the contents of the hold like blood. The oars split and shattered, the splintered remnants streaming upwards. Stormcasts held on where they could, using their weapons to anchor themselves to the rattling deck boards.

Eventually, the galley slammed down with a tooth-rattling crunch. The mast snapped and fell, crushing several rowers' benches. The remaining oars burst into jagged shards, and the keel cracked. The sails were torn loose from the fallen mast by a sudden wind, and flew out over the mire.

Gardus shouldered aside a broken section of mast and rose to his feet. Others did the same. Gardus saw no bodies, smelled no blood, and felt a wave of relief pass through him. Aetius clambered towards him. 'Everyone is alive,' the Liberator-Prime said. 'For now.'

Gardus looked around. They were wedged at the mouth of an inlet, caught among the remains of several barren trees. The mire stretched out around them, flat and featureless. Desolate. 'See to Morbus. Do what you can for him.' He moved to the mast and dragged Gatrog to his feet. The Rotbringer had come through the crash intact, and was still bound tight. He grunted as Gardus slammed him back against the broken base. 'How much farther?'

'It doesn't matter,' Gatrog said. 'This is where it ends.'

'No. Not yet. How long will it take us to reach Desolation?'

'The only way to reach Desolation is to surrender to despair. To fully give oneself over to the King of all Flies.' Gatrog wasn't laughing now. 'You are honourable warriors. Brave. But you are cursed with weakness. Hope still chains you. Until you shed its weight, you will never find the Inevitable Citadel.' He looked away. 'Even I cannot find it.'

'Hope is chaining you as well,' Tornus said. The Knight-Venator made his way towards them, clutching his abdomen as if it pained him. Gardus wondered if he'd injured himself in the crash.

Gatrog ignored him. He seemed shaken. 'Kill me if you wish. I cannot help you.'

Without thinking, Gardus reached for his runeblade. Tornus stopped him. 'I will be convincing him, Lord-Celestant. He will be helping us, whether he is wishing to or not.'

Gardus studied the Knight-Venator. Tornus seemed… different, somehow. His limbs trembled ever so slightly, as if straining against some unseen weight. Gardus caught a whiff of something rancid, like decaying meat. 'Are you injured?' he asked.

'I am feeling sick.' Tornus swayed and Gardus reached out to steady him. 'I am being hot and cold at the same time.' He shook his head, as if trying to clear it. 'Hearing… seeing things.'

'You are not alone.' Gardus turned, searching the mire. Indistinct shapes swayed in the distance, growing closer. A few at first, but every passing moment brought more, until they surrounded the stranded galley on all sides. The wind had picked up. The mist was creeping in on cat-quiet feet. He could hear voices in its gentle susurrus. From the sound of it, he wasn't the only one. Stormcasts crowded the rails, looking out into the grey. Some of them spoke in hushed tones, while others merely stared. A Liberator staggered, clawing at her helmet. Gardus reached her before she got it off.

'No, sister. Leave it on. This place is poison.'

'My children. I… I left them…' Her words came in sharp, staccato breaths. The mist coiled about her like the arms of a lover, and Gardus tried to disperse it. 'They are calling to me!' She tried to pull away from him. 'Can't you hear them?'

'I hear. I see. But they are not here. Listen to me. All of you. Listen!' Gardus raised his voice, silencing the others. 'They are not here. None of them. The spirits of this place are not real. They are lies.' The mist thickened, clinging to everything. He could see the hint of faces within it, and groping hands.

'They are real enough,' Gatrog said. 'This place, the mist, the water, even these trees are made from the souls of the despairing dead. Those who succumbed to Grandfather's blandishments, but lacked the strength to endure the joys they brought. Weak souls.' The Rotbringer spat, in evident disgust. 'And weakness is the mortar with which Grandfather builds his garden walls.'

'But they are not the souls of the righteous, and thus we need have no concern for their murmurings,' Cadoc called out, as he dropped to the deck in a crackle of lightning. The Knight-Azyros rose, beacon in hand. The mist retreated in the face of the glow. The murmurings dimmed. Cadoc laughed. 'Look to my light, brothers and sisters. It is the fire of Azyr, into which I fed a thousand such souls as these. Weak souls, corrupt and broken by the weight of that corruption. Watch them burn.'

He raised his beacon higher, so that the light washed across the deck. Gardus felt as if a weight had been lifted from him. His own light swelled in answer to that of the beacon. He turned, and saw several ghostly shapes standing nearby, watching the Stormcasts. The hazy figures were all over the ship. They retreated before the light. But whenever it turned away from them, they crowded close once more.

Gatrog stood unconcerned amongst a crowd of them. 'They are drawn to the living,' he said. 'To your hopes and desires, for they have none.' He twitched away from an insubstantial hand. 'They will draw you into their embrace, and make you one of them, unless you accept the truth of despair, and have the courage to continue, as all pilgrims must.'

'We are no pilgrims,' Cadoc snarled. He drew his star-blade. 'We are the sword of Azyr, silver and sharp. We are the weapon of the God-King, thrust into the bloated belly of his enemy. As I will do to you, if you continue to yap.'

'Well then, thrust away,' Gatrog said. He lurched forward to meet Cadoc's glare. 'If you wish a fight, you have but to strike off these chains and give me a blade. I will meet your fire again, and reduce it to naught but ashes.'

Cadoc growled and swung the beacon towards Gatrog.

Gardus caught Cadoc's wrist. 'Save your light for the wraiths, Cadoc. His only threat is to your pride.'

For a moment, Gardus thought Cadoc would ignore his command. But the Knight-Azyros subsided. Tornus caught Gatrog by his chains and led him away. Souls shied away from the Knight-Venator, as if something about him disturbed them. Gardus felt a flicker of worry, but pushed it aside as he watched Aetius help Morbus down onto the lower deck. 'Morbus, are you well?'

'Clearly not,' the Lord-Relictor said. His voice was a whisper, and azure cracks ran across his armour. His eyes were burning orbs of fire, lost to the radiance within him. Light flickered in the depths of his mask whenever he spoke. Heat bled off him, causing the air to waver strangely. 'I think I have found a flaw in this particular rite.'

'We should probably tell someone,' Gardus said. He helped Morbus to sit, and sank to one knee before him. 'You're not breathing,' he added, quietly.

'Not a surprise. My lungs are ash. My heart is a knot of lightning. My blood is smoke.' Morbus laughed weakly. 'I am truly the storm made manifest.' He looked up, and Gardus was forced to turn away. The light seeping from the eye-slits of the Lord-Relictor's mask was too intense to meet for long. 'I will not survive this. And when I perish, so too will all those whom I hold safe within me.'

'How long?'

Morbus looked away. 'How long is a storm? A few hours. Days. Perhaps only moments.' His grip on his staff tightened, causing the heat-blackened sigmarite to creak. 'We must find some way to keep moving. If we stay here, we will be consumed by this place. It has already begun.'

Gardus followed his gaze, and saw Tegrus rocking back and forth, muttering to himself. The insubstantial shapes surrounded the Prosecutor, and seemed to be whispering. 'Without the light, we will be overwhelmed.'

'Not if we move, and soon.' Morbus caught his arm. 'We must get to Desolation.'

'We will find Grymn before then,' Gardus said. 'Whatever else, we will not fail.'

Morbus shook his head. 'No. Not Grymn. It is to Desolation that we must go. That is what this has all been about, Gardus. That is why we have journeyed so far. Cadoc is a fool, but he is right about one thing… we are Sigmar's weapon, and we must find his enemy's heart. Whatever the cost, whatever the consequence, we must reach Desolation.' He sagged back. 'Or all of this was for nothing.'

* * *

Tornus staggered away from the others. The pain had been growing since the Hopeless City. Like a seed spreading black shoots through him. He leaned against the stump of the mast, unable to catch his breath. It felt as if there was fluid in his lungs. He was drowning in the open air. He wanted to tell Gardus, or Morbus. Someone. They would know what to do. But he couldn't force the words out. He sagged, head bowed.

It was unlikely that Morbus would be able to help him, at any rate. The Lord-Relictor looked worse than Tornus felt. As if there were a fire building within him, getting ready to explode at any moment. He glanced at Morbus, and saw him sitting hunched on the steps to the forward deck. Gardus knelt before him, and they conferred in low tones. A spasm of pain rippled through him, and he bit back a groan.

'Torglug?' Gatrog asked, watching him. There was a wariness in the Rotbringer's voice as he stood. Or perhaps... worry?

'I am telling you, I am not being Torglug,' Tornus hissed as another spasm of pain racked him. 'I am being Tornus.' He could smell something familiar... the stink of pure water turning sour. Of stone crumbling to mouldy dust, and flesh sloughing from bone. He could hear familiar screams echoing dimly out of the grey.

'Lies,' he whispered. They were just lies, as Gardus had said.

'Nothing here is a lie,' Gatrog said. 'No more than your reflection in a pool of water is a lie.' He crept close, chains rattling. 'I can smell something flowering within you, Torglug. Your hope withers, and new life rises.'

'Quiet.' Tornus blinked, trying to clear his vision. Beads of sweat rolled down, burning his eyes. His stomach was knotted up. The splintered wood of the mast turned to powder in his grip. He whipped around as he half-glimpsed a familiar face. He groped for a name as one shape amongst the hazy masses grew solid.

The apparition moved towards him, her shape wreathed in silent flame. Her body was charred black, with only her eyes remaining unburnt. They were a deep, mossy green, and when they met his, his heart felt as if it were being torn in two. She reached for him, and he stumbled to meet her. What was her name? Why couldn't he remember?

Because you killed her, his shadow said. He looked down. His shadow raised an axe. The burning woman shrank bank, mouth open in a scream that never came. Tornus groaned as the shock of the blow reverberated through his arms. More blows, the echoes of blows long since fallen shuddered through him, and he shook his head, trying to focus.

The smells were stronger now, all encompassing. And he knew them, finally. The Lifewells were burning, and his people with them. His first act as Torglug had been the butchery of all that Tornus had loved. He turned, and saw not the galley or his fellow Stormcasts, but instead... fire. Balefire, burning bright and hungry.

Ancient trees, bastions of bark and aged strength, crumpled in the flames. Burning figures fled, their screams like the sweetest of songs. Other faces pressed in on him from all sides, begging with him, pleading for mercy. And it was mercy he gave them, though not the sort they wished.

Death was the only mercy Torglug had understood. Death was an end to all pain, all hope, all fear. His people had begged him for mercy, and he bestowed it with a swing of his axe. He felt bones crunch beneath his feet, and the heat of a collapsing tree.

'I am not doing this. This is not being me.' He pounded his fists against his head. Somewhere, he could hear Ospheonis shrieking. He wanted to fly, to rise and seek the stars once more. There had been peace there, in the void. Freedom from the weight of his past. But that weight never went away. He had been purged in the fires of Azyr, but some kernel of filth yet remained, and it had been growing ever since he'd entered this realm.

The ghostly screams of the Everdawn tribe rose into a keening wail. Added to their number were the bellowing voices of the Viridian ogors, and the rasping hiss of the sylvaneth. A thousand thousand souls, crying out as one. The names rolled over him. Tree-Cutter. Gut-Spiller. The Despised One. The Woodsman of Nurgle.

Torglug.

Torglug.

Torglug.

Pain. Sharp and insistent. Tornus sank to one knee, arms wrapped about his midsection. He sucked in air for a scream, but no sound came. Bile burned in his throat. He fell to his hands and knees. Vomit spewed from his mouth, splattering against the inside of his helmet. He clawed at the clasps, trying to get it off. He heard voices raised in concern, but couldn't respond. Vomit pooled on the deck.

A hand, thick with fat and muscle, erupted from the puddle. Wide fingers fastened about his helmet and shoved him upwards. Tornus was forced upright as an arm followed the hand. Then a shoulder and a round head, hidden within a corroded helm, topped by a single, curved horn. A moment later, Tornus was dangling helplessly from the apparition's grip.

The Woodsman of Nurgle chortled and lifted Tornus high.

'You are being surprised, yes,' Torglug the Despised said. 'And it is being the last surprise you are having.'

* * *

Gatrog stumbled back in shock as the apparition rose, dragging Tornus from his feet. He recognised the hulking shape instantly, for he had fought beside it often enough. Torglug the Despised. Ironhood the Woodsman, favoured of Nurgle. Hero of the Battle of the Black Cistern.

The featureless helm turned in his direction. 'You are being one of Grandfather's.'

'I am–' Gatrog began.

'In chains.' The great axe licked out, severing the links and gashing Gatrog's arms and chest. 'You are being useless in chains. Find a blade and die as Grandfather wills.'

The bloated creature turned his attention back to his other self. 'And you are being nothing more than an empty vessel I am casting aside.' Torglug hurled Tornus away, and something in Gatrog spasmed in sympathy. For all that he was an abomination, the Stormcast had treated him fairly, and honourably. As well as any knight of the Order. He shook himself, pushing the moment of weakness aside. Tornus was a falsehood. Torglug was Grandfather's truth. And he had come, like one of the old heroes from the songs of the troubadours. Like the stories Goral had told him when he'd been but a squire.

'Ah, cousin, this would have pleased you to no end.' He cast about, seeking something to use as a weapon. Stormcasts advanced on Torglug, shields raised in a vain effort to hold back the bite of the Woodsman's axe. Torglug laughed and swept his axe out in a wide loop, driving them back. The axe reversed course, splintering arrows in mid-flight. The Woodsman was as magnificent as Gatrog remembered.

'Is this being all that is left? How many souls are littering your path, Azyrites?' Torglug rested his axe in the crook of his arm. 'It is hardly being worth the effort.'

'Then by all means, retreat back into whatever nethermost

hell you crawled out of,' Gardus said, pushing his way forward, hammer in hand. 'What are you? A ghost? Or just some twist of shadow and stink?'

'I am being Torglug. And you are being Gardus.'

Torglug brought his axe up, gripping it in both hands. 'Gardus, who is so kindly leading me to Alarielle. Gardus, who is running so rudely through Grandfather's garden. Gardus Shiver Soul, the flydandies of Grandfather's court call you. Gardus the coward. Gardus the weak.'

Gardus drew his runeblade. 'A phantom, then. An echo of failures past.' His voice rang with certainty, and the light that gleamed off him grew so bright that Gatrog had to look away. He paused in his attempts to find a weapon, and stood watching as the two warriors met. Fat sparks of balefire erupted as their weapons clashed.

Torglug roared and cursed as he hewed at Gardus. Gardus, in contrast, fought in silence. Gatrog could not say who was the stronger. He heard a murmur, and turned. The souls of the despairing dead threaded among the Stormcasts, whispering in their ears, or holding their gazes. The ghostly shapes crowded the deck, slowly but surely isolating the warriors from one another. Without Gardus to rally them, without the cursed light of Azyr, they were losing faith. Even the skull-faced shaman was powerless against such persistent murmurings. His body twitched and thrashed, as the dead surrounded him. The spotted gryph-hound stood protectively over him, snapping fiercely but uselessly at the spirits.

Gatrog wanted to laugh, but… didn't. Couldn't. Once, perhaps. But not now. Not after seeing what he'd seen. There was courage here, and honour, though it was in service to a false god. Sigmar was not worthy of such warriors.

This was not victory. Not the sort he'd hoped for, at any rate.

It was a trick. The whispering shapes struck at places no warrior could hope to defend. And though it served the will of the King of all Flies... It was not right.

'And who are you to say what is right, cousin?'

Gatrog whirled. Goral sat on the rail, eating one of the ripe, black apples that grew in the orchards of Festerfane. There were others beside him, knights all – brawny Sir Culgus, who had perished in the Writhing Weald alongside Goral, and young Pallid Woes, with whom he'd earned his spurs. Blightmaster Wolgus, and brave Sir Festerbite. Others, dozens, drifting into hazy obscurity.

'Cousin, have you come to aid me?' Gatrog asked.

Goral took another bite of his apple. His scabrous armour creaked about his swollen frame as he leaned forward. 'In a manner of speaking, fair cousin. I come to ask but a single question... Is your faith waning?'

'No,' Gatrog said.

'Then why do you hesitate?' a voice rumbled.

Gatrog turned and looked up into the frowning, daemonic visage of Count Dolorugus, the hero of the City of Reeds, who had perished in the attempt to summon Nurgle's legions.

The great antlered head dipped, and a sigh gusted forth. 'Surely you see what must be done, gentle Gatrog.'

'I swore an oath.'

'To whom? The Azyrite? You swore one to Nurgle first.'

Gatrog glanced back towards the duel. Torglug seemed to swell in strength, as Gardus' light dimmed. The ending was inevitable. So why then did he hesitate? 'This is not the way,' he said, looking back at his cousin. 'In the songs of Onogal, when did the knights of old ever shy away from a contest of arms, or the truth of despair? But this is not such a contest. It is deceitful. A trick, unworthy of us. Unworthy of the King of all Flies. The beauty of despair does not need to mask itself in falsehood.'

'And again, I ask, who are you to claim that?' Goral finished his apple and tossed the core over his shoulder. 'Who are you to say what is true, and what is false?' He pointed. 'Look. See. She weeps, to see such weakness.'

Gatrog heard the clop of her hooves before he saw her. She who had brought peace to sevenfold warring duchies, and forged from them a kingdom based on the ideals of despair, acceptance and chivalry. The Lady of Cankerwall, in her rotting gown and mouldy furs, her face veiled, her hair bound and coiled about her slim shoulders like a serpent. Her pale hands were clasped before her, as if in prayer, and she smelled of rotting flowers and sour water. Tears of glistening pus dripped from beneath her veil.

Gatrog sank to his knees. 'My lady, forgive me, but I swore an oath.' He knew she was not truly there. Like Goral and the others, she was but a manifestation of this place. But was it a sign of favour, or a warning from the King of all Flies?

'Art thou a true knight, and bold?' Her voice was like the rustle of dead leaves.

He bowed his head. 'I am.'

A pale finger was pressed to his lips. 'If you are, then why do you hesitate? What is honour, weighed against the necessity of the gardener?'

Before he could even attempt to formulate a reply, he heard a crash, and saw Gardus flung to the deck by a blow from Torglug's axe. The Lord-Celestant's runeblade skidded towards him, and his hand twitched for the hilt. A savage heat rose from the weapon, and he jerked back. He looked up as a shadow passed over him. Cadoc Kel plunged towards Torglug, roaring in fury. His attack drove the Despised One back from his opponent. The Knight-Azyros swung his beacon down, like a club. Torglug batted it from his hand with a curse, sending it rolling away.

Cadoc's sword hissed out, adding to the collection of wounds that marked Torglug's corpus. He lunged, blade extended. Torglug avoided the blow with inhuman grace and replied in kind, before his opponent could react.

Cadoc screamed as the blighted axe slammed down on his shoulder, shearing through his armour. His sword fell from nerveless fingers as he stumbled back. Torglug ripped the axe free and the Knight-Azyros collapsed onto the deck. Torglug turned to face Gardus, chortling. Gatrog could see the weakness in the Lord-Celestant's movements. This place, the miasma, it was eating away at Gardus' strength, though he didn't realise it. He faced Torglug, his back to Gatrog. The perfect target.

'I swore an oath,' he said.

'Victory is inevitable,' the Lady whispered. 'All is as the Lord of All Things wills.' Gatrog felt her guide his hand towards the hilt of the runeblade. Despite the heat, and the pain, he caught it up.

He rose to his feet, certain of what he must do.

'Desolation is on the horizon.'

Grymn cracked an eye and looked up at his captor. Spume stared down at him. The pirate nudged him with his axe. 'Thought ye would like to be awake for it.' Grymn tried to push himself up, but Spume's boot thumped down between his shoulders, flattening him. 'I said awake, not on your feet.'

Grymn stared down into the bilges. The slaves who'd once occupied them were nowhere to be seen. 'Dead weight,' Spume said. 'We need speed now, so I had them chopped up and fed to the crew. Rest assured that they did not suffer unduly.'

The Lord-Castellant gave a hollow cry and tried to rise, fingers groping for Spume's fat neck. Spume drove the ferrule of his axe into Grymn's stomach, doubling him over. A single blow from the pirate's meaty fist dropped him back onto all fours. 'Angry, are ye? Mad enough to spit nails, I'd guess. Good.'

Grymn sagged, trying to catch his breath. Everything ached. Every joint felt swollen, his arms and legs felt as if they had been dislocated, his lungs burned. Spume let his axe sink into the deck. 'The maggot-curse has you. But it's slow – takes time. The little buggers chew away at body and soul, and I bet they've never tasted anything like you before.'

For a blood-simple reaver, he's astute, Bubonicus murmured.

Spume twitched. 'I can hear ye, stowaway. And you'll pay mightily for those insults ye toss off so readily. Whoever ye are, your failure is evident. Elsewise, ye wouldn't be walking the maggot-road.' He chuckled. 'You're just a bit of gristle, to be stripped from the bone, and no more than that.' He indicated Grymn. 'This one is the real meat.'

Grymn tried to ignore Bubonicus' growing anger, but it clouded his thoughts as if it had been his own. It was growing harder and harder to tell where his thoughts left off and those of his unwelcome tenant began.

'Ye think your falling into my lap was just happenstance?' Spume laughed. 'Nurgle is called the Lord of All Things for good reason. All that lives serves him in some way. Even a half-life such as yours.' He rolled Grymn onto his side and sank down into a crouch beside him. Thick fingers fumbled Grymn's helmet from his head and sent it clattering away.

Spume grunted. 'Hnh. I expected something else. But you're only flesh and blood after all.' He pinched Grymn's cheek. 'Not for long, though. I can smell the stink of that second soul, rising wild and strong.' Spume slapped him and rose, chuckling. 'Taking a while, though. You're a hard one, no doubt about it. Parched soil, as they say. Hard to grow anything of worth in that.'

Grymn struggled to rise, and Spume casually kicked him back over. 'But it's taken all the fight out of ye. Pity. You'll be hollow and limp by the time we reach Desolation.' The kraken beak in Spume's armpit snapped in what might have been frustration. 'If I had my druthers, I'd rip that stowaway out of you, and set him adrift.'

'A-and if I had m-mine, I'd silence your f-flapping tongue,' Grymn growled.

Spume's tentacles shot forward, wrapping about his head and throat. The pirate rose, dragging Grymn into the air.

'That's what I like to hear,' Spume gurgled. 'Keep that fire in your belly lit. It'll serve ye well, in the nightmare to come. Perhaps, if there's anything left of ye after Father Decay has had his way, I'll find a berth for ye on my ship.'

Grymn laughed harshly. Spume cocked his head. 'And why are ye laughing?'

'Y-you boast so, I assumed that y-you were more than just a-another slave.'

Are you mad? He will kill you, Bubonicus hissed.

Grymn ignored him.

The tentacles tightened about Grymn's neck. 'I'm no slave,' Spume said.

'No?' Grymn met the pallid gaze of his captor and smiled. 'Then why do you hurry so, to do the bidding of another?'

The barbs lining the underside of the tentacles dug into his flesh, and blood spilled down inside his armour.

No! I will not let you do this.

Grymn bit back a groan as something shifted inside him. He

felt as if he had a bellyful of sour wine, and brambles pressing against his lungs and throat. His limbs twitched, and he fought to remain still.

'Ye think ye are the only one trapped here, shiny-skin? There are seas beyond this one, and I would sail them. If that means I must lick the boots of some pampered lubberwort, so be it. All that matters to me is rejoining my armada.'

'A-and it is the nature of daemons to f-fairly reward those who serve th-them, is it?' Grymn's vision was blackening at the edges. He could barely breathe, and his spine ached from Spume's grip.

Then, abruptly, Spume's grip slackened. The pirate let him fall to the deck. 'Ye are a fool, but... maybe a wise one.' Spume retrieved his axe. 'I told ye before, I will not be denied my glory by anyone. Even the Hand of Nurgle himself.' He turned away. 'So have no fear on that score, lubber. You and I will settle up properly, when all is said and done.'

You fool. While I understand the urge to silence his prattling, I will not allow you to endanger us so. Bubonicus sounded fearful. *Not when I am... am...*

'Am what?' Grymn said. 'You think to possess my body? Sigmar made us of sterner stuff than that. Else why haven't you done it yet?'

Bubonicus growled. Grymn laughed mirthlessly. 'You can't.' He tapped his head. 'My mind is a fortress, with walls made of faith. You can scale them, but you cannot take them. Again and again, I have driven you back. I have held you in place.'

And I have held you.

Grymn nodded. 'Yes. Stalemate. If this were a proper siege, I'd give myself odds. But it's not. The best outcome is death. A meaningful one, preferably, but I'm not picky.'

You have no honour.

'A child's insult. Honour is the privilege of good men. You boast of having seen my memories, maggot. Tell me... am I a good man?'

Bubonicus fell silent. After a moment, he murmured, *There is honour in such a death, I suppose. And I am tired. I have fought for the King of all Flies for centuries. I have waged a thousand wars, in a thousand kingdoms, and died a thousand times. But every cycle reaches its end. If this be my final battle, let it be a glorious one. Lay on, friend. And damned be him who cries hold.*

For an instant, Grymn felt a flicker of pity for the creature crouched within his soul. Here was a warrior, lost and damned though he was. What might he have been, had Nurgle not poisoned his mind and soul? Grymn closed his eyes.

'To the death, then,' he said.

CHAPTER TWENTY

MISERICORDIA

Tornus stared in horror at his shadow. The bloated, gargantuan figure that he had once been, and would be again. Despair clawed at the edges of his mind as he forced himself to his feet. He felt as if he had been poured dry and wrung out. His strength was all but gone, perhaps drawn into Torglug, and his wings hung silent and dark from his back. He could not see his bow, and his quiver was empty. It was as if Sigmar had reclaimed all the gifts he had once freely bestowed.

Torglug stood before Gardus, gloating. 'I am thanking Nurgle for this chance to be settling old scores,' he said. 'Ironhood the Woodsman is not putting down his axe yet, no, no. By and by, he will be claiming all of these souls for Grandfather.' He spread his arms, axe hanging loosely from his grip. He swung it up to point at Gardus. 'But for now, he will be taking your head to Desolation, *Steel Soul*.' The words sounded like an insult.

'I do not know how you came to be here, shade, but it will

take more than threats to remove my head.' Gardus lifted his hammer. Blood stained his silver armour, and the thickening mists dragged his limbs down. The despairing dead crowded about him, whispering and clutching at him with insubstantial claws. The Lord-Celestant's light wavered, but did not fade. It was only a matter of time, though. His strength was being leached from him by the clutching wraiths, and Torglug was stronger than ever.

Tornus looked around. There was no help to be had from the others. They seemed blind to what was happening, as if the miasma had claimed their wits as surely as it was stealing Gardus' strength. Even Morbus was afflicted, his crumpled shape shuddering with convulsions as the wraiths crouched about him. Only Cadoc had been unaffected, and he lay unmoving at Torglug's feet.

Torglug's axe looped around, carving a path towards Gardus' neck. Gardus blocked the blow, but was knocked off balance by the force of it. Another blow smashed aside his defences, and a third sent him reeling. Torglug drove the haft of his axe into Gardus' chest and knocked him to the deck. Gardus rolled aside as the axe crashed down. The blade became wedged in the deck. Before Gardus could get his feet under him, Torglug drove a meaty fist into his head, dropping him to his hands and knees.

Tornus took a wavering step towards his shadow. Torglug spun and pointed. 'Be waiting your turn, little lie. I am returning you to oblivion soon enough.'

'No,' Tornus said. Weaponless, he faced Torglug. 'You are being dead.'

'I am being eternal,' Torglug said. 'While you are living, a seed of me is yet remaining. While Tornus is drawing breath, Torglug is gathering his strength.' He laughed. The sound was like oil spreading across water. 'You are never being free of me.'

Tornus lunged, and Torglug caught him by the throat. He lifted Tornus as if he were a child and slammed him down against the deck, splintering the wood. Torglug dragged him up and repeated the process again and again. 'When you are dying here, when your soul is returning to Nurgle's manse, I am being born again. I am rising from you like mushrooms are rising from corpses.' He wrenched Tornus up and held him. 'But I am not killing you yet, little lie. I am wanting you to see what is happening to your new tribe. I am to be slaughtering them, the way I am slaughtering the people of the Everdawn.'

Tornus drove his fist into Torglug's head, crumpling the side of his helm. Torglug roared and hurled him to the deck, hard enough to knock the air from his lungs. Ospheonis shrieked and dived down. The star-eagle had been circling above, uncertain as to what was going on. But it understood now. It ripped and tore at Torglug, causing him to bellow in frustration. He swiped at the bird, driving it away. Tornus tried to rise, but couldn't find the strength. He collapsed onto his back.

A massive, hoof-like foot dropped onto his chest, pinning him in place. Torglug stretched a hand towards his axe. 'Now, you are to be watching as I am taking the head of your new chieftain.'

'Not today, Despised One.'

Torglug turned. A phlegmatic laugh burbled up. 'Is this being a jest?'

'I am Lord-Duke of Festerfane,' Gatrog said, lifting the runeblade in both hands. 'And I swore an oath.' Smoke billowed up from between his fingers, and streamers of blue flame crept up his arms as he lunged and drove the blade into

Torglug's flabby chest. Torglug screamed in incomprehension and backhanded the Chaos knight away. Gatrog struck the mast and sank down, stunned. Torglug snatched up his axe and stomped towards the Chaos knight. Swifter than thought, he buried the pitted blade in Gatrog's chest with a wet thunk.

'No!' Tornus flung himself towards his shadow. Torglug whirled. Tornus slammed into him and drove him backwards. Torglug lost his grip on his axe. Tornus caught hold of the hilt of the runeblade.

'You are not to be killing me,' Torglug said, clawing at him.

'I am. I am killing you this time, filth. As I should have been doing then.'

Torglug tried to pry the blade from his chest, but Tornus held it in place. The celestial energies surged through Torglug's bloated frame, burning him up from the inside out. He clawed at Tornus' helm with charring fingers. 'No,' he gurgled. 'No, not again.'

'Yes, again. And forevermore.' Tornus twisted the blade. He ripped it loose in a spray of superheated bile and turned away from the crumbling shape of his former self. 'Go back to the filth that has being spawned you.' A thin scream tripped across the murky air as, for the second and final time, Torglug the Despised passed from the world and into oblivion.

The light from the runeblade set the wraiths to fleeing as well. They retreated as the last of Torglug crumbled away to nothing. They would return, in time, but for now, they had been sated. Tornus quickly made his way to Gatrog's side.

The Chaos knight was broken. Torglug's axe had cleaved him open, and shattered the bones in his chest and back. There were some wounds even an infernal resilience could not mitigate. 'You are saving me,' Tornus said. 'And Gardus.'

Gatrog chuckled wetly and studied his blackened hands.

'Yes. It appears that our journey is coming to an end.' He looked at Tornus. 'But it has been a pleasure. Such sights have I seen... such glories. And my honour is upheld.'

Tornus sank to one knee beside the dying Chaos knight. 'Why?' he asked.

'I swore an oath to aid thee, and so I did.'

'That is not being the reason.'

Gatrog laughed. 'Maybe not. Maybe I simply saw a chance to pay my debt.' His laughter choked off into a groan. 'I am a true knight, Torglug. That is all I have ever wished to be...' His voice trailed off into silence.

Tornus could think of nothing to say as Gatrog coughed, shuddered, and sagged back into death. Slowly, softly, his body came apart like dry fungus. Tornus rose as the blight-wind swept the remnants up and carried them away, out over the turgid waters. He turned, runeblade hanging loosely in his hand.

'I am not understanding,' he said. Then something Gardus had said came back to him. Mercy was the sharpest blade there was. And for every deed, there was a seed that remained. His grip on Gardus' blade tightened. For perhaps the first time, he truly understood those words. He felt a hand on his shoulder, and turned.

'He died as he lived,' Gardus said. 'That is all any of us can hope for.'

'Could he have been finding redemption?'

Gardus extended his hand. Tornus returned his blade. 'I think, in his own way, he did.' He sheathed the blade and retrieved his hammer. 'And now it is time we found ours.'

The other Stormcasts were slow to recover. Many knelt in prayer, seeking to shore up the foundations of a shaken faith. Some had been wounded in Torglug's rampage, and concentrated on binding up their wounds with shreds torn from cloaks and the tattered remnants of the sail.

Morbus and Enyo crouched near Cadoc. The Knight-Azyros wasn't dead, but that would change soon enough. Blood pooled beneath him, spreading like the folds of a crimson cloak. His war-plate had been torn open, exposing the ravaged flesh within. Enyo had recovered Cadoc's beacon, and Tornus could see that its glow was fast fading.

'I failed you,' Cadoc gasped, as Gardus knelt beside him. 'My faith was not equal to the task, Steel Soul. Forgive me.'

'There is nothing to forgive,' Gardus said. 'You will return to us, with faith and form renewed, soon enough.'

Cadoc tried to laugh, but it came out as a gulping cough. 'I pray that it is so. The realms need cleansing, and who better than the Prince of Ekran to light the fire?' He sagged, gasping for air to fill lungs that had all but collapsed.

Gardus looked at Morbus. 'How long do we have before this place tests us anew?'

'For so long as the beacon lasts,' Morbus said. His voice was dull with pain. 'The power it contains will protect us, but only for so long as it burns. When Cadoc's heart beats its last, so too will the light fade. And we will be defenceless.'

'Can you get us moving?'

Morbus hesitated before answering. 'If the light is freed from the beacon, it might be enough to propel us to where we need to go. After that... it will be up to us.'

'You mean we must shatter the beacon,' Gardus said.

Morbus bowed his head. 'Yes. And such an act may well kill the one who attempts it.'

'I will be doing it,' Tornus said. 'It is being my atonement.' He reached for the beacon, but Cadoc caught his wrist in a vice-like grip.

'No, g... give it to me,' Cadoc gasped. He groped for the beacon with his other hand. 'It is my duty... my responsibility...'

'I am not certain that I can protect your soul, if you perish,' Morbus warned.

'My soul needs no protection,' Cadoc said. 'I am the light of Sigmar's wrath. Let the Dark Gods burn themselves to ashes in my fire.'

At Gardus' nod, Tornus handed him his beacon. Cadoc glared up at him. 'Beware, for I might consume you as well.'

'I am being ready,' Tornus said softly.

Cadoc nodded and gripped the beacon in both hands. Slowly, but surely, he began to prise it open. The light flared, brighter and brighter. 'Say your prayers, Lord-Relictor,' the Knight-Azyros growled as he tore the beacon asunder.

Morbus heaved himself unsteadily to his feet. The azure cracks in his armour were wider, and glowed brightly. A thin shroud of lightning crackled about him as he slammed the ferrule of his staff against the deck. 'Attend me, children of Azyr. Listen, and obey. Who is it that kneels here, before me?'

'Only the faithful,' Gardus said. Tornus and the others echoed him.

'Who shall rise like fire, when all is dust?'

'Only the faithful,' Tornus said, as he sank to one knee. The light slipped from the beacon and rose. Morbus gestured, and the light stretched and wavered. It spilled outwards from itself, doubling and redoubling in size and radiance. Tornus could hear the crash of warring stars and the eternal roar of the celestial cascade. Motes that might have been galaxies and nebulae took shape as the light swelled.

'Who will carry the light of Azyr into the darkness?'

'Only the faithful.'

The words flew like arrows. Tornus felt something within

him stir in response to the light above. The part of him that had been forged anew by Sigmar's hands, the part of him that was as one with the eternal storm, surged upwards to meet and strengthen the radiance. He could see similar motes of light rising from every Stormcast, binding them all to the glow above.

'Only through faith can victory be achieved,' the Lord-Relictor said. The second canticle of the Hallowed Knights. 'Only through faith can it even be conceived.'

Morbus stretched his hand upwards, as if to catch hold of the cobalt light. Instead, at his touch, it burst outwards, streaking to every part of the wrecked galley. 'Who finds salvation in sacrifice?'

'Only the faithful.'

'Who alone shall stand, when all others kneel?'

'Only the faithful.'

'Who shall hold up heaven's foundations, at the end of all things?'

'Only the faithful!'

Tornus and the others cried out the response as one, and the light became blinding. The deck shuddered beneath his feet as radiant blue flame swept across it. The flames consumed and rebuilt the vessel all in the same moment, and what rose from the mire was a graceful echo of what had been. Where before it had been a thing of brutal angles and serviceable design, it was now a craft fit to ply the celestial seas. Fiery sails swelled with a star-born wind, and the twin-tailed comet flickered across their expanse. Oars of lightning lashed out at the murk below, burning away the miasma and reducing the waters to steam.

Morbus, his form wreathed in fire, slammed his staff down once more, and with a peal of thunder, the great vessel began to move. Tornus staggered and sank back, fingers tracing the blackened outline of the twin-tailed comet on his chest-plate. All of the Stormcasts looked as if they had marched through a conflagration. Smoke rose from their armour, and the plumes of their helmets had been reduced to nothing.

Tornus could feel the movement of the oars in his bones, and the rush of searing wind against the curve of the hull. It was as if he and the ship were one. He glanced at Enyo in wonder, and she nodded. 'I feel it as well,' she said. 'This ship is made from the fire of our faith. It is us, and we are it.'

He felt the truth of her words as she spoke them.

'It is being Cadoc who is lighting it though.' He turned, and saw the Knight-Azyros lying still and silent where he'd fallen. The remains of the beacon lay beside him, its casing warped and shattered. Gardus stood over him, his weapons dangling loosely from his hands. Tornus joined him as Morbus sank down beside the body.

'Much is demanded of those to whom much is given,' the Lord-Relictor intoned, setting his hand on Cadoc's ruined chest. Morbus still burned. Cerulean flames rose from his battered mortis armour, obscuring almost all of its detail. Even his skull-helm was alight, with only the black outline of its shape visible. The flames grew brighter, Tornus noticed, as he drew Cadoc's soul into himself.

'Let us just hope that we have something left to give,' Gardus said.

Gutrot Spume stood with one foot balanced on the prow of his galley as it slid towards the gates of the Inevitable Citadel. The upper reaches of Desolation were composed of a ring of once-proud ruins, which spread out about the passage to the sixth tier of the garden as if it were a spoke in a wheel.

Broken walls rose like tombstones, marking the final resting place of long-buried empires.

'A fine place this, eh, Durg?'

The plaguebearer nodded glumly. 'Aye, captain.'

Spume chuckled. 'This place is a true testament to Grand-father's power.' He gestured expansively towards the ruins they sailed through. This place's name was forgotten to all but a few ancient daemon-scribes, and the eldest of Nurgle's tallymen. The capital of a realm-spanning empire, brought to utter ruin by a contagion that broke down the very bonds between flesh, bone, soul and mind. That which had resulted had become fertile soil for the Lord of All Things.

Now, only these few paltry ruins remained. A monument and a warning both. Put to use, as all things must be, and made over into a bastion of plague. Plaguebearers of the Blighted Legion marched in plodding lockstep through the shallows nearby, their scythe-glaives resting on their shoulders. They kept a droning count of the deaths they'd inflicted on the Mortal Realms, naming each and every soul claimed.

Industry thrived here, so close to the garden's heart. A thick cloud of black pox-smoke rose upwards from the tiers below, choking the air and blotting out all light save that of the bale-fire torches that lining the main boulevard. Vessels slid along flooded side-streets, sailing to war. Some went to defend Nurgle's waters. Others to conquer new lands in Grandfather's name.

Once, Spume would have been among them. And soon he would be again.

'You must be proud, reaver.'

He glanced at Urslaug's head, hanging from his belt. The witch had been quiet since they'd left the skaven warrens. 'And ye must be wondering what I intend to do with ye now, eh?' He snatched her up and held her at arm's length. She grimaced.

'I know you well enough to know what my fate is.'

'And yet ye helped me stir the pox-winds in my favour anyway.'

If she'd had shoulders, she would have shrugged. 'Truth to tell, I was getting bored tending my garden.'

Spume chuckled. He gestured, and two plaguebearers rolled a wooden cask towards him. 'By way of thanks, your body, as I swore. Preserved in cankerwine, and ready for its head to be reattached.'

Urslaug's eyes narrowed. 'You've forgiven me my treachery then?'

'Did I say that, now?' Spume twitched his axe meaningfully. The plaguebearers lifted the cask with a shared grunt, and heaved it over the rail. Urslaug screamed in anger. Spume laughed and swung her head out over the water. 'Make your way back to it, if you can. And think on your crimes as you do so. When I return this way again, mayhap you'll have rethought your loyalties, witch.'

'The only thing I'll be thinking of is the best way to strip the blubber from your poxy bones, Gutrot Spume,' Urslaug shrieked. Spume flicked her head after her body, and watched it arc up and tumble down, still screaming imprecations.

'Ah, women,' Spume said, glancing at the plaguebearers. 'Passionate creatures, the lot.'

The daemons stared at him in incomprehension. Spume waved them off, and turned back to his study of Desolation. The gates to the sixth tier hung within a massive stone archway, heavy with moss and slime. They were bronze and grotesquely decorated beneath a patina of grime. Legend stated that they were spoils of war, taken from Khorne's realm during the Wars of Blood. Their size was such that it required a hundred enslaved souls to haul the dripping chains that set the great opening mechanisms in motion.

The souls struggled through deep water, often being submerged entirely as they laboured. Nurglings clustered nearby on makeshift rafts of scum, and pelted the slaves with mucus and filth. Plaguebearers crouched on plinths of stone overlooking the waters. They jabbed at the struggling souls with rust-limned spears and halberds, encouraging them to greater efforts. The gates opened with an explosive creak, sending waves surging up over the rails of the galleys. Slaves were swept away, and nurglings spilled across the water in giggling clumps.

Spume thumped the deck with the haft of his axe, signalling his crew. Drums began to thump, and whips hissed as the rowers bent to their task. As the galley passed through the immense gates Spume heard the thunderous hum of a million flies. Bloated plague drones sped overhead, heading out into the mire. Spume watched them for a moment, then gestured to Durg. 'Go and get our prisoner. He should see this.'

Durg grinned toothily and sloped away. He enjoyed tormenting the Stormcast a bit more than was good for him, but Spume was inclined to be indulgent. After so long, it was almost time to bid the garden, and its stultifying boredom, goodbye. He turned back and leaned forwards, arm across his knee.

Behind the gates, a watery greenish light shone. The light of Grandfather's balefire reflected in the waters that coursed through the entirety of the garden. Unlike the other tiers, Desolation was walled off not simply with stone, but with sorcery. Only those ships blessed by Nurgle, or powerful enough to ignore such enchantments, could safely enter the Inevitable Citadel.

Desolation's wards had only been breached once in its history. The crystal ships of Tzeentch had reached the very walls of Nurgle's manse, during the Age of Blood. The wreckage of that fleet still glimmered in the soft light of Grandfather's hearth. Spume felt a pleasing heat as the galley passed through the light. A sound like the rushing of water filled his ears and, for a moment, he was blind to all save the gangrenous glow. Then they were through, and sailing along a wide canal.

Thick, high walls composed of slime-slick stone rose to either side of the canal. Hunched, toad-like gargoyles with open mouths and bulging eyes crouched atop the walls. They vomited a constant stream of sludgy water into the canal. Oily water vapour billowed upwards in a yellow cloud. Upside-down ramparts crossed above the canal, daemons marching in lazy formation across their inverted length. Parapets stretched vertically towards the sky, intersecting with the upturned ramparts, stubby daemon-engines lining their length. Balefire dripped from the grinning, stylised maws of the fire-throwers, ready to be unleashed upon invaders.

The whole of the citadel resembled a child's broken toy, its pieces cast into the air and frozen in mid-tumble. Spume had heard tell that this place had once been more traditional in its structure, but that Nurgle had grown bored. Now, jungle creepers thick with insect larvae stretched like a web between the dissociated segments, and strange birds nested in the fat roots that emerged from the cracks in the canal walls. Blossoms of an unhealthy hue floated in the waters and, occasionally, Spume caught a glimpse of silvery shapes slipping through the murky depths.

Ahead of him, a second gateway waited, guarded by two warriors of the Rotguard. The massive Great Unclean Ones stood on either side of the canal. They were both clad in battered, disintegrating, half-plate armour, and full-face featureless helms. Each carried an embossed shield as large as Spume himself, and a flail such as only a gargant could wield. The daemons paid no attention to the galley as it slipped between them. Spume watched them warily nonetheless. He remembered Gulax's promise, and had no wish to be caught unawares. The Rotguard were bad enemies to have, whatever the reason. They had much influence in the Court of Ruination in these troubled times.

A clatter caused him to turn. Durg hauled their captive up onto the forward deck, dragging him by his chains. The Stormcast didn't struggle. Spume grunted, somewhat disappointed. This was going to be no fun if all the fight had been beaten out of him. He set his axe over his shoulder and gestured with a tentacle.

'Welcome to the Inevitable Citadel, shiny-skin. It will be the last place you ever see.'

Grymn looked around, blinking against the sudden, painful light. The galley had sailed into what looked to be a vast stone amphitheatre of irregular shape and proportion. Canals ran crookedly through its heart, issuing from a septet of gateways. Haphazardly placed wooden beams rose against the oddly bulging walls, as if holding them in place. Monstrous roots erupted from beneath the paving stones and squirmed in all directions. Colossal statues, obscene in their construction, stood or squatted atop equally large plinths of onyx, marked with weeping sigils. Balefire torches and blighted lanterns cast a sickly glow over everything and, in their light, the statues seemed to twitch and grimace.

Daemons moved like insects among the roots and scuttled through the shadows of the statues. Some wore armour, others

were clad in ill-kept finery. All seemed to have their own purpose, and went about it. Unseen bells tolled throughout the
amphitheatre as the galley slid alongside a fungal wharf, thick
with chattering nurglings and swarms of flies.

At the centre of the amphitheatre, the waters of the canals
drained down into an abyssal cistern through a series of grates
shaped like the maws of great beasts. The rim of the cistern was nearly flush with the floor of the amphitheatre and,
from its mouth, a thick black cloud of smoke rose upwards
continuously.

Overhead, more support beams, each as wide around as two
men, criss-crossed the open air. From them hung thousands
of tarnished and befouled icons. Most were recognisable. The
runes of Khorne, Slaanesh and even the Horned Rat were in
evidence. Captured banners rustled in the smoky air, flap-
ping against hundreds of iron gibbet-cages, each containing
a broken, huddled form.

'The corsair-kings of the Cerulean Seas,' Spume said, looking up. 'Sorcerers and witches, bound to the whims of the
Architect of Fate. And now caged for eternity, at Grandfather's
pleasure.'

'Your kind has ever warred against itself,' Grymn said.

'Not my kind. They were weak.' Spume lifted Grymn's chin
with the flat of his axe. 'As ye are weak. But I am strong.
And will be stronger still, when I am returned to Ghyran.'
He rotated the axe, letting its edge scrape against Grymn's
chin and throat. 'Maybe they'll let me have your skin to hang
from my mast.'

'Come and take it, if you think you can.'

Spume laughed. 'Still some fight in ye, eh? Good. I was worried ye were going to make this no fun at all.'

Would that I had control of your mouth, as I do your limbs,

Bubonicus hissed. Grymn frowned. A wave of weakness passed through him, and he spat out a squirming maggot. Spume crushed it beneath his foot.

'There aren't many as could endure the maggot-curse so long. Ye must be about hollowed out by now.'

Grymn said nothing, too busy trying to control the surge of bile that rushed through him. Memories not his own crowded against his thoughts, making it hard to focus. Bubonicus had redoubled his efforts, desperate to conquer Grymn's will before they reached Desolation. Gradually, he'd lost control of his limbs, of his body. He could feel maggots squirming within him, smothering him from the inside. Pain radiated through his bones as they gnawed steadily away. His prayers had kept them at bay, but not for much longer.

Our battle is soon done, Bubonicus whispered.

'But not yet,' Grymn muttered, as Durg flung him to the deck. The daemon planted a warty foot between his shoulders and held him down. 'And if you have any hope of victory, you will leave me be.'

Bubonicus fell silent. Whatever else he might be, the creature was no fool. His fate was tied to Grymn's for the moment. Grymn blinked sweat and blood out of his eyes. He tried to focus on Spume. The Rotbringer sank to his haunches.

'There are matters yet to settle between us, before I hand your carcass over.'

'To your masters, you mean?'

Spume made a sound halfway between a growl and a laugh. 'Call them whatever ye like. Makes no difference to me. But I will have my just due of you.'

'Hardly a fair fight,' Grymn said, glaring up at him.

'I'm not interested in fair.' Spume waved Durg back. 'But I will give you one last chance to draw blood, if you like.'

A trick. He intends to humiliate you. To break you.

'I know,' Grymn said, heaving himself to his feet. Bubonicus made no attempt to stop him, though Grymn couldn't say why.

'Still talking to that rotten seed, eh? Well, pay attention.' Spume spun his axe and drove the haft into Grymn's stomach. He staggered back, and felt Durg's lash kiss his back. It couldn't cut through his armour, but the force of the blow dropped him to one knee. More plaguebearers crowded around, carrying cudgels and whips. They struck at him from all sides, and the thorns of the whips tore ragged gashes in his face.

'Whoever ye are in there, ye chose the wrong body to usurp. Bad luck, that.' Spume thrust himself through the knot of plaguebearers and used his tendrils to batter Grymn, knocking him sprawling. 'Good luck for me, though. Kept him weak, kept him from escaping. I should thank ye.' He struck Grymn in the side of the head, causing his world to spin. 'But, in truth, I was hoping for more of a challenge.'

Arrogant brute. To torment a captive so – and for what?

Spume caught Grymn in the chest with a kick and sent him rolling across the deck. He wheezed, trying to catch his breath. Something inside him was broken. The maggots were agitated. They squirmed from the wounds on his face and plopped to the deck. He tried to push himself up, but Bubonicus held him tight.

Surrender, and I will see him off, Lorrus. I will take his head, and cast it at the feet of his masters. Surrender!

'No,' Grymn said. Something pressed against his eyes from behind. He was blind. Maggots filled his mouth, his lungs. His heart strained against a shroud of squirming bodies. He felt something grip his soul in iron claws and threaten to rend it to pieces.

Surrender, damn you. I will not perish at the hands of a worthless braggart.

More memories. A young knight, riding through a sweetly scented garden beside a lady fair, her face hidden behind a veil. Of the burning, bitter taste of the sacred waters of Nurgle's own broth. Of the strength, and the glory of a life well lived in service to a Dark God. Vile images spattered across his consciousness like acid, but all with one common theme.

Despair. Surrender.

And that Lorrus Grymn could not do. 'I am the shield of the faithful,' he grunted, forcing the words out. 'I am the rock upon which the faithless break.' Whips hissed. Cudgels fell. New pain blossomed amid the old. 'I will die before I give up.'

You will, won't you? Never have I met a soul so stubborn. Your very marrow aswarm with maggots, and still you fight. Still you resist. Why?

'I have my honour,' Grymn whispered.

Bubonicus fell silent. And then feeling flooded Grymn's limbs. A whip snapped out and he raised a forearm. The lash tightened about his bracer, and he grabbed hold of it, jerking its wielder close. Durg grunted in confusion as Grymn's fist connected with its eye. The daemon screamed as its eye burst and Grymn's fist continued on, erupting out of the back of its skull. He ripped his arm free and shoved the dissolving body away.

'If you want me to fall, you'll have to do better than that.' He pushed himself to his feet. He felt feverish. His joints ached and his stomach churned. But he had control of himself again. He raised his chain, ready to meet Spume's charge.

You are brave, Lorrus. I am proud to know you.

'Quiet,' Grymn snarled.

'Ye can barely stand,' Spume said. He spun his axe with an easy grace.

'Barely,' Grymn said. 'And yet, here I am.' He pulled the chain taut.

'Not for long.' Spume stomped towards him, axe raised. 'I'll deliver you to the Lord of All Things in pieces, if I must.' The axe swept down.

Now!

At Bubonicus' warning, Grymn pivoted. He cast a loop of chain about the axe as it fell. He twisted aside, hauling the weapon out of Spume's hand and sending it whirling towards the mast. The massive blade slashed through ropes and chains before embedding itself in the slime-slick wood. Spume roared and launched himself at Grymn. The Lord-Castellant attempted to wrap his chain about the Rotbringer's throat, but Spume was quicker than he looked. His tentacles snared the chain, and jerked Grymn off balance.

The Stormcast leaned into the fall, tackling his tormentor off the upper deck. They crashed down among the rowers' benches, scattering the souls there. Grymn felt new strength flood him as he drove a fist into Spume's head, denting the pirate's helm. 'What are you doing?' he demanded.

Helping. I cannot defeat you, so I will lend my sword to your cause.

'I need no help from you.'

Spume reached up and caught him by the head. 'Take what ye can get, shiny-skin.' He drove his skull into Grymn's, knocking him back. Spume rose, shaking off bits of broken bench. Grymn snatched up a wide chunk of wood and struck the Rotbringer. Spume stumbled, and Grymn hit him again. The wood came apart in his hands. Spume roared and lunged, groping for his throat.

The kraken, Lorrus – strike the kraken!

Grymn ducked beneath Spume's lunge and made a grab

for the snapping beak. Tentacles entwined about him, but he caught the lump of muscle and clacking mandibles and gave it a wrench. Spume screamed shrilly. Grymn twisted the struggling mass, and hauled Spume around bodily. He caught sight of plaguebearers closing in on them, coming to aid their captain. It was time to end this.

He forced the pirate to his knees, and swiftly looped the chains around his throat. 'Now... now we come to it,' Grymn said. He twisted the chains, tightening the improvised noose. 'You wanted a reckoning? Here is your reckoning.'

Spume clawed at the chains, trying to free himself. Grymn drove his knee into Spume's back. Something snapped and Spume gurgled. He flopped forwards, yanking the chains from Grymn's grip. He writhed on the deck like a dying fish, slobbering curses. Before the plaguebearers could react, Grymn was among them.

He barrelled towards the mast. When he reached it, he ripped Spume's axe free and beheaded the closest plaguebearer. Whirling the axe about, he chopped through limbs and weapons alike, forcing the daemons back. Grymn fought his way back towards Spume, intending to remove the creature's head with his own axe.

'Hold.'

The word echoed in the sudden silence. Grymn turned, panting.

The galley's arrival had drawn a crowd. A phalanx of plaguebearers slouched towards the ship, accompanied by something far worse than they.

The Great Unclean One was enormous. Far larger, even, than Bolathrax had been. It sat slumped atop a massive palanquin, borne aloft by hundreds of mutilated souls. Their broken, disease-ridden forms were bound together by rusty chains and fraying ropes. They were bent beneath thick, roughly hewn logs, upon which the palanquin rested.

The daemon wore what appeared to be robes of state beneath the dirt and mould. Its flesh spilled through great rents and ragged tears in the robes, as if it had outgrown them over time. A tarnished gorget of beaten bronze squeezed tight about its flabby neck, and it wore an ornate breastplate of the same, marked with unpleasant agricultural motifs – unnatural grains waving against bloated moons, and pockmarked scythes. Thick, scaly fingers were draped over the heavy pommel of an enormous sword, which rested between the daemon's bandy legs. Seven crooked antlers sprouted from its round, toad-like skull. They rose up and met above its head to form the tri-part rune of Nurgle. A monocle of cracked, discoloured glass rested in the folds of one beady eye.

Father Decay, Bubonicus whispered. *The Hand of Nurgle himself. Lord High Admiral of the Plague-Fleets. Lorrus – you must surrender, now. Or both our souls are forfeit.*

Grymn shook his head, trying to focus. 'No.'

If you surrender now, you will live on in me. But if you do not, I – no. No.

'Is that the Maggot of Chivalry I hear, scrabbling in my prize? How came you here, Champion of Worms?'

The daemon's voice cut through Grymn like a rusty blade. His stomach heaved, and he blinked back tears of blood.

'Have you resorted to theft of another's crop? Or is it mere happenstance?' The daemon shrugged. 'No matter.'

Father Decay gestured, and Bubonicus screamed. Grymn screamed with him, for the pain was unbearable. He felt as if he were burning up from the inside out. Smoke spewed from his pores, nose and mouth, coalescing above him into something that might have been a face. The daemon chuckled.

'Ah, Bubonicus. A handsome lad, in your day. It is no won-der my dear cousin was so enamoured of you. But all things end, save that which Grandfather wishes to continue. Your time is done, your battles won and lost.'

The smoke began to dwindle, congealing as it did so, shrink-ing into a solid, smooth marble the colour of gangrene. It floated into the waiting palm of Father Decay. The daemon removed its monocle, spat on it, and returned it to its place before closely examining all that remained of Bubonicus. 'Yes, handsome indeed. Perhaps I shall return you to your sweet Lady, as a token of my esteem.' As it dropped the marble into its robes, it turned its attention to Grymn. 'And now for you. Long have I waited for you.'

Grymn stumbled. The axe slipped from his nerveless fingers as the creature's gaze pierced him to his very soul. 'You are a riddle without an answer. A soul plucked from the grasp of its rightful owners by a thief and a coward. You are a poison cup. A prize to be claimed, but fatal to possess.'

The words punched into him, stealing the ebbing strength from his limbs. He fell back against the mast, unable to draw a steady breath.

'Aye, he is a prize – mine.'

Spume had got to his feet. He reached for his axe. 'I brought him to you, daemon. I have done as you asked–'

'Commanded,' Father Decay rumbled.

Spume twitched, and pressed on. 'Where is my reward?'

Father Decay was silent for long moments. Then it sighed. 'And what do you want, Lord of Tentacles? What reward will satisfy a soul as greedy as yours?'

Before Spume could speak, the daemon raised a hand for silence. A plague drone hummed around Father Decay's head and its rider leaned close to whisper in its master's ear. When the message had been delivered, the greater daemon leaned back and laughed, low and long.

'You want a reward, do you? Well then, here is your chance to double it, corsair. Our guests have arrived at last. Much diminished in number, but still shining with the light of their cursed faith. Go, Spume – bring them to me, and I shall reward you more handsomely than even you can conceive.' The daemon flung out a hand, indicating the gateway.

Grymn laughed, though it hurt. Spume's hand tightened on the haft of his axe. The kraken beak in his side snapped and squalled, and his tentacles thrashed. But only for a moment. Then they stilled, and Spume straightened.

'So ye say, daemon. But fair warning – I can conceive of a great deal indeed.'

CHAPTER TWENTY-ONE

THE INEVITABLE CITADEL

The ancient bronze gates burst from their hinges with a scream of tortured metal. The azure galley passed through the fire and smoke, propelling itself on stalking bolts of lightning. Where the ship passed, it left a trail of destruction behind it. Daemons burned in its wake, their dolorous cries echoing down the length of the canal. Rot flies fell twitching from the air, their wings burnt to cinders by the holy radiance. The sludgy waters boiled away to a foul mist, and the walls buckled as lightning played across them. The water-spewing gargoyles toppled from their perches, and water spewed through the walls.

Arrows fell from the inverted ramparts above, and the Stormcasts responded in kind. Explosions rocked the noisome air as crackling skybolt arrows met those of the daemon-archers. The balefire engines on the vertical bulwarks vomited streams of green flame, which dissipated as they splashed across the cobalt vessel's hull.

Crouched by the mast, Tornus braced himself as another burst of green flame washed over the hull. The ship rocked slightly, but did not falter. Tornus sought out Morbus, standing atop the stern, his staff planted before him. Head bowed, the Lord-Relictor took notice of nothing save his prayers.

A sapphire radiance shone from him, almost blinding in its intensity. The shapes of fallen Stormcasts stood arrayed about him, as if warding him from harm. Tornus saw Cadoc among them, his soul burning as brightly as the beacon he'd carried. Someone caught his arm, startling him. He turned and saw Enyo.

'It is time, brother. They are coming, and we must clear the way.'

Tornus nodded and glanced down at his quiver of arrows. It had refilled itself upon Torglug's second demise, but slowly. And not to its fullest capacity. If one was connected to the other, he did not know, but he was glad that the enchantment had been restored. He had a feeling he was going to need all the arrows he could get.

He followed Enyo to the prow, where they were joined by Tegrus and his Prosecutors. Mathias and Azar were the only two of the winged Stormcasts remaining, besides the Sainted Eye. They both carried heavy shields, claimed from the bodies of fallen Liberators. Tegrus had a warblade strapped to his back, its hilt rising between his wings, and a hammer in each hand. A filthy bandage was tied tight about his thigh, where the sigmarite had been broken by a blow from a plague-bearer's blade. 'Let us be about it,' Tegrus said. 'I grow weary of the scenery here.'

Enyo laughed. 'Your forbearance is impressive. I was weary of it not long after we arrived.' She gestured to her star-eagle. 'And poor Periphas hasn't stopped complaining.'

Tornus glanced up at his own companion, perched on the rail above. Ospheonis screeched and flapped his wings, as eager in his own way as Tegrus was.

Gardus was waiting for them on the forward deck, Tallon by his side as ever. 'We cannot stop. Not now. So give them something to worry about.' He spoke confidently, though Tornus noted there was tension there as well. They were close now, they could all feel it. To fail here would be worse than to have never come at all. 'Act swiftly. Morbus cannot keep us in the air for much longer. We must reach the inner sanctum of this place soon.' He unsheathed his runeblade. 'Who will be victorious?'

'Only the faithful,' Tornus said. The others echoed him. Gardus nodded.

'Only the faithful. Now, go.' He swept his sword out, and pointed.

Tornus and the others advanced to the tip of the prow, breaking into a run as they drew close. As one, they leapt into the air and sped away from the galley. A single flap of Tornus' wings was enough to carry him out ahead of the ship. Azar kept pace, if barely. Enyo shot past them, already nocking an arrow.

A wedge of enemy galleys sailed down the canal towards them. Among the ships was a familiar vessel, the one they'd been chasing since they'd arrived. That it was here now was a good sign. It meant the Lord-Castellant was somewhere nearby as well. The black galley hung back slightly, letting the others pull ahead.

Above the galleys, a swarm of plague drones spread, blanketing the air. Tornus banked and pulled up short, trusting in his wings to hold him aloft. He drew, nocked and loosed in a blur, filling the air with death. Enyo did the same, clearing space for the two Prosecutors to use their shields to bash themselves and Tegrus a path towards the lead galley. At the last moment they broke apart, rolling away and allowing Tegrus to hurtle downwards. His hammers spun and tore gaping wounds in the deck.

The Sainted Eye swooped upwards and away, having made his pass. The galley wallowed, smoke gushing from below decks. The Prosecutors moved to repeat their tactics on the next vessel, trusting in the two Knight-Venators to watch over them.

Tornus twisted and spun through the air, loosing arrows as fast as he could. As the azure galley drew close, many of the plague drones broke off and plunged towards it, like moths to a flame. Tornus let them go, turning his attention to the ships below. Balefire arrows sped upwards, but fell back uselessly, unable to reach the flying warriors. The Prosecutors didn't have to get close to employ their celestial hammers, and they reaped a heavy toll on the ships below.

But the black galley yet remained, as if waiting for something. Pox cauldrons had been set up on its decks, and a foul smoke rose into the air above it. Enyo swooped by, picking off the crew of a wallowing vessel one by one. Tornus sped after her. 'There – that one,' he cried. 'It is being the one we are chasing.'

'I see it,' she said. They flew towards it. Plague drones dropped towards them from above, the daemonic riders thrusting at them with wide-bladed spears. Tornus caught a spear just behind the blade and jerked its wielder out of the saddle, sending the daemon plummeting to the canal below. More rot flies closed in, the plaguebearers on their backs waving festering blades enthusiastically.

Enyo dipped away from a darting proboscis, and sent an

arrow thudding into the insect's bulbous eye. Tornus lost sight of her as another fly slammed into him, its serrated claws scrabbling at his war-plate. Ospheonis shrieked and tore at its head, eliciting a high-pitched buzz of agony. Tornus snatched an arrow from his quiver and rammed it into the insect's brain, silencing it. Its rider hewed at him, even as the creature fell away, carrying the plaguebearer with it.

The galley was just below them, attempting to nudge its way past two other wrecked vessels. Whoever its captain was, he seemed determined to reach his goal, regardless of the consequences. The poison smoke from the pox cauldrons on deck had forced the Prosecutors to fly lower than they intended, and a fusillade of arrows rose to meet them. A moment later, Tornus realised the strategy at work.

Several of the daemons on the deck carried heavy nets, weighted by chunks of stone. Azar, forced to swoop low by a volley of arrows, became tangled in one of the nets and plunged to the deck.

Tornus dropped after him without hesitation. As the Prosecutor slammed into the deck of the ship, plaguebearers converged on him with chortles of glee. Tornus reached him mere moments before the daemons did. He clubbed one from its feet with his bow and whistled for Ospheonis. The star-eagle streaked down, talons spread. Tornus swung his bow in a wide arc, driving the crowd of daemons back.

Arrows sprouted from the deck in a circle about them, and several daemons fell. Enyo struck the mast of the ship and perched there, an arrow nocked. 'Cut him loose,' she shouted, as she sent a plaguebearer tumbling over the rail, an arrow transfixing its throat. She pushed away from the mast and shot away, out over the deck. Tornus followed her advice while the crew was otherwise distracted.

As Tornus tore away the net, Azar uttered a muffled warning. Tornus spun, bow raised. An axe slammed down against it. A familiar, hulking figure was behind it. 'Quicker than lightning, aren't ye?' Gutrot Spume gurgled. 'Or so ye fancy yourself. But even lightning can be bottled, with a bit of skill.'

'I am being quick enough,' Tornus said, straining against the weight of the axe. Torglug had confronted Spume more than once during the many wars that ravaged the Jade Kingdoms. The pirate had been a braggart even then, boasting of conquests beyond the stars and beneath the seas. And, unfortunately, he had the strength to back up those boasts, and a certain raw cunning.

Spume's tentacles writhed, slipping away from the haft of his axe and about Tornus' bow. With a guttural laugh, he jerked Tornus off his feet and sent him flying. 'Ye butchered the rest of the fleet good and proper, but I'm made of sterner stuff than that.' Spume raised his axe as Tornus clambered to his feet. 'I'll collect a tally of silver helmets, and make them into chamber pots for my crew.'

Tornus didn't waste breath replying. He leapt backwards, avoiding the blow. He heard a shout, and saw Enyo dragged down by several plaguebearers. Her wings sliced through the nets that tangled her, but she was quickly surrounded. Spears splintered on her armour, driving her back. Tegrus and Mathias swooped to aid her.

He lost sight of them as Spume slashed at him again, nearly sending him over the rail. 'I knew ye winged moss-brains would come first, so I planned accordingly. I'll gut ye and hang your wings from my mast.' He turned. 'But first, to stop that glowing scow from getting any further. Bring out the wyrmbows, ye lubbers!'

Five massive shapes clambered up from the lower decks,

grunting and slobbering. Tornus recognised the creatures as ogors, despite the malformations which afflicted them. Their pale green flesh was puffy with inflammation, and iron muzzles were hooked into the flesh of their jaws. Heavy limbed and scarred by branding marks and obscene runes, the hairless brutes wore iron collars and manacles, which bound their thick hands to their barrel chests. On their broad backs were mounted heavy ballistae. Plaguebearers crouched on their shoulders, manning the siege weapons. Heavy loops of anchor chain clattered from the barbed heads of the ballistae bolts. The loose ends of the chains were swiftly affixed to rings set in the decks by chanting slaves.

Tornus grasped the nature of Spume's scheme immediately. 'Talbion,' he muttered. Memories of fire and blood surfaced, and an old guilt with them. He glanced back and saw the azure galley sweeping towards them, heedless of any threat.

'Aye, so you've heard of my exploits, then,' Spume chuckled. 'How I hooked and plundered those flying islands for their treasures. And I'll do the same here. I'll drag that flying boat down and drown her crew in filth, as Grandfather wills.' His axe thudded down, nearly taking off Tornus' arm. As Tornus twisted aside, Spume turned and howled, 'Fire!'

The wyrmbows fired with a great creaking. The barbed bolts flew upwards and thudded into the hull of the galley. The ogors shuffled back, pulling the chains taut. Spume laughed and spun his axe, nearly decapitating Tornus.

His laughter ceased as the galley did not stop. Nor did it slow. Instead, lightning crept down and played across the deck, incinerating daemons and scorching the rotting wood. The black galley shuddered as it was slowly dragged around by the momentum of the flying vessel. Spume stared upwards in stunned silence. 'No,' he snarled. 'No – quick, ye lubber-worts, up the blasted chains!'

Daemons scrambled for the chains, intending to climb them and board the vessel above. But cobalt fire spread down the chain, one link at a time. The first daemon to make the attempt reeled back, arms crumbling to ash. Spume cursed and began to shout for them to cut the chains. Tornus took advantage of his distraction and slammed his bow across the back of Spume's head, staggering him.

Abruptly, the stern of Spume's vessel rose out of the water as the glowing galley bypassed it. Lightning crawled across the deck, and the sails burned. Daemons and slaves slid or fell towards the prow as the deck timbers began to splinter. The mast swayed, dangerously close to snapping in two.

Spume rounded on Tornus as the latter rose into the air with a flap of his wings. The Rotbringer's tentacles caught his leg, and Tornus was forced to carry him upwards. Beneath them, the black galley split in two with an agonised groan. 'Took my ship, I'll take your head,' Spume roared, waving his axe.

A glowing arrow, blazing with celestial energies, sank into the open beak of the kraken. The star-fated arrow tore Spume free of Tornus' leg and hurled him into one of the canal walls. The pirate struck the wall hard enough to crack the ancient stonework and fell into the scummy waters with an echoing splash.

Tornus gave Enyo a nod of thanks as she flew towards him, followed by Tegrus and the others. 'I did not hit him clean,' she said. 'Even with an arrow such as that, he might yet survive.'

'If so, we have no time to hunt him down – look,' Tegrus said. He pointed to the archway at the end of the canal, where two massive Great Unclean Ones in heavy armour waded towards the approaching galley, weapons in hand.

With a sinking sensation, Gardus recognised the creatures wading towards the galley. 'Rotguard,' he said. The armoured daemons had dealt the Hallowed Knights heavy losses in the Ghyrtract Fen, and again later, in the Athelwyrd. They were preeminent among the warriors of Nurgle's sevenfold legions.

'At least there are only two of them this time,' Feros said, raising his hammer. 'Seven was a bit many, even for us.'

Despite the apparent humour, Gardus sensed the underlying tension in the Retributor-Prime's tone. The Rotguard had been responsible for Feros' Reforging, crippling the warrior so badly that Gardus had been forced to grant him the mercy of death. He glanced at the Heavy Hand. They had never spoken of that moment. Did Feros even remember what Gardus had done?

The Retributor-Prime looked at him. 'I'll have the one on the left. He looks rambunctious.' He thumped the haft of his lightning hammer against the deck. 'With your permission, obviously.'

'Obviously,' Gardus said. 'Stay your hand for the moment.' He turned, sword raised. 'Solus, slow them down. Aetius, bring your shields up here.'

'Easy enough,' Solus said, motioning several of his Judicators to the prow. The rest of the archers continued to loose volley after volley into the inverted ramparts overhead, or at the plague drones that pursued them. 'Aim for the visors, brothers and sisters,' Solus continued, as he and Aetius led their warriors to the prow rail. 'Nothing distracts better than an arrow to the eye.'

The Judicators began to loose as soon as they reached their

new positions. Sizzling arrows struck the approaching behemoths, scorching their armour and blistering their sagging flesh. But the daemons didn't slow. Instead, they hunkered behind their great shields and continued to wade towards the galley. Displaced water slopped against the walls of the canal as the daemons advanced into the volley.

'Hnh. Tactics.' Solus took aim. 'I hate it when they're smart.'

'They're just using shields,' Aetius protested. 'It's hardly a cunning stratagem.'

'You use a shield.'

'Yes, but that's different.'

'Oh?' Solus said, tracking the closest of the daemons. It was moving slightly ahead of its fellow, by a hair's breadth.

'Yes,' Aetius insisted. 'There's a subtlety to it that–'

'Shh. I'm aiming.' Solus loosed his arrow. It struck the immense shield of the closest Rotguard and ricocheted off, to vanish behind the shield of the other. The daemon gave a bloodcurdling cry and staggered, shield dipping. For an instant, it left itself open. The Judicators loosed without prompting. Arrows pierced rotting flesh. The daemon roared again, shaking its head, momentarily deterred.

The other continued to advance. It swung its great flail and struck the hull of the galley, causing the vessel to shudder. Then it cast aside its shield and reached for the rail, as if to hold the ship in place. Gardus sheathed his runeblade, grabbed the rail and vaulted over, ignoring the shouts of Feros and the others. He dropped onto the head of the Great Unclean One, bringing his hammer down in the same instant. A thunderous crack sounded, and the crude helmet split down the centre, sliding away from the monstrous skull. Dazed, the daemon dropped its flail and groped for him. Gardus ignored it and struck again. Unnatural flesh tore and bone splintered.

The Rotguard stumbled back against the wall of the canal. 'Fall,' Gardus snarled, as he batted aside its hands and brought his hammer down a third time. 'Fall, damn you.' Thunder rolled, and the daemon slumped with a groan of protest. The galley slipped past it. The second Rotguard had recovered, and it lurched towards its companion, flail swinging. Gardus jumped, and the Rotguard pulverised the head of its fellow.

Gardus hit the edge of the canal with a crack. Pain shot through him, but he pushed it aside and clambered to his feet. The dead Rotguard collapsed in on itself, its body venting noxious gases. The remaining daemon turned ponderously, flail swinging. Gardus threw himself out of the way as the weapon cracked down, splintering the stones of the canal. It swatted at him with the rim of its shield, trying to crush him, and he dropped to the ground. The shield slammed into the wall, sending jagged chunks of stone crashing down.

Panting, he clambered to his feet. He was at a disadvantage. The creature had size and strength on its side. But as long as it was concentrating on him, it wasn't paying attention to the others. Out of the corner of his eye, Gardus saw the galley passing through the gateway.

The Rotguard loomed over him, flail swinging. Arrows sprouted from its helmet, distracting it. A moment later, a winged shape dropped down onto its head. A warblade sang down, piercing the helmet and the head within. Tegrus gave the blade a twist, and ripped it free. The Rotguard toppled into the canal with a grumbling sigh.

'Lord-Celestant, do you require aid?' the Prosecutor-Prime said, the body of the daemon settling beneath him. Foul gases spurted from its folds of fat as it dissolved. Overhead, the remaining Prosecutors, as well as Enyo and Tornus, circled.

'A lift would be appreciated,' Gardus said, waving the miasma aside.

'Then be taking my hand, Steel Soul,' Tornus called out, as he swooped low. Gardus reached up and was yanked off his feet by the Knight-Venator. They sped after the galley. Behind them, what was left of the enemy fleet was in disarray, unable to pursue.

They caught up with the galley a few moments later. Past the archway, the canal spilled into an enormous amphitheatre. The air reverberated with the sound of plague-bells and the thudding of drums. Swarms of flies spun lazily overhead in an infernal dance. Hordes of daemons were arrayed before them, armed for war. Their droning chants duelled with the noise of the bells for prominence. Behind the serried ranks, black smoke billowed upwards from the mouth of a cistern.

The galley shuddered in its flight. The cobalt fires flickered, flared and began to dim. Morbus' spell was fading. The galley dipped, its prow crunching into the ground with a booming crack. Lightning roared out, ricocheting amongst the ranks of daemons. Ancient statues crumbled as the power of Azyr washed over them. The galley bulled forwards, smashing aside anything in its path as it carved a smouldering trench through the stonework. A Great Unclean One staggered away, body aflame. Plaguebearers were incinerated mid-chant. The massive beams that rose against the walls cracked and splintered as lightning played across them.

Gardus said a prayer for those still aboard, even as Tornus carried him in pursuit. The galley came to rest at the edge of the cistern. A conflagration of sapphire flame roared up, swirling into the air. Tornus dropped Gardus to the ground as Morbus led the survivors out of the inferno. The fire had burned their armour clean of filth, and as Gardus and the others approached, it did the same to theirs.

Morbus alone remained alight after leaving the fire. Even his reliquary staff was aflame. The blue fire flickered and snapped and, as it did so, Gardus felt the light within him respond. He had been glowing since they'd entered the citadel, but now it blazed as brightly as it had the day of his Reforging. He looked around, counting the survivors. Barely twenty left now. It would have to be enough.

He let his hand fall to the hilt of his runeblade. 'Who will dare walk through the fire?'

'Only the faithful,' Morbus intoned, his voice echoing within itself. The souls of all those within him spoke as he did. He struck the ground with his staff. Lightning shimmered along the stones.

'We are the faithful, and the light of Azyr shines upon us, wherever we make our stand.' Gardus turned. The daemons were massing anew, regrouping in the wake of the galley's passage. 'Any sign of him?'

'His soulfire is close,' Morbus said. 'He is here.'

'Good. I would hate for this to have all been for nothing.' Gardus surveyed the forces arrayed against them. 'Was this a mistake, Morbus?'

Morbus was silent, for a time. Then, 'No. I think – I know – this was meant to be.'

Before Gardus could ask him what he meant, a commotion among the ranks of the enemy drew his attention. The ranks of daemons parted, allowing a massive palanquin, borne by hundreds of chained souls, to pass through. On the palanquin, a singularly enormous Great Unclean One lolled, clad in filthy robes of office and rust-splotched ceremonial armour. Seven antlers sprang from its round, batrachian skull. They met above its head to form the tri-part rune of Nurgle. A monocle of stained glass rested in the folds of one swinish eye. A large sword lay across its knees, its sheath made from the shaggy hide of some great beast.

Worst of all, however, was the silver shape that hung crucified from the front of the palanquin. Lorrus Grymn was shrouded in chains, his head bowed, his body limp. Nurglings clung to him with almost affectionate possessiveness, their giggles audible even at a distance.

'Welcome, Garradan, welcome,' the Great Unclean One boomed. 'Long have I desired to meet the soul who ran Bolathrax to his doom, and banished poor Pupa Grotesse.' The daemon heaved itself up on its palanquin, causing the enslaved souls beneath to moan in agony. 'Both of them dear friends, it must be said. Brothers of boil and bubo, if not blood.' One great yellow eye narrowed in a conspiratorial wink. 'Still, bygones, eh?'

Gardus did not reply. Instead, he sank to one knee and began to pray. As one, the Stormcasts fell into battle formation. Liberators moved to the fore to shield the remaining Judicators. Feros and his warriors surrounded Gardus. Morbus stood apart from them all, silent and watchful. Molten sigmarite dripped from his hands and torso, forming a smoking puddle on the stones.

The daemon cupped a hand to its head and said, 'Are those… pleas, I hear?' It slapped its belly and laughed jovially. 'Too late for that, my friend. Far too late. You have well and truly wedged yourself into this mire. And all of your free will.'

Gardus closed his eyes. He continued to pray, letting the words layer over one another. Let the creature talk. He was building a wall. One prayer at a time. As he prayed, he wondered if Morbus was right. Had this all been preordained?

Was this Sigmar's will? But to what purpose? Was it simply a show of defiance, or something more?

The daemon was still talking. 'I have been remiss. Allow me to introduce myself. I am called Father Decay. I am a lord of the Court of Ruination, and the Hand of Nurgle. And I am the architect of your destruction.' The daemon waited, as if expecting applause. When it received no response save silence, it removed its monocle, rubbed it on its robes, replaced it and leaned forwards on its palanquin. 'Well? Have you nothing to say, Garradan? From the very first moment you dared set foot in the garden, I have teased you and tweaked you, drawing you further into my grasp. I had my poppet draw you in, and away from the Gate of Weeds. Even now, my servants attack through that portal you so obligingly left open.'

Still silence. The daemon said nothing Gardus hadn't already known. If it thought to dishearten him, it had severely misjudged him. The remaining Stormcasts stood like statues, arrayed for battle along the rim of the pit. Then Tornus stepped forwards. His steps rang like a hammer strike on an anvil. He drew an arrow from his quiver as he walked. Gardus made to stop him, but a look from Morbus stilled his protest. This too was meant to be.

'He is having nothing to say to you, monster. But I am.'

'And who might you be?' Father Decay grumbled, all trace of its former good humour gone. 'I do not wish to waste words on some little soul. Wait.' It made a show of sniffing the air. 'You smell... familiar.'

'We are meeting once, in another life.' Tornus lifted his arrow.

Father Decay squinted. 'And what is that?'

'It is being the weed in Nurgle's garden.' Faster than the eye could follow, Tornus nocked and loosed the star-fated arrow. It shattered the daemon's monocle and pierced the eye behind it, eliciting a deafening shriek of agony. The creature bucked on its palanquin, overbalancing it. Souls were crushed as the daemon was dumped onto the ground. An enormous fist slammed down, shaking the ground and crushing several unlucky plaguebearers as the daemon continued to bawl.

Gardus' head snapped up, and he lunged to his feet. Behind him, the remaining Judicators loosed their own arrows, sending the volley into the packed ranks of daemons. 'Enyo, retrieve our Lord-Castellant,' Gardus said, as he started towards the wounded Great Unclean One. 'Solus, Tornus, keep them off our backs. Feros, Aetius, with me.'

Daemons tried to interpose themselves, but Aetius and Feros smashed them aside, clearing Gardus a path. Father Decay heaved itself up, an oily ichor spilling from its ruined eye, and clawed for its sword. 'You dare?' it snarled. 'You dare strike the seventh son of Nurgle?' Its blade swept out in a murderous arc. Gardus twisted aside and summoned the enchantment in his war-cloak. A barrage of glowing hammers struck the daemon, punching steaming craters in its flesh.

The sword slammed down, chopping through the ground. It became lodged in the mouldy stones, and Gardus leapt onto it, swiftly scaling Father Decay's arm. The Great Unclean One's remaining eye widened as Gardus lunged, runeblade slashing out. The creature screamed as the blade opened the flesh of its face. It reeled, clutching at Gardus. He dropped to the ground and spun, hammer cracking against the daemon's knee. Spongy bone ruptured, and the creature sprawled across the ground.

'No, no, *no*,' Father Decay groaned, as it tried to heave itself over. 'This is not how the game is played. This is our place of power, our garden... it isn't *fair*.'

'This is not a game,' Gardus said, striding towards the creature. 'It was never a game.'

'Cheat!' Father Decay vomited a stream of effluvial discharge. It steamed away to nothing as Gardus' light swelled. The daemon covered its good eye and tried to squirm away. 'No, you are cheating somehow. Cheating god. Thief. Usurper!' It continued to curse and moan, even as Gardus planted a foot on the side of its bloated skull. 'We've already won, you can't change the way the game is played.' Its flesh sizzled and blackened as Gardus' light washed over it. 'No,' it moaned. 'No, I was promised victory.' It stretched a hand out towards the cistern. 'Papa, help me. Help your child...'

'There is no help for you. I have died, and I live again. I am the light and the fire, and I will burn this garden clean.' The tempestos hammer rose, its head crackling with energy. Father Decay's final shriek was cut short as the blow collapsed its skull. A cracked monocle rolled free of the decaying morass.

Gardus turned. Daemons massed on all sides, eager to avenge their fallen lord. Behind the ranks of plaguebearers, massive Rotguard lumbered into motion. Plague drones swooped overhead and lolloping beasts appeared, yanking against the chains of their daemonic handlers. A thousand and one ways to die, with no reprieve in sight. 'Aetius – get them into line,' he barked. 'We make our stand here.'

'Well, it's not as if we can go anywhere else, is it?' Grymn called out, as Enyo deposited him on the ground nearby. 'Of all the idiotic, vainglorious things you could have done, you chose this one.' He sank down as Tallon scrambled towards him, shrieking joyfully. He bowed his head, murmuring softly to the gryph-hound for a moment. Then he looked up. 'You shouldn't have come. It was obviously a trap.'

'Obviously,' Gardus said. He flipped his hammer around and extended the haft to Grymn. 'And yet, here we are.'

Grymn accepted the hammer with a nod of thanks. 'I suppose we should make the best of it then.' He glanced at Morbus, eyebrow raised. 'You're on fire.'

'I hadn't noticed,' Morbus said.

Grymn didn't smile. 'Spume?'

'We sank his ship, and Enyo put an arrow in him.' Seeing Grymn's frown, Gardus shrugged. 'We were in a hurry.'

'That's your problem. Always in a hurry. You never think.'

'Brother, while it is good to hear your voice, perhaps we should save the lectures for another time.' Gardus glanced at Tornus. 'If it comes to it, I want you and Enyo to make for the realmgate, as quickly as you can. There is no reason for all of us to perish here.'

'I am to be staying here,' Tornus said, drawing an arrow from his quiver. 'Here is where I am supposed to be.'

'And I as well, Lord-Celestant,' Enyo said. 'You will need my bow.'

Gardus looked at them and nodded. 'So be it. Do what you can. We must – eh?' He turned at a shout from Tegrus. The Prosecutor-Prime had swooped out over the cistern, and was now plunging back towards them. He struck the ground and rolled, clawing at his helmet. Pox-smoke rose from his armour, and the silver was marred by black motes. Gardus knelt beside him, trying to help without knowing how. 'Tegrus, what is it?'

'It's coming,' Tegrus said, his voice almost shrill. He thrashed, as if trying to free himself from the clutches of something only he could see. A moment later, a dull boom echoed up out of the cistern and washed over them. Gardus felt his heart pause in its rhythm, and gasped, clutching his chest. Nauseated, he saw several Stormcast fall to their knees, retching. The daemons had stopped their advance and fallen silent, seemingly expectant.

Another boom, like the collision of distant stars. Gardus tasted blood. He'd bitten his tongue. Tallon shrieked loud and long, every feather on the gryph-hound's neck stiff and flared in fear.

'What is that?' he asked, already knowing the answer.

'The Lord of Flies himself,' Morbus said. The Lord-Relictor strode past them towards the edge of the cistern. Gardus rose quickly and followed him, after waving the others back. They knew enough to hold their positions, unless otherwise ordered.

Through the ragged shroud of smoke, Gardus saw what lay below the Inevitable Citadel, at the heart of Nurgle's garden. Almost immediately, he closed his eyes and turned away, unable to bear it.

It was impossible to describe. Impossible to comprehend. To his eyes, it was a wallowing swamp of black stars and dying worlds, of rotting galaxies alive with immense, writhing shapes as large as nebulas. Cosmic maggots, gnawing at the roots of infinity. Galactic plagues, eating away at the very flesh of existence, reducing all that was to leprous ruin in their unending hunger. It was a dark mirror of Azyr, corrupted, reduced, strangled. All glory vanished, all hope quashed. A thunder of screams echoed upwards, driving him back. A million million voices, raised up in anguish and despair. Forever crying out for that which would never come.

Again, the world shook. The reverberations were the death knell of the worlds below, Gardus knew, though he could not say how. Worlds claimed by Nurgle, realms older than Azyr or Ghyran, now broken and ground into filth. He felt sick.

He wanted to see the clean stars of Azyr once more, even if it meant enduring the Reforging. But still the voices cried out, crying for aid, for him.

Garradan... help us...

It hurts... why does it hurt...

Everything is burning... help us...

Garradan...

Garradan...

Help us...

The voices assailed him from every side, filling his head, squeezing his heart. He staggered, and felt Morbus' hand steadying him. Another tolling of the death knell.

Down below, something began to crawl out of the black heart of that cancerous infinity. It was no shape, and all shapes. Fat and thin, a plume of smoke, a puddle of oil, spreading ever upwards. There were eyes in the smoke, as round as cold, dead suns, and teeth that stretched in a grin as wide as the horizon. Fingers like comets clutched at the void, as the Lord of All Things stirred from his manse, and began the long, arduous climb to his garden. Moons crumbled beneath that impossible bulk, and stars were snuffed out.

'He is coming,' Morbus said, hollowly. 'An honour, of sorts.'

Gardus closed his eyes. 'He is coming for me. I escaped once before. I should not have. My fate was written the day I stepped through the Gates of Dawn.'

Gardus stepped away from the edge of the cistern. He did not wish to see the swamp of dead universes swirling below, or the thing rising from within them. The thing that had been trying to claim his soul since before the burning of Demesnus Harbour, in one way or another. He looked up, and saw the others approaching. 'Stay back,' he roared. He looked at Morbus. 'Keep them back. Keep them from seeing that, if you can.'

'Soon that will not be an option.'

Gardus shook his head. The ground trembled beneath his feet. It felt as if the garden were set to tear itself apart. Perhaps Nurgle had grown bored, and had decided to reshape it all again. 'Much is demanded–' he said.

'–of those to whom much is given,' Morbus said.

'Lead them to glory, Morbus,' Gardus said softly. 'Temper them, as I might have. Be the light that guides them.' He took a breath and stepped to the edge of the cistern. His hands tightened on his weapons. He wanted to run. To leave this place. To see the stars again. But the voices cried out, and he could not turn away from such pain. He would not. Whatever the cost.

'What do you think you are doing?'

'If Nurgle wants me, I will go to him. I will carry the light of Sigmar's wrath into the dark, as the only the faithful can.'

Morbus laughed softly and extended his staff, blocking Gardus. 'I think not.'

'What?'

'I think I have waited all of my life for this one moment,' Morbus said. 'I was ancient before I heard Sigmar's call. And I have only grown more ancient still in the centuries since. I am old, and I am tired, but I have one storm yet left in me. A storm bolstered by the souls of the living and the dead alike.' He looked at Gardus, lightning trailing from his eyes. 'I think you are wrong, my friend. This is not your doom. It is mine.'

'Morbus,' Gardus began. Morbus flicked a finger and Gardus was hurled backwards by a flash of celestial energies. He struggled to his feet, smoke rising from his armour.

'I know now why I came here with you. In death, we prove ourselves worthy of life. The fifth canticle.' Morbus unclasped the remains of his cloak and let it crumple to the ground.

He cast aside his staff. 'Our souls are pure, and by their light is darkness banished. I hold an army within me now. You are the sword. Grymn is the shield. But I am become the hammer stroke, which puts an end to the conflict.' He stepped to the edge of the great, cosmic cistern. He stared down into untold abysses of foulness, into the very eyes of the Lord of All Things.

And Morbus Stormwarden laughed.

He spread his arms. Lightning swelled out around him, melting the stones to slag, and driving back the mass of daemons which surrounded the remaining Stormcasts. 'This is why we are here, Gardus. This is the first blow, and the last. This is the settling of a question millennia old.'

Gardus lunged, reaching for him. Morbus leapt. He fell into the black, a shining comet of azure. The rising presence paused in its ascent. Something that might have been a hand, miles across and as wide as a universe, reached up to intercept the light. Fingers closed. The light was gone. Snuffed.

Nurgle screamed.

The light returned. A spark, at first. Then a blazing column of fire and heat, spearing upwards through the black, pursued by the agonised screams of a daemon-god. Twenty souls, thirty, more, all those who'd fallen in this diseased realm, rising up, at last, to the forges of Azyr. The light swept out as it rose, filling the amphitheatre. Daemons screamed as they were reduced to floating motes of ash. Everything wavered and came apart, reduced to shards of darkness. The light grew brighter and brighter, until it was the only thing Gardus could see. He felt a wrenching sensation deep within him. And then he was rushing upwards, carried on wings of lightning and thunder.

Below him, he could see the darkness returning in the wake

of the light's ascent. He could hear the enraged bellows of a consciousness as old as the stars. Neither Nurgle nor his garden could be so easily destroyed. But they could be hurt. They could be reminded of why they had once feared the storm. And should do so again.

Reminded. Warned. Challenged.

Who shall carry my light into the darkness? Sigmar's voice whispered.

'Only the faithful,' Gardus said.

He closed his eyes, and let the light carry him home.

CHAPTER TWENTY-TWO

ONLY THE FAITHFUL

Kurunta sent the plaguebearer's head spinning out over the realmgate with a blow from his broadsword. 'It's been long enough,' the Knight-Heraldor growled, shoving the daemon's headless body aside. 'I'm starting to get worried.'

'Starting,' Angstun repeated, incredulously. 'Starting?' The Knight-Vexillor crushed a daemon's skull with his warhammer and rounded on his fellow Stormcast. 'They've been gone for seven days. And these attacks are growing worse with every passing hour.' A plaguebearer lunged for him, blade raised in both hands. He whirled his standard about and clubbed it from its feet. He drove the end of the standard down into its chest and gave it a twist, silencing the creature's groan of protest.

All around them, the battle for the chamber was in full swing. Every warrior that could be spared from the evacuation efforts was down here, fighting against the daemonic intruders. Liberators formed a living cordon around the only way in or out, with a thin screen of Judicators to break up the momentum of the enemy. Machus and his Decimators waded into the thick of battle, further reducing the pressure on the Liberators' shieldwall.

But it wasn't enough. The enemy's numbers were steadily increasing – for every one that fell, three more pulled themselves up out of the muck. And the flickering light of the Lord-Castellant's lantern was dim and barely perceptible. The realmgate was close to opening fully and, when it did, the daemons would flood through in an unstoppable horde.

He still wondered whether or not this whole affair had been some sort of trap. The broken remnants of the Order of the Fly had assaulted the walls, bleeding themselves white in an attempt to retake their citadels. Though he had driven them off, the distraction had almost cost them control of the realmgate. Kurunta had nearly been overwhelmed before Angstun had managed to lead several retinues' worth of reinforcements to his aid.

Since then, it had been a near constant battle. The daemons continued to squeeze through the gate and fling themselves at its defenders. It was a grim reminder of those early battles in the Ghyrtract Fen, and the Grove of Blighted Lanterns. A war of attrition that the Hallowed Knights must ultimately lose, unless something turned the tide.

Angstun hoped that Yare and his followers had made it to safety. He had ordered their evacuation over the old man's objections. If the citadels were to be overrun, Angstun had no intention of allowing the deaths of the prisoners they'd freed. The retinues he'd left to oversee the final stages of the evacuation would be enough to shepherd the mortals to safety, if it came to it. They had orders to escort the mortals to the Living Citadel, where they would be safe. Angstun wondered if he would miss his conversations with Yare, when he was Reforged anew. Would he even remember the old philosopher, or would Yare become another face without a name, lodged in the roots of his consciousness?

'Angstun – watch yourself,' Kurunta roared.

Angstun snapped out of his reverie and whirled as a blade skidded from his shoulder-plate. He caught the plaguebearer in its swollen abdomen, bursting it, and doubling the creature over. It clutched at him with swollen fingers as he tried to yank his hammer free of its guts. He finally succeeded and, with a snarl of satisfaction, shattered its skull. It sank to its knees, dissolving. Sweeping its remains from his hammer with a flick of his wrist, he turned towards the bubbling waters of the realmgate. 'It is time to close this gate, Kurunta,' he said. 'One way or another, this invasion will be halted.'

'What of Gardus and the others?' Kurunta protested. He backhanded a daemon, catapulting it away from him. More of them clawed at his legs, their half-formed bodies trailing off into trails of sludge. 'We cannot simply abandon them.'

'And what would you have me do? Follow them?'

'I can do it. Allow me to lead a few–'

'No,' Angstun barked. He smashed a daemon to the ground and started for the bubbling black waters. 'I will seal the portal. You fall back with the others. Command of the Steel Souls falls to you. Retreat to the Living City and – eh?'

Something was happening at the heart of the realmgate. Where before it had only been black, now there was a spark of light. The water began to roil, more than ever before. The daemons had not yet noticed that anything was amiss, and continued to press their attack. Streams of light pierced the surface of the water. The shattered remnants of Grymn's warding lantern responded, the glow in its depths strengthening.

Where the light washed across daemonic flesh, it blackened and disintegrated. Some daemons turned, cyclopean eyes widening. The black waters turned grey, and then white, as the light swelled up – up, washing out over the chamber. The grime and filth that stained Angstun's war-plate began to smoulder and flake away. 'What in Sigmar's name…?'

Kurunta laughed. 'Exactly. In Sigmar's name.' He drove his sword point first into a struggling daemon and lifted his war-horn. He raised it to his lips and blew a single note – a rallying call. The sound resonated through Angstun and, suddenly, he understood.

'Gardus,' he said. He turned, raising his standard high, so that all the Steel Souls might see it. 'Make a joyful noise, my brethren. Our brothers and sisters return to us. Sing to them, sing so that they might hear us, and know we are waiting.'

As one, the Hallowed Knights began to chant, softly at first, and then more loudly. A song of praise and gratitude. A song the first men had sung to welcome Sigmar to their feasting halls. A song taught to all the sons and daughters of the fourth Stormhost. And for the first time in a long time, Angstun joined his voice to those of his warriors.

Plaguebearers burned. Their droning chants became garbled and soon dripped away into nothing. Some still fought, even as they were reduced to ash. Others simply collapsed. The realmgate shone like the sun. Shapes breached the surface, wading towards solid ground. Angstun recognised Gardus… Enyo… and Grymn. A sense of relief filled him as he caught sight of the Lord-Castellant. There were others as well – Feros of the Heavy Hand, the unconscious form of Tegrus slung over one shoulder. Aetius Shieldborn, supporting a limping Solus. Less than twenty had returned, but that was more than he'd expected.

And Tornus. The Redeemed One had an arm about the waist of a wounded Liberator, and was helping her to shore. Relief warred with – not anger, but surprise. He had not expected the Knight-Venator to return. Perhaps Tornus had not expected it either, for he stared about him in obvious bewilderment.

The light continued to grow and, within it, he thought he glimpsed the ghostly shapes of the fallen, rising up. Thunder rumbled, far above. One by one, the ghostly shapes were whisked upwards in flashes of lightning. The last was more recognisable than the others, for all that it was a ragged, threadbare thing.

'The Lord-Relictor,' Kurunta murmured, in awe. 'His soul, it's…'

'More powerful than any of us ever imagined,' Gardus said, as he approached. His armour was blackened and bent. He removed his helmet, revealing burnt, bloody features. 'He carried us all, living and dead alike, out of the garden, in the moment of his death.'

'What happened in there?' Angstun said, as he and the Lord-Celestant clasped forearms. 'You look as if you've been through a war.'

'We have,' Grymn said, limping towards them. His gryphhound paced by his side. The light began to fade and with it, the realmgate itself. The waters had dried away to nothing. All that remained was a crater set into the floor of the chamber. A chamber that no longer had a purpose. The floor began to tremble, and the ancient pillars shifted on their bases. Cracks ran up the walls.

Angstun turned and barked an order to retreat. The Stormcasts decamped, leaving the shuddering chamber behind. They made their way carefully to the surface, as all around them, the citadel shuddered in what felt like its death throes. Chunks of rock fell, and corridors collapsed in on themselves just behind the retreating Stormcasts, as if some unseen power were sealing the chamber off, now that its purpose had been served.

They emerged into the light of a new day, accompanied by a cloud of dust. Thunder rumbled overhead, and the sky was dark and fierce. Angstun heard a shout, and saw a group of mortals, accompanied by several Stormcasts, hurrying towards them. Yare was among them. 'Yare, I told you to leave,' Angstun said, as the blind man was led towards him by several followers.

'And I did. Then I came back.'

'More sophistry,' Angstun said, unable to restrain a chuckle. The old man beamed cheerfully and groped for the Knight-Vexillor's arm.

'Stop grumbling and help an old blind man. I can feel the warmth of Gardus' light. Has he returned?'

'I have, Yare of Demesnus,' Gardus said. He looked down at the old man and placed a hand on his shoulder. 'You asked me a question before, do you remember?'

'Of course. I'm blind, not forgetful.'

Gardus smiled. 'You asked if I spoke the truth. I never answered you.'

'Will you do so now?' Yare asked, smiling slightly.

'No. Because I do not know the future. All I can say is this… while I stand, I will do my best to protect your people from the storms to come. I swore an oath, many years ago, to see that no harm befell those in my care, and I will uphold it, unto death and beyond.'

Yare nodded and glanced unseeingly at Angstun. 'And that, my friend, is both an echo of a truth and the truth itself. Wouldn't you agree?'

Before Angstun could reply, the sky cracked open, disgorging multiple strikes of lightning. The ruins of the citadel shuddered in sympathy with the storm. As the glare faded, figures in silver and amethyst war-plate were revealed.

Astral Templars, draped in barbaric totems and chanting fierce war cries, marched out of the smoke of the strike. At their head, Lord-Celestant Zephacleas Beast-Bane strode forward, hand raised in greeting. 'What's this? I was told you got yourself lost in a garden again, Steel Soul. Now I come all this way to find you're here after all?'

'As if you had any doubts, you great oaf,' Lord-Celestant Cassandora Stormforged said. Her Hallowed Knights marched in silent precision behind her. 'Still, it is a shame. I was almost looking forward to coming in there after you.'

'You – how did you know?' Gardus asked, startled. He glanced at Angstun, who shook his head.

'I sent no word, my lord. As you ordered.'

'Sigmar saw that light of yours shining in the dark,' Zephacleas said, as he removed his helmet. He flashed a gap-toothed smile. 'He said you'd only gone and invaded the realm of the Ruinous Powers, *again*. And this time you'd had the gall to take a whole chamber with you.'

'We were sent to lend aid, should it be required,' Cassandora interjected. Then, more hesitantly, she said, 'The skyhosts are claiming to have heard the screams of a wounded god, echoing out on the realm's black rim. What happened, brother?'

Gardus hesitated. 'I am still not sure. I know only that we carried our light into the dark, and out again.'

'It sounds like I missed a good fight. Again.' Zephacleas shook his head. He grinned. 'Still, always tomorrow, eh?'

'Yes,' Gardus said.

Overhead, the clouds were clearing, as the Storm of

Sigmar rolled on, carrying the tidings of war elsewhere. The Lord-Celestant peered at the sky as if seeking something, and Angstun wondered what it might be. A moment later Gardus nodded, as if he'd found it. 'And whatever tomorrow brings, we will meet it, and emerge victorious. We are the faithful, and we can do no less.' He drew his runeblade and held it up, so that it caught the rays of the rising sun.

'Who will be triumphant?' he thundered.

'Only the faithful,' Angstun roared, joining his voice with those of the others. With Feros and Aetius, Solus and Enyo. Even Tornus, who met his gaze and nodded. And as their voices rose and became one, he thought he heard the voices of those who had fallen cry out with them. A cry that would echo throughout the Mortal Realms, now and forevermore.

'Only the faithful.'

'Only the faithful.'

'*Only the faithful!*'

ABOUT THE AUTHOR

Josh Reynolds is the author of the Warhammer
40,000 novels *Fabius Bile: Primogenitor, Fabius
Bile: Clonelord,* and *Deathstorm,* and the novellas
Hunter's Snare and *Dante's Canyon,* along with
the audio drama *Master of the Hunt.* In the
Warhammer World, he has written the End Times
novels *The Return of Nagash* and *The Lord of
the End Times,* the Gotrek & Felix tales *Charnel
Congress, Road of Skulls* and *The Serpent Queen.*
He has also written many stories set in the Age of
Sigmar, including the novels *Eight Lamentations:
Spear of Shadows, Nagash: The Undying King, Fury
of Gork, Black Rift* and *Skaven Pestilens.* He lives
and works in Sheffield.

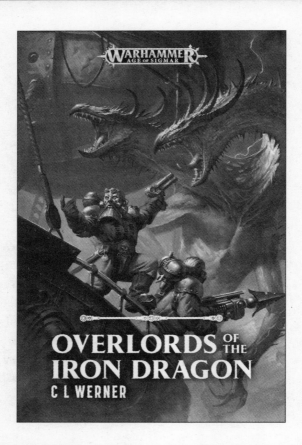

The sorcerer's face curled back in a leering rictus, exposing the blackened stumps of bone hidden behind his lips. There was something almost batrachian in his visage, bulbous eyes jutting from puffy folds of skin. Unlike the flesh around them, there was no softness in Khoram's toadlike eyes, only a rapacious hunger as they stared both outwards and inwards.

Possibilities and potentialities, the twistings of doom and fate, the shadows of futures yet unmade. Scenes of glorious victory and visions of annihilating disaster, each waxing and waning like the falling sands of time. The ebb and flow of prophecy was unrelenting and unforgiving. The weak of mind were consumed by the ordeal of divining insight from the tide of omen and portent, driven mad by their inability to confine such knowledge into purely mundane perceptions. The weak of spirit lost themselves in the cosmic expanse of the infinite, flesh and soul obliterated as they surrendered to the Cyclopean enormity where past and future united into a single moment that defied the mortal conceit of time. Humanity had been the first and least of the sacrifices Khoram had rendered to his black arts.

The sorcerer was a tall man, his body disfigured by the manifold blessings thrust upon him by his dread god. Grossly mutated, his robes and armour folded awkwardly about his frame. The side of his neck bulged with a hideous feathered growth, pushing his head down towards the opposite shoulder. One hand, the less malformed of his extremities, gripped a long staff. The other hand, ending in elongated, boneless digits, beckoned to the fist-sized sphere of glass that hovered around his head. At his summons, the sphere came to rest, floating just before his eyes.

Wind rippled the sorcerer's robes, disturbing the feathers of the growth on his neck. The beast upon which he stood shuddered, shifting slightly as it adjusted its flight through the darkling skies, high above the bleak hills of Shadowfar. The sorcerer's boots were gripped by hairy tendrils that emerged from the creature's back, melded into its very substance. The flattened, ray-like daemon could no more divorce itself of its rider than it could shed its own organs. Its corporeal form had become subsumed by Khoram, existing as an extension of his own. Through the skies of Chamon it would carry him until such time as it was dismissed and its physical mass dissolved into vapour. There would always be another daemon ready to enter the Mortal Realms to replace it when the sorcerer was in need.

Khoram's wormy fingers reached out and curled around the scintillating sphere, little ribbons of steam rising where his cobalt-hued skin rested against the glassy surface. Even flesh that had been transformed by the blessings of Mighty Tzeentch wasn't immune to the corrosive touch of temporal abeyance.

'Mighty is your power, oh Orb of Zobras,' Khoram hissed to the gleaming sphere. 'You are prophecy manifest. Prediction given physical form.' He felt the heat in his fingers gradually lessen. The sorcerer thought of the great seer who had created the orb. 'Zobras sacrificed much to achieve you,' he told the relic. 'At the height of his power he commanded daemons to forge you from the essence of time and dream. You are the pinnacle of his magic.'

The flattery spilled off Khoram's tongue, tasting bitter in his mouth. By arduous rite and obscene ritual, the sphere had been soulbound to him, orbiting him like a captive star. To command the orb was never enough, however. It had to be appeased. Zobras had ignored the will of the relic he had created and in the end it had betrayed him when the armies of Chaos laid waste to his theocracy. The prophet's ruin was a warning, a reminder to remain humble before the Dark Gods.

'Reveal to me the path of things yet to become,' Khoram enjoined the orb.

He stared into the sphere, peering into its thousands of facets. Each one bore its own story, its own interpretation of how the future would unfold. Trying to concentrate upon all of them would be futile, an effort that had driven lesser sorcerers mad. Khoram, however, had received one blessing from his god that made all the difference.

'There! There!' The words sounded from the feathered growth on Khoram's neck. A tiny face peered out from the midst of the feathers, clusters of black eyes fixated upon the orb's planes. 'There!' the homunculus repeated.

Khoram diverted his attention from the images his parasitic daemon had rejected. He depended upon the creature's guidance to lead him to the most propitious of the visions. A connoisseur of lies, the tretchlet unerringly sniffed out the truth for its master.

The sorcerer's eyes gleamed as his familiar drew his attention to the image playing out within one of the facets. The moment he focused upon the image and his mind digested the scene, the other surfaces around it changed. Now they exhibited a new array of futures, possibilities derived from the initial prediction. Again, Khoram felt the tretchlet guiding him to the most truthful of the prophecies. Mustering his resolve, he tore his gaze away from the orb. It was unwise to peer too far ahead at one time. Therein lay the route of obsession and the madness of infinity.

Looking away from the orb, Khoram gazed out across the cloud-swept skies. Ugly fogs of scintillating amber cascaded through the atmosphere, thrown aloft by the forests of spytepine that infested the hills far below. Buzzing swarms of tiny blot-midges flocked to the amber, greedily glutting themselves on the shimmering motes of hardened sap. Those that fed too lustily became weighted down by their feast, crashing onto the slopes below, their carcasses fertilising the very trees that provoked their downfall. The flux of Change in action, from benefactor to exploiter, from predator to prey. The role played one moment was but a mask that could swiftly be torn away, either by expedience or by the whims of fate.

Khoram's left hand closed tighter about the whorled runestaff he held. Glancing down at the daemon upon which he stood, the sorcerer drove the spiked butt of the implement into one of the scarred grooves that circled the creature's forward edge. The disc-shaped thing snarled in irritation as the goad jabbed at it. Wormy tendrils tried to writhe up from underneath the daemon's body, but their reach was incapable of threatening the mortal on its back. The creature let out another snarl, the shudder of its annoyance shivering through its substance up into Khoram's feet. The circular daemon floated upwards, racing towards the height to which its master directed it.

The roar of battle crashed upon the sorcerer's ears. The skies below him were filled with conflict. Savage warriors draped in kilts of sapphire and malachite soared through the air on daemonic chargers similar to the one Khoram rode. Fiery chariots harnessed to still larger daemons careened across the atmosphere, trailing plumes of smoke and flame in their wake. Bird-faced half-men glided about the fray, borne aloft upon shrieking daemon-steeds and loosing arrows of bone from bows cut from the tendons of gargants.

The warhost of men and monsters spiralled around a clutch of fantastical craft. Great ships soared over Shadowfar, supported by metal cupolas suspended above their decks. From prow and stern, each ship directed an array of weaponry against their tormentors. Beams of golden light streaked out at masked warriors, punching through their flesh as they solidified into bullets just before reaching their targets. Harpoons rocketed away from cylindrical launchers fixed to the decks, the spears impaling howling beastmen, leaving them dangling against the keel until the chains fitted to the projectile were reeled back in.

From the decks, from armoured baskets fastened to the cupolas and the sides of the hulls themselves, the crew of the sky-vessels directed a determined defence. Pistols belched shot into the very faces of the attackers, larger snub-nosed weapons spewed blasts that shredded the wings of beastmen and scoured the hides of daemons. Axes and pikes were employed to deadly effect, hacking through the beaked faces of the monstrous raiders or plucking warriors from the backs of their steeds to send them plummeting to the earth far below.

'How unfit for the storm are our foes,' Khoram mused, the tretchlet gibbering in agreement. The crews of the sky-vessels were utterly unlike their vicious foes. They were shorter and stockier, broadly and stolidly built. Most wore bulky armour of heavy metal plates, their faces locked inside helms with glowering masks and golden beards. 'They lack the grace and agility of those born to the skies. Brutes of rock and stone that seek to conquer the tempest with their puerile inventions.'

The sorcerer shook his head. 'The duardin are a meddle-some breed. Whatever the peculiarities of their creed they invariably demand great effort to dispose of. More effort than some are willing to expend.'

As the thought came to him, Khoram gazed back into the orb. Responding to his mind, the facets shimmered and displayed a new array of images. Each facet displayed the same Chaos warrior standing upon the back of a daemonic disc. He presented a gruesome aspect, his baroque armour still dripping with the sacrificial blood used to anoint it before the fighting. Dismembered fingers dipped in wax were plastered about his gorget like hideous candles. Veiled by the smoke rising from the smouldering fingers his horned helm was an indistinct suggestion of shape and motion. Only the nine eyes that stared from the jumble of visors scattered across the helm's face exhibited any clarity, shining through the smoke like angry embers.

'Tamuzz is in a particularly wrathful humour,' Khoram told his homunculus.